# MOHAWK WOMAN

**Forge Books by Barbara Riefe**

THE IROQUOIS SERIES
*The Woman Who Fell from the Sky*
*For Love of Two Eagles*
*Mohawk Woman*

# BARBARA RIEFE

# MOHAWK WOMAN

A TOM DOHERTY ASSOCIATES BOOK

NEW YORK

MOHAWK WOMAN

Copyright © 1996 by Barbara Riefe

This book is printed on acid-free paper.

Design by Lynn Newmark
Map by Ellisa Mitchell

A Forge Book
Published by Tom Doherty Associates, Inc.
175 Fifth Avenue
New York, N.Y. 10010

Forge® is a registered trademark of Tom Doherty Associates, Inc.

Library of Congress Cataloging-in-Publication Data

Riefe, Barbara,
    Mohawk woman / Barbara Riefe.—1st ed.
        p.   cm.
    "A Tom Doherty Associates book."
    ISBN 0-312-85704-7 (acid-free paper)
    1. Mohawk Indians—Fiction.   2. Mohawk women—Fiction.   I. Title.
PS3568.I3633M6   1996
813'.54—dc20                                                    95-40771
                                                                    CIP

First Edition: January 1996

Printed in the United States of America

0   9   8   7   6   5   4   3   2   1

This book is fondly dedicated to
Charles Arthur Frydenborg

# CONTENTS

|  | Place Names | 9 |
|---|---|---|
|  | Map | 11 |
|  | Cast of Characters | 13 |
|  | Prologue | 15 |
| PART I | People of the Twilight | 17 |
| PART II | Summer of Discontent | 69 |
| PART III | The War Road | 121 |
| PART IV | The Heart of *Augustuske* | 151 |
| PART V | The Vane of Fate | 205 |
| PART VI | Enemies, Time and Distance | 235 |
| PART VII | The Test of Devotion | 285 |
| PART VIII | Flight | 307 |
| PART IX | Dark Days Coming | 357 |
|  | Epilogue | 379 |
|  | Author's Note | 381 |

## PLACE NAMES

Tenotoge—*Mohawk castle*
Schandisse—*Mohawk castle*
Onekahoncka—*Mohawk castle*
Onneyuttahage—*Oneida castle*
Te-ugé-ga—*Mohawk River*
Shaw-na-taw-ty—*Hudson River*
Kanawage—*St. Lawrence River*
O-chog-wä—*Richelieu River and Falls*
Unandilla River
O-jik-ha-dä-gé-ga—*the Wide Water—Atlantic Ocean*
Tree-eater Mountains—*Adirondacks*
Tongue Mountains
Green Mountains
Ganagawehas—*Catskill Mountains*
Cahonsye Ononda—*Zwart Mountain—Black Mountain*
Oetsira Ononda—*Fire Mountain*
Kä-ne-gó-dick—*Wood Creek*
South Bay
Champlain marshes
Fort Anne
Fort Nicholson
Fort Carillon
Fort St. Frédéric
Fort Dion
Ile-la-Motte
Shogahu—*Sokoki village*
Talldega—*Sokoki village*
Mission of St. Joseph—*Jesuit mission*
O-ne-ä-dä-lote—*Lake Champlain*
Andia-ta-roc-te—*Lake St. Sacrement (Lake George)*
Skä-neh-täh-da—*Albany*
Stadacona—*Quebec*

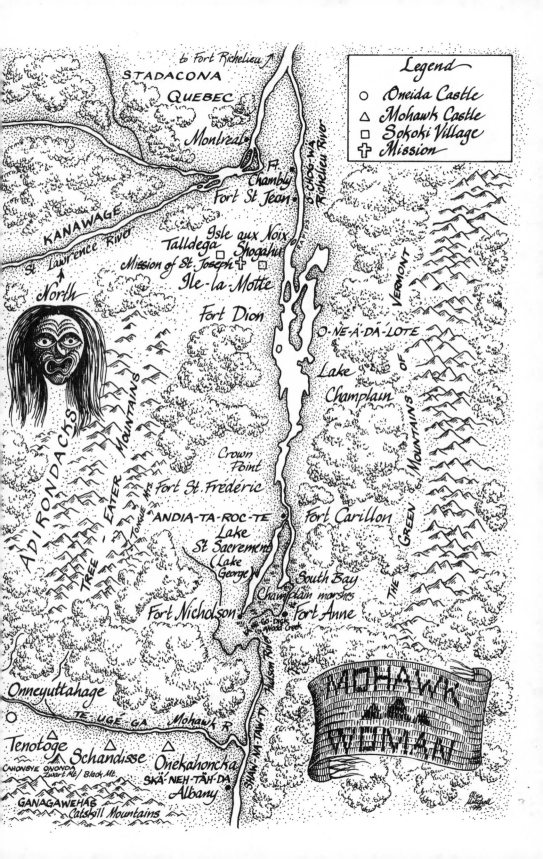

## Cast of Characters

### Mohawks

O-ron-ia-ke-te—*Touches-the-sky, Sky Toucher*
Tenäte Oÿoghi—*Singing Brook*
Tékha Ochquoha—*Burning Wolf, Singing Brook's brother*
O´hute Onega—*Green Water, Singing Brook's mother*
O-̈kla?—*Snowflake, Sky Toucher's mother*
Onea Onà·kara—*Stone Antler, Sky Toucher's deceased father*
Cahonsye Osto—*Black Feather, Singing Brook's deceased father*
Hah-Kooks—*Winter Gull, chief of the turtle clan, of the Mohawk*
Tiyanoga—*Hendrick, chief of the bear clan, of the Mohawk*
Ondach Ohonchwa—*Kettle Throat, chief of the wolf clan, of the Mohawk*
Cayere Tawyne—*Four Otters, Sky Toucher's friend*
Wotstaha Onirares—*Wide Shoulders, Sky Toucher's friend*
Christittye Etsi—*Copper Man, warrior-scout*
O-ne-ha-tah—*Porcupine, tribal elder*
Esteronde—*Rain, childhood friend of Singing Brook*
Crage Otsíhsto?—*White Star, Singing Brook's friend*
Azotsioha—*String-of-beads, Singing Brook's friend*
Endathatst—*Looking Glass, Medicine Man*
Quane Onawy—*Big Teeth, warrior-scout*
Serande—*Marten, Rain's friend*
Owanisse·nekwaŕ—*Yellow Tongue, wife of Winter Gull and purported seer*
Onea Canonou—*Stone Pipe, Caughnawaga, Oneida, warrior*

### Oneidas

Tékni-ska-je-a-nah—*Two Eagles, chief of the bear clan*
Margaret—*his wife*
Swift Doe—*Two Eagles' sister-in-law*
Tyagohuens—*Splitting Moon, warrior, Two Eagles' friend*
O-dat-she-dah—*Carries-a-quiver, chief of the turtle clan, of the Oneida*
Hat-ya-tone-nent-ha—*He swallows-his-own-body-from-the-foot, He Swallows, chief of the wolf clan, of the Oneida*

Quane Onente—*Large Arms, warrior*
Waghideria—*Sweat, warrior*
Canyewa Tawyne—*Little Otter, Benjamin, Two Eagles' and Margaret's son*

### English

Colonel Douglas Dorr—*commander at Fort Anne*
Captain Graham Hasty—*assigned to Fort Anne*
Captain Thomas Flood—*assigned to Fort Anne*
Major Alden Carver—*assigned to Fort Anne*
Lieutenant Walter Dumbarton—*New York Governor Hunter's emissary*

### Dutch

Jan Pieter Van Brocklin—*trader and double agent*

### French

Cavagnal Pierre Rigaud de Vaudreuil—*governor of Quebec*
Etienne Le Moyne Saint-Vallier Ramesay—*the turkey cock, governor of Montreal and colonel commanding the raiding force*
Paulette Lamaire—*Ramesay's mistress*
Captain Marcel Dussault
Major Gagne
Major Claude Piquet—*commandant at Fort Dion*
Sergeant Loubet—*attached to Fort Dion*

### Sokoki-Abnakis

Jankanque Karackwero—*Very-beautiful-sun, Stone Pipe's woman*
Ka-ta-kwa-je—*It-was-bruised, Sokoki warrior*
Na-wah-tah-toke—*Two-moccasins-standing-together, Sokoki warrior*

### Jesuits

Antoine Valterie Sebastien Xavier Fresnais—*father superior at St. Joseph Mission*
Julian Alain Clouet—*priest*
Emile Hiroux—*priest*

# PROLOGUE

IN THE SPRING of 1609, Samuel de Champlain encountered a band of Mohawk warriors while exploring the Mohawk Valley. In the fight that ensued he killed three chiefs with his arquebus. At the time the Mohawks were the most powerful and most belligerent tribe in the Iroquois Confederacy, but within a few years Mohawk dominance of the lucrative fur trade centered in Fort Orange (Albany) began to diminish.

The Mohawks turned to the Dutch, and later to the English, for help in protecting their trade and territory against the French. Alliance with the English was to involve the tribe in the protracted struggle between France and England for supremacy over the New World, ultimately dooming the Mohawks, the Keepers of the Eastern Door of the Iroquois Confederacy, as a sovereign nation.

# I
# PEOPLE OF THE TWILIGHT

# 1

IT WAS THE month before the month of the berry moon. In the swampy floodplain of the stream that flowed beside the Mohawk castle, the spicebushes were laced with tiny, subtly fragrant yellow-green flowers. Fire-red trillium crouched in the shadows of lofty sycamores preparing to burst into leaf; on the woodlands floor, baggy white Dutchman's-breeches hung above pale green, lacy leaves. The setting sun ambered the area and nature rested in silence before night spread its wings over the lands of the Iroquois to rouse the katydid chorus and the jingling voice of the spring peeper.

The stockade timbers surrounding the castle of Tenotoge thrust lancelike into the darkening sky, and the sounds of activity within came muffled to the ears of the young warrior and maiden. O-ron-ia-ke-te—Touches-the-sky—stood leaning against a tree, arms folded, his coppery skin glowing in the waning light, his expression glowering. From the bristling two-inch-wide roach cut strapping his otherwise shaven head, to his twined corn-husk moccasins he portrayed discouragement. He was called Sky Toucher not for his height—though he stood just above six feet—but for his climbing ability. In seconds he could pull himself effortlessly to the top of the tallest tree, rivaling the gray squirrel in speed and agility. Cross-legged on the ground before him, the fringed hem of her *ga-ka-ah* pulled just above her gleaming knees, aimlessly twisting a blade of grass, sat Tenäte Oÿoghi—Singing Brook—named for her dulcet voice. Her complexion was fair, discernably lighter than Sky Toucher's, although her long hair, parted in the center and separated into the two braids of an unmarried woman, was as black as his. Her huge, limpid eyes, looking anxiously up at him, appeared even darker. Laughter came faintly from the castle, riding on the warm breeze and deepening his gloom.

"We are doomed," he murmured.

She sighed impatiently. "So you keep saying, so often you must secretly wish it to be."

"*Neh!*" he flared.

"Then do not say it; ignore the shadows, look for light. Our two hearts are one. Think of the power that gives us. There is no boulder so big we can not push it aside."

"There *is* Tékha Ochquoha."

"My brother does not control my life."

"He is not the only stone in our path. Remove them all and we still could not live here, not as man and wife. He would make it impossible."

"That is the bone of it; you fear him."

He bristled. He admired her willingness to stand up to her brother but that did not alter the reality: everyone was against their marrying. They could not even find favorable signs in dreams, a bad omen.

"If you do not fear him, do not talk so."

He growled in frustration. "He pours his objections, his hatred of me into O´hute Onega's ears."

"You think she listens? My mother's mind is her own and *she* does not *hate* you. And I can defy Burning Wolf, you can at least try to."

"I do!"

She rose, and he took her in his arms. In the faint light of the dying day her face glowed. Embracing her he could feel his discouragement ebb. She stroked his cheek, letting her fingertip linger at the corner of his mouth, asking a smile. It came weakly. He kissed her then frowned as back came his discouragement.

"My gift of venison in exchange for your marriage bread is starting to rot in my chamber. Our mothers, our relatives, everyone knows it is there, who it is for. Everyone shakes their heads, snickers, waits. For what?"

"Look at me. We . . . *will* . . . be . . . married."

"When?"

"Patience. I . . . will talk to O´kla?"

"*My* mother?"

"*Nyoh,* get her to talk to O´hute Onega," said Singing Brook. "With both of them on our side, Burning Wolf's words will become as hollow as reeds."

"It still will not discourage him. He will see everyone ganging up against him as a challenge."

Singing Brook searched his eyes, her own eyes welling with worry. "You *do* fear him."

"Stop saying that!"

"Then why raise your voice? Why do your cheeks burn?" She ran her fingertips across his cheek.

Anger heating his stomach, he growled his words. "I can handle Burning Wolf."

"That is what *I* am afraid of. You will fight, blood will spill, one of you will kill the other."

"It does not have to come to that. I will . . . talk to him."

"Stay away from him," she warned. He hates the sight of you because of your father."

Which was central to the problem. Burning Wolf blamed Sky Toucher's father for the death of his own father, considering Onea Onà·kara's—Stone Antler's—cowardice as the cause of both men's deaths at the hands of the Abnakis allied with the French nine years earlier, in 1701. Others in the tribe agreed with Burning Wolf, and yet the often-recounted incident had become so garbled that what actually happened seemed impossible to ascertain.

Sky Toucher ached to know the truth; he did not believe his father had played the coward. Perhaps Cahonsye Osto—Black Feather, Singing Brook's and Burning Wolf's father—was the culprit. Possibly neither man was. But until Sky Toucher could prove otherwise, Burning Wolf and others poured the milk of cowardice down the back of Stone Antler's shade in the Village of the Dead, and would forever.

At that, even if Sky Toucher could prove his father blameless, it was doubtful Burning Wolf would accept it. So like the pain of a wound that refuses to heal, the breach continued between the two warriors. And more than once Burning Wolf announced that he would take his sister's life and then his own, rather than see her marry "coward's seed."

His opposition did not serve his purpose as well as he believed; if anything, it inspired even deeper affection on the part of the lovers. Sky Toucher, although he would never mention it to Singing Brook, knew that one day he would have to fight Burning Wolf to the death.

In the world of the Iroquois, the lovers were an anomaly.

Iroquois young men and women were not supposed to fall in love. Love, even affection, was ridiculed as an emotional failing in the nature of the whiteskins. The Iroquois did not even require a contract between the parties to be married. Only between their mothers. When a mother considered her son mature enough to be married, she looked about her for a maiden, who, she either knew personally or from friends, would be right for her son in disposition or temperament. The two mothers negotiated and reached a decision. Meanwhile, the concerned parties were entirely ignorant of what went on until the announcement of their marriage. Up to that time it was likely neither even saw the other. Neither party ever objected, for they received each other as a gift of their parents. To refuse to do so invited disownment.

When the parties were told that they were to be married, a simple ceremony sealed the bond. On the day following the announcement, the maiden was conducted by a few female friends to the longhouse for her intended. With her she brought a few cakes of unleavened corn bread, which she presented to her prospective mother-in-law upon entering the house, as proof of her usefulness and of her domestic skills. After receiving the marriage bread, the mother of her betrothed gave his gift of venison, or other meat, to the mother of the bride. This ratified and concluded the contract.

Singing Brook and Sky Toucher knew that many in the tribe disapproved of their relationship, considering it a liaison from which no respectable marriage could possible result. The Mohawks, Oneidas, Onondagas, Cayugas and Senecas, the tribes of the Five Nation Confederacy, observed the same stringent rules of marriage; and in marriage, as well as in their pre-marital arrangements, they allowed no place for the whiteskins' love.

Singing Brook and Sky Toucher defiantly disagreed, even flaunting their independent thinking, which did not help their cause. In each other's arms they had discovered passion, and having tasted it, quickly came to thrive on it. They did not disguise the fact that all they wanted in life was each other.

He took her hand, leading her deeper into the woods. On a bed of pine needles in their secret place, they lay naked listening to the night voices and touching their stars together. She had been born three years to the day after he, and each had been marked at birth with a perfect white star at the base of their thumbs. The discovery that both had stars and that no one else in the tribe did was what had brought them together in the first place.

## 2

TORCHES FOUGHT THE darkness in the Council House of the Mohawks, flames sprang from a crackling fire, smoke gathered thickly under the elm bark roof. Leading the Council were Ondach Ohonchwa—Kettle Throat—chief of the wolf clan, obese, flabby, his skin as brown and wrinkled as a walnut shell, his little eyes gleaming like ocher wampum beads, and Hah-Kooks—Winter Gull—chief of the turtle clan, gaunt, consumptive, riddled with arthritis, perpetually glum. The two flanked Tiyanoga—called Hendrick by the Dutch—chief of the bear clan. Hendrick, who carried fifty scars on his wiry body—the most obvious one appearing to extend his mouth around to under his ear—was brilliant, calculating, a born leader, and more experienced than any other Iroquois chief in dealing with the English. Now, though, he was reduced to fighting a delaying action while watching the erosion of his people, the gradual shrinking of their territory, the coming of twilight for all the Iroquois. Some suspected that he was weary of opposing the inevitable, even past the point of caring. His helplessness was written in his pensive eyes, his irresolute posture, and his near inertia.

The Council House was surrounded by low, windowless longhouses, each about thirty feet wide and upwards of eighty feet long. The castle, enclosed by a tall palisade, and called Tenotoge, was one of only three Mohawk castles still standing, the other seven having been destroyed or abandoned. Tenotoge was the westernmost of the existing castles, the one closest to the border of Oneida Territory. East of it stood Schandisse and further on, close to the confluence of the Mohawk and Hudson Rivers, stood Onekahoncka.

The warriors sitting in on the powwow were concerned. "What

will come of this, I wonder?" whispered Wotstaha Onirares, Wide Shoulders, to his friend Cayere Tawyne, Four Otters, beside him.

"Is not the answer to that hanging from the war post outside?"

"That is a question, not an answer. Their red tomahawk is an invitation."

Four Otters turned sharply. "Not for me. That one battle all of us took part in last year was my first and last."

Along with the warriors, numerous elders crowded the Council House, the stink of sweat mingling with that of rancid dog meat and smoke. Wide Shoulders studied the four whiteskins sitting opposite the chiefs, their leader the colonel, Dorr. He had been droning on about the ever-worsening political situation, making it sound as if the world would end if the Mohawks did not join what the English called Queen Anne's War.

"Look at them," snickered Wide Shoulders. "The smoke is making them sick."

"Not Dorr, he is used to it."

"Look at the one with the skin like snow, his eyes are so watery he cannot see."

Wide Shoulders chuckled. The air was stifling, but Dorr, he knew, was comfortable in the company of warriors wrapped in blankets or, in warm weather, wearing only breechclouts. Used to the stink of the bear grease many smeared on their bodies, to the Mohawks' haircuts, to the tufts of hair some wore in their ears, the beads others fastened to their noses with a thread hanging down to their lips. Wide Shoulders gave the colonel credit: unlike other whiteskin long knives, Dorr at least made an attempt to understand and respect Mohawk ways and values.

Three squaws shuffled in, carrying bark trays and picking up the bones littering the earth floor. Their blankets were impregnated with bear grease and vermilion made from red iron oxide. They wore men's shirts sprinkled with vermilion, earrings, bead or animal-tooth necklaces, bracelets and a winding blue kilt that came to their knees. Their footwear was not the warriors' twined corn-husk summer moccasins but instead deerskin, worked with black, red and yellow, with porcupine quills and fringes of scarlet-dyed wolf hair.

Four Otters grunted. "He, Dorr, should not have driven the

red-painted hatchet into the castle war post when they came in.
That is taking it for granted that we will go back to war."

"We will."

*"Neh."*

"Watch and see."

Now Kettle Throat was gently reproaching the colonel for his
presumptuousness, presuming that the Mohawks would again flock
to the banner of his chief with the gold hat, Queen Anne. Dorr
let him rattle on without defending his action, shifting his legs so
a squaw could retrieve a bone. The bones would be given to the
dogs yelping outside, many of whose own bones were destined for
the same fate.

Dorr, Wide Shoulders knew, was the most experienced among
the four whiteskin long knives present. Trained as an artilleryman,
he had served in the army since the age of sixteen. Intensely pa-
triotic, politically sage and opportunistic, he was also tough and
resourceful. Unlike many English officers, he did not panic under
fire—that trait the Mohawks had witnessed in the engagement the
previous fall.

"I do not like Dorr," murmured Four Otters.

"What is to like or dislike with any English?"

"Last time you could see, he did not hesitate to shed Mohawk
blood before spilling any redbacks', given the choice."

Wide Shoulders grunted. "And what choice do we have but to
side with him? Without English guns and protection, Tenotoge,
Schandisse and Onekahoncka would be destroyed by the lace-cuffs,
and our people massacred by the French moccasins."

Beside Dorr sat Thomas Flood, who had come with him across
the O-jik-ha-dä-gé-ga on a wooden island five summers before. In
his fifties, the fat, red-faced Flood was able, brave and fought like
a madman until he became too drunk to stay awake. Hasty, a
captain of militia from Albany, was also present. He was less than
half Flood's age but had fought boldly with him and Dorr in the
victory last year: a victory as hollow as a gourd, for the English
and the tribe had lost nearly 150 men, the Mohawks, 80 alone.

Now Kettle Throat began to adduce his reasons against continued Mohawk involvement. As Dorr listened, his face did not
darken with the disappointment flooding Dumbarton's face. The

lieutenant had been sent by Hunter, the governor in New York, to sit in on the talks. At first sight of him Wide Shoulders saw an official spy in silk, lace and black cockade. Dorr, too, knew what Dumbarton was.

Kettle Throat concluded, "It comes to this, Dorr. Our people have seen too many red days, lost too many brave warriors fighting with your guns against the lace-cuffs." He squinted, setting his fat jaw, trying to look resolute. Suppressing a grin, Four Otters elbowed Wide Shoulders.

"Some of us think that you are in a conspiracy," Kettle Throat added.

Dorr, haggard from lack of sleep, looked up sharply. "I don't follow you, Kettle."

"That the English and the French are secretly friends, and pretend to fight only to kill off those of us foolish enough to choose the warpath."

"Chiefs on both sides," interjected Winter Gull, nodding vigorously.

Hendrick, the youngest of the three chiefs, grunted agreement.

"So that in the end," Winter Gull went on, "instead of stealing our lands you only have to move onto them, for there will be too few of us left to drive you off."

"Great Chief, with all due respect, that is a most distressing, most unfair allegation. Totally wrong. We fight to protect your proud people from the threat of the French yoke."

"A yoke is a yoke," muttered Winter Gull, "French or English. We have always fought with your guns and have the graves to show for our loyalty." Guttural agreement threaded through the gathering. Dumbarton sniffed disdainfully and waved away smoke. Wide Shoulders did not like him. He was no soldier, he was too much lace and too sweet a smell. He belonged with the women in Albany dancing and drinking tea, not in a serious powwow.

Winter Gull went on. "Dorr, before you came to these shores our warriors were fighting under English long knives against the lace-cuffs. For seven harvests it lasted. When the time came to make that peace the English deserted us, leaving us to choke down Frontenac's terms."

"In payment for our help to you, we were humiliated," added Kettle Throat.

Winter Gull went on. "And even before those long years of red days, many of our people accepted the honey that the black robes poured into the cups of their ears, accepted the cross and Je-sus and became Praying Mohawks."

"And moved up to Caughnawaga near Montreal. And sided with the French," said Dorr. "And do you blame us for that?"

"You ask us to take the knife to our blood brothers?"

"You have before, great Chief, to defend yourselves. It is in your interests as well as ours that you remain loyal, see this through to final victory. English armies are poised to overwhelm Canada. In six months most of the French survivors will be returning home. From that day on you will live in peace."

Kettle Throat grunted. "Better from this day on. *Neh,* it is decided, Dorr, no more will we paint our wampum red for you English."

"Rubbish!" shrilled Dumbarton. All eyes flashed toward him. "'Od's fig, don't you see? They're bloody afraid!" He scowled at the chiefs.

Silence fell like a stone. The squaws, almost done picking up the bones, stood staring with the warriors and chiefs. Wide Shoulders elbowed Four Otters and held his breath. Dorr looked shocked. The lieutenant leveled a finger at Winter Gull. "Isn't that really it, you red bugger? You dread having to face their guns; your vaunted warriors can't stand pain, they're afraid!" Winter Gull returned his glare, his expression indifferent. Then he looked at a warrior, Christittye Etsi, Copper Man, seated close to the fire. "Speak up, damn you!" snapped the lieutenant.

Copper Man thrust his hand into the fire and held it there. Wide Shoulders sucked in a quiet breath. Stunned, Dorr watched with the others as the flesh began to melt like candlewax and catch fire, blistering. A faint, sickeningly sweet odor arose, fighting with that of rancid meat. The hand trembled but stayed in the flame, the only sound the soft sizzling of burning flesh. Then slowly Copper Man withdrew his hand. The flames on it died, wisps of smoke curled upward as he shoved his hand behind him.

"Can English long knives stand pain?" Kettle Throat asked Dumbarton.

The Lieutenant set his jaw. On his knees he pulled his lace-trimmed sleeve a few inches up his arm and started his hand toward the fire. Flood moved to intervene, but Dorr's hand on his arm stopped him. Reaching the flame, Dumbarton jerked back his hand.

"Ridiculous! Showing off! I'm talking about the pain of a blade, a shot! I'm talking about—"

"Shut up!" snapped Dorr.

The powwow was over. Wide Shoulders watched Dorr glare at the too sweet-smelling one. Then smile at the chiefs.

"It's late, great Chiefs, great warriors all. We will presume on your patience and your time no further." He got up, dusting off his rear. "With your gracious permission, Kettle Throat, Winter Gull, Hendrick, we'll talk again. There's time. I thank you, I thank you all for inviting us, giving us the chance to discuss it, and bid you good night. Gentlemen?"

Outside they gulped in the fresh air. Dumbarton flared. "Beastly savages, cowardly scum! They—"

"Lieutenant," interrupted Dorr, his voice barely above a whisper. "May I call you Walter?"

"Of cour—"

"Walter, we'll be riding back to camp now, a bit prematurely, thanks to your enthusiasm. You needn't bother coming; it would be out of your way. Better you get on your horse and ride back to New York City."

Preparing to mount, Dumbarton frowned. "Out of the question, Colonel. I'm here on assignment from His Excellency the governor . . ."

"I know, I read his letter that you showed me. All the same, just do as I ask; get out of here."

By now, Dumbarton was in the saddle. Dorr snatched the lieutenant's reins and slapped the horse's croup. It bolted and galloped off, Dumbarton fumbling for his reins. Hasty laughed uproariously. "You think he's got enough face powder to hold him till he's back in his mother's arms?"

"I think we've smelled the last of him."

"What'll Governor Hunter say?" asked Flood, producing a bottle of rum, downing a quarter of it and passing it to Dorr.

"Not much," said Dorr, drinking, then offering the bottle to Hasty. "Not as long as we bring our red friends back into the fold. We will. Don't look so worried, Thomas, you didn't expect them to run outside and throw their arms around the war post, did you? They'll come around; they know which side their bread's greased on. Savages they may be, but they're not stupid."

"You could see warriors in there itching to fight," said Hasty.

"That's what we want, red loyalty. Trust me, chaps, we'll all be back bleeding together again. And those three feathered apes know it. That Hendrick's as sneaky as a snake in your boot, doesn't say two words, but he's the brains of the three and despises the idea of throwing in with us again. But he knows they have to. They chose sides a long time ago; they can't switch now and can't stay out of it no matter how loudly they down our invitation." He pointed at a pack of whelps fighting over the bones. "There you have it, chaps, visible proof it's a dog-eat-dog world."

# 3

WIDE SHOULDERS AND Four Otters emerged from the Council House with the crowd. Four Otters caught a firefly in his small fist, the cold, yellow light pulsing through the slits between his fingers. His smirk said "I told you so."

"I knew even before we sat down the chiefs would turn him down. That settles it, we do not go back to war." He released the firefly. It ascended, joining others, a tiny earthbound galaxy challenging the lofty giants.

"They said the same thing last time," muttered Wide Shoulders. "They were still saying it just before we left to fight. We will go back."

Four Otters, who barely came up to his friend's shoulder, shook his head and patted his knife. "I will say it once, try and remember: never again will I draw this for any English."

Wide Shoulders scoffed and waved this away. "You call yourself a warrior? At heart you are a basket weaver, a Munsee." He shoved him playfully.

Already a young giant, Wide Shoulders was still growing; he delighted in taunting the smaller Four Otters. Some thought Wide Shoulders jealous of his friend's quickness and superiority with weapons. But the two were inseparable, and both just as close to Sky Toucher. They had been *four* close friends before Many Wounds, the philosopher and elder of the group, the only one with prior experience in battle, was killed by an Abnaki arrow in the ambush that had triggered the fighting the previous fall.

"Tell me the truth," Wide Shoulders went on, "is it that you are afraid? Is the powdered whiteskin with the big mouth right?"

"*Neh.* I have already fought, I do not have to prove I have a spine. Did you not listen in there? Kettle Throat said it: we must have the approval of the whole Confederacy to go to war, all five tribes. We could never get it even if we wanted it. The Senecas and Cayugas are dead against fighting the lace-cuffs. Think about that: if they side with the lace-cuffs, they will not have to fight, the Hurons and Abnakis will do it for them. If they side with the redbacks, they will have to."

"They will if they side with the lace-cuffs," said Wide Shoulders. "Their long knives will insist on it. I do not care what you or the chiefs say, we will fight. The voice in my bones tells me so."

"Your *voice in your bones* is an *onewachten.*"

"*Neh,* it never lies." Wide Shoulders sobered. "We have to fight. If the English lose, we lose. Everything. I figured that much out last time and it is true. We are tied together like the arrowhead to the shaft. We do not want it, we do not like it, but that is the way it is. Do you think Sky Toucher will go back?"

Four Otters grinned. "Only if Singing Brook lets him."

"He would not let us go without him."

"Let *you,* not me."

"You will come around. Where is he, anyway?"

Four Otters snickered. "Where is he always after dark? Let us go sneak up on them."

Wide Shoulders grunted. "No sneaking, he will feed your knife to you. What do you think those two will end up doing? They know they can never marry."

"They can if they run off," said Four Otters. "Come . . ."

They had made love, and now was the time Singing Brook enjoyed almost as much, the time for the tender caresses and sweet words and vows that brought them slowly down from the peak of their passion. Around them the woodlands were unaccountably silent. Even the voice of the breeze was stilled. Sky Toucher kissed her, framing her face with his hands, gazing down into her eyes. The sadness in his own touched her heart.

"I am sorry," he murmured. "I just do not think my mother can help us with O'hute Onega. I think we should just leave, go far away."

"Where?"

"Out of our territory, across the Shaw-na-taw-ty to Mohegan lands."

"And become Mohegan? *Neh.*"

"Then cross the border to Onneyuttahage, become Oneida. My cousin Two Eagles would welcome us."

"Look at me. We are Mohawk, not Mohegan or Oneida. Besides, that would be running away, the coward's choice. Our mothers do not deserve that. The gossip would be embarrassing, painful for them. Please, let us at least try my way."

"Even if both approve, there is still Burning Wolf."

She jerked erect, scowling, then began to dress. "How many times must I say it? I do not care what my brother thinks about anything!"

"Shhhh, he is still your brother. All right, all right, tomorrow talk to my mother. Try and make her understand. But if you fail, we leave. What else can we do?" He kissed her, letting his mouth linger against hers, and felt her tremble slightly. "Our problem is we are in the wrong place," he murmured. "Wrong to be Mohawk, to be Iroquois. In another place, in a country across the Wide Water it would not be like this. We would be free to do as we please."

"We are free if we tell ourselves we are," she said. "I want you, I want your children, your life and mine like two vines twisted together so tightly nothing can separate them. We can make it so, we can!"

He grunted, suddenly depressed. As she kissed him, the woodlands came to life, as if approving: katydids, cicadas, the insistent, continuous trilling of the black-horned tree cricket. And overhead a host of white-and-yellow acre moths came undulating toward them through gossamer moonlight.

"We are going back to war!" a voice sounded.

Sky Toucher jumped up, straightening his breechclout. Already dressed, Singing Brook gaped in disbelief. Wide Shoulders came lumbering up, Four Otters following. Sky Toucher scowled and started to reprimand them, Singing Brook cut in.

"What are you talking about?" she asked.

Wide Shoulders explained, interrupted frequently by Four Otters, who disagreed with his assessment of the situation. But the bigger man was more persuasive. Singing Brook turned her glance toward Sky Toucher and held his eyes as worry seeped into her own.

"*Neh,*" she murmured.

"Oh, not right away," said Wide Shoulders. "The chiefs are against it, but in time they will come around. Even if they do not, there will be warriors who will join Dorr. I will." He thumbed his heavily tattooed chest proudly.

"Not me," said Four Otters. "How about you, O-ron-ia-ke-te?"

"You will come," said Wide Shoulders. "You must!"

As Sky Toucher looked Singing Brook's way, she lowered her eyes. "This comes at a bad time for us," he muttered.

"You knew it was in the wind," said Wide Shoulders.

"To hear you, you are already on the warpath," said Singing Brook. "Why not wait and see what is decided?"

"She is right," said Sky Toucher. He looked from one to the other. "You have delivered your *good news,* you can leave."

"Are you coming?" Four Otters asked.

"*Ísene!*"

They laughed and started away.

"There will be no more fighting," said Sky Toucher to her,

striving to sound resolute. "Not for Tenotoge. The redbacks and lace-cuffs can kill each other off like starving wolves; we do not have to get into it."

"Are you trying to convince me or yourself?" She threw up her hands. "This is all we need. I will be a widow before I am even married."

He said nothing, there was nothing he could think of.

# 4

RAIN CAME LATER that night, thrashing the longhouses, stopping just before dawn, leaving the mountains to the south shrouded in a bright white haze. In rolled fog to fill a yawning clove a short distance from Sky Toucher, and the early morning mists swirled eerily around the mountain before him. By the time he reached it and began climbing, through the talus at the base, where bloodroot and fuzzy miterwort flourished, the sun had emerged brightly. Up the steep trail he picked his way to a sheer rock face, the trail wandering off to his left to circle the face. Rejecting the trail, for following it would take him far out of his way, he began to pull himself carefully up the rock, finding holds with his fingertips, easing himself gradually upward, gaining the same holds with his bare toes, having left his moccasins hidden below.

Time moved backwards, spring retreating from the land as he cleared the sheer rock and continued his ascent through stands of oak and hickory. Raccoons and woodchucks trundled about. Fifteen hundred feet up, the Dutchman's-breeches had just recently broken into leaf. Purple and white violets blossomed in profusion. Climbing out of the oak and hickory through a grove of beeches, he came to sugar maples and smooth yellow violets among the purple and white ones. He spied a black bear lurking on a shrub-festooned ledge above him and far to the left.

As he climbed he thought of Singing Brook and her mission to his mother this morning. He pictured them discussing the problem, his mother's expression grim. He had asked to join them, but

Singing Brook wanted to go alone, to avoid pressuring O꞉kla?—Snowflake. He grunted. Even if Singing Brook won over his mother, how would that help with her own family?

Whatever the outcome, he had to do his part, and this would be the start of it. Which brought him to thoughts of Burning Wolf. Why *did* Burning Wolf hate him? They hardly knew each other. Why did Burning Wolf blame him for his father's suspected wrongdoing?

What exactly had Stone Antler done? Sky Toucher could only hope that the answer lay at the top of the mountain. He had sought it there previously from Gâ꞉oh but had been unsuccessful; still, he had to keep trying.

He had told himself earlier that even if he got knife-steel-proof of his father's innocence, Burning Wolf would reject it. But since then he'd changed his mind. Clearly, if he could prove his father guiltless Burning Wolf would have to accept it, or look a fool in the eyes of others in the tribe. And that would end the matter. His task was twofold: secure proof, persuade Burning Wolf it was genuine.

Up, up he moved swiftly, nimbly. At eighteen hundred feet silvery, broad-boled beech reappeared along with thick, dark-green hemlock and yellow birch. Spring flowers that had already gone to seed in the woodlands around Tenotoge abounded here: lily of the valley, starflower, yellow violets of a variety different from those below, these showing dark-green, downy leaves with a glossy sheen.

At the end of the steepest stretch of the climb, he came to a gently sloping terrace cut by numerous small streams issuing from springs in the mountain bedrock behind the slope. Boulders in all sizes were strewn about the old woodland of tall sugar maples and white ash.

For a time the land ascended more gently, and hemlock took possession of it, inhibiting wildflower growth, mosses and lichen displacing blossoms. Higher and higher he climbed, coming to where the trees thinned and squirrel-corn plants were in early bud. Still higher, clawing his way up the face of a fifty-foot cliff, he found the ragged edge of winter, the land cold and windswept, with no sign of greening and old snow lingering stubbornly in the shade of boulders.

He was now within two hundred feet of the summit, not tired, although his fingers ached slightly from pulling his weight up the sheer face of the cliff immediately below. Overhead a turkey vulture floated on the updraft from a ledge, hanging motionless. Filling his lungs with the chill air, he resumed climbing and reached the summit, a small grassless plateau strewn with rubble. Seemingly securing it in place, three pinnacles rose high, the tallest upwards of thirty feet and flattened at the top. Near the base of one of the shorter pinnacles a clove yawned pitch black and so deep one could barely hear a stone land—at least one thousand feet straight down, he guessed.

The chill wind gusted with occasional fury. This was the highest mountain nearest Tenotoge: the Dutch called it Zwart Mountain. To the Mohawks it was Cahonsye Ononda, Black Mountain, from the blackness it assumed at sunrise. Facing north, cupping his hands around his mouth, he called as he had three times before, to Gä̃oh, the Bear, the Father of Winds; Gä̃oh, the North Wind, asking him to summon from the Village of the Dead the spirit of his father Stone Antler.

"*Kä-ooga-sar-da-ne-do. An-di-äh* Onea Onà·kara!"

This he repeated four times. The wind blew fiercely in his face, and the pinnacles seemed to tremble at its force.

"Gä̃oh, Father of Winds, bring me the spirit of Onea Onà·kara, my father. I must question him."

To his surprise and elation Gä̃oh responded; blasting, howling, wailing, whining and then making a curious undulating shrill sound that was neither wail nor whine. It lanced his eardrums, and in it he heard a single word rejecting his entreaty. A second time he asked, again he was denied. He was preparing to ask a third time when Gä̃oh spoke in many words, telling him that it would be pointless to summon Stone Antler's spirit. Sky Toucher's heart sank. He was about to give it up when Gä̃oh spoke again, asking to hear his questions. *He* would do the asking.

Sky Toucher's heart rose against his ribs. "I want to know, Father of Winds, how he died in the war nine years ago," he said.

"He and Cahonsye Osto, Black Feather. They fought in battle together. What happened to them?"

Gẵ-oh blew shrilly with no words, then rested and resumed howling furiously. The sun stood straight overhead warming Sky Toucher's pate. To the west rose Oetsira Ononda, Fire Mountain, so called from its appearance at sunset. To the south beyond the Mountain of the Winter Moon threaded the Unadilla River. To the north the Te-ugé-ga, the Mohawk, threaded northward back to its source. And in the west Lake Oneida spread its silver.

Sky Toucher held his breath and waited. The howling ceased abruptly, supplanted by a rolling wail, like a woman's high-pitched singing. The words came distinctly: not, to his surprise, Stone Antler's words, but those of the shade of an Abnaki warrior, who identified himself and had witnessed the deaths of both fathers on that fateful afternoon.

His words came clearly though Gẵ-oh.

Incriminating Black Feather. A courageous warrior, afraid of no man, he had unaccountably lost his nerve, panicked and fled the battle. Stone Antler, his friend, had followed to bring him back. The two found themselves cut off and surrounded. Both were killed but clearly Black Feather, not Stone Antler, was the coward.

Gẵ-oh ceased. All was silent. Sky Toucher sat, hanging his head, deep in troubling thought. He had his explanation at last, and from an eyewitness. But it neither satisfied him nor relieved his mind. He would have to go back to Burning Wolf and tell him the truth about his father. But Burning Wolf would never believe him, never. He would accuse him of trying to shift the blame and despise him for his deviousness.

He could see only one solution: somehow, he would have to induce Burning Wolf to come up here so that he could hear the truth with his own ears. Could he? Could Singing Brook? Could anyone?

His sigh was more of a groan.

The wind resumed, not furiously, not howling or even whining, not Gẵ-oh. He had given Sky Toucher the explanation he had sought for so long, he was gone.

# 5

THE ODOR OF cookfire smoke from the passageway seeped into Snowflake's chamber in the longhouse, stinging Singing Brook's eyes and nostrils. Nervousness seized her as she let drop the entrance flap behind her. Ordinarily, she felt comfortable in the company of Sky Toucher's mother. She was fond of her and her warm feelings toward Snowflake were reciprocated in kind. Perhaps not today.

Snowflake sat on the earth floor leaning against the platform on which her bunk was built. The shelf above it was crammed with bowls and kettles, other cooking utensils and extra bear robes. Under the platform snowshoes, bows and winnowing baskets were kept, while suspended from the rafters were skeins of tobacco, all sorts of dried fruits and vegetables, salted fish and braids of corn.

In shallow dishes were quantities of purple clam shell beads and white beads fashioned from the cylinder of the whelk, both colors appropriate to peace, not the hostilities that rumor insisted would soon engulf the Mohawks. Between the two dishes was a dish with only a few undrilled beads of both colors.

The Iroquois strung wampum on cards for use in minor tribal transactions and wove it into belts to convey messages, record treaty stipulations, carry on condolence ceremonies when chiefs or loved ones died and for other religious and social purposes. Snowflake used a steel drill bartered from a Dutch trader, a distinct improvement over earlier bone drills. The beads were strung on nettle fibers or deer sinew to form the wampum strings, several of which were tied together in a bunch at one end.

Snowflake looked up from her drilling as Singing Brook entered. The older woman had been pretty in her youth but life, tragic and demanding, had drained away her beauty. She had lost her husband and Sky Toucher's sister.

Premature fissures creased her forehead, etched into her cheeks and around her small mouth. She was blind in her left eye, which looked out at the world as white as the winter visitor whose name she bore.

She smiled greeting. Singing Brook read it pessimistically as sympathy: Snowflake knew why she had come and knew as well that she would be sending her away disappointed. Sky Toucher's favorite word lately came back to her: doomed. Snowflake would not want to become involved.

Working meticulously, Snowflake finished piercing a white bead. She held it up, peering through it at her visitor.

"Why so worried looking, my child? Sit."

Singing Brook cleared her throat and looked about like a wary bird protecting its food. "I have come to ask your help, O-kla?."

"In what?"

"Ahhh . . ."

By now Singing Brook's throat had become as dry as sand, she felt as if her voice would crack. She would stammer and croak and make a fool of herself in front of this woman whose help they so desperately needed. She would look witless, too immature to be wife to any man.

"Go on," said Snowflake.

"He and I wish to marry."

"Why?"

"Why?"

"Why Touches-the-sky?"

"He . . . holds my heart, and I hold his. With our eyes we see only each other."

"No one else? Neither of you?"

"No one."

"And so my son has sent you to plead your case."

"*Neh, neh,* it was my idea. I want you on our side, to help us with my mother, my family."

"Help you how?"

"You and my mother are good friends . . ."

"Green Water and I have been best friends since back before either of you was born."

"*Nyoh.* O-kla?, my mother will listen to you. My words do not reach inside her ears. When I try to speak of him she closes them to me."

"Which should tell you that she disapproves."

"But she has no reason to!"

"Shhhh, do not excite yourself."

Snowflake was attacking another bead, fixing it in a stick of hard wood with one end split like a vise. Her drill was imbedded in the end of a hawthorn spike. When she had drilled the hole halfway through she stopped and started on the opposite side. Singing Brook watched uneasily as the work progressed and Snowflake said nothing further, concentrating so intently on her work it was as if she'd forgotten her visitor. The only sound was the soft gouging of the drill. Singing Brook was tempted to repeat her comment regarding her mother but held back fearing that the older woman would think she was talking too much. At last Snowflake looked up and spoke.

"I have a question for you, my child. Do you think it right for me to stick my spoon into your family's soup?"

"Your son is half of this," said Singing Brook.

"Will he approach Green Water?"

"*Neh.* Only because of Burning Wolf."

"Only because of Burning Wolf. I have heard it said that your brother would prefer to kill you before he will let you marry my son."

"He has no right to speak so!"

"He is your brother and the warrior of your household."

"That does not give him the right to interfere in my life."

O꞉kla? shrugged. "Maybe he is just being overly protective. Would you condemn him for that?"

"I do not care what his reason is. I ask you, O꞉kla?, I beg you, will you speak to my mother?"

The deerskin flap lifted, a familiar face appeared: O´hute Onega—Green Water. She carried undrilled beads in a small basket, adding them to the depleted quantity in the dish in front of Snowflake. She came in with a smile of greeting for her friend, but at sight of her daughter her expression darkened.

Snowflake nodded, gesturing for her to sit.

"Leave us, Tenäte Oÿoghi," said Green Water.

Singing Brook started up. Snowflake touched her arm.

"She can stay."

Green Water shrugged. She sat cross-legged opposite her friend. Snowflake finished drilling the other side of the bead, held the hole up to her good eye, approved it and tossed it in the white bead dish. She then selected a bead cut from the purple spot in a clam shell.

"Singing Brook has asked me to speak to you on her behalf."

Green Water bristled. She was younger than Snowflake, shorter, pudgy, less comely. Her nose was too large and slightly flattened, causing the nostrils to flare, her eyes set too far apart with a shining plane between, but her skin was unlined.

"Why do you not come to me, your mother?" she asked Singing Brook coldly.

"How many times have I tried?"

Green Water sniffed and looked away. "It is useless, Daughter. You cannot break the rules and expect my approval. It would be an insult to our people."

"That is what annoys you. Not him, not our marrying, but what others may think!"

"Shhhhh," said Snowflake.

"But it is so unfair!"

"Be quiet," said Green Water. "Your selfishness blinds you to what is proper here. Look at me. I and I alone decide who you will marry. Snowflake decides who her son will. Neither of you has a say. Blame yourself for this situation. You have ruined any chance you might have had to marry with your presumptuousness and impatience." She shook an admonishing finger. "You cannot disregard tradition and expect to have your way. That is not how marriages are made among our people."

"Listen to her," said Snowflake. "She is right. It is not. Although not all our marriages are . . . conventional. Green Water, does she know how you and Black Feather married?"

"That has nothing to do with this," grumbled the other.

Singing Brook looked puzzled. Her mother looked suddenly angry, as if in the next instant she would reach out and throttle Snowflake.

Snowflake sniffed, unfazed by Green Water's scowl. "Is it not the same? You and her father, she and my son? Now, do you tell her or do you wish me to?"

"O꞉kla? . . ."

"Child, your mother and your father—"

"All right, all right! We met . . . we were attracted to each other, we . . ."

"Ran away together when their mothers disapproved," said Snowflake.

"We came back."

"Two years later with two children. So . . ." Snowflake paused and leaned forward. "Is not this the same as what you two did?"

"It is *not*," snapped Green Water.

"You are right, it is not. *These two are not running away. She is trying to reason with you!*"

Silence followed. Mother refused to meet daughter's eyes; Snowflake's single good eye shifted back and forth between them as she let her words sink in.

Suddenly Green Water flared. "What do I care if you marry him?" she rasped. "You think I hate him? You think me heartless? Toward you, my only daughter? It is your brother, your uncles and aunts—"

"Not my uncles and aunts, only Tékha Ochquoha," murmured Singing Brook.

"Is he not enough?"

"He is not anything in this."

"Tell him that."

"I have. It is like talking to a stone," Singing Brook replied.

"I have a question," said Snowflake. Having drilled the purple bead through on both sides, she squinted through the hole. It looked imperfect, so she attacked one side with the drill. "Can you not handle your own son, O´hute Onega?"

"I will thank you not to stick your spoon into our soup," rasped Green Water.

"Sky Toucher is *my* son, is he not?"

"*Nyoh,* and you should be talking to him the same way, discouraging him."

"I am curious," Snowflake went on. "Does Burning Wolf know how his father and mother married, without approval?"

"That, too, is no business of yours," snapped Green Water.

Snowflake nodded. "You are right. But this, their desire to marry, is. I approve. Will you?"

Singing Brook held her breath. Her mother glared at her briefly but gradually her eyes softened.

"Will you speak with your son?" Snowflake persisted.

"I . . . will think about it. I must go, I have *gwä´ onondä* cooking."

She left abruptly, the flap dropping behind her. Snowflake looked at Singing Brook and grinned.

"Patience, child, patience."

Singing Brook's heart sank. What good would patience do? No matter what her mother said to him, however she approached it, Burning Wolf would not budge in his opposition.

══ 6 ══

BURNING WOLF GOT his name from an incident. Bitten by a she-wolf protecting her young, in retaliation he clubbed her senseless and burned her alive. At the time he had just turned fourteen. He emerged from the experience proud of his bravery and resourcefulness. No one in the tribe had ever known anybody to burn an animal alive; some praised him, others saw his action as pointless.

He was not a big man but was strong and quick with his knife and his temper. Unaddicted to thinking, impulse governed his every action. He was slow of foot and not agile. His sister's good looks he shared but unlike Singing Brook he was vain. His superior attitude was ill-calculated to win people's good will so he had few friends. He was, however, considerate toward and devoted to his mother and aunts, as well as his sister. Snowflake rightly contended that he opposed Sky Toucher's marrying Singing Brook because he was overly protective of his sister. Perhaps, too, he thought no man good enough for her, an opinion not uncommon among older brothers. Singing Brook was one of the few people who stood up to him; she refused to put up with his teasing when she was young and refused to let him influence her thinking now that she was a grown woman. This he saw as ingratitude; brother and sister were not on the friendliest terms even before she turned her eye toward Sky Toucher.

"You are not shaking the buttons, Cayere Tawyne," said Burning Wolf. "You cannot hear them rattling in your hand."

He stood watching Wide Shoulders and Four Otters play the deer-button game. Eight deer-horn buttons about an inch in diameter were polished and slightly burned on one side to blacken them. The player shook the buttons and threw them. If six turned up the same color, it counted two, if seven, it counted four, and if all eight, it counted twenty.

"You should make him shake properly, Wotstaha Onirares," Burning Wolf went on.

The winner took as many beans from a pot of fifty as he made points by the throw and continued to throw as long as he won. The player who took all the beans won the game. It often took hours.

"You cannot win," growled Wide Shoulders to Four Otters. "I feel luck in my bones."

"So why *is* he winning?" asked Burning Wolf.

The game was being played on the ground outside Sky Toucher's longhouse. Both ignored the intruder. Neither wanted him to join the game. Besides, he would have refused if invited to play and they knew it, but this did not discourage him from commenting.

"Watch him shake, Wotstaha Onirares. That is not a proper shake, can you not see?"

If Wide Shoulders did he was not about to acknowledge it to Burning Wolf. Sky Toucher came through the open front gate. At sight of him Burning Wolf frowned, sending his hand to his knife.

"I want to talk to you," said Sky Toucher coming up to him. The players paused to watch. "Outside."

"You have nothing to say that would interest me, cowardly dog."

Four Otters sucked in a breath, stiffened and exchanged looks with Wide Shoulders.

"You have called me that for the last time," said Sky Toucher.

Burning Wolf leered. "Listen to him, the worm is getting its back up. Are you challenging me, worm?"

"When you hear what I have to tell you, you will know how wrong you are. Your coward's moccasins belong on somebody's feet but not my father's."

"His shame shrivels his bones in his grave, and you know it. Oh well, I have nothing to do. Let us go, this should be interesting." They started off, the others stopped playing to follow.

"Give us some privacy, will you?" rasped Sky Toucher.

The two walked outside. To their right, women were hoeing in the cornfield. Green shoots were already showing. Beyond the field where the woodlands resumed two men were bringing in a buck suspended from a pole between them. Sky Toucher knelt, picked up a twig and began aimlessly drawing in the dirt to avoid looking at his listener.

"You accuse my father of being a coward and causing your father's death, *neh?*"

"Not an accusation, worm, the truth."

"You are right about one thing. In what happened, there was a coward."

Sky Toucher told of his ascent to the mountaintop and his conversation with Gá̃oh. Even before he could finish Burning Wolf began scoffing.

*"Onewachten."*

"I do not lie. Nor does Gá̃oh. My father's father was able to speak to Gá̃oh, my father, too. All the elders can testify to that. I spoke to him; he got it from an Abnaki shade who was there that your father was the coward who cut and ran, not mine."

*"Onewachten!"*

*"He* was the deserter." He stood up bringing his face close to Burning Wolf's glare. "Gá̃oh said it. I say let us both forget it, push it back where it belongs under the dust of the nine years."

"You lie," snarled Burning Wolf, "and I can prove it!"

"Good, this is your chance. Come with me up Black Mountain. I will summon Gá̃oh, he will tell you what he told me."

"Gá̃oh talks to *you?* That is good, that is funny!"

"Come, Tékha Ochquoha, when you hear the truth you will not think it so funny."

"I should climb all the way up there just to prove you a liar?

Wait, wait, I get it, this is a trick. You want to get me up there and pull a cowardly trick—"

"No trick." Sky Toucher studied him archly. "Why are you so afraid of finding out the truth?"

Burning Wolf waved him away and started to turn back. "You waste my time, *onewachten*." He stopped abruptly, scowled and took a step toward Sky Toucher, his hand again going to his knife. "Who else have you told of this?"

"No one."

"You tell my sister and I will cut your heart out."

"Ahhh, you *do* believe me!"

"*Neh*. I just do not want to hear of you spreading this shit about the castle, you talking to Gắoh."

"If you are so certain I lie, why not come up with me, prove that I do."

"I do not need to bother. I know what happened nine years ago. So do you, only you are ashamed to admit it. Ashamed of him who stuck you in your mother's belly."

It was useless, no surprise to Sky Toucher. Nothing was to be gained by pressing it further. He could kick himself: in his eagerness to apprise Burning Wolf, he'd let himself be carried away. He'd talked too much, pointing the finger at Black Feather, even though that was where it belonged. Gắoh had assured him that Stone Antler was innocent. He should have let it go at that, let Burning Wolf hear the rest from Gắoh or the Abnaki shade.

A wild thought struck him: if he could track down one of the Abnakis who had been present and seen with their own eyes who the coward was—

No, ridiculous. What should he do, pack up and trek north into Abnaki Territory, enemy territory, question everyone he came upon? Besides, everybody who was there and saw was probably dead after nine years. Even if he did locate someone, what would they have to gain by helping him, a detested Mohawk?

He watched Burning Wolf walk back to the deer-button game. He must think this through, find a way to prove it to him. The words out of Gắoh's mouth would do, if only he could get Burning Wolf up there . . .

He walked back and was preparing to enter the longhouse, when Singing Brook emerged. They touched the stars on their hands.

"I spoke to your mother."

"What did she say?" he asked eagerly.

"She approves of us."

"Good, good, good. Great!"

"Do not celebrate so soon. My mother came in, she heard it all and still has to decide. And are you forgetting Tékha Ochquoha?"

How he wished Burning Wolf was dead and out of the picture! The urge to kill rose in his throat and formed a lump.

"What is it?" she asked. "Why that face? It frightens me."

# 7

SKY TOUCHER'S CAMPAIGN to convince Burning Wolf of the truth became an obsession, although he made no mention of it to Singing Brook. She had no idea of the importance that he placed upon establishing his father's innocence. Had she known, she would likely have told him he was wasting him breath trying to change Burning Wolf's mind. Her brother did not want to know the truth, acknowledging it could greatly weaken his opposition to Sky Toucher. And since the truth branded Black Feather as a coward, this, his devoted son would surely hold against Sky Toucher for as long as he lived. It was a nest of adders; further stirring threatened disaster. But Sky Toucher refused to give it up.

The sweet-smelling flowers, spring's later arrivals, adorned the woodlands floor: scarlet columbine and bluebell, false hellebore— pheasant's eye— and jack-in-the-pulpit shared their nectar with the bees and butterflies. The buds of the bush honeysuckle and barberry were already opened to add baby leaves to last fall's red berries still clinging to their twigs. Spring grew older as Sky Toucher wrestled with his predicament. It preyed on his mind so he began having trouble sleeping. In time, he decided on the only feasible course of action open to him that he could see: consult Gä̀oh a second time, plead with him to tell Burning Wolf the truth. One did not have to climb to a mountaintop to speak with the North Wind. In winter it assaulted Tenotoge, rattling the palisade fence, sneaking under the bark sheet siding of the longhouses. He remembered seeing his father address Gä̓oh from a corner lookout platform high on the palisade. It was late spring, but the nights still retained unseasonable coldness, when Gä̓oh blasted his final farewell to the lands of the Iroquois, before settling into his cave for his summer's sleep.

It took Sky Toucher a week to reach his decision. During that time Green Water continued hedging on her promise to decide, and Singing Brook concluded ruefully, knowing her mother, she would probably drag it out until summer's end.

"I will speak to her," announced Sky Toucher grimly as they walked beside the stream through the glow left by the sunset as vividly red as a cardinal. Singing Brook stopped to sit on a fallen tree, elbows and knees, chin clamped to her palms. Her mood was uncharacteristically somber; she had not smiled since they started out.

"*Neh.*" She shook her head.

"Why not? She has no bad feelings toward me, not like your brother's hate."

"It is not a question of bad feelings. She is making up her mind."

"Is she? Is she even thinking about it?"

"She promised she would."

"What is taking her so long?"

"This is a delicate situation. She sees it as such. If either of us interferes, pushes her, it could tear it like you tear a spider's web in your path. And we would have to start all over, for all the good that would do."

He flared angrily, ripping a branch from the deadfall, flinging it into the water. "Wait, wait, wait, I am sick of it!"

"Do you think I like it?"

"If we cannot talk to her, what about *my* mother?" he asked.

"She has done her talking. She cannot press it anymore than we can."

He calmed down. He watched a fat spotted pickeral frog leap

from stone to stone across the stream. He held out his arms. When Singing Brook arose he embraced her. "What do you think?" he whispered. "About Green Water? You must sense that she is leaning one way or the other. Women always feel such things. Which way?"

"I think towards approval. I think in the end she will resent Tékha Ochquoha trying to bully her. Oh, he knows better than to say anything but the look in his eye whenever your name comes up . . ."

"At least she will make up her own mind, that is something." He exploded, startling her. "I could kill him!"

"Shhhh, that is foolish talk."

"It is all so unnecessary; he has no reason to do this to us."

"He thinks that he does."

His sudden outburst spent, he plunged into brooding. "He will never move out of the way, and we will never marry, unless we run off."

"*Neh!*"

"Why not? Others do."

"I could not. It would be so wrong, I would not want to live with that on my conscience."

"My mother told me that your mother and father—"

"I am not my mother and father!"

The roseate glow surrounding them deepened as the day ended. The black bird of night slowly settled its great wings over the woodlands. He kissed her; she shook her head and sighed and held him with pleading eyes. He hated this helpless feeling, the reins of their lives in the grip of others. The way she stared at him made him feel weak, his upper body losing its sinew. His heart swelled in his chest, filling it, pressing against his ribs. Taking his hand, she cupped it on her small breast. With their eyes, with hunger in them, wanting, they made love. But in their eyes, too, were desperation, resignation, defeat. Frustration set him tingling.

They removed each other's clothing in silence. He spread out his breechclout, and she lay on it. The stream sang softly like a mother to her child, the night sounds began. They lay close, caressing each other, loving tenderly; her hand found his member and began stroking it to hardness. She quivered in anticipation, panting softly, finding her lower lip with the tip of her tongue. Her eyes grew huge. His finger gently drew the honey of love from her place. Her excitement intensified, she rolled her hips and gave a little cry.

The stars moved closer, closer still, and watched. They lost themselves in each other, drowning, surrendering to the wildness that possessed them. When at last, gasping for breath, he lifted his lithe body from hers and settled on his back she seized his hand and kissed it fondly. They lay quietly listening to the night and the stream and gazed at the watching stars.

"Are you content?" she murmured.

"Always. With you. Never when we are apart, carrying this stone inside me."

"It is the same for me."

Silence.

"What are you thinking?" she asked.

"What else?" he rasped.

"Clear your mind. Think back, remember when we first met?"

"Our eyes touched and it was like an ember bursting, a great flame shot up between us, touched us, singed us . . ."

"With love. I remember I felt as if I were suffocating. It was so sudden, so unexpected. Discovery." She rolled on her side and kissed his cheek lightly. He held her. "How did we go so long before that, ignoring each other?" she went on.

"We were blind. I could not see you, you could not see me."

"How *could* you see me? I was a skinny rag, all bones, eyes too big for my face and always staring. All eyes and teeth and scraggly hair."

"Beautiful hair, it gleams like a raven's wing. I can almost see my face in your hair."

"Back then it was hideous, it flew off in every direction. I could not tame it even with bear grease."

"Beautiful, it has to be for your face."

"Seriously, did a flame really go up?"

"*Nyoh,* and burned my heart." He sobered. "It still hurts and will forever."

"*Onewachten.*" She pushed him playfully. "But I love to hear it." Her smile faded, worry creased her brow.

"What?" he asked.

"What are we to do?"

The sudden weakening of her resolve surprised him, *he* was the pessimist. "*Do?* Leave. Tonight. Just go."

She kissed him. "Do not keep saying that, it is too tempting."

"If you love me you will leave."

"Do not put it that way, that is unfair."

"I am sorry."

"There is only one right way to do this and we are trying." She held his hand and touched her star to his, holding it. A curious warmth radiated under her flesh. "Make love to me again. Like the good husband that you are. And you are my husband in my heart."

"*Nyoh,* my wife."

A hermit thrush landed above them and sent forth its sweet, reedy tremolo in agreement. The stars continued their staring, the myriad night sounds swelled in symphony.

# 8

NEAR THE BOUNDARY that separated Mohawk from Oneida Territory, within sight of the Main Trail that led to Lake Oneida, stood Onneyuttahage, the single Oneida Castle remaining from the days when twenty-seven castles dotted the six million acres of Oneida lands. In construction Onneyuttahage resembled Tenotoge, although it was slightly larger. Surrounding it were patches of woodland. Northeast of the castle a cornfield stretched toward the Te-ugé-ga, the Mohawk River. Within the palisade stood twenty-four longhouses separated by wide streets. Unlike Tenotoge, Onneyuttahage boasted no Council House. Meetings were held in one or another longhouse.

Outside the castle, amongst a number of graves marked by low palisades painted scarlet, stood Tékni-ska-je-a-nah—Two Eagles—who three years before had been elevated to chief of the bear clan. By his side was his wife of eleven years, Margaret Addison, an Englishwoman who had come to North America to marry a French captain of dragoons stationed at the time in Quebec. In the months that it took her to reach there, with the help of Two Eagles and his friends, her fondness for the Oneida blossomed into love. Arriving in Quebec she was reunited with her husband-by-proxy, Captain Pierre Lacroix, only to reject him, return with Two Eagles to Onneyuttahage and marry him. A year later their son was born—Canyewa Tawyne—Little Otter—Benjamin, after his English grandfather.

Three days before, husband and wife had buried Benjamin on what would have been the boy's tenth birthday. He had died accidentally. In the three days that had elapsed since his funeral, his father continued stunned, unable to understand or accept the tragedy. Margaret's initial shock had changed to a bitterness so potent, so deep-seated it became all but impossible for husband and wife to communicate. How long this black passion would control her, Two Eagles could only guess, but it shut out the world and everyone around her, including her husband.

They stood in silence looking down at the freshly mounded grave. His hand reached for hers but she moved hers away. Hesitantly, he set his arm around her shoulders; she did not move but did not press into it or otherwise acknowledge him. He felt as if he were holding a stone.

Then she turned to face him, the bright sunlight setting her light blonde hair shining nearly albescent. It was a glorious day filled with the sights, the sounds and scents of spring, asserting its presence at its peak before giving way to summer. The sky was the blue of an indigo bunting, the few clouds as white as new snow, the breeze soft and invitingly warm. But Margaret saw and felt nothing other than the rain and darkness inside.

"Margaret . . ."

"Mmmmmm?"

"I have been thinking. I think we could . . ."

"Could what?"

He cleared his throat self-consciously and plunged ahead. "Have another *cian*."

She stared. "Another child? To replace *him?*"

"Not replace . . ."

"No, no more children. I couldn't do such a heartless thing, not a second time."

*"Heart . . . less?"*

"What do you call bringing a child into this? This struggle to survive? This savagery? Human life as cheap as dirt! No, never again!"

"You are unhappy living here."

*"Living?* Is that what you call it? How about fighting to survive? Look around you, all your friends are dead. Aunt Eight Minks is, both of Swift Doe's husbands, her son, nearly everyone we know struck down before their time. To be born into this is a curse. Ten years old and dead, murdered by this damnable wilderness!"

"I just thought—"

She set a hand against his cheek. "I know, and you're not wrong to want another son. But I can't, not here."

"I am sorry."

*"Sorry?"*

"About this place. But it is all we have: this wilderness, the hard life, the dangers. We make the best of them."

"You do. And do very well, considering. Even *I* make the best of them." She set her cheek against his chest. He embraced her, towering over her. "But this is *too* painful, unbearable. When you think of how much he survived, the illnesses, the injuries, the insect bites, the time he fell out of the tree and fractured both arms. The time he nearly drowned, nearly froze to death. He was nearly bitten by a snake before, remember? Blue Creek of all people killed the filthy thing just in time. To come through so much to such a stupid, needless death. And so young, a baby . . ." Tears glistened. "No, no more children. I'll not risk putting us through this ever again."

"Do you ever wish that you and that black cloak Wilson made it away from Boston on the wooden island?"

"Ship."

"To England, back to your father's longhouse?"

"And leave you? Never, that would have been as hard to bear as this is."

*   *   *

Benjamin had run ahead of her, scrambling up the rock, standing tall on it, spreading his skinny arms. He would be tall, approaching his father's six feet seven inches. He resembled his father in so many ways, which delighted her.

"Come, come!"

"Slow down," she panted, out of breath.

"It is just up a ways. Wait till you see the bones. They're warrior bones."

"I'll bet they're deer."

"You'll see. Come, come!"

She had never seen the cave before, despite its location fairly close to the castle. Bushes concealed the entrance so well one could stand two paces from it and not realize it was there. He pulled the bushes aside.

"Warrior bones!"

They were deer ribs.

"What is that ghastly stench?" She covered her mouth. "I'm not going in there—you, either."

"You promised!"

"We can see it fine from here."

"Little Elk, Dawn Maker and me went all the way to the back."

"I, not me. Good for you, and don't you dare do it again."

"Come just inside—"

"No, Benjamin. It's getting late; your father'll be wondering where we are. Let's go back."

He came back through the bushes, letting them snap behind him, looking hangdog. She was feeling sorry for him when she heard the hissing. For an instant the danger failed to register, and by the time it did the rattler had struck. She saw it in the air, then saw it drop, swing about and start through the grass. Benjamin screamed, she screamed, and ran to him. She examined the punctures.

"Lie down," she ordered.

"It hurts!"

"Lie back! And don't move. Don't move!"

"I want to see—"

"Down!"

She stripped off her belt and made a tourniquet about a third of the way up his leg, then snatched his knife from his belt, cut twin crosses and began sucking out the venom. It tasted like acid. She spat. She sucked and sucked, he grew impatient as the shock wore off and the pain eased slightly. "That's enough."

"Shhhhh. Hold still."

She kept it up until her cheek muscles became so weak she could no longer use them. His leg by now was badly swollen.

"It's starting to hurt bad again, Mother."

"I know. Clench your teeth." She checked and retightened the tourniquet. He complained, so she loosened it slightly. "Listen to me, I've done all I can. We need help getting you home. And that leg has to be kept lower than the rest of you."

"Make a travois and drag me home."

"No, in the time that would take I could be there and back. I'll run and get your father." She glanced warily about.

"It's gone," he said. "They never stay around after they bite."

"Cross your fingers. Hold your knife just in case. And don't move. Here." She found a large stone, setting it under his knee. "Knee up, heel down, the bite down. Don't move your leg. How do you feel?"

"I'm okay, it's nothing."

She woke up sweating furiously, her mind a jumble. It was so real, every phase, every detail. She shuttered her eyes. Images flashed: the bushes, the cave mouth, the snake striking, Benjamin screaming, working on him. Leaving desperately afraid, but having no choice. Running for help. Splitting Moon standing outside the front gate talking to O-dat-she-dah—He-carries-a-quiver—chief of the turtle clan. Sight of the chief raised thought of the death from snakebite of Sho-non-ses—His Longhouse—chief of the bear clan before Two Eagles.

When the three of them came within sight of Benjamin he was sitting up grinning. "I'm all right, I'm all right."

That night his aunt, Swift Doe, insisted on dosing him with medicine made from the root of the wild yam, which the Iroquois relied on to dilute all venoms. He drank four cups and went to sleep. The pain had left him. Margaret paced his chamber all night. He sweat, she wrung out the cloth across his forehead a hundred times. When dawn came, she tried to rouse him. It was useless. Her screams woke Two Eagles.

He lay beside her, from his expression his sleep deeply troubling. Benjamin's death he had taken with the stoicism she expected of him, holding his feelings tightly inside, letting them fuel and expand, releasing the pressure in the privacy of their chamber, in sleep.

She gently woke him. For the first time since Benjamin's death they made love. Never had she been so complaisant, never had her need for him been so desperate.

TENÄTE OŸOGHI SAT with O´hute Onega in her mother's chamber. Her impatience with Green Water was becoming increasingly hard to conceal. She simply had to know which way her mother was leaning. They were sorting *o-ne-ha-tah* quills into piles of similar thicknesses and lengths. White with brown tips, they had been stored in the bladder of an elk and hung from the rafters above Green Water's bunk in company with the dried fish, tobacco, fruits and vegetables. Mother and daughter sat at the corners of a blanket facing each other.

As she sorted, Singing Brook repeatedly glanced up at her mother, until Green Water felt her eyes.

"I have not yet decided," she said and returned to her sorting.

"Why must it take you so long?"

Green Water reached into an elm-bark bucket of water bringing out two large handfuls of quills which had been soaking for about an hour. Shaking off the water, she spread them in a line before her, then picked up one of the dry piles, immersing it in the water. And ignoring her daughter's question.

Knowing her mother's love of procrastination, Singing Brook

did not expect a decision this soon, all she was hoping for was a comment on the situation, something that might betray which way Green Water was tending: something for Sky Toucher.

Green Water cleared her throat. "I remember when your father and I came back after being away for two years. From the moment we walked through the entrance gates, me with a baby in each arm, the looks on people's faces. On my parents' faces, on your father's parents'. They shot arrows with their eyes."

"Because you ran away."

Green Water stiffened resentfully, them relaxed and shrugged. "Maybe that was part of it but most was because we married without our mothers' permission, without their even suspecting what we were up to. We denied them the right to choose our mates. It was not until we left that we realized what a terrible thing we had done, how badly and needlessly we hurt both, how we made them look in others' eyes. We were gone. They had to stay and face everyone. It was humiliating."

"Would it have been as bad for them if you got married and did not leave?"

Green Water sniffed disdainfully. "How should I answer that? How would I know? We did what we did and that was that."

She settled into herself, her anger subsiding as quickly as it arose, giving way to a rueful sadness. Singing Brook could see her mother's mind whirling back to that time as she sighed heavily and turned to flattening a quill between her teeth. Next she would poke a thread hole in it with her steel awl. Then she would thread the quills on sinew and sew them to Burning Wolf's buckskin shirt in an old tribal design.

"You and my father must have loved each other very strongly," ventured Singing Brook.

"*Love?* What is that word, *Asseroni?*"

"Not European, English. We . . . have no word for it in our language."

"What does it mean?"

"I have told you."

"Tell me again."

"*Love* is what he and I feel for each other. A feeling stronger than feeling."

"A squirrel bigger than a squirrel? What gibberish."

"I mean tremendously strong, so strong our hearts join, become one heart and we . . . share it."

Green Water sniffed. "Pretty words. And meaningless. Our language has no word for it for good reason: there is no such thing."

"There is."

"Are you English or Mohawk? You borrow their words. What next, their ways?"

"I cannot help how I feel about him."

"You can and you should. But *neh,* you would rather bring embarrassment to your family."

"Like you did."

Green Water glared, seething.

"I—am sorry, I should not have said that."

"You are thinking it, you say it."

"I said I am sorry."

"Good."

"You are like stone!" burst Singing Brook. "You talk, you say nothing, you hear nothing, see nothing, feel—"

"Because you make no sense, you and your *love.* Why? Because of the anger that burns in you. You are like the porcupine. He cannot eat when his quills are up. You cannot think right when yours are!"

Green Water began piercing the shirt front with her awl. When she was done she would put holes in the drying quills. As she worked her anger again seeped out of her, releasing the tension from her face.

"Try and understand, Tenäte Oÿoghi, I do not oppose this thing because I am annoyed or hurt or afraid of what others may think. I am not so small-minded. I simply want to spare you two what your father and I were put through."

"O-ron-ia-ke-te and I know what to expect. We do not care what others think."

"Not even the chiefs and the clan mothers?"

"It is not their business."

"A marriage in the tribe is everyone's business!"

"It is no one's!"

Green Water finished poking the design into the shirt front and turned to piercing the quills. Singing Brook eyed her stonily.

"We could run off," she murmured.

"Is that a threat?" Up came her mother's head sharply. "Go, no one is stopping you."

"*Neh,* we cannot, that would be cowardly."

As the words came out, she realized that she'd insulted her mother. She sighed to herself. There seemed to be no chance of winning this game. They'd gone about falling in love all wrong; they should have kept their feelings to themselves rather than display them for all to see. Flaunting them was an open affront to both their mothers, to everyone in the tribe.

What could they do now, apologize? Ask forgiveness for their brazenness? Focusing on the pile of quills directly in front of her, she sensed that Green Water had stopped poking holes and was staring at her. She raised her eyes to look and was relieved to see no anger in her face; her expression was more like the sympathy she had seen earlier in O꞉kla?'s face the day they talked.

"I am sorry, my daughter. I can see your frustration and it pains me deeply, believe that or not. Your problem is you have set a rabbit trap and caught a wolf, *neh?*"

"I set no trap. Neither of us did anything, it just happened, our *problem,* as you call it, is . . ."

"That you love."

"And I will until the day I die!"

"Or until I introduce you to another."

Singing Brook threw up her hands, nearly upsetting the bucket. "You refuse to understand!"

"Mmmmm. Maybe not. Maybe I am just beginning to. I promise I will think about it with great seriousness. I said that before, I know."

"Tell me one thing, *Distan,* just to satisfy my curiosity. Is it Tékha Ochquoha or your friends? The clan mothers? *Everyone?*"

"None of them."

"Who then?"

"Me. This worry inside me is like a *ka-goo-sa* that bites and burrows under the skin. If your father and I never went through it, if our mothers picked us out and put us together like our parents' mothers did, perhaps this would not trouble me so. Is it so heartless of me to want to spare you what he and I went through?"

"We can handle it. We are not children."

"You are not but I still do not think you can handle it. You have no idea what you are letting yourselves in for. You have sorted enough, get sinew from the basket under the bunk, short pieces. Tie up each pile. Put those we will not be using back in the bladder."

"*Nyoh, Distan.*"

She finished filling the bladder and hung it in its place. Her mother suddenly seemed reserved. Whatever was troubling her showed in her flashing eyes that avoided Singing Brook's. Had she decided?

"What is it, *Distan?*"

"It is no use; it is heartless of me to drag it out. My answer is *neh.*"

Singing Brook shot to her feet. *"Neh!"*

"Shhhh, do not make a scene. I have discussed it with your brother. You know he is very strongly against it."

"I do not care. It is none of his business."

"Sit."

"I will not! You cannot do this to us!"

"Are you not forgetting something? You asked me. Now, because I give you the answer you do not want, *I* cannot do this? Your selfishness is showing, child. *Nyoh, child.* Children cannot accept being crossed, denied."

"I am going."

"Go."

"For the last time—"

"For the last time *neh,* I will not approve of your marrying him."

# 10

Sky Toucher talked for hours before Singing Brook finally agreed to accompany him to Onneyuttahage to visit his cousin Two Eagles. With no options left them, they would leave Tenotoge and settle with the Oneidas. Scarcely more than two hours on foot separated the two castles, with the territorial border about midway between. The Oneidas were as Iroquois as the Mohawks, each tribe considering the other cousins. Two Eagles and Sky Toucher literally were cousins, about fifteen years apart in age, oceans apart in experience, and long-time friends.

Splitting Moon came barging into Two Eagles' and Margaret's chamber. Just outside the flap the firepit showed blackened fragments of Benjamin's cradleboard, which Margaret had saved. Now she wanted no reminders of him. Gone was his clothing, given away; his weapons, the bear claw he had used as a target when, at the age of five, his father began teaching him how to use a bow and arrow.

"Your *rackesie* is here!" exclaimed Splitting Moon.

"O-ron-ia-ke-te here?"

"With a woman."

Two Eagles and Margaret exchanged glances. "We haven't seen Sky Toucher in what, two years?" she said.

Outside Sky Toucher approached, holding up his hand. "*Nyah-weh ska-noh, Rackesie* Tékni-ska-je-a-nah."

"*Nyah-weh ska-noh, gayah-da-say, Rackesie* O-ron-ia-ke-te."

Two Eagles introduced Margaret, whom Sky Toucher already knew. He in turn introduced Singing Brook, whom neither Margaret nor Two Eagles had met before. They stood outside the entrance to the longhouse in the warm sunlight. Splitting Moon stood off a short distance watching, until Two Eagles' scowl sent him away.

"Something serious has come up that I want to discuss with you, Cousin," said Sky Toucher.

"First let's go inside and have something to eat and drink," said Margaret.

"*Neh,* later," said Sky Toucher. He glanced apprehensively at Singing Brook. From the way she nervously worked her fingers and looked about, like a doe protecting its fawn, it seemed as if she had come with him against her better judgment.

"You two go inside," said Margaret to Two Eagles. "Tenäte Oÿoghi and I will go for a walk." Singing Brook smiled approvingly.

The warriors sat on the chamber floor. On the wall over the bunk hung Two Eagles' *ga-swĕ-̇dà*, the string of wampum beads awarded him upon his elevation to chief of his clan. On the floor sat a chunk of chert from which he had been chipping rough, triangularly shaped *cache* arrowheads.

He offered his guest a cooling cup of *go-qua-hackt,* made from the tips of hemlock twigs boiled in maple syrup and cooled.

"I see trouble in your face, *Rackesie,*" said Two Eagles, and resumed his chipping, using a tool fashioned from a buck antler.

"Trouble all through me."

Two Eagles picked up a rough arrowhead, examined it, and began pressing off small flakes. Working swiftly and deftly, he shaped it then began cutting in the barbs along first one edge then the other.

Sky Toucher heaved a sigh and began his explanation.

Margaret and Singing Brook, meanwhile, had taken an immediate liking to each other and were chattering like old friends, neither noticing that their steps had led them in amongst the gravesites at the side of the castle. Benjamin's grave, the low palisade newly painted, stuck out prominently among the weatherbeaten older graves. Singing Brook noticed Margaret glance at the grave and her smile fade.

"Someone you know?"

"Our little boy Canyewa Tawyne, Benjamin."

"Oh *neh!*"

Margaret told her what had happened. "For three days I was in shock, then I became bitter. Now I feel guilty."

"Why guilty?"

"I should have saved him. He was big for his age; I didn't think I could carry him, that trying to would only speed up the poison in his veins. Now I know I should have tried. The poison must have raced through him like lightning. It got past the tourniquet before I tightened it. Everything I did was just too late, too late."

"It sounds to me like no one could have done anything more for him. You must not feel guilty."

"So Two Eagles says but I can't help it. Let's get out of here, go and sit by the stream. So you and Sky Toucher want to marry, only your family's against it?"

"It is my brother: we cannot get by him so O-ron-ia-ke-te wants to leave Tenotoge, come and live here."

"You'd be most welcome. Two Eagles would be very pleased; he's terrifically fond of Sky Toucher. Oh yes, he'd be delighted. But you don't want to come, is that it?"

"Running away would be wrong."

"But if you've no other choice . . ."

"It is not a choice I want to make."

"Please come."

They sat by the stream tossing rose-mallow blossoms into the bright water, watching them float away. A marten poked its button nose around the trunk of a spruce, fastening its snapping black eyes on them, staring. On a branch above it a dusty rose-red purple finch landed, raising its voice in a rich melodious warble.

"I only came today because I feel sorry for O-ron-ia-ke-te," murmured Singing Brook. "None of this is his doing."

"None is yours."

"He tries hard to be patient but gets terribly upset over it. Is Tékni-ska-je-a-nah patient?" Margaret rolled her eyes, and Singing Brook laughed and seemed to relax. "Of course O-ron-ia-ke-te has his faults. For one thing he can be terribly stubborn."

Margaret set a hand on her shoulder. "My dear, you don't know what stubborn is until you've dealt with Two Eagles."

"Was anybody in the tribe opposed to your marrying?"

"Practically everybody. Oh, not Eight Minks—his aunt, who was really more his mother—she was a friend when I most needed one. And his friends didn't oppose it; we'd gotten to know each other. But everybody else was against me. An English whiteskin? Outsider? Interloper? Poor Two Eagles."

"You should see your eyes when you say his name, you love him like O-ron-ia-ke-te and I love."

"Mohawks and Oneidas are not supposed to love."

"Please, I have heard that so much my ears burn in my sleep. I cannot help how I feel, neither can he."

"Who can? It's easy to see you have *o-goch-que-na-dik,* reservations, but you'd really be welcome here. We'd love to have you. And no one will look down their nose at you. Leaving your family, your friends, all that's familiar, won't be easy, just ask me. But love really does conquer all things. I think Virgil said that: he was a Roman poet."

Singing Brook stared blankly. Margaret laughed.

"He was right. It happened for us, it can for you. Don't let this chance pass by, don't waste the years ahead wallowing in regret. The deer runs by, grab it by the antlers."

Becoming bored with eavesdropping, the finch flicked its brown tail and flew off. The marten persisted in staring.

"He fills my heart," murmured Singing Brook. "My man. Even though sometimes he's like a little boy."

"He's male, isn't he?"

"If he cannot get his way, he pouts. Or mopes about muttering to himself."

"Or grunts and won't look you in the eye."

"*Nyoh, nyoh.* And he loses everything—"

"And you always know where to find it."

"*Nyoh.*"

"Two Eagles goes fishing and expects me to clean his catch. He goes hunting—"

"And you have to skin the deer and cut it up. And if he traps a rabbit or beaver you do the dirty work."

"Not anymore," Margaret said. "We share it. It's called training. It begins right away in your first week of marriage. You musn't put it off. Oh, there's so much you have to learn."

"O-ron-ia-ke-te is messy. I bawl him out for not picking up his chamber. And he has this habit of tossing aside his bowl after eating, without wiping it. Or claims he forgets to."

"They all do. Put your foot down," said Margaret.

"And he'll promise to meet me at such-and-such a time at such-and-such a place and forget or show up much later."

"And blame it on his friends."

"*Nyoh, nyoh!*"

"These things are baggage they all carry. Does he refuse to tell you when he's ill or in pain?"

"I have to drag it out of him like a deep sliver."

They bandied about masculine idiosyncrasies, faults and flaws like shuttlecocks in battledore.

Meanwhile, Two Eagles listened as Sky Toucher poured out his problem.

"You feel that strongly you should marry her," Two Eagles cut in.

Sky Toucher nodded resolutely. "I intend to, nothing can stop us!"

"You have made up your mind to leave Tenotoge."

"How can we stay?"

Two Eagles had finished three arrowheads to his satisfaction. He now began affixing them to shaft heads; later he would fletch the shafts. "Others leave their families, their old lives to go and live elsewhere. I do not see that as any big problem. But you want to move here."

"*Nyoh*, it is the perfect solution. Up to now there was a chance that O´hute Onega would relent and approve of our marriage, in spite of Tékha Ochquoha. She might have closed her ears to him, but now she says *neh*."

"Moving here, both of you would have to become Oneida."

"I—*nyoh*."

"The move would be permanent and you could not live here permanently as Mohawks. You would have to give up being Mohawk." Two Eagles leaned forward, lowering his voice. "Leave your tribe, O-ron-ia-ke-te, your property, your heritage. The heritage of your father and his father all the way back to before memory. Are you prepared to take such a drastic step? Do not misunderstand, I would be delighted to welcome you both into our tribe. I do not need to describe how I feel about you, how we feel about each other.

"But you must think very seriously what you will be doing; it is the step of a lifetime, a step from which there can be no turning back, *neh?*"

"I . . ." his cousin stammered.

"You cannot take a tribe off like a pair of moccasins."

"I thought about everything." Sky Toucher clucked grimly.

"Except that."

"Except that. I pushed it aside, I guess because I did not want to think about it."

"Adoptees come into all Iroquois tribes all the time, so many during and after the red days. Mohegans, Munsees, Abnakis, Susquehannas, Hurons, warriors from tribes all around us. And Oneida warriors go from here to other Iroquois castles when they take wives. But that is not the same." Sky Toucher grunted and nodded.

"My marriage to Margaret is different," Two Eagles explained. "I have never known an Oneida couple who left here to be adopted by another tribe. It has never happened. There is something about it that—disturbs me, O-ron-ia-ke-te."

"But it is the only solution."

"Is it? Or the easiest solution? Have you talked with Tékha Ochquoha, I mean really sat down and opened your hearts? Gotten his reasons out of him so that you can tear them like meat?"

"His reason is our fathers, I told you."

"I heard, but could there be others? You must get inside his head."

"With my tomahawk!"

"I am being serious. To change from Mohawk to Oneida for this reason is . . ."

"Wrong, say it."

"I think it is. You are impatient, you would rush into it. Consider it for what it is, a last resort. And you have time and a way to go before you reach it. She is very pretty."

This signaled an end to the discussion. Sky Toucher let it go. Two Eagles was not wrong and not putting him off. He had opened his heart and out had come sincerity as expected. His own heart opened, letting in discouragement. He had not considered how serious it would be to leave Tenotoge permanently. How it would look to Mohawks and Oneidas alike, how it would affect her. It wasn't something to be approached lightly. She would agree. She had no enthusiasm for the idea.

But Two Eagles' suggestion that he sit down with Burning Wolf was much easier voiced than attempted. He wouldn't get six words out before Burning Wolf threw them back laced with sarcasm and insult.

"Did you hear me?" Two Eagles asked. "I said she is very pretty."

"*Nyoh.*"

"Do not look so, it will all work out. You will make it, I am sure. How is your mother?"

"All right. She approves of our marrying, for all the good that does." He groaned. "You have no idea how I feel about Tenäte Oÿoghi."

"You love her."

"More than that, deeper, much. Oh, she has her faults. She can be headstrong, she tries to tell me what to do, she has a temper."

"Tell me about stubborn women with tempers. Who does not have shortcomings? Only when you hold her, your eyes close to all of hers, *neh?* She lifts your heart out of you into the clouds. So you can touch the sky, O-ron-ia-ke-te."

"She does. There was one day last winter when it was so bitter out nobody stirred from their chambers. That day we did not see each other. It was the longest, heaviest day of my life. I thought it would never end. That night I lay awake until the great horned owl called his last and went to sleep. I could not stop thinking about her, seeing her face fixed before my eyes. She is my heart, my world."

"And will be always. So be patient and think about approaching her brother. Maybe both of you . . ."

"*Neh,* he and Tenäte Oÿoghi get along like two wildcats in the same hole. It is useless; we are doomed."

Two Eagles rose and set a hand on his shoulder. "This is not my favorite cousin talking. *Neh,* it is a Huron dog with his yellow spine stuck up his arsehole."

They stayed until twilight, but hope for a solution had drained from Sky Toucher and he could not conceal his discouragement. They started for home when the bats came out of their caves to feast on the white-marked tussock moths, dotting the gathering darkness by the millions.

\* \* \*

"What did he say?" Singing Brook asked.

"We cannot move to Onneyuttahage. It was a mistake. I made a mistake."

"Can we talk about it?"

"Why waste breath? It is pointless. Everything is. We are doomed."

# II
# SUMMER OF DISCONTENT

# 11

B INDING THE SHORT hairs from a gray squirrel's back into a small
brush, Sky Toucher had wedged the brush into the split in a
stick the thickness of an arrow. Singing Brook had mixed the
crushed root and fruit of the sumac with bloodroot and berry juices
to create a vivid crimson color. Now they sat opposite each other
in their private place; she had removed her moccasins. He held
her foot, and dipping the brush in the clay cup of paint, painted
her little toenail in a single, meticulous stroke.

"Perfect," she murmured.

"Hold still."

The sun standing straight overhead, finding its way through the
leaf canopy, set the color gleaming. He painted the toe next to it,
the middle toe, scraping his brush between dips on the edge of the
cup. She eyed him lovingly. The palm of his hand set against her
sole sent a slight tingling into her foot and up her ankle. Her heart
picked up its pace. So engrossed was he, he did not raise his eyes
to look at her. In swiping paint on the toe next to her big toe his
hand slipped slightly, daubing the flesh. He reached for a piece of
deerskin, using a corner to wipe off the excess. Only then did he
look at her.

"I love you," he said.

He said it often, as did she, this foreign word that had no
meaning in their language. She had a sudden urge to lean forward
and kiss him hungrily but resolved to wait. He finished and sat
erect, tilting his head from side to side, assessing his work, nodding
satisfied.

"Good?" he asked.

"Perfect, I told you."

"You cannot stand up until they are dry. Give me your other
foot."

A wood pewee, its olive-gray feathers fringed with white, alit
on a branch just above their heads and lifted its voice in its *pee-
ah-wee* song, the last note rising. It sang again, a third time, then
flew off. Sky Toucher dipped the brush, drew off the excess paint

on the lip of the cup and started on her other foot. When he had
finished he held both her ankles and blew lightly on her toes one
by one.

"They will be dry when the sun finds itself halfway down its
path."

"Kiss me, my husband."

He spread the deerskin, setting her heels on it and, crawling
forward on hands and knees, kissed her lightly. Her response was
not so light. She took his mouth ravenously.

They stood gazing into each other's eyes.

"I must go," he whispered, his tone verging on the apologetic.

"Where?"

"Up Black Mountain, I . . . must speak to Gấoh."

"What about?"

"I . . . cannot tell you."

"Oh? We plan to marry, in our hearts we already are, and yet
you would keep secrets from me?"

"I promise I will tell you everything in time."

"In time?"

"Please. Accept that and trust me, I would never deceive you."

She turned from him and picked a delicate pink spring beauty.
She held it to the sun; if she held it long enough it would open,
showing its deep pink veins.

"Are you going?" she asked.

"Where?"

"Do not play games with me, you know I mean the war. Rumors
are swirling about the castle like dust dancers. Look at me and tell
me you are not going. Cayere Tawyne is not, neither are you. The
last time you put me through fire waiting and wondering; never
again."

"Tenäte . . ."

"I will not argue about it, not even discuss it. I do not want it
in my mouth. All I ask is for you to tell me you are staying home.
If Wotstaha Onirares goes, you will let him."

"Do not make me say such a thing. Besides, it may not happen,
we may none of us go back."

"It *will* happen, it has happened so often to our warriors, why should it stop now? Every day I hear . . ."

"Rumors. Old-woman gossip, people talking about something they know nothing about. It is getting late, I must go."

"Go!"

She turned and walked away.

He would return to the mountaintop to summon Gã́oh and ask his help in enlightening Burning Wolf. As he ascended, he tormented himself with questions. Was this a strategy of desperation? What else could one call it? Gã́oh was not an old sachem or Medicine Man one could question at one's convenience. He was a god-oracle not overly interested in the affairs of mere men. Could he be bothered with the problems of two men who simply could not get along? Were not such situations legion?

Sky Toucher was within a few hundred feet of the summit when it began to rain, making the highest stone face a more dangerous climb than it was in dry weather. He picked his way up it carefully, ascended through the brush-studded area and finally reached the top. As he stepped onto level ground the rain let up and stopped, the sun burst forth radiantly. An omen? Had the rain been sent to discourage him from completing his ascent? Was it Gã́oh's doing?

He looked about; nothing had changed since his last visit. The rubble appeared undisturbed, the clove, a splitting of the mountain, still yawned nearby. On the opposite side a fissure ran to the edge of the summit and dropped about twenty feet before closing.

He stood thinking about Singing Brook. Not telling her why he'd really come up was deceitful. This was the first time he'd deceived her. He tried to tell himself it was for her own protection but in his heart he knew he was only trying to avoid arguing over her brother. She would have told him to let what happened nine years ago sleep in the dust. He should, only he could not.

Standing in the shadow of the tallest pinnacle, he faced north. The wind had lost strength after the shower and did not buffet him about as it usually did, gusting only occasionally. He waited for it to pick up. He was still waiting when he heard a sound below: a stone loosened and bounced down. He went to the edge and looked over. Less than ten feet below a man was climbing, pulling himself up as he himself had done, hand over hand, using the projecting bushes. The arrival glanced up at him. His expression was pure hatred.

Burning Wolf. He reached the plateau glowering.

"You followed me . . . ," began Sky Toucher.

"Did you not invite me up here?"

"But you said . . ."

"I changed my mind."

"So you do believe me."

Burning Wolf snorted. "Are you as dense as you are cowardly, *onewachten?*"

Burning Wolf pulled his knife and assumed an attacking stance, bending slightly, his blade upward at an angle, his face masked with loathing.

"Put away your tooth, I do not want to fight you," Sky Toucher snapped.

"Of course you do not, worm, because you are a coward. But you cannot avoid me. I came up here to kill you."

*"Neh."*

*"Nyoh.* So you have no choice but to fight."

"This is stupid!"

"This is the only way out of your problem. If my foot slips on all this rubble, I fall and you kill me, your troubles are over. No one will stand in your way to my sister. But if you die, as you surely will—" He tossed his knife to his other hand and began slowly circling. *"My* problem is solved."

"Stupid."

"Coward!"

"Your brain has turned upside down in your head."

"Worm. Draw your tooth!"

Burning Wolf began closing on him. Sky Toucher backed away, stepped on an unseen rock and nearly fell. Recovering his balance, he pulled his knife. The sun caught the blade, causing him to blink.

"That is better. Look at your eyes, they are welling with fear. Are you afraid because you know I am better with a tooth?"

"You are slower."

"We shall see."

They feinted, circling slowly. Burning Wolf attempted the first thrust; Sky Toucher sucked in his stomach, leaping backwards. So close did the point come he imagined he felt it prick him. Now Burning Wolf came roaring at him. Sky Toucher slipped to one side as he swept by. Burning Wolf stopped clumsily, nearly losing his balance, spun about and came back at him. Sky Toucher stood his ground; toe to toe they swiped away at each other's bellies. Then Burning Wolf switched hands and brought his knife upward toward Sky Toucher's heart.

He threw himself to his right; his foot coming down on a stone, he fell. Scrambling clear, he jumped to his feet, just in time to avoid the death blow, the other's knife two-handed coming straight down between his shoulder blades.

He whirled and backed off. On came Burning Wolf plodding, swinging his knife from side to side. Sputum threaded from his lips; redfaced and panting, his eyes gleamed evilly.

Sky Toucher ducked under the swinging blade and threw himself against the other's knees, toppling him. Burning Wolf bellowed angrily, crabbed clear, and up on his feet came screaming at him.

Sky Toucher swiveled sideways just in time; Burning Wolf rushed by. He tried to stop, teetered on his toes and screamed shrilly. His momentum carried him forward; over he fell, down he plunged, his shrieking sustaining all the way to the bottom of the clove.

Ceasing with a faint thud.

# 12

SKY TOUCHER KNELT at the edge of the clove and peered down. As he expected, he could see only as far as the sunlight permitted. He cocked an ear and could hear nothing. But what could he expect? No living thing could survive such a fall.

He sat back and pondered the situation. It couldn't be worse. Everyone who knew he climbed up here would assume that he'd lured Burning Wolf up and pushed him to his death. Would anyone believe that they had fought fairly, that he'd eluded Burning Wolf's thrust, he'd rushed past him to the lip of the clove and . . .

Could he convince Singing Brook of the truth? Her mother, her family? His friends? *Any*one?

He plunged into deep thought. The sun slipped down the sky, the wind rose, swirling dust around him. No need to consult Gã̃ oh now, too late for advice. Too late for Burning Wolf. And for him, as well?

"Shit!"

His heart thundering, he examined all aspects of the problem. A thought struck: Burning Wolf lay dead at the bottom, not a mark on him other than the injuries incurred in his fall. No wounds from the fight, not a scratch, nothing but broken bones. If he could climb down and somehow carry Burning Wolf's dead weight all the way back up, he could bring him home and tell everyone what happened. His honesty would certainly be in his favor.

But would anyone believe him? Would *she?*

On the other hand, he could leave and hope that Burning Wolf had told no one he intended to climb the mountain. Undoubtedly true, inasmuch as his sole purpose in coming up was to kill. So if he did leave Burning Wolf's body it would never be found.

But that would be worse than dishonorable, it would be cowardly, yielding to Burning Wolf's accusation. Could he live with that on his conscience? Could he look in Singing Brook's eyes whenever her brother's name came up and pretend he knew nothing about his disappearance? Should he hope that everyone would think Burning Wolf had run off? Why would he?

"Shit!"

He pondered his dilemma. Why look for ways out of it? At heart *was* he a coward? Again he crept to the edge and, shading his eyes, squinted down. He could see and hear nothing. Digging a chunk of salted venison out of his belt pouch he began chewing it for energy.

He had to go down.

He lowered himself over the edge and surprisingly, feeling with his toes, found immediate footing. Descending about fifteen feet, he came upon many gouges in the wall, more than he needed, making descending even easier than he could have hoped for.

Coming back up carrying the dead weight would be the problem. Impossible? He wished he had rope but he would have to go halfway back down the mountain to find slippery elm or hickory and dig out the inner bast. And he had only his knife, no axe. And would have to fell at least three reasonably large trees to get rope enough for his needs. Weaving it would take him at least two days.

But it would be so much easier than this: climb down, tie the body, back up, pull him up. Laborious, back-breaking, he'd have to rest every few minutes. A tedious job, but not perilous like this.

Down, down, down he made his way, frequently failing to find holds in the pitch darkness, groping about with his free hand until his supporting arm ached so it threatened to wrench from the socket. Finally, he located a hold and resumed his descent.

He guessed he was about three hundred feet down, the air getting close and uncomfortably warm, when his upper-arm muscles and the backs of both legs began to tighten. He tried to rest, hanging on with one arm, supporting himself on one leg, discouraged, thinking that if it was this hard going down, what would coming back up be like?

Down, down, sweating furiously now, every bone, every muscle in all four limbs burning with the strain. Down, down. His luck changed suddenly. He came to a ledge jutting out a full two feet. A chance to rest at last. He looked down but could see nothing. He felt about him for a loose stone to drop to check the depth but could find none. He had heard the body land but there had been no way of judging how far it had fallen. From here it could be another six or eight hundred feet.

He filled his lungs, flexed his arms and legs and resumed descending.

# 13

THE BOTTOM OF the clove was wet underfoot. Feeling about he established that Burning Wolf's body lay face down. He determined that his neck and back were broken, as well as both legs.

His skull was split; Sky Toucher could feel part of the brain protruding, soft and moist to the touch.

Picking up the body, he slung it over his shoulder and groaned aloud. It was as heavy as a full-grown buck. Looking straight up he could see a tiny round patch of blue sky. It looked miles distant but had to be less than five hundred feet; it might just as well be five hundred leagues. Balancing the corpse precariously he got firm holds with both hands and started up. If he could make it to the ledge he could rest as long as he liked before continuing.

He could not make it to the ledge, could not get thirty feet up. He quickly lost all strength in his arms and was about to fall when he tilted his shoulder and let the body slip off. It thumped to rest below. He continued his climb.

# 14

WIDE SHOULDERS' PROCLIVITY for sharpening his knife had narrowed the blade to near half its original width. Four Otters teased him for his eagerness to go to war.

"We are going, and I will be ready," declared Wide Shoulders, and began miming attacking his enemy.

"You have got it as sharp as a whiteskin's beard tooth. You will go, get into battle and lose it. Some Abnaki *odasqueta* will end up shredding corn with it," Four Otters predicted.

The two were working on their dugout canoe, watched at a distance by a knot of small boys. Their project had already consumed nearly a month. The work went slowly possibly because it was not that important to either of them. The trunk they were working on—burning, digging out the charred portions, carefully shaping the interior—was taken from a tall, straight hickory free of knots and other defects. About eighteen feet long, it was kept off the ground with three logs, evenly spaced, set crossways. The cavity was about half hollowed out.

"Where is O-ron-ia-ke-te?" Four Otters asked. "He should be helping with this drudgery."

"With her," said Wide Shoulders. "Where else?"

"*Neh,* she is cutting up a she-moose her brother shot; I saw her. Sky Toucher was not around. He must be up on his mountain again." He shook his head, frowning. "He will not find the solution up there, with his problem down here."

Wide Shoulders finished cutting out a stubborn chunk of wood from under the bow. "He should cut it out of their lives," he snapped. "Like so." He pulled out the piece and cried out as a splinter jabbed into his thumb. Four Otters laughed as he watched him, grumbling, extract it.

"Getting rid of Burning Wolf *would* solve his problem," he said, "but that will never happen."

"That is so; if they were to fight it would be a grudge fight. They would be banished."

A fact of Iroquois life and fixed in every warrior's mind. To risk reducing the tribe's manpower merely to gain dominance over one's rival or enemy was considered a crime justifying severe punishment by the chiefs and clan mothers.

"Still Sky Toucher will end up fighting him," asserted Wide Shoulders. "Burning Wolf will see to that. And he will kill him before he lets his sister marry him."

He picked up one of the two torches and probed the area he was working on.

"Look!" Four Otters pointed toward the main gate.

Looking haggard with worry, loping in came Sky Toucher. They called to him. He waved without glancing their way or slowing his pace, ran by them and went into Singing Brook's longhouse.

"What is bothering him?" Four Otters asked.

"Bad news from Gâ-oh," said Wide Shoulders.

Four Otters dropped his axe into the canoe. "Let us go see."

"Leave him alone," replied Wide Shoulders.

Sky Toucher found Singing Brook in her chamber scraping the hide of her brother's kill. She looked up as he entered and gasped.

"What is it? What has happened?"

He looked about, dropped to his knees in front of her and spoke in a whisper. "Not in here!"

"What? Tell me!"

"Shhhh, outside. By the stream. Come."

Minutes later they sat by the stream, the castle beside them rising through the trees. Small white-flowered floating hearts and showy bladderwort crowded both banks beneath the grass; red- and white-spotted trout glided by.

"Must I drag it out of you?" she burst.

"Your brother is dead."

She gasped, her eyes rounding. "You killed him!"

"*Neh!* I . . . did . . . not. Please listen. I will tell you exactly what happened."

As he told her step by step she seemed to sink into herself. He was not halfway through his explanation when she began trembling. He slipped his arm around her shoulders.

"He did not see the clove. I think he did not know it was there. He ran toward it, I stepped out of his path, he tried to stop. Too late. I was nowhere near him when he fell. I know I threatened to kill him but that was just my frustration talking. I would never. How could I face you if I did such a thing? And it would destroy any chance we had to marry."

"We *had*."

"You think it is gone now?"

"What do you think?"

"Look at me, I say it again, I did not start the fight. You must believe me."

She searched his eyes. "I do." His shoulders slumped in relief, he exhaled loudly. "You would never do such a thing; it had to be all Burning Wolf. He never takes the time to think, just blunders ahead." She framed his face with her hands. "We must go back."

"Are you all right?"

"Of course I am not *all right!*" She sighed. "I am sorry. It is done, and there is nothing we can do to change it. I feel like the whole world has crumbled into pieces. Now we must look into the coiled rattler's face."

"*I* must."

"You will have to be the one to tell my mother. I cannot support you, you understand."

"*Nyoh.*"

"Come."

* * *

They found Green Water with Snowflake in her chamber, talking
and laughing. Green Water sobered at sight of Sky Toucher in a
manner that suggested she felt a responsibility to.

"Mother," began Singing Brook. "O-ron-ia-ke-te wishes to
speak with you."

"About your marriage, I know. You wish me to repeat my
*neh?*"

"*Neh,*" said Sky Toucher, "about something else." He avoided
his mother's staring eye.

"Speak," muttered Green Water.

"If you would come outside with me."

"What is going on?" Snowflake asked.

"Please, O´hute Onega."

They walked down the passageway to the rear entrance. Sky
Toucher pushed it open, they slipped outside. He suddenly felt
very nervous, a feeling unusual to him. Green Water eyed him
indifferently. He bit his lip and looked away.

"Tékha Ochquoha is dead."

She tensed and jerked slightly then flung her arms around her,
gasping, teetering from side to side. *"Neh, neh, neh!"*

He watched her stiffen against the shock. Quickly, he told her
what had happened. She heard him out silently and motionless,
her arms at her sides. Then sat down hard. He assessed her admiringly: she would not wail or carry on. Like all Iroquois women,
her spine was iron. She looked up with tearless eyes.

"His body lies at the bottom?"

"I tried to bring it up, it was too heavy."

She grunted and immediately focused on the task ahead. "Get
your friends, get others, take rope with you. Bring his body home,
he must be properly buried."

"I will see to it. I was going to. I say again, Green Water, I
did not kill him."

He caught himself; he was doing it again, talking too much.
She had not accused him, not even with her eyes. Had he now put
suspicion into her head? What a mouth he had, and the brain of
a slug!

"Do I blame you?" she asked. He shook his head and hung it. "Let me tell you something for your ears only, not my daughter's, not your mother's, no one else's. I have always had deep and very warm feelings for my son but I was not blind to his faults. I know what he was, and what you describe in this is Tékha Ochquoha, so there is no need to keep telling me you did not kill him.

"But one thing puzzles me: why did he follow you up there? Why this time when he never did before? What went on between you two that I do not know about?"

He told her without elaborating that the deaths of both their fathers had become an issue between them. He told her of his efforts to get the truth from Gâ'oh, that he finally was able to, only Burning Wolf refused to accept it.

"You are putting fog around what you are saying. What 'truth' about your father and my husband?"

"That my father Onea Onà·kara was no coward in the war."

"They were killed in the same battle, your father and my husband. Some think Onea Onà·kara was the cause of Cahonsye Osto's death."

"They are wrong. I have it from Gâ'oh, from the shade of an Abnaki warrior who was there and saw both killed. They . . ." he paused, "died bravely."

"Did they?"

"Tékha Ochquoha believed my father guilty of cowardice that caused Cahonsye Osto's death as well as his own. He held it against me. That was his reason for objecting to the marriage."

Green Water shook her head. "Not so. It is not you or your father, it never was. My son did not want his sister to marry anyone. No man was good enough for her. Outsiders think from what they see that they hated each other, and perhaps there was ill-feeling. But deep down he worshiped her. I know my son, O-ron-ia-ke-te, and that is the truth of it."

"It *was* an accident, O´hute Onega; it did not have to happen."

She shrugged. "Knowing him, it did. He was his name, inside he *was* fire."

"I still think he had a special hate for me."

"You mean because of your father." Again she shook her head. He helped her to her feet. "Let me tell you something which you are to keep secret. From her, from everyone. I found out what happened in the war nine years ago; I heard it from one of the warriors who died of sickness less than a week after they came back and brought home the dead. This man was a lookout sitting hidden in the top branches of a tall tree. He first told me that Cahonsye Osto died bravely. I should have let it go at that." She shook her head and walked a few steps away before turning back. "I should have accepted it. But I asked myself why would he put it that way? Why not just say he was killed in battle? He kept saying *bravely* too often. I could not help suspecting that there was more to what happened out there. Possibly something Cahonsye Osto did wrong, or did not do that he should have, and this man wanted to spare my feelings. I kept at him.

"He finally told all on his death bed, that Cahonsye Osto was shot while running away; his brave stomach for battle filled with milk. I kept it a secret from all four boys and from Tenäte Oÿoghi. What was to be gained by telling them such a terrible truth? The day came when Tékha Ochquoha was my only surviving son. He kept asking about his father. He became more curious as he got older; he wanted to know every detail of his life. He assumed his father died bravely and was very proud. I worried that he might spread that around, that others had seen what the lookout saw and were keeping the truth quiet for my sake. Tékha Ochquoha could make himself look ridiculous and when he found out it would crack his heart. I told him the truth. Not his sister. She does not know any of it."

"Then he knew all along?"

"*Nyoh.*" She eyed him. "Now so do you. Of course, you already knew from Gǎoh. But you will keep my embarrassing secret. Will you help recover his body?"

"*Nyoh,* of course."

"And if anyone accuses you of killing him up there, I will tell what happened. They will believe it from me, *neh?*"

His heart enveloped her. His whole life he had known her and had never seen this side of her, never imagined it existed. Her candor lifted him and he understood why his mother so loved and respected her.

His heart relieved, they returned to Singing Brook and Snowflake. On the way he thought about the situation. How *would* the tribe react to Burning Wolf's death? Even with Green Water on his side? He sighed inwardly. Knowing people, he could foresee their reaction.

No one he knew (apart from Burning Wolf) had any particular prejudice against him. He realized that only when the average person is pressed to decide between the logical and the titillating, he usually has little trouble choosing. In such situations the truth seems to have little value.

There was a bright side: the tragedy might possibly serve one good purpose, to revive his and Singing Brook's chances. Could that happen? Despite all the reasons she had given Singing Brook, had Green Water refused her approval only from fear of her son?

# 15

THE BEST THAT Singing Brook could get out of Sky Toucher was that he would not run off to war without first sitting down and discussing it. At least that would give her the chance to marshal her objections and oblige him to listen to them. She could not order him; he had to be persuaded.

They were married, in light of Burning Wolf's death, without the customary ceremony: they simply gave their consent to be man and wife in the presence of others serving as witnesses. The previous day the bride-to-be was conducted to her intended husband's longhouse by her mother, her two aunts and a few friends. With her she had brought the traditional cakes of unleavened bread, presenting them to Snowflake. Snowflake returned Sky Toucher's gift of venison. But the mere giving of consent the following day did not satisfy the bride; afterwards, they went into the woods to their private place and were married a second time under the eyes of a red squirrel who had just given birth to four little ones, a number of birds and a fawn that happened by and stood eyeing them curiously. The couple knelt facing each other and clasped hands.

"You are my husband now and forever," she murmured. "I am yours, you are mine, nothing can ever come between us."

"Nothing," he murmured. "If you die before I do I will give my knife to my heart, so that we will travel together to the Village of the Dead and be with each other always."

"Always."

She had fashioned a garland of harebells. She placed it around his neck, twisted it once and placed the other end around her own. They touched their stars, held them together and kissed.

He held a fistful of ripe strawberries over her, squeezing them, letting the drippings fall and puddle in the concavity of her stomach. Then he spread the pulp from below her breasts down to her place. She trembled excitedly as he raised to his knees and, bending, began tonguing the crimson pulp up through the valley between her breasts. Then slowly eating downward. Her nipples erect, her hand gripped his nape, pulling his head to one side, setting his hot mouth against her belly.

He licked gently, gradually becoming more voracious, moving about, crushing and spilling more fruit down onto her belly, consuming it greedily. Returning to the path of the pulp leading down to her place, he devoured it inch by inch, licking away the bright stain remaining. When he came to her place, where the trail ended, he crushed one more handful of fruit, pulling her lips gently open to receive the sweetness and mix with her honey. He bent his head. She moaned.

A week passed, bringing the last day of the berry month and to the earth came the month when the bee balm bursts into fiery red, inviting the hummingbird and monarch butterfly to drink from its rough and shaggy cup.

Kettle Throat, Winter Gull and Hendrick met in privacy in the latter's chamber. They sat in a triangle filling and lighting their pipes with tobacco from a skein hanging above their heads and puffing in silence, relaxing, arranging their thoughts. All three had ruled their Mohawk clans—the wolf, turtle and bear clan respectively—for many harvests. Both Kettle Throat and Winter Gull were respected, both honorable men, but neither was cut from the same sinew as Hendrick, Tiyanoga—chief of chiefs of the People of the Place of the Flint. Recently he had returned from visiting London with two other Iroquois chiefs. There he had been honored by Queen Anne and presented with gifts. At hundreds of council fires his voice had been the most eloquent. How many scalps had his knife lifted in defense of his people? He had defeated his enemies red and white with courage and cunning. Kettle Throat and Winter Gull merely ruled in his large shadow.

"So it is agreed," said Kettle Throat. "We will not paint our wampum red this time."

"When Dorr returns we will give him no warriors," said Winter Gull.

Hendrick pursed his thin lips and studied the slender column of smoke rising from the bowl of his pipe. His index finger found the end of the scar that started under his ear, tracing it along its length to the corner of his mouth.

"Refusing him our help is not strong enough," he murmured in his gravel voice.

Kettle Throat grunted. "This gives it strength. We cannot break faith with our blood brothers, the Senecas, Cayugas, Onondagas and Oneidas in the confederacy."

Hendrick shook his head. "Not strong enough, either. Have we not broken with them before and gone our own way? You two agree that we should stay out of it this time."

"You do not agree?" Kettle Throat asked.

"I think we are overlooking the reality of the situation. Because we do not want to face it."

"What *reality?*"

"That English and Mohawk destinies are like the vines of the *sku-nak-su,* woven so tightly together no one can separate them. That we have come too far together: the alliance that began as words is now carved in old stone."

Winter Gull growled in annoyance. "Then you do not agree with us."

"I did not say that. All I am saying is that by staying out of the fighting this time we are only postponing the inevitable. But I will not go against you two. Although I think the excuse we must give

Dorr when he comes again should be the truth, that the ranks of our warriors have become so thinned we do not have the men he needs. That is the horse we must ride until it drops." Again he shook his head. "We are like a wolf caught in a trap and surrounded by hunters. Stay caught and he dies, get free and his fate is no better."

The others nodded. "You do the talking when he comes back," said Winter Gull.

Hendrick grunted. His pipe had gone out, he flung it aside in frustration. This business with the English was tearing him. He was only in his forties but his fondness for fighting was waning. Should the tribe cling to neutrality, the inevitability of disaster dogged his thoughts day and night. And yet if they acceded to Dorr's demands and the next battle turned out as bloody as the last one, Tenotoge would only survive as a tribe of old men, women and children.

Still, Hendrick and his fellow chiefs seemed unwilling to confront one critical issue: over recent years the Mohawk warrior had become almost fiercely independent, no longer accepting his leaders' decisions without question. Many warriors disobeyed their chiefs outright, so many in some instances, that singling out the rebels and punishing them proved impossible.

But, at least at the moment, Singing Brook was giving no thought to war, to Sky Toucher's possible departure and life without him. He had solved a minor problem.

Combs ordinarily fashioned of elm bark were crude and broke easily. He had removed intact the spine and ribs of a brook trout, carefully cutting away one row of ribs and shortening those on the opposite side to uniform length. This she had submerged in a bowl of black paint made from powdered iron ore boiled with oak galls. Repeated dippings formed a coating which gradually thickened, creating a comb much more durable than those made of elm bark.

They sat naked in a shallow pool in bright sunlight hidden from curious eyes by a wall of tall reeds, she with her back to him. He washed her hair with a shampoo that mixed chamomile with soapwort that not only cleansed it but also brightened it. He worked up a thick lather, massaging it in, her hair cascading black and gleaming down to her waist. His fingers dug deeply, moving slowly, invigorating her scalp, bringing a delicious sensation that stirred her down to her place. It also brought a drowsiness, despite the refreshing coolness of the water. When her hair was completely lathered he scrubbed it thoroughly, working upwards toward her scalp, massaging it.

This done, he moved backwards, bending her backwards until her head was just above the surface of the pool. He then dipped double handfuls of water, spilling it, rinsing her hair, restoring the gleaming blackness that rivaled that of a raven's back in bright sunlight. When he was done rinsing she sat up and he began combing it, drawing the comb from her center part all the way down to the ends in a single stroke. He combed steadily for a while before rinsing it a second time and combing it again. When almost all of the water was drawn from it, both got up and made their way to the nearby bank. She lay on the grass and together they fanned out her hair to dry in the sun.

Before it dried completely she rubbed in a decoction of the powdered roots and leaves of nettle boiled in water, which helped to preserve the natural color. Then he combed it for her one last time before she braided it into the single braid of a married woman and fixed it in place with a small wooden tablet covered with embroidered deer hair.

# 16

THEY SAT FACING each other beside the stream, having invaded the realm of a flight of lace-winged butterflies. Sunlight set the fliers' diaphanous wings gleaming like gold leaf, as they lazily propelled their small bronzy-green bodies around Sky Toucher and Singing Brook. She held up a large apple, dipping it in the water, skinning it before she handed it to him. He held it out, she bit, the crunching sound intruding on the softly droning chorus and the stream music. She chewed slowly, crushing the pulp, savoring its juiciness, then held the apple for him to taste. He bit and chewed even more deliberately, savoring the sweetness; the juice trickling

from the corner of his mouth she took on her fingertip and spread
on her tongue. He took back the apple, holding it close to inhale
its aroma. He held it for her, and she eyed him over it, slowly
sinking her teeth into it. In turn, they proceeded to consume it,
taking ever smaller bites as it diminished in size.

The dragonflies flitted around them, binding them together with
invisible threads. Unmindful of their capture, their eyes never unlocked, not even to glance at the apple. When it had reduced to
a slender core she grasped the stem and pulled it free. Breaking
the core in two, she pushed half into his mouth, the remainder
into her own. Sweeter than honey was the core juice. It dripped
and ran down her throat while with the tip of her tongue she pushed
the seeds to the front of her mouth out over her teeth. He did the
same. One by one she retrieved the seeds from his mouth, he from
hers, his fingers crossing her lower lip, resting briefly on it sending
a tingling through her. The seeds disposed of, they savored the
last of the sweetness lingering in their mouths, continuing to stare
at each other, unwilling, unable to free each other's eyes. And the
dragonflies circled, weaving on.

They had returned to the castle and were entering their chamber
when they heard excited voices outside the longhouse. Colonel
Douglas Dorr was arriving with his escort, dismounting, coming
forward to greet the three chiefs. At sight of the scarlet uniforms,
the swords and muskets and the bloodshed they so starkly sym-
bolized, Singing Brook's heart sank.

Sky Toucher looked her way. "Do not be upset," he murmured.

This was not how she had planned it. She'd wanted to discuss
it at length with him, without rancor, without raising their voices.
She had thought about talking Four Otters into trying to dissuade
Sky Toucher; she'd seen his friend by himself two days ago and
wanted to run to him, talk to him. But she could not bring herself
to do it. It didn't seem right, using him to change Sky Toucher's
mind, even if Four Otters were willing to try. They could end up
arguing, which would be unfair to Four Otters.

"Why must you go just because Wotstaha Onirares is so eager
to? Must you follow him like a faithful dog?"

"He is not *eager,* he feels that he must go. If the English lose this time, we lose everything. They will have to pick up and move south or maybe even leave, go back home on their wooden islands. Without their guns to protect us, the French moccasins will overrun Iroquois lands while the lace-cuffs stand by grinning. It will be get out or be massacred. Or become the lace-cuffs' slaves. If we got out where would we go? Where is there no tribe already occupying good land? We would have to fight from then on; the days would be red from the day we leave here. Is that what you want?"

"But why you? Will your knife, your gun make such a big difference? You make it sound like the fate of the whole tribe hinges on you."

"You think my head is that big?"

"Never mind, I do not want to talk about it now. Tonight we will sit and discuss it without you losing your temper."

"Or you."

"*Nyoh.*"

The powwow was set up just inside the entrance gate for every Mohawk to witness and take part in if they chose. The three chiefs sat opposite Dorr and a major of militia whom he introduced as Major Alden Carver from Connecticut, an intimidatingly large man with a barrel belly and multiple chins bedding a massive face. In a startlingly high-pitched voice, he squeaked out his acknowledgment of welcome. As was the custom when visitors arrived, women brought food. They passed *Gă´oñ´wă´s,* bowls, among the officers and men, with *atog´washäs,* spoons made from curly maple knots. Everyone's staple, *ogon´sä'ganon´dä,* succotash, was served, the green corn stripped from the cob and thrown into a pot of beans which had nearly finished cooking, and the mass simmered together until both ingredients were done. *Ojiké tàhdä´wa,* salt from a woven corn-husk bottle, was available for those who wished to season the dish. There was also *sateeni,* roast young dog meat, and *aque,* venison. And to wash it all down parched corn coffee, *o'nīstagi,'* was offered. The corn was well burnt and parched on coals, scraped from the cob, thrown into a kettle, and boiling water was thrown on it. Then the kettle was placed over the fire again for a few minutes.

"*Gŭk´wa,*" croaked Winter Gull, "*E$^n$ sádĕ koni.*"

They would most certainly *eat* the food. Unlike Hendrick, Kettle Throat and Winter Gull spoke little English. Hosts and visitors got along mainly with gestures and much smiling on both sides. The meal consumed, the utensils taken away, Dorr cleared his throat and was preparing to speak when Hendrick held up a hand.

"The answer, Dorr, is No, we cannot send our warriors to fight again. They are too few, our losses have been too heavy."

A low rumbling ran through the watching crowd. Singing Brook could tell from their expressions which warriors disapproved. Wide Shoulders was one.

Sky Toucher made no sound, and Singing Brook resisted looking for his reaction.

Hendrick went on. "No longer have we the strength to bleed and die for our friends the English. See for yourself, Tenotoge had not that many warriors left. It is the same with Schandisse and Onekahoncka."

"We must refuse you," added Winter Gull in Mohawk, Hendrick translating for Dorr.

From Hendrick's expression Singing Brook could see that he was not afraid to stand up to Dorr or any whiteskin. Still, Sky Toucher had told her that Wide Shoulders had told him that Hendrick agreed only reluctantly with Kettle Throat and Winter Gull to stay out of further conflict. In his heart, Hendrick felt the same as Wide Shoulders and Sky Toucher. Would the warrior chief's true sentiments surface in the days to come?

"Why do they not leave us alone?" she rasped.

"Shhhh, you should be pleased. Dorr has his answer even before his question."

"I hate him. I hate all of them! They wear red like the blood our warriors spill for them, like a reminder to taunt us. Why do they come here? Why do the French? They have their own lands across the *O-jik-́ha-dä-ge-́ga*, why force us to fight over *our* own lands? It is disgusting! *'Oueda!'*"

"Shhhh, people are looking at you."

Dorr was speaking. "Great chiefs, we do not come this time to ask for your brave warriors." A rumble of surprise ran through the onlookers. Winter Gull's jaw sagged as he gawked. Both Hendrick's and Kettle Throat's brows bunched in puzzlement. "How many times have they bled and died by our side? For their service to the Crown all English are eternally grateful. All we ask this time is a small favor. Only twelve brave men, not to fight but to act as scouts." He looked toward Sky Toucher, smiling. "I recognize Sky Toucher there. He fought bravely in the ambush last fall and before that was the best scout we had—our lookout up at the top of a tall tree watching for the enemy. He was invaluable. Sky Toucher, we need you badly. And eleven others. That's all, no warriors to fight, no guns, no danger. Only scouts."

Singing Brook flinched as fury seized her. No danger? More danger than fighting, skulking about in enemy territory trying to stay out of their way and at the same time find out what they were up to! Scouts died as easily, as often as warriors facing enemy fire. And death was even worse for scouts, no quick bullet in the chest. If captured they were tortured to death.

This was a whiteskin song designed to put the chiefs' good sense to sleep. Honey poured into their ears. All three looked relieved, they would agree, they would jump at the chance to sacrifice only twelve compared to two hundred.

"*Neh!*" she shouted. Everyone looked her way. Sky Toucher grabbed her arm. "No warriors, no scouts! Why should we die for your chief with the gold hat? For what? Our blood in exchange for your promises that you do not keep, gifts we never see?"

"*Ogechta!*" snapped Kettle Throat.

"Shut up yourself!" She flung an arm, dismissing him, dismissing all, and turning, strode off toward the longhouse. Sky Toucher came after her. "Do not say anything," she muttered, "not a word."

All eyes that had followed her departure, now turned back to the chiefs, Dorr and his men. Wide Shoulders stepped out of the crowd.

"I will go," he said in English, "I will scout."

Dorr beamed. "That's one, who's next?"

# 17

CONSIDERING DISCRETION PREFERABLE to valor, in spite of Dorr's glowing compliment, Sky Toucher did not return to the powwow to volunteer. Moments after he and Singing Brook went inside the longhouse, Wide Shoulders came bursting into the chamber beaming. He found husband and wife sitting far apart, staring at the floor in silence woven with tension.

"I am going!" declared Wide Shoulders.

"We know," muttered Sky Toucher, not looking up.

"You are, too!"

Singing Brook glared savagely at Wide Shoulders. He swallowed.

"Not now," growled Sky Toucher, "get out, please, I will see you later."

"He *has* to come, Tenäte Oÿoghi . . ."

Again she scowled. Sky Toucher sighed, got up and pushed his friend gently through the door.

"Your heart is set on going and you know it," she said tightly.

"I have not said a word."

"Your face says it all. Why do you look so sheepish if your mind is not made up? You betrayed me, as well. You chose without discussing it, despite your promise to me."

"We will discuss it, we will."

"What good will it do; you will still go. I know you better than you know yourself. You are as stubborn as a child." She started up.

"Tenäte Oÿoghi, where are you going?"

"Out."

"Not—back to the pow . . ."

"*Neh!*"

She was gone. Seconds later Wide Shoulders came back in.

"Thank you, *friend,*" murmured Sky Toucher.

Violet clouds were shearing off pieces of the setting sun when she returned, marching purposefully in on Sky Toucher and Wide

Shoulders. She began pulling clothing, moccasins, other personal items down from shelves and tossing them on the bunk.

"What are you doing?" Sky Toucher asked, feeling Wide Shoulders' eyes boring into him.

"Moving out. What does it look like?"

"But we were going to talk—"

"We can talk until our brains turn upside down. We have already talked it to death, why drag it out? We talk, only neither of us listens."

"Do not go, Tenäte Oÿoghi."

She turned to him, her eyes glistening tears. "Do not come to see me. I do not want to see you. I would rather be alone."

Moments later, a moosehide sack filled to bursting slung over her shoulder, she left.

# 18

SINGING BROOK AND other wives were not the only ones opposed to Mohawk involvement. O-ne-ha-tah—Porcupine—a tribal elder, was fiercely against it. At his insistence a council meeting convened, which Sky Toucher and Wide Shoulders attended. Wide Shoulders, the only volunteer at the earlier powwow with Dorr, remained confident that others were on the verge of joining him. Evidently, O-ne-ha-tah suspected as much.

He raised a withered hand asking to speak. He was an early convert to Protestantism, one of the few Tenotogeans still remaining in the Valley to embrace Christianity. He was very old, wise and deliberate in his thinking, and when he spoke the chiefs and clan mothers listened, even though lately his mind did not seem as clear, nor his memory as sharp as before.

"One thing no one has mentioned," he said in a tremulous voice, raising a bony finger for emphasis. "It does not matter how many men we put into their war, one or hundreds, it is the same to our enemies. The French moccasins will threaten us, burn our corn, burn our castles, kill our hunters in our own territory. I say do not give Dorr one man. I pray to God we do not. God and

Jesus Christ will frown upon us if we do, for we are only inviting deaths that would not occur if we stay out of it altogether. Why call God's wrath down upon us?"

Hendrick grunted. Not a Christian, he disliked and distrusted Jesuit black robes and Protestant black cloaks equally. He likened them to wasps, only the stinger of their preaching did not stop paining; their efforts to convert were impossible to discourage, short of spilling their blood. He mainly resented them because they assumed that the Iroquois had no religion, which was as wrong as it was presumptuous. And those Christians who did credit the people with beliefs usually belittled them. He was fond of Porcupine, as were his fellow chiefs, but none had any fondness for his religion, and his concerns over the use of Mohawks as scouts they refused to take seriously.

"What Dorr is asking for is much better than for warriors to fight," said Hendrick. Virtually everyone present nodded agreement.

"It is the same," insisted Porcupine. "If we take part, even just as scouts, French moccasins will come here and burn us down as they burned Caweoge, Schatsyerosy and other castles. Sending scouts will show whose side we are on, bringing death and destruction to our people. Then we will feel God's wrath in all its fury!"

On he ranted until Kettle Throat interrupted, politely thanking Porcupine for his opinion. Then Kettle Throat commanded the council fire to be strewn, signaling an end to the discussion.

Women! Sky Toucher growled in frustration and hurled a deer bone against the wall of the chamber. Women's minds and men's minds followed wholly different trails over every issue. You talked about a problem with a woman, and it was as if the two of you were talking about two different things. Women saw everything differently from men. Neither's eyes could fit the other's sockets.

This was so because women viewed things with the eye of their place, his father used to say, from between their legs. He recalled his mother laughing when his father said it. She insisted it wasn't true, it was just that men's and women's brains were as different as a bear's brain from an eagle's. Not that women's brains were upside down in their heads, just different.

Or was it a game women played? Did they *pretend* to see things differently, just to be contrary? At times it seemed they felt it their duty to disagree, and to point out that the man was wrong, blaming his wrongheadedness on his "man-ness," another way of saying his skin was too thick, he was incapable of applying his feelings to the situation in the way that a woman could; he could not see beneath the outer skin, not see into the heart of the thing. Whatever the case, their way of thinking was peculiarly their own and traveled over trails no man could find, much less follow. No wonder men and women arrived at different camps!

Of course things went on in his head Singing Brook could not understand. But that was different, he was a man.

Still it came down to this: whatever a man decided, it clashed with her view, so it had to be wrong. Worst of all, you could never tell what a woman was thinking, while *she* always seemed able to see inside a man's head and knew exactly what he was thinking. How did they do that?

When he got to be thirteen and stopped looking through girls and began looking at them his mother told him a story about a hunter out hunting with his squaw. He shot a moose but only wounded it. Charging, it would have trampled him had he not defended himself with his knife. He was quick and agile and managed to kill the moose. He was proud of his courage, of his success in surviving a dangerous situation and saving them both.

But his wife didn't see it that way. She thought he should have made a clean kill. Wounding the creature caused it unnecessary suffering, apart from putting them in grave danger. She told him she would not eat its flesh or preserve its hide, because he had made it suffer so. She found fault with him for failing to make a clean kill. Then Sky Toucher's mother asked him which of them was right, husband or wife?

He remembered saying that the husband was because every kill cannot be clean, such things happen in hunting and the wife shouldn't find fault with him for it. His mother had smiled and said—and he could recall her every word—"Maybe both were right."

He wasn't sure he understood but he didn't pursue it. It was, after all, just a story. But now, thinking back on it, he could see her point.

The sun warmed the Te-ugé-ga, the Mohawk River, as the cumbersome dugout canoe butted rather than slipped through the placid water. It was heavier and slower than either an elm-bark canoe or birch-bark and required considerably more physical strength from its occupants. But it did have its advantages. It was so solidly built it required no thwarts. There were no seats. The paddlers knelt in the bottom. It was virtually indestructible, never needed repair, and it generally outlasted the men who carved it.

Four Otters, sitting in the bottom between Wide Shoulders and Sky Toucher, had dropped a fishing line.

"This is like paddling a rock." Sky Toucher, at the stern, groused as he bent and dug his paddle deep.

"We are against the current," called Wide Shoulders over his shoulder. "Cayere Tawyne, did he tell you she left him?"

"*Ogechta!*" snapped Sky Toucher.

"Why shut up? You think it is a secret? By now it is all over the castle."

"*Ogechta!*"

"You can get her to come back," said Four Otters. "Do not volunteer to scout for Dorr."

"You think I would refuse now that she has done this? What would others think?"

Four Otters pulled in his line and rebaited his hook with a fragment of smoked venison. "They are only asking for twelve."

"And you had better speak up, O-ron-ia-ke-te," said Wide Shoulders, "before others beat you to it. And please, do not tell me *ogechta* again. I will have to come back there and dump you into the water. Besides, you know you are going, you want to, have to, why put off volunteering?"

"Is this all there is in that bean-size brain of yours?"

Wide Shoulders swiveled about and rested his dripping paddle across the gunwhales. "Will she come back?"

Sky Toucher ignored the question, avoided his eyes. Would she? *He* was supposed to be the stubborn one, but she was proving a match for him.

"Not right away," said Four Otters.

"Why not?" Wide Shoulders asked.

"Will you stop your rattling tongues?" Sky Toucher berated them. "You are like two old *odasquetas!*"

Four Otters went on. "Because she is not a reed that wavers in the breeze, she has an *orochquine* like an *aquidagon,* an ox, *neh?* And this way she forces you to stay home."

"No one *forces* me to do anything I do not want to do!" Sky Toucher snapped.

"You will stay home or never see her place again, am I right, Wotstaha?"

"*Nyoh.*"

"*Ogechta!*"

Four Otters yelled. He had hooked a small rainbow trout. It leaped surprisingly high before twisting about and plunging downward. In that instant a belted kingfisher dove from straight overhead. Its oversized head and neck built to absorb the shock of the water, it gripped the slippery fish in its spearlike bill, snapped Four Otter's line and flew off to a nearby branch where it began whacking the fish and tossing it in the air. The three of them watched it openmouthed as it began eating the head first, then stopping, waiting for its stomach juices to reduce the fish in size to fit down its throat.

The mounting tension was broken, Four Otters exploded in anger, Sky Toucher began laughing, joined by Wide Shoulders.

# 19

I WARNED YOU not to marry him," said Green Water, "but who can tell you anything? Now here you are fighting like two angry foxes who have rutted together!"

"Stop it!" rasped Singing Brook. "We—did not *fight.*"

"What do you call it? You knew he was stubborn but you had to go storming into marriage."

"I do not want to talk about it, not with you."

"Would you like me to leave my own chamber?"

Green Water held up Burning Wolf's buckskin jacket, to which she had earlier sewn the porcupine quills. Singing Brook watched her mother pick away at the decorations. Annoyance set her awl flying. There was no man left in their immediate family to wear the jacket, so it would be ornamented instead with a narrow edging of white beadwork, and perhaps a bit of silk ribbon in contrasting color. Green Water would gather it at the waist and shorten the sleeves so that she could wear it herself.

"I do not want to fight," murmured Singing Brook.

"Is expressing one's opinion *fighting?*" Green Water shook her head. "So what now?"

"It is up to him."

"It is up to you; you are the one who left. Do not expect him to come crawling after you."

Singing Brook eyed her entreatingly. "How can I stop him from going away?"

"You cannot. Do you think I could stop your father from going to fight back when he and Onea Onà·kara left? I had more sense than to try."

"You should have."

"Oh? Are you saying it was my fault that he got himself killed?"

"I did not mean that and you know it!"

"All I know is that your marriage is broken in pieces and you sit around mooning like a *cian* who has lost her favorite husk doll."

"What can I do?"

Green Water paused in removing the quills to stare stonily. "*Now* you want my advice. When you were thinking of marrying it was worthless. Look at me. Only you can solve your problem. If I advise you to do this or that we both know you will not do it. Why give my breath to words your ears will reject like so much noise? You are a grown woman, if you cannot figure these things out . . ." She sighed and clasped her hands in exasperation.

"Forget it! And forgive me, I thought you cared."

Green Water studied her, shaking her head slowly. "You must have an *onea* for a brain, a stone. Your first fight and neither of you can deal with it. And I am supposed to feel sorry for you?"

"Never mind!" Singing Brook got quickly to her feet.

"Where are you going?"

"What do you care?"

Outside she seethed. Her fury and frustration compressed her lungs, making breathing difficult. Going back to him was out of the question, staying in her mother's longhouse appeared just as impossible.

Men!

*Deep down* he had to go, he said. He could not live with himself if he did not! And what about her? What about living with his wife, recognizing her viewpoint, deferring to her wishes? He'd hardly be alone if he didn't go. But he'd made his mind up long before the English arrived and he was picked out of the crowd. She could kill Dorr for that! Why pick him? Why not Wide Shoulders?

Why couldn't he stay home? she asked. It was more than stubbornness. He saw it as his chance to prove he was immune to her influence and even if wrong, even disastrously, his judgment came first. Hers counted for nothing.

She couldn't blame Wide Shoulders; even his influence was pretty much balanced off by Four Otters'. No, Sky Toucher's decision was all his. She could make no sense of his argument that the English had to win the war, that if the French did the Mohawks, if not all the Iroquois, were doomed.

Even if he was right, what difference could one man make? And whenever she brought it up he went wild, which proved he felt guilty about it or wasn't as sure of himself as he pretended. Or secretly feared she was right. Or feared she might change his thinking if he listened.

How strange. You chose someone and married him because you loved him. Only after did you discover hidden weaknesses, flaws which, had you suspected them before the marriage, might have made you think twice about going through with it. Still, she'd handed over the marriage bread without hesitation, thinking she could get him to change his mind.

"Stupid!"

But what fired her frustration more than anything was the fact that he was ready, even eager, to bleed and die *when nobody asked him to.* Dorr she considered nobody. And she was out of it, kept out by her husband's ego, his stubbornness. She had no influence on him.

"I could kill him!"

# 20

THE SEPARATION PUT more of a burden on Singing Brook than on Sky Toucher. Everyone in the castle knew that their marriage brazenly violated tradition. Some saw it as the spoiled act of two self-indulgent people, a deliberate insult to the clan mothers and the chiefs. In every look directed her way she saw "I told you so." She felt that people were laughing at her. She blamed Sky Toucher and wanted to leave, to escape the staring and gossiping.

But she decided to stay. The long days of *otteyage* found her in her old chamber, in her mother's longhouse, until Green Water all but pushed her out the door. From then on she spent much of her time as she had before she married, in the company of her friends: Crage Otsíhsto⁷, White Star, Azotsioha, String-of-beads and Esteronde, Rain, a child of twelve, whom the older women let tag along with them. Beautiful she was and would be a beautiful woman, as comely as White Star, who glided like a shadow, and was statuesque and so sensuous-looking as to take a man's breath away. Wide Shoulders worshiped her from a distance, hesitant to approach her because he feared rejection, claimed Sky Toucher and Four Otters.

String-of-beads was not blessed with White Star's extraordinary beauty; actually, she was rather plain-looking, but her vivacious personality was more appealing than somber White Star's. String-of-beads liked Four Otters, but he seemed to have no interest in any woman. He did not display homosexual tendencies and Sky Toucher had never even hinted that he might be a berdache; still, Singing Brook privately wondered about him.

She was standing outside String-of-beads' longhouse with her when she spotted Sky Toucher coming toward them with Four Otters, the two of them arguing, walking with their heads down.

"Come!" Singing Brook grabbed String-of-beads' arm and hurried her up to the front entrance, to get around the other side, out of sight.

"What is the matter?"

String-of-beads glanced back to where Singing Brook had been looking and saw the two heading in their direction.

"You two are ridiculous," she rasped. "If you want to avoid seeing each other why does not one of you move out of the castle? Make it easy."

"I do not want to talk to him."

"You know everybody is smiling at you, clucking, talking behind your back. When you do this you play into their hands."

"What do I care?" Singing Brook retorted.

"You know you will get back together one day."

"Not soon. Right now I cannot stand the sight of him."

"Words, your face denies them."

They watched the two friends pass, still talking heatedly.

"Good," Singing Brook remarked. "Now we can relax for a while."

String-of-beads laughed.

*Otteyage* lazed on, the sun shone brightly for the crops, the rainfall was sufficient, no further word from Dorr was forthcoming. In the cool evenings enormous flocks of tree swallows came swirling in to roost in the marshes near the Mohawk River. In the meadows vast splashes of purple appeared as the loosestrife bloomed, signaling August's arrival and with it the *Ah-daké-wä-o,* the Green Corn Festival, a four-day celebration eagerly anticipated by all five Iroquois tribes. The corn planted in May was now green and fit for consumption, marking the beginning of the season of plenty. Tenotoge came alive with feasting and rejoicing.

The first day of the festival opened with the introductory speeches by the chiefs and elders celebrating the gift of the three sisters, corn, beans, and squash. The feather dance was held in midmorning, followed by the War dance: the two great dances of the Iroquois. Both featured up to twenty-five costumed participants, distinguished for their stamina, endurance and spirit. The dancers appeared in their finest apparel, including *gä-kä-ah, gus-to-́wah and gisé-hǎs,* the kilt, the headdress and leggings. The deerskin kilt fringed and embroidered with porcupine quillwork, was secured by a belt and descended to the knee. The headdress, the most conspicuous part of the costume, boasted a frame consisting of a band splint, adjusted around the head with a crossband arching over the top, from side to side. A cap of net-work enclosed the frame, and a silver band completed the lower part. Hanging down was a cluster of white bald-eagle feathers. A single larger feather, usually taken from the wing of a golden eagle, was set in the crown, inclining backwards from the head. It was secured in a small tube, which was fastened to the cross-splint, allowing the feather to revolve.

The deerskin leggings were fastened above the knee, descending to the moccasin. They were ornamented with quillwork on the bottom and side, the embroidered edge at the front. The dancers also wore ornaments on their wrists, arms and necks, with deer-hoof rattles at their knees.

The Feather dance began with two singers chanting. After the drums sounded, the turtle-shell and gourd rattles chattered, and down came the dancers on their heels in rhythm, shaking the ground. The crowd roared approval. Sky Toucher and Four Otters danced; so vigorous were their movements and gestures that in seconds their flesh was gleaming and dripping sweat. The more grotesque the dancers' movements, the more manly they looked, the Mohawks believed. The traditional hour-long dance was a contest that taxed even the strongest warrior's endurance. Round and round went Sky Toucher, flinging his limbs, pirouetting, whirling, charging this way and that before the eyes of his wife, who gazed impassively, trying her best to look through him.

But watching him dance, meeting his eyes every time he turned her way, saddened her. She missed him so, it was almost as if death had wrenched him from her. Her expression reflected her mood, for she was suddenly conscious that her friends were staring at her.

"He will come to you," said String-of-beads reassuringly, setting a hand on her friend's shoulder. Singing Brook had declined her invitation to move in with her.

"I am the one who left."

"So go back home to him" said White Star.

"*Neh!*"

"But you should see your face. You yearn to so much, it is twisting your heart."

"What I would like and what is right are two different things. Stop talking about it and watch the dancing," said Singing Brook.

"You should see your face," said White Star again.

"Shhh," murmured String-of-beads, rolling her eyes at her friend's tactlessness.

Singing Brook ignored both of them. Sky Toucher whirled, stopped abruptly, tried to avoid her eyes but failed. She so distracted him, he momentarily lost his rhythm, stumbling and nearly falling. Even when he moved away from her side of the spectacle, putting most of the other dancers between them, he continued to feel her eyes. Four Otters moved up close to him.

"You look filled with rain."

"Never mind."

"Her eyes are only for you."

*"Ogechta!"*

"Do you miss her?"

Sky Toucher made as if he didn't hear, moving away, at length finding himself back around the other side of the troupe, positioned all but squarely in front of her.

"Good dancing." White Star told him; Singing Brook frowned, then fastened her eyes on the ground.

Sky Toucher moved on. How he detested this, being alone all night and thinking instead of sleeping. He felt hollow without her, and depressed, every waking minute. It was all so stupid, unnecessary . . ."

Women!

What made them think they were entitled to run a man's life? Did marriage give them permission to? It was his life, his decision. Why must she interfere? What Mohawk wife told her husband what he should do in anything? None he knew; was she bent on being the first? Couldn't she understand after all their discussions that it was impossible for him to give in? If he yielded, Wide Shoulders would never let up on him. He could hear him now, wondering aloud which of them was the squaw in the family, who made the decisions. Everyone could not help but judge him a coward if he stayed home. When Dorr picked him out of the crowd, Sky Toucher felt as if his chest would burst, he was so proud. He felt as tall as the palisade, with all eyes on him, admiring him. Refusing to go back to war could only turn respect and praise into accusations of cowardice, into disgrace. Did she really want that for him?

She wasn't slow-witted like her friend White Star; it was simply that she couldn't see his side of it. She could see nothing beyond the two of them, the English situation was inconsequential. And she was convinced that if he did leave, he would never come back. It seemed not to occur to her that if he didn't, others would think him afraid to go. How would he hold up his head then?

If only they had it to do over, they could have left together when he first suggested it, before Burning Wolf's death. Maybe not to Onneyuttahage, but there were other places; it didn't have to be another castle. Her parents had done so.

If they had left, they could be living by the Shaw-na-taw-ty or somewhere between the river and Onekahoncka, still in Mohawk Territory, if that was so important to her. But at the end of the world, as far as Tenotoge was concerned. Gone, forgotten, and never to see Dorr come back with his request for volunteers, not even know about it. That would have pleased her and solved everything.

The music stopped abruptly; the dance was over. Some dancers dropped to their knees, exhausted, others supported themselves hands on knees gasping the burning out of their lungs. He felt a bit dizzy. Four Otters come over, Wide Shoulders appeared. They started talking. When he glanced over to where Singing Brook had been sitting, she and her friends were no longer there.

# 21

T HE DUST SETTLED, leaving the site of the Feather dance trampled as hard as stone. Winter Gull took his place in the center of the circle of celebrants. Low conversation ceased as he raised a hand.

"We thank our mother, the earth, who gives us life. We thank the rivers and streams for their precious water. We thank all growing things which feed and protect us, cure our illnesses, heal our wounds. We thank the corn and her sisters, the beans and squashes, which keep our bodies strong and healthy. To the bushes and trees which yield us their fruit we give thanks. We thank the moon and stars which give us their light while the sun sleeps. We thank our grandfather He-no, who protects us from witches, monsters and reptiles, and gives us his rain. We thank the sun that looks down upon our mother the earth with the eye of life."

"We thank all," chorused his listeners.

Fire was brought on a bark tray. Winter Gull knelt, a hush fell over the gathering and the ceremonial burning of tobacco began. Another dance followed, though the exhausted Feather dancers did not take part. Afterward, the crowd broke into groups and played games until near sunset, when everyone sat down to the traditional day's-end feast. *Sagamaté* was brought in three huge steaming kettles. The diners filed by, scooping up handfuls of the succotash, filling their bowls. There was also smoked fish and salt venison, fresh moose meat, rabbit and dog meat, vegetables, fruit and heaps of a variety of nuts.

Sky Toucher and Singing Brook purposely sat with their friends some distance from each other. She was not sure that he saw her, for he did not look in her direction. Unable to resist the temptation, she stared, willing him to look at her and eventually he did so. He had been laughing at something Four Otters said, but when he turned and saw her, a shadow darkened his smile and he looked sharply away.

Why? She could see others watching them, looking for just such a reaction. Why must he play to them? Didn't he understand that, apart from reflecting on her, it made him look childish? In that instant, when he averted his glance, the inclination to return to him came speedily to mind. She shook it off just as fast. That would be crawling back. Why give him the satisfaction!

Was he losing weight? Was he eating properly? He had not gone to his mother's chamber. Crage Otsíhsto? had told her she'd heard he was cooking for himself or eating with friends. Was he able to sleep? Was he taking proper care of himself, his clothes, the chamber? He was no more or less helpless than any other man, but when a woman wasn't around, men did tend to ignore the necessary daily tasks of washing things, airing out the bunk, keeping straight the contents of the shelves. How *was* the chamber? She wished she could look in without his knowing it.

She sighed. It seemed six whole moons since she left. She missed him. She never dreamed it would be this bad.

Now Sky Toucher forced himself to avoid looking her way. He grinned and laughed at everything Wide Shoulders and Four Otters said to make her think he was in the best of spirits, not lonely, not missing her. He laughed almost continuously until he began feeling foolish. Sobering he flung a rabbit bone over his shoulder and muttered, "I hate this, it is—*a-di-ho-ga.*"

"Awkward, *nyoh,*" said Wide Shoulders, "it must be."

"It is like we are both naked and everybody is staring at us."

"True. Very *a-di-ho-ga.* So what are you waiting for? Go and ask her to come home."

He couldn't bring himself to do it. Thinking back, he should have been the one to leave, only it hadn't occurred to him. Her walking out certainly came as a shock, she hadn't even given him time to protest.

"When do you think she will come home?" Four Otters asked.

Sky Toucher only frowned.

"Ask *her,*" said Wide Shoulders.

When would she? From her expression every time they saw each other, not soon. How long could a person stay angry? One usually reached a point where you had to consciously strain to continue it; pretend, to keep from losing face. It seemed so foolish. *He* wasn't angry with her, he hadn't been from the start. Was that supposed to give him satisfaction?

She had left her mother's longhouse and was now living with String-of-beads in the longhouse situated nearest the rear entrance to the castle. Should he put aside his pride and go and see her? Would she talk to him? What would they say that they hadn't already discussed? She hoped to change his mind by leaving him, presumably planning to stay away until he did. If he approached her, she would see it as capitulation. He could envision the triumph in her eyes as he walked in, even before he could get a word out.

He could not change his mind. He would not. The sooner she

accepted it the better for the both of them. One thing was sure, if they didn't get back together before he left, they probably never would.

"Going to her and talking about it would not be so bad," murmured Wide Shoulders. Sky Toucher started slightly. Uncanny, it was as if the other had been walking through his head, seeing his every thought. "What does either of you have to lose?"

Sky Toucher shook his head. "All our talking only tightens the knot."

Wide Shoulders seized a quantity of succotash between his fingertips, spilled it down his throat and belched. "But time has passed; maybe by now she is thinking differently, maybe beginning to see your side of it. A little . . ."

"If she is, why does she not come home?"

"Maybe her pride will not let her. It is the same with her as with you, *neh?*"

"What does her mother say?" Four Otters asked.

Sky Toucher sniffed, his voice suddenly sounded weary, "I do not know, I do not care. Eat."

The second day of the Green Corn Festival began with an address by Kettle Throat. It was followed by *Gä-na-o-uh,* the Thanksgiving dance. In steps and music it duplicated the Feather dance, the only difference between them being the brief thanksgiving speeches inserted between the individual songs. The sun was almost to the top of the sky when the front gate was thrown wide and in trouped a host of Oneidas, men, women and children, Onneyuttahagens come to join the festival, bringing their *baggataway* team, to play the game the French called lacrosse.

As played by the Iroquois, *baggataway* was the bloodiest of blood sports, brutality in constant motion, with many a match ending in death for some players and injuries to most. It was the highlight of the annual four-day festival and called for lengthy preparations on the part of the host Mohawks. A field five hundred paces long with no lateral boundaries had been cleared. Twenty-foot poles with crossbars forming goal posts were erected at either end.

O-dat-she-dah—Carries-a-quiver—chief of the turtle clan, Hat-

ya-tone-nent-ha—He-swallows-his-own-body-from-the-foot—chief
of the wolf clan and Tékni-ska-je-a-nah—Two Eagles—chief
of the bear clan—led the visitors. Carries-a-quiver returned the
painted and beribboned invitation stick, formally touching it when
Kettle Throat held it up signaling acceptance of the challenge.
Tumultuous cheering came from the spectators, who would wage
bets on the outcome, offering furs, skins, utensils, trinkets, French
scalps, English coins, knives and muskets. Members of the opposing hundred-man teams painted their bodies and drank sacred
medicine provided by their Medicine Men, who were pronouncing
incantations, each believing his magic would strengthen his own
team and weaken the opponents.

Final preparations for the match consumed most of what remained of the second day, before both camps settled down to enjoy
the day's-end feast. When darkness fell the players on both sides
danced, whipping themselves up into a combative frenzy.

The next morning, almost as soon as the sun freed itself from
the horizon, the rival teams lined up at opposite ends of the field,
whooping and screaming loudly. The two Medicine Men, one from
each tribe, stepped forward to officiate, although they were mostly
occupied in keeping out of the way of the screaming, charging
horde. Porcupine walked slowly to the center of the field, looked
toward one end, looked toward the other, and as a rumble rose
into a thunderous cheer, threw a deerhide ball stuffed with dry
corn into the air and ran as fast as he could out of harm's way.

Their backs still stinging—earlier, the players had been
switched into near-madness by their women—the players charged,
wielding their webbed sticks furiously, one in each hand. Sky
Toucher ran with Four Otters on one side, Wide Shoulders on the
other, whooping. Among the Oneidas coming at them was Splitting
Moon, who was a superb *baggataway* player, very fast, very durable. Two Eagles, who had no liking for the game, had never
played it seriously.

The two sides slammed together. In the flurry of legs, flailing
sticks and falling bodies, in the screaming and yelling on the field,
on the sidelines, in the massive cloud of dust slowly rising, violence
exploded. Sky Toucher had yet to even see the ball since it was
tossed up as all around him players swung their sticks, cried out

in pain and retaliated, smashing at their opponents. He saw Four
Otters go down, two men running over him, one planting a foot
squarely on his cheek, causing him to roar. Up he sprang, and,
ignoring the play, started after the offender. Sky Toucher caught
his arm.

"Never mind!"

"There is the ball!" shouted Wide Shoulders and started for it.
Four Otters elbowed him aside and picked up the chase. Sky
Toucher still had not seen it until Splitting Moon came hurtling
by, carrying it on his webbed stick, only to have it batted away.
The pounding feet were like thunder ascending from below ground,
crashing against Sky Toucher's ear pans, merging with the shrill
continuous whooping. Somebody swung a stick solidly against his
back knocking him forward, forcing him to shift his feet nimbly to
stay upright. Down went Four Otters, the ball slamming into his
temple. Sky Toucher saw that his right shoulder had been dislo-
cated and hung awkwardly from the socket. Four Otters bellowed.
Wide Shoulders bent over him, elbows out, both sticks swinging
lightly, fending off the players around them.

"What is all the noise?"

"My shoulder . . ."

"*That* hurts? It is nothing."

Sky Toucher crouched and straightened Four Otters' arm, then
tried to push it back into its socket. Four Otters roared. Wide
Shoulders laughed raucously. The players around them had thinned
out. Two older men ran out onto the field, grabbed Four Otters
by his ankles and pulled him off, his face contorted, his jaw working
up and down.

Somebody nearby had scooped up the ball and was moving with
it toward the Onneyuttahage goal. Defenders besieged him, knocking at his stick and at him as they tried to recapture the ball. He
passed it to another man who sent it flying through the goal. The
cheering on the Tenotoge side of the field was ear-splitting and the
players on the scoring team began cackling derisively like turkeys,
taunting their opponents for letting in the goal. By now a score of
players on both sides had been knocked out of the match. Two
men Sky Toucher saw looked almost dead as they were carried
off, both motionless, covered with blood and gaping white-eyed.

Then he discovered he was bleeding down the side of his head and his back where an errant stick had raked it from his shoulder down to the small. Dust had ground into it, causing it to sting furiously.

More and more players were carried off, helped off, dragged off, including Splitting Moon with a gash to the forehead. Finally the opposing sides were reduced in numbers by nearly one third, opening the game up, making it possible to move, pass and score more freely. Margaret and Two Eagles watched with Singing Brook and her friends, none of them with much enthusiasm, except for String-of-beads who had already cheered herself hoarse. The score was six goals to five in favor of Tenotoge when the ball came bouncing into Wide Shoulder's stick webbing and he started for the opposition goal. He was attacked from all sides. His teammates tried to form a protective ring around him but the Oneidas broke through. As his stick was knocked from his hand, the tide turned, and the Oneidas started toward the Mohawks' goal, striving for the tying tally. The goalie had been knocked down, and lay on his back shifting his upraised knees, seemingly unaware of what hit him. Ignoring his back wound, Sky Toucher raced ahead of the play and threw himself across the goal mouth deflecting the shot.

The crowd roared, he did not hear it; a thump on the head had knocked him senseless.

He came to, lying on his side. Gazing anxiously down at him was Singing Brook. But seconds after he opened his eyes, she saw that he was not badly hurt and wordlessly hurried back to where Two Eagles and Margaret were talking to Splitting Moon, whose head had been bandaged. Singing Brook had said nothing to Sky Toucher and he didn't get a chance to speak. Supporting himself on one elbow, he could see his cousin and Margaret with Splitting Moon, now sitting up, but by now there was no sign of Singing Brook.

He felt the side of his head. While he was unconscious someone had applied a salve. Wide Shoulders and Four Otters stood over him, the latter's arm in a deerskin sling. Sky Toucher smelled the salve, recognizing it as healing herb, a medication made from the crushed root and leaves of comfrey. The long gash down his back had also been attended to. He did not ask who had taken care of him, preferring to believe it was Singing Brook.

*cop.1*

By this time the match was over, the last injured players were being dragged and carried and helped off, the dust was beginning to settle.

"Who won?" he asked.

"They beat us eight to seven," said Four Otters.

"Only because we lost our best shot blocker," added Wide Shoulders. "Up, you cannot lie there all day."

"Only one player dead so far," added Four Otters. "This was not nearly as wild as last year's match."

They helped him to his feet. He looked over toward his cousin, Margaret and Splitting Moon hoping Singing Brook had rejoined them. But she was gone. He had noticed her concern for him when her eyes met his, but that look turned to impatience when she saw that he was not seriously hurt.

And yet in the instant before she turned away he was sure he saw something quite like longing. He had seen it there too often before to be mistaken.

# 22

THE GREEN CORN Festival concluded on the fourth day with the peach-stone game. Six stones, blackened on one side, were placed in a bowl, the bowl slammed into a blanket on the ground and the number of black sides up totaled. All six black sides showing counted twenty points, five counted one point. From his opponent, each thrower received beans as counters. The first player to accumulate a hundred beans won the game. Games sprang up all over the *baggataway* field. Betting was heavier on the peach-stone game than on the *baggataway* match, some warriors even wagering their weapons.

Other gambling games commenced, as well as contests: *gä-na´-gä-o,* hurling a spear through a ring rolling on the ground, arrow shooting, both for distance and accuracy, foot races, wrestling. In the final competition, a single contestant stood at the foot of a tree, and when a squaw dropped a stone, a warrior standing to one side shot an arrow straight up, and up the tree scooted the climber. When the arrow fell to the ground the climber marked the high point of his ascent with a colored ribbon. Despite the wound in his back, Sky Toucher easily defeated eleven challengers.

Singing Brook watched his victory as shouts of approval came from all sides. It was she who had treated Sky Toucher's cuts the day before while he lay unconscious, but only later did she realize that his head and back injuries offered her a valid excuse to return to him.

In leaving him, in fact, she had broken tradition. When an Iroquois wife wished to rid herself of her husband, she merely placed his belongings outside the door. When he found them there he knew what it signified: *he* left, no questions, no discussion. But though Singing Brook and Sky Toucher had separated, divorce hadn't occurred to either of them.

After eating she and String-of-beads started back to the long-house. String-of-beads looked at her and clucked.

"Your mind is whirling like bees around the hive. You are thinking about him, *neh?*"

"Mmmmmm."

"That cut down his back does not look like it is in any hurry to heal. It will need more tending to, and for some time."

"He has his mother to look after him."

"He has a wife."

Singing Brook paused before entering String-of-beads' long-house, looking aimlessly up at the black bear head mounted over the door. "So? Am I to return to him? Should I let him think I give in?"

"You should put that aside for now. His condition is what is important. He needs the healing herb salve put on at least three times a day. He cannot do it himself, and it should be dressed to keep it clean. If he were my husband I would apply a *che-gasa*, a poultice."

"Mmmmmm."

"This is not the time for foolish pride, Tenäte Oÿoghi."

"I do not have any foolish pride, you know why I left him. My reason is just as strong now as it was back then. I cannot stand him, his . . . his stubbornness."

"Show me a man who is not stubborn." String-of-beads' grin

showed a missing tooth in one corner of her mouth. "Or woman either. That is the heart of it, you know: stubbornness. You two are like lynxes crouching, staring at each other, neither budging. It has to end sometime. Do you not see that this is your chance?"

"To go crawling back?"

String-of-beads groaned and threw up her hands.

"All right, all right," Singing Brook went on.

"Then you will go back. Say *nyoh*."

Singing Brook said nothing but assent was in her expression. It *was* over, she simply could not go on like this, lonely, miserable. But she would not go back tonight; darkness, the privacy, the silence, their bed would offer a temptation too hard to resist. Tomorrow morning would be soon enough, after the Oneidas left and the excitement of the festival died down. Yes, then she would go back, tend to his injuries, say not one word about their "problem," let him be the one to bring it up. *Had* he changed his mind? Was he even thinking about doing so? She glanced at her star. Did he still look at his own? He must. How permanent their stars were, as fixed and constant as the stars that held the night against the sky.

Go back. It was high time one of them stood tall in this. A thought struck her, a lever that just might budge the lynx off his haunches.

# 23

Two EAGLES AND Margaret visited Sky Toucher in his chamber. Neither brought up the fact that he and Singing Brook had separated. She'd made no mention of it when she and her friends joined the two Oneidas to watch the *baggataway* match, but later Margaret had seen Singing Brook run to Sky Toucher's side, minister to him and leave him when he came to. And sensed intuitively that something was wrong between the two. Her absence from the chamber confirmed it. Even the usually unobservant Two Eagles had noticed.

"Where is Tenäte Oÿoghi?" he asked bluntly.

"Two Eagles . . ." rasped Margaret.

"She left me," said Sky Toucher. He lay on his side sparing his afflicted back. He felt very discouraged, she had approached and treated him, only to leave before they could talk.

"Why?" asked Two Eagles.

Margaret scowled at him. "It's none of our business."

"He is my *rackesie . . .*"

Margaret stirred the heated kettle of *gwä´ onondä,* corn soup with berries, and set out bowls. Noticing that they were not all that clean, she washed them thoroughly in the water kettle, along with three spoons. As she worked Sky Toucher tried to defend his decision to join the English by appealing to Margaret's patriotism.

"The English whiteskins are the Mohawks' only hope."

"Are they really?"

"Margaret . . ." began Two Eagles.

"Fiddlesticks and rot! It's absolultely amazing, it must be something in the air, so many of you catch it. Tell me, O-ron-ia-ke-te, what have the English ever done for any Iroquois?"

"For one thing they protect us against the French moccasins," said Two Eagles. "Besides, we have always fought on their side."

"Tradition. *Gu-nä-saqueda.*"

"More than that," said Sky Toucher. "If we stay out of this war and the French win, the Abnakis, the Ottawas and their other moccasins will overrun us. We will be the payment the French give them for their help."

She flipped her hand, flinging this away. "O-ron-ia-ke-te, get this straight in your mind: the English are not our friends, they don't care about us. We're like bugs they find in their beds; they'd rather we weren't around. Worse, they *use* our people. You two worry so about the Abnakis and others, what about the colonists? Don't *they* already overrun our lands, steal our furs, our game, our women, kill our hunters? English, all of them, and here in droves."

"But do they want to massacre us," Sky Toucher asked, "like the lace-cuffs?"

"Do not bother, *Rackesi,* she hates the English, she sees no difference between English and French."

"Would you mind letting me answer the question? They would

love to *massacre* us. I know them, how they think, what motivates them, what makes an Englishman tick."

" 'Tick'?" asked Sky Toucher.

"Behave like he does and with such consistency. They think they're the only true civilized nation on earth, that all others are born to be subject to them. God smiles on them to the exclusion of every other race. They see themselves as the emperors of the world and they no more care about the wants, the needs, the rights, the aspirations of others than the man in the moon. They are the greatest users in history, and they're using the Iroquois. Using you, O-ron-ia-ke-te, if you're so foolish as to volunteer. Tenäte Oÿoghi can see that, why can't you?"

"It is not that simple," said Two Eagles, tasting his soup.

"You think we are blind?" Sky Toucher asked. "We cannot see how they are? It comes down to this, they are two snakes, the French and English, both want to drive us out. But the French snake is poisonous, the English is not. If they win out in the end at least they will not massacre us."

"If the French snake wins he will not hesitate to," added Two Eagles. "From the Ne-ah´-gä te-car-ne-o-di to the Shaw-ne-taw-ty, they will exterminate us like flies."

"The greater of two evils," murmured Margaret.

"The greater of two evils." Two Eagles nodded. "Which makes my *rackesie* right and Tenäte Oÿoghi wrong. Let me speak with her, O-ron-ia-ke-te."

"You'll do nothing of the sort," snapped Margaret. "Stay out of it. Eat your soup before it gets cold."

"I will stay out of it. You explain it to her."

"No thank you."

"She is not stupid," said Two Eagles to Sky Toucher. "She will come around. It is like swimming across an ice cold river; no one likes doing it but if it has to be done . . ."

"You wouldn't be planning to join them?" Margaret asked.

"Did I say that? I did not hear me say that."

"We'll discuss it on the way home. Eat."

Sky Toucher looked at one then the other. They squabbled like he and Singing Brook had. How he wished she would come back so that they could squabble again.

# 24

SINGING BROOK BROUGHT none of her things back with her. Walking into the chamber after saying goodbye to Two Eagles, Margaret and Splitting Moon at the entrance gate, she found Sky Toucher lying on his side, his face lined with pain. But as he looked up in surprise, his expression changed to pleasure. Or was it relief?

"You have come back at last, Tenäte Oÿoghi."

"How is your cut, O-ron-ia-ke-te?" She examined it. "It looks angry, like a red snake crawling down your back. It must hurt."

"It is healing."

"How would you know, you cannot see it."

"It is beginning to itch."

She shook her head. It looked as if a strip of flesh as wide as her thumb had been peeled away. She heated water and carefully washed off the healing herb before applying more of it. Then she examined the cut at the side of his head.

"This *is* healing, it is your back we should worry about."

"You did not bring your things home. You will?"

"We shall see." She resolved to put that out of her mind for the moment.

"You are here, that is all that matters. Does it mean you have changed your mind, you approve of my leaving?"

"You will leave whether I approve or not, *neh?*" He lowered his eyes. "So go."

"With your approval. I must have it."

"I will not give it. Just go, scout, fight if you want. Only do not expect me to be here when you get back. *If* you do."

"So now you threaten me . . ."

"No *threat,* it is what *I* must do. I am your wife, I have some rights in this. I have the right to choose whether I stay or leave."

"It is still a threat." He smiled thinly. "Besides, where would you go? You would not leave Tenotoge by yourself. Oh, *nyoh,* I agree you have rights, you can choose. Even threaten me, but you cannot change my mind."

She shrugged. "Maybe you will come to your senses. Hungry?"

She cupped his shoulder as he started up. "I will go to String-of-beads' longhouse and get your things," he said.

"Do not bother."

"Then you are not staying?"

"I asked you are you hungry? You must be. Prop up and I will hold the bowl for you."

She ended up feeding him. They talked little the rest of that day, avoiding the obvious subject for the obvious reasons. But the little they did talk softened her resentment toward him. And being home, being this close, made her feel better.

Would she leave come nightfall? As time went on she felt less and less inclined to do so. The hours passed, the shadows flattened, lengthened, joined, darkness blotted out the lavender twilight, the harsh, barking *quawk* of black-crowned night herons came from the marsh. He prepared to go to sleep. He threw back the bear robes, moving over to give her room. She stared down at the empty place and shook her head.

"I am going back to String-of-beads' longhouse."

*"Neh."*

"I would rather."

"But why did you come?"

"To look at your cuts."

"Come to bed, Tenäte Oÿoghi, please." He patted the side of the bed and held out his hand.

"I am still very angry."

"I know . . ."

"Only you do not care."

"Please do not start, we are both too tired to argue. Get into bed. If you do not want to *sinekaty* we will not. But I want to feel you close beside me; your side has been cold too long."

"Mmmmm."

She undressed and got in beside him, their bodies touching, his warmth sending a thrill radiating down to her place. She stifled a sigh and rolled over, putting her back to him.

She lay under the sprawling willow tree where they placed their clothing when they swam in the pool around the bend in the Te-ugé-ga, the Mohawk River. She sensed he was lying beside her.

She turned her head; his body was dotted with golden droplets where the sunlight found his skin. He had a feather, and he began tickling her, caressing her nipples lightly, dragging it down her stomach to her place: circling it teasingly, touching again and again before moving down to inside her thighs. He explored her all over, down to her ankles, back up to and over her shoulders. She could barely feel it but it aroused her, setting her flesh pulsing; gradually it came to feel as if a tingling blanket was spreading over her.

Her eyelids flickered, parted, closed, she sighed soundlessly and wriggled beneath the blanket, causing it to fall apart here and there, to her surprise.

She looked up, saw him standing over her smiling down, the sun haloing his head through the branches. He was dropping flowers: rose and lilac shooting stars, pouch-shaped vivid yellow lady's slippers, drooping red and yellow columbine bells, forming a coverlet over her, except where she had disturbed them with her movements. He began dropping whole handfuls. She sat up, tumbling them from her shoulders and breasts into her lap, retrieving some in her cupped hands and inhaling their sweet fragrances.

Discovering him, the mingled scents, the music of the passing water, the quiet beauty of their surroundings, filled her with a comfortable warmth. He did not speak, nor did she, both hesitant to intrude upon the mood, fearful of breaking the spell that kept their eyes on each other.

She awoke. Her eyes became accustomed to the darkness. He slept soundly by her side. She leaned over and kissed his forehead. She was home; it was good.

# III
# THE WAR ROAD

# 25

TWO EAGLES SAT with Carries-a-quiver and He-swallows-his-own-body-from-the-foot in Carries-a-quiver's chamber. They were discussing the possibility of the Oneidas' return to the war-path. No Oneida warriors had taken part in the fighting the year before near Fort Anne, at the southern terminus of Wood Creek. It was there that the Mohawks had lost nearly eighty men, a critical factor in turning Hendrick and his fellow chiefs against the tribe's continued participation in Queen Anne's War, whenever and wherever it again erupted.

Two Eagles half-listened to the other two chiefs, his thoughts occupied with his and Margaret's conversation on the way back from Tenotoge. Sky Toucher's decision to volunteer had upset her a good deal more than she showed in his cousin's chamber. Margaret appeared convinced that Two Eagles had also made up his mind to go. Against his better judgment, he fell into discussing it with her, at first casually, in the end heatedly. The louder he got, the less he convinced Margaret that he would stay home this time.

He'd made the tactical mistake of agreeing with Sky Toucher that the Iroquois had little choice but to side with the English. Again. *Forever* was her word. He knew implicitly that Splitting Moon, though wisely staying out of the argument, was nonetheless itching to get back into the fighting. And in Onneyuttahage not a few others were already cleaning their muskets and sharpening knives and tomahawks.

They returned home, Two Eagles to this meeting called a few minutes after they walked in the gate. All three clan chiefs saw the English through the same eyes, reluctantly, even—to an extent—bitterly, as the tribes' only hope of survival. To choose the narrow and precarious path of neutrality would only alienate them from the colonists. Siding with the French was even more unthinkable.

"So what it comes down to," said He-swallows, "is that we must give them warriors to keep alive the fire of friendship."

Two Eagles grunted. "The Mohawks keep it alive with only scouts."

Carries-a-quiver shook his head, squinching his face in reaction to another headache. "We cannot. How many scouts does Dorr need to cover the War Road? Besides, the Mohawks have already spilled blood for him; we have yet to this time. Sooner or later he will come asking for warriors. Coming back from the Green Corn Festival He-swallows and I came up with an idea."

"What idea?"

"Perhaps, and this is just a suggestion, you could lead a delegation to Fort Anne, sit down and talk to Dorr."

"Why me?"

Carries-a-quiver chuckled without smiling and indicated his pale blue, totally blind eyes. "How would these eyes find my way there? And my headaches are worse than ever. Our friend here is even older than I and ailing." He compressed the wad of tobacco in his right cheek against a toothache.

Two Eagles glanced at the chief of the wolf clan. He-swallows looked incapable of making it as far as the front gate, without a litter. A scrawny wraith had taken the place of the once lean and muscular man. His bones protruded, his flesh hung, his talon-hands shook. He complained of aching feet, but the rotted teeth he had carried for years, his principal distress, had all fallen out.

However, he did not let his pains affect his cheerful disposition. In his day he was considered the Oneidas' ablest mediator and in the seven years of war, despite his advanced age and his chronic infirmities, he had led the warriors of his clan with honor and distinction, nearly losing his life in the final days.

While Carries-a-quiver and He-swallows piled on additional reasons why Two Eagles should be the one to go to Fort Anne, Two Eagles thought about what Margaret would say about his *talking war* with Dorr. That it wasn't his own idea wouldn't help much. Yet he couldn't see how he could get out of going. He did not look to *see*, he wanted to go.

"Fifty warriors might satisfy him," said Carries-a-quiver, "maybe even fewer."

He-swallows nodded. "But take care you do not make an outright offer of help."

"Take care not to take me for stupid," Carries-a-quiver flared. The whole reason for going is to sound him out, find out how many troops will be joining him, how powerful he will be, find out many things."

"*Nyoh,* and by going to him instead of waiting for him to come to us, we will be in a better position to bargain," piped He-swallows, nodding vigorously.

As if trying to convince himself, Two Eagles knew. A sigh rose in his heart. He knew little about Dorr, apart from what others, most of whom had never met the man either, said about him. He was reputedly brave, cool under fire, a good soldier—a rarity among the English. He had been a captain under Colonel John March in the defense of Fort Casco against Beaubassin, the Firebrand, seven years before. He had also taken part in last year's expedition organized to follow the Lake Champlain route to the St. Lawrence, to destroy Quebec, but the troops only reached the southern end of the lake before the project was abandoned for lack of funds for supplies and ammunition.

Never having met Dorr, Two Eagles was eager to talk to him, to get to know his weak points and his strengths. For he was convinced that if not this coming fall, eventually the red-painted hatchet would be driven into the war post, and the Oneidas would be back into the thick of it. It was either fight or invite certain annihilation.

"Plant the seed," said Carries-a-quiver. "Lead him to think we *might* be interested in helping."

"Please, if I am to go, you must trust me to handle him properly."

"He is right," agreed He-swallows. "Two Eagles is not an ox that has to be guided with a stick."

"From what I hear, Dorr is typical of the breed," Two Eagles went on. "All their officers have the same opinion of us, our situation. That we are afraid of what will happen if we do not side with them. So even when Hendrick, Kettle Throat and Winter Gull say *neh* he does not have to force *nyoh* out of them. He knows they will come around. Like us. Like the Onondagas." He tapped his temple. "He is smart first to ask only for scouts. After spilling so much Mohawk blood last fall he moves cautiously, like an *adiron*. Smart."

"Feel him out," said Carries-a-quiver. "You are very good at that."

"I said I would go," said Two Eagles. "No need to drip honey into my ears."

Margaret and Swift Doe were braiding corn, which they would hang from the ridge pole and crossbeams, to preserve over the coming winter months. Swift Doe was the widow of Two Eagles' brother Long Feather. She had subsequently married Bone, the Mohican adoptee and Two Eagles' close friend, who had also died. She still retained her beauty, despite the rigors of her life. But the sweetness that had marked her personality had soured. Her tongue had become tart, her outlook on life resentful. In addition to losing two husbands, her oldest son had been killed by raiding Montagnais some ten years before. While mourning for him, she had flirted with suicide but Margaret's devotion and gentle control over her had pulled her through.

A pile of corn husks rose between them as the stripped ears were lined up in rows against one wall. Neither looked up when Two Eagles entered and broke the news.

"Back to war," said Swift Doe, shaking her head in a manner that suggested he was personally reponsible for the situation.

"*Neh.*"

"What do you call it then!" flared Margaret, looking up for the first time. "Why so deceitful? At least O-ron-ia-ke-te tells Tenäte Oÿoghi the truth."

"How do you expect me to tell you what I do not know? Maybe when I get back after talking with Dorr. Not now, so do not accuse me of *ech-ka-wa-ne.*"

"Oh, stop it," muttered Swift Doe. "You know very well what you two will talk about: when will the blood start painting the ground?"

"Did he tell you that? Do you have his ear?"

"How many warriors do you need, Dorr?" Margaret asked. "Fifty, a hundred? We have more, take them all. Give us muskets for hunting, trinkets to play with and our blood is yours to spill as you please."

Two Eagles scoffed. "That is stupid talk."

"Is it?" Margaret asked. "How many Mohawks did he lose last fall?"

He shrugged. "Thirty, forty . . ." He was beginning to wish he hadn't walked in.

"A hundred at least!" shrilled Swift Doe.

"Not that many."

"One Oneida would be too many," said Margaret.

"Must we? *Two* of you shooting fire arrows at me? Margaret, I did not ask to go to Fort Anne."

"And didn't hesitate to agree to."

"I am the only one who can go."

"Only you do not have to," said Swift Doe. "No one *has* to. What are those two broken down *ochtahas* trying to do, get every Oneida over the age of fourteen killed off? Will you three be happy then?"

"This does not concern you," rasped Two Eagles. "Your sons are not old enough to go."

"I am not talking about them but about us, the whole tribe!" She stabbed between her breasts with her thumb. "And we, Onneyuttahage, *are* the whole tribe, all that are left, thanks to your wonderful wars. With three times as many warriors in the Village of the Dead as we have walking around here, thanks to your English masters. Thank Dorr for me, for all of us. Tell him to keep up the good work."

Two Eagles was visibly uncomfortable. "I must go," he murmured. "Find Splitting Moon and whoever else I can get to come with me."

"Don't let us detain you," snapped Margaret. "Go bow to your lord and master." She eyed Swift Doe. "At that, it'll no doubt end up a wild goose chase, he won't tell him anything. When he wants warriors he'll just spring it on us, like he did the Mohawks last fall."

Two Eagles went out. Everybody has an opinion, even those who don't take part. Especially those who don't take part.

# 26

SKY TOUCHER SHIFTED to another limb near the top of the great white oak rising at the corner of the castle of Tenotoge. No breeze, no voices challenged the night. He could look almost straight down into the darkened castle. Under each rounded roof whole families slumbered. Under the roof of his longhouse he envisioned his and Singing Brook's chamber, the bunk, the bear robes covering her as she slept gently breathing, shifting her lithe body, finding refuge from the beast-threat of their impending separation in dreams.

He looked upward at the stars, millions pulsing, holding the black blanket in place. Soon now the star hunter with his dogs would round the north star, overtake the bear and slay him. The hawk would rise and point south, as would the fat green darning needles, monarch butterflies, hosts of species. This oak and its brothers would drop their acorns and he and Singing Brook would awaken each day to find themselves with woodlands, brooks and rivers between them and each would look at their stars and wonder and worry about the other. As he gazed upward the blanket seemed to lower, bringing the twinkling night closer and heightening his feeling of isolation. Here, between heaven and earth, belonging to neither, he had a sudden urge to let go, spread his arms, kick and launch himself into the night, fly upward until the stars were all around him and he could not see the earth through those swarming below.

But that would mean leaving her and he could not; could not let go of this great tree anchored to the earth that she slept upon. Could he let go of her tomorrow, look into her sad eyes, release his arms, turn his back and walk away with Wide Shoulders and the others? She would not plead with him not to leave. They were past that; she was resigned to it.

He descended sure-handedly, nimbly, touching the cool earth with his bare feet and going back inside the castle. She was asleep when he crawled in alongside her. He slept. He could not estimate for how long, but when he woke up he found her awake, staring at the preserved food- and tobacco-festooned ceiling.

"How long have you been awake?"

She shrugged. He raised and peered through a crack in the elm-bark siding.

"The night is dying."

She uncovered her arms and held them for him. He held her, they snuggled under the robes, reveling in each other's warmth. His chest warmed her breasts. He did not touch them with his hands. To the Iroquois, arousing a woman by fondling her breasts was taboo, for they belonged to the child. Below in her place an aching began to feel his hardness throbbing inside her. Groping, she found his growing erection as he sheltered her place with the flat of his hand. They kissed and his fingers slowly spread the warm lips. His probing finger moistened her and she moaned as he slowly drew her honey. Their mouths and tongues and fingers began exploring each other in the play that arouses all the senses. The darkness filling the crack in their chamber wall was visibly lightening when he flung away the reins of control, kicked off the robes and swung his body over hers. Vising him, she gripped his stone-hard buttocks with all her strength to pull him fully inside.

They held each other without moving, breathing softly, each feeling the separate fire rise, their hearts thumping in unison. The light in the crack in the wall grew brighter. Easing their grips, they began. She bucked to hurry him but he refused to. Then gradually he began thrusting faster and faster, furiously, wildly.

Beyond the Shaw-na-taw-ty the sun poured its gold across the shoulders of the Taconic Mountains. They lay panting in silence, their eyes shuttered, withdrawing into their thoughts, each thinking about the other, about the torment of separation. The day she most dreaded had arrived. Dorr's men would be coming to take away the volunteers.

Sky Toucher had recovered from his back wound. He was fit, prepared for whatever mission they might give him. She had packed cranberry bread and salt venison for him for the four-sleep trek to Fort Anne. They would journey down the Te-ugé-ga to where the rapids tangled the river and tumbled it into the Shaw-na-taw-ty, there abandon their canoes and head north overland. He would be bringing his knife, his quiver filled with flint-tipped arrows, his best ash bow and tomahawk. He had no musket. Those given the Mohawks the previous fall had to be returned when they left for home. Wide Shoulders had heard that when the twelve arrived at the fort they would be issued new muskets. Sky Toucher doubted it. Silence and furtiveness were a scout's chief assets in the field. Still, a few scouts, Copper Man among them, certain that the rumor was true, planned to leave their bows behind.

Copper Man—Christittye Etsi—was the warrior who had thrust his hand into the fire at the powwow months earlier. His hand had come to resemble in shape and color a turkey vulture's talon. He could still use it as well as his other hand but it looked repulsive; he hid it behind him. Wide Shoulders and Four Otters had told Sky Toucher what he'd done, he told Singing Brook. She thought it a high price to pay to make a whiteskin fool look even more foolish.

Snowflake and Green Water stood in the longhouse doorway watching Sky Toucher and Singing Brook say their goodbyes. Not caring that it might strike those around them as unseemly, he embraced her and she laid her head against his shoulder.

"You will be careful," she murmured.

"*Nyoh.*"

"Eat properly, get your sleep, cover up against the night cold. I packed you extra moccasins."

She shuddered, as if shaking off a ghost, as she fought back tears. He smiled, hoping to bring a smile to her face. He failed to.

"How long will you be gone?"

He shrugged. "That is up to the lace-cuffs, *neh?*"

She averted her eyes, turning to brush them with the back of her hand, and walked off a few steps, her back to him. He caught up with her, turned her and kissed her passionately, Green Water and Snowflake looking away in mild distress. Others saying their goodbyes drew in their breaths and shook their heads disapprovingly.

Captain Hasty, wearing a blue coat with the lapels faced red, a long garment of coarse linen reaching to the knees and held in place by a sash, stood with four militia just inside the entrance gate waiting. Wide Shoulders came up with Four Otters.

"Ready?" Wide Shoulders asked. Sky Toucher grunted. Wide Shoulders jerked a thumb at Four Otters behind him. "I have talked to this one until my throat burns."

"Why bother?" Four Otters grinned. "Is it that you need me along to protect you?"

Wide Shoulders scowled. "Do you know what you are doing? Breaking us up, that is what!" He held three fingers tightly together under Four Otter's nose. "Three like one, almost since our mothers took us off our cradleboards. Three last fall in the fight near the lake. Three in everything. Until now. Now you stay home with the women and children and let us—"

"*Ogechta!*" snapped Four Otters. "I am tired of hearing it. O-ron-ia-ke-te, when they send you out up there keep your eyes and ears as sharp as your tooth. And see that you come back to us on your feet. Good luck, old friend. Good luck to you," he added to Wide Shoulders and walked off ignoring Wide Shoulders' calls.

"Leave him alone," said Sky Toucher.

"You misunderstand, I do not call him coward, that is not the point. He should be coming!"

"In O-ron-ia-ke-te's place," murmured Singing Brook.

"*Neh, neh,* the three of us, three. Always, always." Wide Shoulders caught himself and looked at one then the other. "Forgive me, I am not thinking, you two want to be alone."

They kissed one final time and touched stars. Then he walked off toward Hasty and the escort. The other scouts were already assembled, impatient to leave. Singing Brook appraised the four colonials. They wore scraggly beards, with hats as misshapen as if they'd been pulled through hollow logs. One wore brown, the other three blue watch-coats, homespun breeches. One had on moccasins in place of boots. They looked not soldiers but farmers, who should be holding pitchforks or plow handles in place of their muskets. As well, they looked untrustworthy, as if they did not care, or appreciate what the Mohawks would be doing for them. These twelve were not their allies; they saw the scouts as dogs to be

brought along to *sniff out* the enemy. How precious was Sky Toucher's life to any of them, even Dorr? If Sky Toucher got himself
captured and tortured to death would they care? If they found his
body would they bother to bury it?

Four Otters was right, they were being used. Brazenly, un-
ashamedly. All of Sky Toucher's arguments, all his reasoning were
meaningless. He had not convinced her, had he even wholly convinced himself? *They were being used,* that was the heart of it.

She watched as he joined the others. He did not look back.
Suddenly furious, seething with disgust at the whole business, she
could not stay to watch them leave. Pushing between her mother
and Snowflake she stormed into the longhouse.

# 27

ONE WEEK TO the day before Sky Toucher and the other scouts
departed for Fort Anne, Two Eagles, Splitting Moon and two
other Oneidas, Quane Onente—Large Arms—and Waghideria—
Sweat, named for his all but unabating predisposition—set out
along the Te-ugé-ga to the almost identical spot where Hasty and
his group later planned to abandon their canoes and continue north
on foot to Fort Anne.

Two Eagles and the others came through the trees along the
narrow trail to sight of Wood Creek, which ended just below South
Bay, and Fort Anne. There they saw the new flag of Queen Anne,
displaying the three lions of England, the lion of Scotland, the
fleur-de-lis and the Irish harp, flapping bravely high on its pole.
The fort was an irregular square of four bastions, built of timber
cribbing, filled with earth and gravel, and faced with logs. Arming
the ramparts were small cannon, swivels and mortars. Within the
walls there were wooden barracks for a permanent garrison of
about four hundred men, storehouses, casements and a magazine.
The fort was capable of resisting the strongest infantry attack, and
even that of light artillery. Though against heavy artillery in a siege,
it stood little chance. It badly needed a ravelin, a wedge-shaped

outer work to protect the weak western side, and the walls should be raised an additional three feet, to bring them to a height of twenty feet. But those who had built it were not experts in such specialized construction.

A wedge of Canada geese honked by overhead, the whiteness of their bellies and the color of their powerful wings lost in blackness against the sun.

"I still do not understand why we bother to come all the way up here," grumbled Splitting Moon, setting his palm against the head of his outmoded tooth-ball tomahawk in his belt. Stumpy, powerful, he delighted in crushing enemy skulls like pumpkins with his favorite weapon, one not popular with the majority of Iroquois warriors, who preferred the conventional pipe tomahawk.

Towering over him, Two Eagles seemed to question his intelligence.

"Are you saying you do not understand your own langauge?"

"What I do not understand is coming up here to meet with him," replied Splitting Moon. If he wants our warriors to fight, can he not come to Onneyuttahage and ask?"

"I have explained all that. And there is more to it. This is a chance to look into Dorr's eyes and see what goes on inside his head that does not make it to his tongue. Very important. I want to know what sort of man he is, what kind of leader. Maybe what his plans are, what he thinks of us, many things. We do not need French moccasins attacking us, burning our castle like the Montagnais did ten summers back, when Hare and Eight Minks and so many others were killed. Tell me, Tyagohuens, is it not in our best interests if we can help Dorr to prevent it?"

"The Mohawks are not giving him warriors," complained Sweat.

"They cannot afford to, they lost too many men here last fall. So many from Tenotoge alone we Oneidas are now almost equal to them in numbers."

"And so our warriors should die," Sweat asked, "to give the edge back to Tenotoge?"

Two Eagles stopped short and stared at each of the three in turn. "For the last time, we will not be offering Dorr so much as a rusty knife in the hand of an old squaw. *We are here to find out what he plans, what he knows, what is going on behind the trees. Is that clear? Is it!*"

"No need to scare the birds," muttered Large Arms.

He resembled Splitting Moon in physique but was younger, much wilder, not an easy man to control. But Two Eagles had asked him to come along for a good reason: little escaped his keen eye. He could be counted on to see and hear things that he, Splitting Moon and Sweat might miss.

A sentry called out as they approached.

"We are friends," said Two Eagles in English. "Come to speak with your Colonel Dorr. A delegation from Onneyuttahage, from Chiefs Carries-a-quiver and He-swallows-his-own-body-from-the-foot."

"Advance!"

So low was Dorr's office ceiling it forced Two Eagles to bow his six feet seven inches until he could make it to the nearest stool. There was a rough table, an intricate inlaid cherrywood sideboard, two chairs in addition to Dorr's chair behind his desk. On the wall behind him was a crudely drawn map of the area showing the War Road up to the St. Lawrence and including Montreal, but not Quebec, situated outside the margin.

Dorr was in his shirtsleeves, his jacket on the back of his chair, his collar undone, his wig sitting on the desk amidst a clutter of papers, a quill and ink pot, a ledger and, oddly, a Bible. The room smelled of stale rum and hadn't been cleaned in weeks. The colonel looked slightly bleary-eyed to Two Eagles, perhaps from a combination of too much drink and too little sleep. Bags bulged beneath his eyes, and repeatedly he looked about to stifle a yawn. But he was in good spirits, prepared to assume without notice the role of gracious host. Two Eagles introduced himself and the others.

"Oneidas," murmured Dorr, "come all the way from—"

"Onneyuttahage."

"Onney-yutta-hage, I'll remember that. Where exactly is it?"

"Near Lake Oneida in the west, just across the Mohawk border."

"Ah, ah, ah. Well, before you tell me why you're here let's

have something to drink. Chase the dust and pick you up out of your weariness."

He served rum, babbling on about nothing in particular, talking continuously as if silence was taboo. The door creaked open. Major Alden Carver started in behind his huge belly and many chins; seeing that Dorr was engaged, he stopped and started to back out.

"Come in, Alden, join us."

Dorr introduced his visitors, forgetting Sweat's and Large Arms' names.

"They've come all the way from . . ."

"Onneyuttahage," said Splitting Moon.

"A delegation. Oneidas, our loyal allies for lo these many years. Always there when we need them." He raised his tumbler. "To the Oneidas, princes of the Iroquois, bravest of the brave."

Two Eagles suspected that the Mohawks were the only Iroquois he was familiar with, and had no idea how well the Oneidas had served the Crown over the preceding half-century.

Dorr emptied his tumbler and refilled it. "To your great chiefs. Ahhh . . ."

"O-dat-she-dah, Hat-ya-tone-nent-ha and Tékni-ska-je-a-nal," said Splitting Moon. "This one is a fool, a fool," he added in Oneida to Two Eagles beside him.

Two Eagles laid a hand on his arm to quiet him. "Carries-a-quiver, He-swallows and me, Two Eagles," he added, thumbing his chest.

"Wonderful, marvelous. And what can we do for our good and loyal friends, the brave Oneidas?"

Splitting Moon and Large Arms were fidgeting, Sweat frowned. Two Eagles sighed to himself. This long knife talked so much and said nothing. In serious discussion did he intend to hold back information, cover up his reluctance to confide in them with meaningless chatter? Had he already decided to send them home with their ears full of honey and nothing of substance for Carries-a-quiver and He-swallows? He emptied his glass, passing a hand over it when Dorr, leaning against the front of his desk, tried to refill it. "We have come to ask what you plan against the French. Will it be attack or defense? What do you know of their plans? How big will your army be?"

"Ah ah, you've come to offer your sevices!"

*"Services?"*

"Ah, ah." He swung around his desk and sat leaning back, lacing his fingers over his belt buckle, yawning slightly, blinking his red-webbed eyes. "All is at a standstill at the moment, neither side moving troops."

"But you have sent for Mohawk scouts."

"We must be prepared. What will transpire a fortnight from now is anybody's guess. So, how many men can the brave Oneidas give us this time?"

Two Eagles sighed inwardly. And how many times after *this time?*

Dorr chuckled. "All you can spare and fifty on top of that, eh?"

Two Eagles cleared his throat. "We are here to warn you that you cannot rely on the Oneidas for warriors *this time.*"

Splitting Moon and Long Arms exchanged looks, Sweat looked sharply at Two Eagles

"Oh come now," murmued Dorr, "Five hundred?"

Splitting Moon sniffed. Large Arms rolled his eyes. Sweat appeared to be searching for something he'd dropped on the floor.

"You needn't commit yourself," Dorr went on. "All we ask is that your bravest, your most experienced warriors be on alert. Sokokis, Montagnais, Ottawas, Caughnawaga Mohawks, Canadians, French regulars, could come swooping down in vast numbers, burn Onneyhugatag, massacre your loved ones, decimate the tribe before we can come to your aid. How much better for the Oneidas if your brave warriors join us before that can happen, march out with us, meet the enemy and annihilate them?"

Two Eagles grunted.

"I beg your pardon?"

"I said nothing."

"Ah, on the contrary, you've said a great deal. You've come here and proclaimed your loyalty to our gracious queen." He leaned forward. "That's really why you've come, right? You do see the proverbial handwriting on the wall."

"What wall?"

"What handwriting?" asked Splitting Moon.

"Never mind, never mind, let's go on. Feel free to ask anything you please. If I can answer I shall."

"Where will you send your Mohawk scouts?" Two Eagles gestured to the map behind Dorr. The colonel circled his hand over the War Road. "All over."

"How many men can the French put into battle? Soldiers, Canadians, French moccasins?"

"You tell me."

"If I could I would not ask you."

Dorr and the Oneidas fenced until the shadows lengthened and the sun sought refuge behind the Tree-eater Mountains. It became even more evident that if Dorr knew anything of substance he preferred to keep it to himself. Two Eagles didn't like it, intuitively aware as he was that the colonel did not trust him.

Two Eagles changed the subject.

"My cousin will be joining you to scout."

"Which one is he?"

"O-ron-ia-ke-te."

"Ah yes, Sky Toucher. Excellent man. Natural-born scout. And climbs like a monkey."

"His wife is against his coming."

"I could see that the day I picked him out of the crowd at the castle. Wives the world over are against their men going to war. I can sympathize but they do blind themselves to the inevitable consequences if we fail to fill the ranks when hostilities threaten."

Two Eagles grunted.

Dorr went on. "Sky Toucher will turn out the best of the twelve, you watch. We'll be greatly dependent on him. Oh, greatly."

The Oneidas were invited to stay the night, given quarters at the end of a barracks, with a partition separating their beds from those of the soldiers. They sat drinking spruce beer and discussing the meeting with Dorr.

Two Eagles was fond of spruce beer, concocted from well-boiled tips and twigs of the spruce tree. When they began to fall apart, they were skimmed off and molasses added to the liquid that remained. After it cooled yeast was added and allowed to work for a few days until the beer was ready to drink.

Sweat snickered. "You and Dorr were like two wolves trying to corner the same deer, coming close again and again but not touching it, lunging, snapping at the air, until it finally got away from you. And we have found out nothing, he tells us nothing. *Oueda,* shit. *Onneyhugatag!*" He spat.

"He is an *onewachten,*" murmured Large Arms.

"You say he lies?" asked Splitting Moon. "Why would he? No promises were made on either side, no numbers decided on, he gave no details. Like Waghideria says it was all smoke."

Large Arms shook his head. "Lying does not always need words; it was in his eyes, his look, his tone. He is not to be trusted, Tékni-ska-je-a-nah."

Two Eagles grunted, sipped his beer and studied the floor.

"They could sit here in this stinking box for the next two summers and never see the French," said Large Arms. Again Two Eagles grunted, scowled, spoke.

"And lace-cuff moccasins could be attacking Onneyuttahage while we sit here. He knows what every English with a musket knows. If the red days start again and keep going we have to help them. Like the Mohawks and Onondagas we have no choice." The others grunted. "Blow out the fire stick, let us sleep. We will be leaving early tomorrow before the stars die."

"What is the hurry?" Splitting Moon asked. "The rum is good, this spruce beer, they feed us—"

"They can keep their liquor and food, we are going home. And sit and wait and wonder like before. Margaret was right, coming here was chasing the goose, a waste of good hunting time."

Dorr sat with Flood and Alden Carver in his office, their feet up on the desk. The hour was late, the colonel and Flood were decently drunk.

"Clever chaps for savages," said Dorr. "Especially the tall one. Come here to feel me out. Itching to know what's going on. Only they should have kept going on up to Quebec, get their answers from the frogs."

Carver snickered. Flood's head jerked as he woke up. "What did I miss?"

"Nothing," said Dorr. "Go back to sleep."

Carver patted Flood's arm. "He was just saying those red devils are worried sick something's afoot that they won't be up to handling. They practically demanded our protection."

"Not exactly," Dorr said. "Oh yes, they want to protect themselves, want *us* to. And we shall." He snickered. "In exchange for all the warriors we can get out of their chiefs."

Carver slapped his knee resoundingly, snapping Flood's head back a second time. "Why do we bother?" Dorr jerked and stared at the major. "Really. They're too bloody undisciplined to be of any help. When the shooting starts it's like trying to manage a pack of wild hounds. Most don't understand English, and those that do pretend they don't. Stick a musket in their hands and they're as likely to shoot themselves in the foot as the enemy.

"Wouldn't it be a blessing if we could round up every last Iroquois, stand 'em up against the northern tribes, sit back and watch 'em jolly well massacre each other? Burn down each other's villages, kill their women and children. And we ship the survivors somewhere out beyond Lake Ontario? Or turn the northeast upside down, give it a rattling good shake, spill 'em, sweep 'em in a hole and fill it in?"

"Dream on," muttered Dorr. "Only wake up a bit more pragmatical. The Iroquois, Alden, are our burden, the price we pay for the opportunity to battle it out with the frogs for possession of this glorious wilderness."

"Punishment for our sins," mumbled Flood and fell back asleep.

"Be a good fellow, Alden," Dorr went on, "get a couple of off-shift sentries in here to put him to bed." He lowered his feet, stretched and yawned. "I'm turning in. And take heart. Your dear friends, the savages, will be up and out of here before reveille. But of course we've the Mohawk scouts coming in with Graham." He turned about and checked the wall map. "Onneyhugatag, Onneyhugatag, where the devil is it? Is it even on here? Ever hear of it? Know anything about the *Oneida* tribe?"

"Not a blessed thing, Douglas, they can't be very large or important, just another bunch of painted howlers. Cannon fodder with feathers, eh?"

Carver laughed at his own joke.

# 28

GRAHAM HASTY WAS trying to learn Mohawk. Not doing particularly well at it, finding it unexpectedly difficult. But Sky Toucher admired his persistence and patiently accommodated him. Since departing Tenotoge, Sky Toucher had come to like the captain, like his cheerfulness, his kindliness and consideration. No prejudice lurked beneath Hasty's unassuming manner; he treated the scouts as he treated the militia, as equals, as friends. The party moved along the trail in single file, Hasty in the lead, Sky Toucher behind him.

"Hands," said Sky Toucher.

"*Osnotsa,*" said Hasty.

"Feet?"

"*Ossidau.*"

"Nose?"

"Ahhhh, *oneyat* . . ."

"*Oneyatsa.*"

"*Oneyatsa.*"

"Tongue?"

"I . . . don't know."

"*Owanisse.*"

"*Owanisse.*"

"Nose?"

"*Oneyatsa.* Tongue, *owanisse.*"

"Good, you speak good Mohawk."

"You speak better English. Face it, you're a better student. Your woman is very beautiful, O-ron-ia-ke-te."

"Wife."

"Very *jankanque.*"

"Very beautiful. Where did you get that word?" Sky Toucher asked.

"Words about women are the first ones you learn in any language, after the swear words, no? And Mohawk has no swear words."

"Say *neh. Neh* is no, *nyoh* is yes."

"It was easy to see that she was dead against your coming."

"Mmmmmm."

"Colonel Dorr speaks very highly of you. The day we came to Tenotoge and asked for scouts and he picked you out of the crowd he told us after that you were a natural."

"What is that?"

"Born to scout, it comes easy to you, natural."

Sky Toucher grinned.

"He wanted you before anybody else."

"Where will he send us? Me and Wide Shoulders. Wherever it is we must stay together like last time."

"That should be all right with the colonel."

A Cooper's Hawk sent its distinctive loud *cack-cack-cack-cack* down from a treetop. They stopped to listen, though they could not see it. Then straight as a bullet, it dove vanishing under the underbrush, reappearing clutching a baby hare.

"Tea snack," murmured Hasty.

"What is going on up around the Kanawage?" Sky Toucher asked as they resumed walking.

"The St. Lawrence; see, I know. Nothing I've heard, except a rumor that Vaudreuil, the governor, has his eye on this area. Fort Carillon, where Lake St. Sacrement almost joins Lake Champlain, is their southernmost post. It's in the wind that they want to move up Champlain to South Bay, along Wood Creek and wipe out Fort Anne then Fort Nicolson to the west. It'd open up the whole of the Mohawk Valley to them. They could do it, O-ron-ia-ke-te."

"*Nyoh,* Lake O-ne-ä-dä´-lote makes it easy."

Hasty turned and stared. "Champlain. Yes, *nyoh,* exactly. No woodlands, no tree-to-tree fighting, just glide up it pretty as you please, as big a force as you need, artillery and all and overwhelm our pitiful little post and Nicholson."

"When will they come?"

"Oh, as I say it's only a rumor, and if it does happen it won't be overnight, but the longer the rumor persists the more probable it becomes in the minds of the commanders. The more concerned Colonel Dorr and Colonel Fleming at Fort Nicholson become.

Which is why he's called for you and your friends. You'll be our eyes and ears from here to the St. Lawrence. Excuse me, Kanawage."

Sky Toucher grunted. Now in the middle of the afternoon, they were drawing close to their destination. Rounding a bend in the trail, Hasty pulled up so sharply Sky Toucher bumped into him. Ten yards ahead they spied a civilian, a small man so bulging of chest he resembled a pigeon. He was about forty, his complexion almost as dark as the two braves with him, both armed with muskets. He was dressed in a suit of dark blue cloth trimmed with gold braid. His neck-cloth and handkerchief were ruffled and laced. His hose was dark red, pulled up over the knee and fastened under his breeches, and his buckle shoes had high insteps. His hat was cocked on both sides and worn over a periwig of medium size without powder. He was eating a hard-boiled egg.

"Jan Pieter Van Brocklin," murmured Hasty, and described him as the son of a Dutch dominie in Albany, a confidante of Colonel Francis Nicholson and probably a spy for the French. He kept a trading post close by Fort Anne. He recognized Hasty and waved.

"Captain Hasty . . ." He came forward, introducing himself. "We haven't had the pleasure before," he added, switching his egg to his other hand and grasping the captain's hand. "But I heard you'd gone down to Tenotoge to pick up your volunteers. On your way home, I see."

"Amazing, Mynheer Van Brocklin, your ears must be the biggest in the territory."

"Always keep this one to the ground," said Van Brocklin, tapping his right ear. "How delightful bumping into you. Splendid, splendid, I'd ask you to detour to my little trading post for a snifter of brandy and a good cigar but I assume you want to get back. I'll not detain you, perish forbid I upset Colonel Dorr. Do give him my warmest salutations, if you will." He stepped aside, pushing his two companions to one side to allow Hasty and the others to pass. *"Ga door,* Captain."

Once out of earshot, the four militia crowded around the captain.

"Who was that?" asked one.

"A two-legged snake in the weeds. Jan Pieter Van Two Tongues, the colonel calls him. As devious as they come; nosy, unprincipled, dangerous." He grinned at Sky Toucher. "I wish we could spare a couple of you to watch his trading post, see where he goes, who visits him. A snake in the weeds in ruffles and lace. Let's go on."

# 29

SINGING BROOK WORKED with the other women collecting the last of the crops, mainly pumpkins, from the cornfield, and turning over the soil. It was hot for October, the work tiring, and she was not in the best mood. She thought of the stream and cooling water that would be hers at day's end and paused in her hoeing to swipe sweat from her forehead. She thought of Sky Toucher.

Would he survive? If he did make it back, in what condition? And would he go back a third time? Most likely, so she could again feel the clawing at her heart when they parted. How many times before he was killed? She sighed loudly. Esteronde, the child Rain, worked nearby. She rested, leaning on her hoe, and smiled. Singing Brook had been watching her work. Even the old women, who did nothing but gossip and saw nothing but one another stared at her. She seemed unaware of her gifts, which made her even more attractive. Singing Brook did not think of her as rain but more a wide-eyed fawn.

"Thinking about O-ron-ia-ke-te?" Rain asked.

"I cannot stop."

"He will be all right, they all will."

Singing Brook bristled. "They will be run down and caught like foxes, and tortured to death."

"I . . . am sorry."

"*Neh,* forgive me." She leaned on her bone-bladed hoe. "Being without him I can stand, but wondering what will happen is eating at me so I cannot sleep. It is the same with him."

"How do you know that?"

"I feel it."

"That is not knowing."

"It is the best knowing, the most genuine. I know what he is feeling at any time."

Rain laughed merrily.

"Do not believe me but it is true," Singing Brook said. "I need only close my eyes, clear my mind, touch my star and before long what he is feeling comes to me. Not where he is or what he is doing, it is not like that. Only what he is feeling."

"And can he feel what you do?"

"He has never said."

"Has he felt pain yet?"

"I do not think he and Wotstaha Onirares have been sent out yet. But when he feels pain I will know."

"Hey, you two," called Green Water. "Are you working or talking? Look!" She pointed east. A fat black cloud was coming toward them. "It will be here before you know it; can we get done before it does?"

# 30

SINGING BROOK WAS bitten in the knee by a *quo-ada*, a deer tick. She had been walking in the grass by the stream with her friends and Rain when the tick struck. She pulled it off, squashing it between thumb and forefinger. The bite stung viciously for a few seconds but when String-of-beads dashed cold water on it the pain went away. They returned to the castle and Green Water rubbed the pulverized bud of the soothing, sweet-scented balsam poplar on the bite: *tacamahea*. Singing Brook had been bitten many times before. No one walking in the grasses by the stream could escape the ticks, spiders and other insects infesting the area. But as if to confirm that it was not something to worry about, the pain did not return.

That night she lay abed thinking about Sky Toucher as usual, cheered by the fact that she had felt nothing of his pain or discomfort. Her star did not pulse; for the time being, she felt he was uninjured, presumably safe. Most likely, the volunteers had not yet been sent out to scout, at least not all.

She lay listening to the wind set the palisade creaking. The nights were growing colder, the stars sharper in the heavens. Gâ oh would be returning to the lands of the Iroquois, bringing *augustuske,* the freezing cold, the deep snows that kept all but the hunters inside and the passageway fires burning continuously. Happily, before that there would be a period of warm, calm, hazy weather when leaves fell in bunches, like a flock of birds that turns suddenly in flight. A time when the warriors took to the hunting trails, when the birds took the last of the grapes, those too sour to eat. At that time Nonahbazhoo would smoke his pipe for several days before he fell asleep for the winter. First would come stormy, cold weather, the Squaw or half-winter, to be followed by Indian Summer. A bluish haze would envelop the world and there would be the clean, musty smell when Hatho the frost spirit, skinned the puddles with ice no thicker than moonlight on the bark of a tree, and froze the insides of the leaves, releasing pungent vapors into the crisp air.

The wind resumed its assault. Stars she could not see pulsated tirelessly, burning the blanket of night. The moon's face showed the answer as to when he would return to her. But even were she able to see it she did not have the power to interpret it. Some did. Owanisse-nekwar´—Yellow Tongue, Winter Gull's wife—claimed the ability, although others pointed out that her predictions always came in the form of "I-told-you-sos," after the event.

"Come home to me, O-ron-ia-ke-te, my love. Home to stay."

# 31

USHERED IN BY the bully Gâ'oh, *augustuske* assumed dominance. Virtually overnight, life abandoned the lands of the Iroquois. Snow fell early and plentifully. The hickory fires burned continuously in the longhouses; except for the hardiest hunters, the people stayed indoors to escape the ringing cold. In the woodlands the rhododendrons and laurels curled up their leaves needlelike, pointing them straight down, to ensure their survival. Winter's sounds were brittle, desiccated: the muted crackling in the wind of stiffened leaves clinging to oaks and beeches, the hollow rattle of dry seedpods, the crunch of weed husks underfoot, before the snow turned the world as white as the winter moon. At Fort Anne the smoke climbed from the chimneys in slender columns only to be snatched by gusts of wind. Gâ'oh blew tirelessly, reveling in his reign, mailing the woods in relentless cold. In late December the temperature dropped, the wind howled off the frozen bay and Dorr's men hunkered down to await *tegenhonid,* spring, or the enemy, whichever was first to arrive. In January *augustuske* caught its breath; the thaw was brief but timely and welcome. Then, having renewed his strength, Gâ'oh blew in the bitterest cold of the season.

The main topic of conversation at Fort Anne—when the men weren't complaining about the weather, the rations, the shortage of supplies, their cramped quarters, scurvy induced by a scarcity of fresh vegetables, the deficient sanitary facilities, fever and dysentery and boredom—was the imminent attack. It hung like a swarm of hornets over their heads, keeping nerves on edge, patiences short, tempers volatile. Dorr assembled his officers in his little office. There were no windows, no ventilation; the candles sputtered and smoked in the wind that filtered through the cracks in the log walls. It was growing colder, and the fire in the little cast-iron stove had died. Only two of the twelve Mohawk scouts had not been sent into the field, the active ten being scattered about north of Lake Champlain, around Crown Point and as far away as the south bank of the St. Lawrence.

# 32

CAVAGNAL PIERRE RIGAUD de Vaudreuil, the French governor in Quebec, suffered from ulcers. He blamed the English for his pain, specifically the enemy's presence at the south end of Lake St. Sacrement, Fort Nicholson and Fort Anne blocking the spread of French dominance into the Mohawk and Hudson Valleys. He paced, he fumed, he suffered until an idea struck him: if both forts could be destroyed before winter ended—when attack would be least expected—in the spring that followed, Canadian forces could pour down the opened War Road and overrun the enemy. His Majesty's territory would be expanded as far south as Albany.

He summoned Etienne Le Moyne Saint-Vallier Ramesay, governor of Montreal, and placed him at the head of the invading force. Ramesay had never been in battle. His rank of colonel was purely honorary, but for months he had loudly trumpeted his desire to get into action. He was bored with his office, the politics, the petty bickering among the priests and the soldiers, the savage hunters that used Montreal as home base, the half-savage fur traders. He wanted a change, he wanted recognition, he wanted saber glory.

That he was wholly inexperienced, his mettle unproven, did not seem to trouble Vaudreuil. With a grand soirée in honor of himself, Ramesay accepted the commission.

His raiding party was made up of a handful of regulars, seven hundred Canadian militia and more than fourteen hundred Algonquins, Sokoki Abnakis, Ottawas and Mississaugas, plus fifteen Caughnawagas. By this time the French had grown weary of the Praying Mohawks' dissembling and put little value in their professions of loyalty, suspecting they were secretly reluctant to face their Mohawk Valley cousins in battle. The black robes painted the enemy as rapists and murderers, godless men red and white, but the Caughnawagas' religious conviction was as half-hearted as their loyalty to King Louis.

Vaudreuil made a wise decision in his selection of Ramesay's troops. French regulars were proving poor bush fighters, their training ill-suited to the woodlands. For such unorthodox combat, for stealth, for ambush, they had proven themselves all but useless. Woodlands fighting was a method of warfare their officers could not understand and were powerless against, as were their English counterparts. The Canadians, on the other hand, and a growing number of English colonials readily adapted to woodlands fighting; in effect it was no different than defending their farms and villages against marauding Indians.

Ramesay's raiding party, more than two thousand strong, reached the mouth of the frozen Richelieu River and started up it dragging their artillery on cumbersome sledges. They would have covered fifteen miles or more a day in milder weather, even more unencumbered by heavy guns. In deep snow and freezing weather they averaged fewer than five miles a day. But they were fortunate in that virtually every step of the route ahead would be negotiable over snow-clad ice.

However the persisting cold proved a staunch adversary: horses died from exposure, weapons froze, men suffered frostbite, snow-blindness and other afflictions. Three days from Fort Chambly two men froze to death on sentry duty and within sight of Fort St. Jean a blinding blizzard struck, wreaking havoc among men, horses, equipment.

At Fort Anne, Colonel Dorr got wind of the raiding party and summoned his last available scouts. Captain Hasty was present when Sky Toucher and Wide Shoulders walked in. Dorr greeted them warmly and indicated the map.

"Last we heard they're about eight or ten leagues north of the headwaters of the Richelieu. They'll pass the Isle la Motte here and start up Lake Champlain. Common sense suggests they'll come all the way up the lake past the marshes here and continue on to South Bay. Which means Ramesay intends to attack us first, before Fort Nicholson."

"What if they come up Lake O-ne-ä-dä´-lote and cross into Lake Andia-ta-roc-te?" Wide Shoulders asked.

"A possibility, of course. But this route would be easier. And the land is level from Fort Anne to Fort Nicholson, while up here, crossing from Lake Champlain to Lake St. Sacrement they would have to climb and drag their artillery up over and down the other side. Now I don't have to tell you what you'll be up against in the weather. It's brutal out there and no promise of let up. It won't be easy." He pointed out the route. "You'll cross and head up Wood Creek, over to South Bay, down Lake Champlain east of the mountains until you sight them."

Hasty cleared his throat. "We want to know their approximate strength, how much artillery they'll be bringing and what it is specifically if possible."

Sky Toucher frowned. He didn't know one cannon from another, except that the mortars were fat, stubby.

"They are all the same," said Wide Shoulders, "they spit the big balls and break your ear pans they are so loud."

Dorr smiled indulgently. "We'd like to know their sizes. Especially the mortars. As you say, they're the fat ones like we have that throw a ball high into the air." He gestured. "Whatever their size, their maximum effective range is only about nine hundred yards, about from here to the creek. It would be most heartening if we could stop them before they cross the creek."

Dorr lit his pipe, eying them through the smoke. "Ideally, when you find them we'd like one of you to stay and keep an eye on them while the other gets back here fast as he can and reports. Their strength, their artillery. As to numbers, we already have a rough idea, but I particularly want to know how many redsk—*Indians* they have." He slapped the desk with both hands and rose from his chair. "That's it. It's late, be packed and ready to leave before dawn tomorrow. Godspeed and good luck."

"Be careful," said Hasty, "be very, very careful."

The cold next morning when they started out was indeed brutal. Not a whisper of wind, only gnawing, numbing, relentless cold. Even the dying stars looked frozen and the water barrel outside the magazine door had frozen solid, splitting and spreading the staves into a wooden flower. They wore snowshoes, they moved slowly to conserve their strength, crossing Wood Creek and following it north toward South Bay.

And so they pressed on for three bleak, bitter cold days.

# IV
# THE HEART OF
# *AUGUSTUSKE*

# 33

Down fell the snow in a solid curtain of flakes the size of a man's thumb, blinding them, heaping their fur caps and shoulders. The wind rose howling, flinging snow at them and adding to the drifts on every side. Sky Toucher could not make out Wide Shoulders' back six paces ahead. He was having trouble with one of his snowshoes. Cursing the cold, the discomfort and the inconvenience, he knelt.

"Wait!"

Wide Shoulders came back, beating himself with his arms. Muttering, Sky Toucher tightened his strap; it broke. Furious, he picked up the snowshoe and would have smashed it against a tree had Wide Shoulders not caught his arm.

"You will need that. Cut a strip from around the top of your winter moccasin. It will do nicely. I know, I have done it."

The strap repaired, they pushed on. An hour later the snow began letting up and shortly reduced to a few flakes. In the metallic sky, a feeble sun struggled to show itself. They stepped over a deadfall and ducked under a toppled pine. Delicate flakes shot by Sky Toucher in sudden gusts. Was it getting colder? The sun wasn't just pale, it was dying; the wind was taking over the world. It bit and burned his cheeks; he adjusted his rabbitskin muffler. Gusts slipped between the trees scooping up powder, setting it whirling like maddened war dancers. How far had they come? How much further to South Bay? They could not possibly reach there before dark. And what was there? More barrenness, snow, cold.

An hour later night came to cloak the frigid land. The Mohawks stopped and hollowed out a spot near the protection of a low boulder—poor cover, but the only one available. Wide Shoulders found a fallen oak and broke off branches for firewood. Sky Toucher found slender twigged bladderwort and seedbox stalks poking above the snow. The two of them bent over the little heap of fuel as Sky Toucher got out his punk.

"Careful," warned Wide Shoulders. "Do not drop it."

Sky Toucher said nothing. Holding a few of the seedbox stalks, he made sure they were dry and gently poked the ends into the cob. They caught at once but went out as soon as he exposed them to the air.

"Let me," said Wide Shoulders.

"Just stay hunched over, keep the wind away."

On the fourth try, he managed to light the fire. Up it blazed. Wide Shoulders piled on his sticks.

"Not too many," cautioned Sky Toucher.

They made the fire strong enough to defy the gusting wind. Wide Shoulders suggested elevating the end of a rotted log on a rock a few inches above the flames, but Sky Toucher dismissed this.

"We must not show our smoke."

"The smallest fire shows smoke. Who will see it? Even their forward scouts have not yet reached the end of the upper lake."

"You know that for certain?"

"It makes sense."

"Forget the log."

Wide Shoulders slapped his arms across his chest and hugged himself, gritting his teeth. "It is so cold the fish in the lake must be freezing to death."

Sky Toucher scoffed. "The lake freezes only so deep. No matter how cold it gets there is always water."

"How do you know? Have you swum under the ice?"

"I have ice fished, I am not blind."

"You are in a good mood."

"Leave me alone."

"She tangles your brain up so all you do is worry like an old squaw," Wide Shoulders scoffed. "You cannot think straight about anything anymore."

"Leave her out of it!"

"You have been miserable since we left. Why did you come? You should go home."

"Do not tell *me* what I should do!"

"I tell you for your own good."

Sky Toucher scowled but said nothing further. The fire crackled merrily. They had eaten shortly before noon; neither was hungry. Their stomachs were accustomed to one meal a day, always taken before the sun reached the roof of the sky. It was believed by all the Iroquois tribes that consuming less than one's appetite demanded kept one fit and strong. While overeating invited gluttony; a tendency of the elders and the matriarchs, it was diligently avoided by all warriors.

"The fire burns my face while my arse freezes," complained Wide Shoulders.

"So turn around."

Wide Shoulders' laugh broke the tension between them. He threw an arm around his friend. "Do not worry about her, O-ron-ia-ke-te, she is fine, and getting used to your absence from the bed."

"That is what I am afraid of." Sky Toucher grunted. "At least we can see daylight."

*"Daylight?"* Wide Shoulders looked up.

"I mean the battle," Sky Toucher explained. "The lace-cuffs come down, attack the fort, the redbacks drive them off or are beaten, and it is over, we go home."

"The trouble is the lace-cuffs may not show up for many sleeps, maybe not till *tegenhonid.*"

Sky Toucher snorted. "You heard Dorr, they are on their way. Our scouts sent down word."

"That does not mean they will come straight down. They could stop anywhere and wait till warmer weather."

The thought disturbed Sky Toucher. No one had suggested such a possibility till now. Was Wide Shoulders right? Would it be a long, drawn-out business, its pace dictated by the weather?

"Holding off makes no sense," rejoined Sky Toucher, aware that he sounded like he was trying to convince himself.

"I am only saying—"

"I heard you."

"Maybe they *will* come straight down."

"They will. I have to shit."

"Me, too. Be careful your arsehole does not freeze before your *oeuda* gets all out."

They defecated and returned to the fire and built a wall of sticks to protect it from the wind. Then they cleared separate places, lay down and fell asleep.

Sky Toucher dreamed the same dream he had dreamt almost every night since leaving Tenotoge. He saw her in their favorite place, where they rendezvoused to talk and plan their future, and made love in privacy. It was beautiful there with grassy mounds, butterflies flitting about the wildflowers, the birds relentlessly dueling in song, the sunlight spilling through the trees and at twilight the amber glow that settled over the place bringing silence and the peacefulness she so loved.

He held her, feeling her warmth blend with his own. His love for her dizzied him, it was a wild thing in him, a creature he could not control. When he found her mouth with his the world around them would retreat, sights and sounds. When they made love time stopped, suspended like a hummingbird over a flower. And in their afterplay, when the twilight gave way to night, silence majestic and solemn consumed them before the insect voices began, rising in song to the stars.

The wind dashed snow against his exposed cheeks, waking him. He glanced about. Wide Shoulders snored nearby, pillowing his head on his mittened hands which he had wrapped in his rabbit fur muffler. The fire had reduced to embers. The few visible stars looked frozen, brittle, as if in the next moment one then another would shatter and fall in pieces around them. The wind rose setting the trees creaking in mournful chorus, bringing the cold winding about him like a bear robe. He shivered, his blood felt chilled in his veins, turned to sludge. It felt as if ice were filling his lungs and breathing was uncomfortable. Even the tender flesh around his eyes felt frozen. He lay back down his partially exposed face inches from the embers. The wind bit them, setting them flaring. Wide Shoulders snored on smiling.

With luck they would reach South Bay tomorrow, then head north between Wood Creek and the lake, up to the southernmost tip of the northern lake across from Fort Carillon. There they would settle in and wait for the raiding party. Sky Toucher would climb a tree (a hemlock or pine, for the hardwoods were leafless and would offer no cover) and sit in the wind all day watching for signs of them. All he would have to see would be one scout preceding the main body of troops.

*Would* they come down Wood Creek as Dorr thought? It made sense, hauling their cannon on sledges. If they did, he and Wide Shoulders would get ahead of them and one of them make it back to the fort.

Planning it, it did not seem complicated or dangerous; the main thing was to stay out of the way of their scouts. The French would have two on the points, one on each flank, at least one trailing.

He fell asleep with Wide Shoulders snoring in his ears, too close, but then the sound drew further and further away until it faded into silence.

The last sound to reach his ears was the wind.

 **34**

THEY HAD REACHED South Bay starting down the lake passing the Champlain Marshes. Every night seemed colder than the last. The sun rarely showed itself, and the wind blew tirelessly. Then a low cloud cover obscured the sky, threatening more snow.

Shortly before darkness that night, they camped and tried to start a fire, but the cob cylinder containing the glowing punk slipped from Wide Shoulders' grasp and fell hole first into the snow. Snatching for it, he only managed to drive it deeper. Snow plugged it full length, extinguishing the precious fire. Sky Toucher threw up his hands and swore viciously. Wide Shoulders mumbled a vague excuse for his clumsiness and blew on his reddening fingers.

The wind rose viciously, flinging snow at their faces, teasing them in their discomfort.

"What now, clumsy dog!"

"It slipped."

"It slipped!"

"*Ogechta!* I do not need your mouth singeing my ear pans. It is no great calamity. We will make a pump drill."

"A bow and shaft."

Wide Shoulders fashioned the bow from a pliant elm branch,

making the string from a strip of his winter moccasin top. Sky Toucher sharpened the shaft around which the strip would be wound. Using grass as tinder, they drilled into a piece of bark and presently the friction sent up a tiny wisp of smoke, the grass caught, sticks were piled on, the fire was made.

"You and your temper," groused Wide Shoulders. "Are things not hard enough? Must you bite my head off? How far to the headwaters of the creek?"

"How would I know? I have never been up this far before in my life."

"You might have heard—"

"Who from? When? How? In a dream?" Sky Toucher stood up. *"I hate this!"*

Wide Shoulders sneered. "So go home. If you do not have the stomach for the stew, do not eat it."

"Do not tell me what to do!" Sky Toucher looked about angrily. "There is no firewood here, not a stick. I will go find some."

"Find some hemlock bark, it burns warmer than anything. Or hickory, even beech or birch."

"And what will you do meantime, sit and stare at the fire?"

"One of us has to watch it," said Wide Shoulders.

"You shouldn't have started it without wood."

*"You* started it, you worked the bow."

Sky Toucher waved this away and scanned the overcast. No stars shone through it. He could smell more snow coming. He felt miserable: his body stunk under his clothing and was beginning to itch. His crotch was sore from the continual rubbing of his trousers. They had not fit properly since the first time he pulled them on. His snowshoes, old to begin with, were threatening to fall apart. He thought gloomily that he would have to fashion a new pair from scratch, which would mean sacrificing the leather risers in his moccasins for the needed rawhide, thereby exposing his lower legs to the cold.

His muffler kept slipping down and the wind had already burned his cheeks crimson-raw. His upper body ached, his legs were sore, he had raised a blister on his instep. He had no tetterwort juice to rub on it to prevent infection and dry it up. His teeth ached with the cold, one in particular. If the pain persisted he would have

Wide Shoulders examine it, and if it was rotted beyond salvage, he would knock it out with the butt of his knife.

What he wouldn't give for a hot meal, a warm bed with Singing Brook beside him, the fire blazing in the passageway. Let it snow, let it freeze the lakes to their mud—with her warmth, her tenderness, all his petty ills would vanish and he would be whole and hale again.

Wide Shoulders interrupted his reverie. "Where is that wood?"

"Coming. Quiet down, your voice carries for miles."

"The fire is going out, hurry!"

In the passageway outside her chamber door, Singing Brook fed the fire and studied her star. It seemed normal, it did not pulse. But intuition told her that something was going on with Sky Toucher. She winced and examined her calf, where she'd been bitten months before. The area was hard and slightly painful to the touch, and now showed a red mark the size of the tip of her little finger.

She dressed warmly and went out. Green Water was not in her chamber. But at Snowflake's she found the two mothers drinking *o'nīstagi*, coffee made from parched corn and a popular winter drink.

"Where did you get that?" Green Water asked when Singing Brook showed them the mark.

"It is my old bite that you put *tacamahea* on last fall."

"There is poison under the skin," said Snowflake.

"What poison?" asked Singing Brook.

"What was it bit you?"

"A spider, a tick." Green Water pressed the spot hard with her thumb causing Singing Brook to suck her breath in sharply. "The *tacamahea* did not cure it. What else is there?"

Green Water shook her head. "These young girls are all alike. They do not bother to learn what medicines to use, what salves or powders. They do not need to know anything as long as Mother is around."

"You need something to draw the poison," said Snowflake. "A *ga-na-tow-a-ke*."

"Again, what did it feel like when it happened?" Green Water asked.

"It stung."

The mothers' eyes met. "Button snakeroot," both said.

Snowflake got a quantity of the salve out of her medicine basket from the shelf over her bunk and handed it to Singing Brook. "Rub it in well three or four times a day. And when you go to bed rub it on again and cover it."

"Have you any scarlet sumac?" Singing Brook asked.

"What for? It is a bite, not a wound. Or are you suffering from diarrhea?"

"*Neh,* for nightmares."

They stared. "You are having nightmares?" her mother asked.

"I will be, starting tonight."

"Over him?"

"*Nyoh,* something is happening, something dangerous."

"Her star," said Green Water to Snowflake, both smiling.

Singing Brook hesitated to speak. Why bother, she told herself. As she got up from the dirt floor, dull pain lanced through her lower back, her hand went to it.

"Are you pregnant?" Snowflake asked.

"*Neh.*"

"What is the matter with your back?" Green Water asked.

"Nothing, just a twinge."

She thanked them and left with the salve.

## 35

SINGING BROOK TOOK to her bed. All her energy had deserted her. She developed a painful rash on both thighs, her buttocks and under her arms. Her joints ached furiously; muscle cramps and pains attacked her all over, chills and fever persisted, nausea struck occasionally, forcing her to vomit. She had little appetite due to her sore throat.

Green Water and Snowflake tried a host of medications, but nothing helped in the slightest. For three days the patient purged herself, abstaining from all grease, eating only the white flesh of white birds. Despairing, the two mothers called in Endathatst— Looking Glass—the Medicine Man. Before he arrived an assistant came to the chamber to search for anything that might destroy the "life" of the medicine, such as vermin, decaying meat, soiled garments. The patient was isolated. Then the ice in the stream was broken and water dipped *downstream,* not up, into a bowl. Everything was now ready.

Endathatst came in. He was huge, muscular; even advanced age had not diminished his vigor. He had been the tribal Medicine Man for more than half a century, keeping his reputation intact and his person respected, even held in awe. His entire body was painted black except for his head and face which were colored red. In all seasons of the year, even during the hottest months of summer, he dressed in the skin of a bear he had slain in his youth to acquire its powerful spirit.

In his role as tribal healer he carried with him at all times a bag of secret conjures and talismans to ward off evil spirits and rid the patient's body of bad medicine. Among the tools of his trade were dried human fingers, deer tails, rattles and a variety of curative herbs. His knowledge of plants and roots was far greater than any squaw's and he was careful to keep secret much of what he knew, to be revealed only at the hour of his death to some friend or relative.

Nightly he sprinkled his baskets, his wrappings and his bags with tobacco. Early each morning he chanted in words alien to his fellow Mohawks, looking straight into the rising sun.

Outsiders might see his prescriptions as mundane: for colds and fevers boneset tea mixed with prickly ash bark might be used; for stomach ailments sassafras and golden seal proved efficacious. Yet he contended, and his patients believed, that the medicines themselves were not effective, but rather the magic they contained.

His was a unique spiritual power, one denied to everyone else in the castle, and one which all Mohawks implicitly believed in. He had cured diseases of the blood, set broken bones and treated battle wounds. There was no ailment he would not attempt to cure.

In Singing Brook's chamber, he immediately began dancing, shaking his turtle-shell rattle filled with flint corn and cherry stones and accompanied by an old squaw beating a water drum. He danced until his black body dripped with sweat and his long hair stuck gleaming to his scalp. Into near-exhaustion he danced while Singing Brook watched and wondered if he could cure her.

Never had she felt so ill, so weak, in such pain. It gripped her like an eagle's talons grip its prey. Fever raged through her, pain afflicted every joint, her heart beat wildly, her head ached so it brought tears to her eyes. And the rash spread.

The drumming and rattling stopped. Now Endathatst stood over her staring down with his frightening eyes. His bear skin lay on the floor at Green Water's feet. The drummer withdrew, leaving Endathatst and the two mothers. Part of the passageway fire was brought in on a bark tray and set in the center of the floor. Into it he cast pinches of tobacco, that the sacred smoke might lift his chant to the spirits.

Water was poured into a cup, and the first medicine packet opened. With a miniature ladle he picked up a pinch of powder. He proceeded to drop three pinches on the surface of the water in three spots, the points of a triangle. If the medicine floated the omen was good, if it clouded the water the results were considered doubtful, and if it sank, death could be predicted with some certainty, so the medicine was thrown out.

To the relief of everyone it floated. Endathatst sprinkled tobacco over the patient chanting softly; then, with the two women's help, he prepared a number of concoctions: teas, poultices and mixtures of powdered roots, leaves and herbs, putting each one in turn to the floating test. All were found useable. He then pulled back Singing Brook's bed robes and ordered her clothing removed. He applied a salve to the rash, to her entire face and the bottoms of her feet. He gave her teas, he applied poultices, he dosed her with medicines.

When he was done Green Water and Snowflake placed the robes back, sprinkled more tobacco on her and Green Water served Endathatst *onno' kwà,* hulled corn soup and *gai' těn tân' ä''kwă,* cornbread boiled with *awé ōndagon,* purple kidney beans. The Medicine Man ate, sprinkled tobacco over the patient a third time and withdrew, but not before Green Water and Snowflake inundated him with gratitude.

"Now you will be well again in no time," cooed Green Water, coming to her daughter's bedside.

Snowflake nodded vigorously. "It is always a good sign when *everything floats.* You are so lucky."

With difficulty, Singing Brook attempted a smile. She did not feel at all improved. Was it too soon? No doubt. A frightening thought leaped to mind: was it possible that she was not just desperately ill but was dying?

Sky Toucher awoke, the cold striking his face. He could feel his normal aches and pains, but it struck him that they seemed much worse than when he had fallen asleep.

Only curiously it was as if the pain were not his. Sitting up he closed his eyes, cleared his mind and waited. Presently he saw Singing Brook in their bed, her face glistening with sweat, pain twisting her lovely features.

"Wotstaha Onirares!" He shook him roughly.

"Whaaaa—?" Wide Shoulders sat up rubbing his eyes.

"She is *aghihi,* it is bad . . ."

"Who?"

"Tenäte Oÿoghi, I must go back."

"It is the middle of the night."

"I am leaving," said Sky Toucher.

"Wait, wait, let us at least talk about it. If she is sick . . ."

"She is!"

The big man looked puzzled. "How do you know that?"

"I know."

"If she is, what can you do for her? You are no Medicine Man. Endathatst will take care of her, cure her. He is very good. Lie back down, *aghidawe.*"

"How can I sleep? She may die!"

"She is sick, not dying. If you leave now, by the time you get back she will be all better."

"Or dead."

"Do not talk nonsense."

The wind rose, flinging powder over them. Sky Toucher brushed it off. "It is *bad,*" he insisted.

"You *think,* you do not know. You always imagine the worst.

Marriage has turned you into one who can only see the black side, like old Kettle Throat."

"I do not like this being away from her."

"I know, you have told me a hundred times. Look, if you want to go back, go, I will be all right on my own. Go home but not now, leave at sunup. At least you will be able to see your way."

Wide Shoulders' willingness to go on alone stirred shame in Sky Toucher's heart. *Was* he taking the thing too seriously? *Was* she only ill with a cold or fever and would recover in a day or two? She was rarely sick. Her whole family was blessed with good health. As long as he'd known Green Water he had never seen her confined to bed by illness or any part of her body broken.

Wide Shoulders had fallen asleep and was snoring lightly. He lay back down and closed his eyes and at once could feel his star pulsing slightly. Or did he imagine it?

# 36

THE POLITICAL REASONS that had earlier prompted Sky Toucher's return to the battleground, now ruled out his leaving. Also, the job assigned them was hard enough for two men, giving it to Wide Shoulders alone would have been unfair.

This Sky Toucher decided the next morning. His friend wisely did not mention the conversation of the night before, nor did Sky Toucher.

Still, Sky Toucher's concern for Singing Brook persisted, despite knowing how everyone at Tenotoge placed such great confidence in Endathatst's powers. Most of the time his cure magic worked; it had more than once for Hendrick, and for many warriors and their family members. Pregnant women faced with the possibility of losing their babies came to him, and time and again he saved both child and mother. But one aspect of the situation in particular troubled Sky Toucher: the people only turned to Endathatst when the women of the tribe failed to cure whatever ailed the patient. The Medicine Man was the last resort. Sky Toucher intuitively felt that Singing Brook was seriously ill; *so* ill Endathatst would have to be summoned to cure her?

The Mohawks slid steadily northward until midway through the gloomy, gray morning, until both of Sky Toucher's snowshoes gave out. As one frame broke, the other threatened to and all the netting unraveled. From a hickory tree, they cut off two branches. Sky Toucher's arms outcircled and touching fingertips determined the size of the snowshoes. He made them with two bracing cross-pieces—the toe bar and heel bar—three times as long as wide. The frame had a square toe. A space was left open without netting, for walking in soft snow, a characteristic of the Mohawk snowshoe.

While Sky Toucher readied the frames, Wide Shoulders cut his friend's moosehide winter moccasin tops into slender strips for the netting. Not until well into afternoon, with only a few minutes off to eat, did they complete both snowshoes. Sky Toucher tried them on, slid a few paces and pronounced them perfect.

On they went. It began to snow shortly before darkness fell, at which point the temperature inexplicably rose for the first time since they left Fort Anne. But rain fell, too, and underfoot the slushy mire effectively slowed them before they quit for the day. They scoured the area and found a large piece of bark, propping one end up with two sticks, to prevent the fire from going out. Erecting a lean-to for just one night would be too time consuming, so they decided to sleep in the open.

For days now, the severity of the weather had sent all the animals to ground. Bears had been in hibernation since September; raccoons, skunks, porcupines, woodchucks and rabbits went underground or sought shelter in crannies or under overhanging rocks. No deer were to be seen. Even the birds had fled the chill and turbulent air. Since departing the fort, the only life the two Mohawks had seen was each other.

They lay in slush, pelted by it, and feeding the fire under its makeshift shelter. Wide Shoulders escaped from his discomfort into nostalgia.

"Do you remember how we first met?" he asked.

"How could I forget? You shot me in the back."

"You make it sound as if I meant to. I was shooting at my bear-claw target hanging from the branch above your head, and you blundered into the way."

Sky Toucher laughed. "You could not shoot any straighter then than you can now."

"My eye is like a *ska-je-a-nah's* with a musket."

"What a shot. I was barely up to my father's waist and the bear claw was hanging above his head."

Wide Shoulders scoffed, sniffing. "*So?* You did not have to attack me, force me to thrash you. We were the same age and I was twice your size."

"Twice as fat." Sky Toucher sighed. "Remember back then? We practiced shooting with our toy bows at a bear paw. Then a chickadee."

"Then a squirrel or rabbit."

"Then a grouse or a turkey."

"Until we sharpened our aim good enough to kill a deer with a full-size bow. Remember old Uncle Fur Cap?"

"Nonnewarory." Sky Toucher grinned and shook his head, flicking water hissing into the little fire. "Who never took his hat off summer or winter and whose eyes looked in two different directions."

"Always snorting like a sick *semotowanne*."

"He *looked* like an elk too, same big flattened nose, big sad eyes, and always chewing, even if he had nothing in his mouth. But he was a good teacher."

Wide Shoulders nodded. "Remember the time he gathered us all at the council rock? You, me, Cayere Tawyne, all the wolf-clan boys our age. He made us take off our clothes and run to where the streams meet. We had to stay there all day, make a fire from scratch, make a spear, kill a deer or beaver—"

"And make moccasins. Yours fell apart."

"We had to catch enough fish to feed the whole wolf clan. And if we did not do all those things before the sun buried itself in the mountains, he threatened to send the bear-clan boys after us, with weapons, to make war on us."

"What happy days," said Sky Toucher.

"We never knew *how* happy until they were past. Remember mud-smearing? Those summer days when it got so hot it burned your throat to breathe? How we'd run to the mud-hole, cover each other from head to foot with mud, lie in the sun until it baked on while we sweat like pigs. Then we'd claw the mud off each other and jump in the stream. And after, rub each other down with oil."

Sky Toucher grunted. "I remember the time Cayere Tawyne nearly smothered himself. He spit up mud for days."

"Back then there was always something to do. To learn, to enjoy. We did not stand around talking all day like the grown-ups." Wide Shoulders sighed heavily. "It seems so long ago, another life. So much has happened: Gä-nä-esi tas-i-go, dead . . ."

"Poor Many Wounds, he was supposed to get the three of us through the battle that turned out an ambush."

"Poor everyone who was killed that day. By now, all have reached the Village of the Dead."

Neither spoke, each plunging into sad recollection of the hostilities two Septembers ago. Then Sky Toucher broke the silence.

"Remember when we were boys, the first time we tried throwing the snow ski? I could not get the hang of it, it would not slide for me, it always stuck in."

Wide Shoulders chuckled. "Remember the *baggataway* matches back then?"

"I remember one when the warriors from Schandisse massacred our warriors. That had to be the bloodiest *baggataway* ever played anywhere."

"I remember that one. My father did not get out of his bunk for half a moon after. You could hear him groaning clear to the front gate."

Again they were silent, immersing themselves in the past, the happy days before the red days. Down came the sleet, the fire crackled, the little flame writhed as if the elements were inflicting pain. Day after tomorrow they would reach the point where land joined the two lakes, with the longest and widest part of Lake Champlain ahead. Where Mohawk Territory ended and enemy territory began.

# 37

SINGING BROOK'S CONDITION did not worsen but showed few signs of improving. Although the red mark, site of the tick bite, faded away completely, and her rash was disappearing, other, more uncomfortable symptoms remained.

Endathatst, the Medicine Man, kept his distance, which suited his patient. Uneasy, Singing Brook did not confess to her mother or Snowflake that she had little faith in his powers to begin with, and his efforts and the unimpressive results had not changed her thinking.

One afternoon Rain came to visit her.

"Stay on that side of the chamber, dear," cautioned Singing Brook as the girl came in. "You must not catch whatever it is I have."

"What *do* you have, Tenäte Oÿoghi?"

"No one seems to know, least of all Endathatst."

Rain's limpid eyes rounded. "Do you feel awful?"

"Awfully weak. And I ache all over, and—never mind. Something has sneaked inside me, gotten a grip and is squeezing the life out of me." When the girl looked alarmed, Singing Brook managed a smile. "Oh, it is not that bad. The worst of it is the days go by and I do not seem to get any better."

Rain eyed the steaming soup in its pot, the ends of the cords holding the red-hot stone in it, keeping it hot. "Are you hungry? Would you like me to feed you?"

"You should not come too close. You look lovely. I love your hair, the two braids tied together at the ends. So, what are you doing with yourself these days?"

Rain colored slightly and looked away.

"What is it?"

"Nothing. Well . . ."

"What?"

"I have met a boy. Eytroghe—"

"Beads? I know her."

"Her sister Crage Aque, White Deer, married a warrior from Schandisse."

"And?"

"He has a son from a former marriage. They have come here to live. He, the son, is . . ."

"Good looking?" Again Rain averted her glance. "*That* good looking? How old is he?"

"Thirteen summers. His name is Serande."

"Marten. Tell me about him."

"I do not know very much except that he is beautiful."

"Have you spoken to him?"

"I was sitting by the stream alone, he was swimming upstream in a pool with other boys, playing with a deerskin ball. They were very boisterous and splashing about. You know boys. They could not see me. Someone threw the ball over Serande's head and he came upstream to retrieve it. He swam right in front of me. He did not see me at first, then looked up and was surprised. He blushed."

"Because he was naked."

"I turned my head so I could not see. But . . . I did."

"What happened then?"

"He stood before me waist deep in the water and asked me my name. The others were shouting for the ball but he paid no attention. I was so flustered, I could hardly get my name out. He said 'I am Serande. Which is your longhouse?' I told him."

"And after did he come to see you?"

"Not inside but I . . . watched for him and saw him hanging about outside."

"So he is a shy one. But you impressed him."

"I did not do anything."

"You did not have to. He saw how beautiful you are and wanted to know you."

"I am not beautiful."

Singing Brook gave a little laugh. "You are, too. So you have a *rocksongwa gayah-day-sey.*"

Swan blushed furiously. "He is not my boyfriend, I hardly know him."

"But you like each other, you have a start. What else does he have besides his looks?"

"What do you mean?"

"Does he hear the birds, does he see the flowers? Is he *ga-oga-de-näh?*"

"Sensitive?"

"Very important. If he is sensitive toward nature he will be sensitive with you. Not with hands like antler hoes, rough and loud. And his eyes must be only for you, *neh?*"

"I do not know about any of those."

"Study him, find out, they are very important."

"How did it start with you and O-ron-ia-ke-te?"

"Almost by accident. Living in the same castle we looked at each other many times, of course. But one day we looked and *saw* each other for the first time."

"I do not understand."

"We stopped—and took each other in. Our eyes touched and something happened in both our hearts. Then and there we wanted to know each other, know everything. It was . . . it was discovery. Just like when he looked up and saw you on the bank. Did your eyes not touch?"

*"Nyoh, nyoh . . ."*

"And something strange and beautiful happened. And you simply had to get to know each other. You *do* want to see him again?"

*"Nyoh!"*

"And I am sure he is just as eager to see you. Tell me, when he looked at you did your heart race? Did you tingle all over? Did you find it a little hard to catch your breath? Your eyes answer. Lucky you, you have found each other so early, so young. He is not grown enough to go off to fight the French."

"You miss O-ron-ia-ke-te dreadfully, *neh?*"

"I miss him so it is painful. Maybe that is part of my sickness. If he were just out hunting it would not be so bad. But knowing he is in danger, and if he is wounded I will not be there to help him . . ." She turned her eyes toward the wall.

"He will come home safe, he did before."

"Mmmmm." She stared at the beautiful child and felt warmth in her heart for her. An aura seemed to surround her; she glowed.

"Is there anything I can bring you?" Rain asked.

"*Neh,* my mother and O⁻kla? are taking good care of me. I just lie here and wait for whatever it is to get out of me. It will. I will be well again."

"And he will come home to you."

"*Nyoh.*"

She glanced at her star and could feel it pulsing.

The temperature plunged. Mist rose around them continuously. It got so cold Sky Toucher feared it would freeze their marrow, crack their bones, cripple them so they could go no further. They endured three frigid days and nights before a thaw set in. It began sleeting. The next day they arrived at the isthmus of the two lakes, searched about for a well-concealed spot and put up a lean-to. By this time they were soaked through, their moccasins squishing when they walked, their bodies soaked with a combination of sweat and the unabating downpour. Both had caught colds, clogging their nostrils and filling their heads with pressure bringing headaches and aggravating their persistent aching. As their discomfort increased their patience suffered, and they would snap at each other at the slightest provocation. How long the miserable weather would prevail, how long before the forward echelon of the enemy would appear defied predicting. They sat in their leaky lean-to looking out, able to see a small section of the lake between the trees.

"They could have gotten by us, you know," grumbled Wide Shoulders.

"In this rotten weather? We move like slugs. Can they go faster with their big guns?"

"They got by us before."

"In clear weather, and that time they did not bring their big guns."

"They could be coming down the other side of the lake or further east, maybe even through the woods. Who knows?"

"*Ogechta!* Just because you feel miserable there is no cause to paint everything black. They will come down this way!"

"What if they pass by at night while we sleep? How can we count their big guns with our eyes closed?"

"They have to sleep, too, *neh?* They will pass by daylight. We count their guns, and one of us makes it back to the fort as fast as he can."

"Which of us?"

Sky Toucher stiffened slightly. They had not even discussed that.

"We should decide," Wide Shoulders went on. He reached overhead, pulling down two twigs, one longer than the other by half. He put his hands behind his back, shifted the twigs about and brought his fist into view holding both tightly. "Whoever picks the shortest stays, *neh?*"

"All right, all right."

"So pick."

Sky Toucher hesitated. Slowly his hand reached forth. He almost touched one twig, changed his mind, changed it a second time and selected the first twig.

Wide Shoulders opened his hand revealing the longer twig. "I will stay. You go back."

Sky Toucher touched his head. "I drew the shorter one, I lost, I stay."

"*Neh.*"

"*Nyoh,* you won fairly. As soon as we get a look at their guns and can count them, you go. No more talk about it."

"You have a wife, I have no one," Wide Shoulders protested.

"That has nothing to do with it. *Ogechta.*"

They sat in silence, the sleet pelting their cover. Water dripped through in a number of places. Wide Shoulders began stamping his feet.

"They hold the cold," he explained. "They sting they are so cold."

"Mine, too. Let us get the fire going, a real blazer that even this sleet cannot douse. Take our moccasins off, dry them, dry all our clothes."

"What if the lace-cuffs are getting close? They will see our smoke."

"By the time we get this fire really blazing, it will be dark. They will see nothing. Let us get wood."

"We will have a hard time finding any dry."

"Up and off your arse."

Since no dry wood was to be found, they ended up burning green hemlock boughs which made for an extremely smoky fire. Now and again the shifting wind blew smoke straight into the lean-to, setting them coughing. While the fire emitted some warmth, it kept going out; they were unable to dry any of their clothing. They finally let the fire die and sat staring at the sleet plopping into the ashes and sizzling.

"What if we stole a big gun and powder and balls for it?" Wide Shoulders asked.

"And got our heads blown off trying?"

"But if we could get away with just one we could drag it ahead and blow holes in the ice and stop them in their tracks."

Sky Toucher waved this away. "They would see the holes and desert the lake for the woods, continue on down alongside it. It would turn out a lot of work for us for nothing. We cannot stop them, nobody expects us to try. We just count their guns, how many of each size."

Wide Shoulders grunted, then brightened. "If I can get back to the fort really fast maybe Dorr's men can make an ambush, like in those woods where O-ne-ä-dä´-lote flows into South Bay. Surprise them as they pass, slaughter them like they tried to do to us."

Sky Toucher nodded. "Not bad, not bad. Maybe that is what he is planning. Tell him about the thick trees, what a good spot it is for an ambush. He could cut them down like cornstalks."

"*Nyoh.* Look, it has stopped sleeting."

"Come, we will get more boughs, start a blazing fire, dry everything out. And tomorrow morning shoot a deer, get us some fresh meat. Come."

# 38

THE THAW CONTINUED throughout the night. The next morning it was still mild. Wide Shoulders shot a fine buck which the two of them skinned and cut up, cooking the best parts and scattering in the woods the ribs and other cuts of lesser quality. Early

in the afternoon Sky Toucher sought out the tallest pine in the
area and climbed it to the topmost branches. It was cold aloft but
the wind coming from the east did not have Gâ'oh's teeth, Sky
Toucher's clothing was dry for the first time in days, he found a
reasonably comfortable perch, and in general his attitude took a
turn for the better.

Late that afternoon, his eyes fixed on the lower reaches of Lake
Champlain and Fort Carillon, he heard a noise. Far away and very
faint, at first he wasn't certain it was a musket shot until he saw
blue smoke rising above the treetops. He called down to Wide
Shoulders.

"Did you hear that shot? They are coming!"

"I heard no shot."

"I can see the smoke."

"It could be just a scout out hunting. They could be as far as
two days from here."

"It is the lace-cuffs I tell you!" Sky Toucher noted the position
of the sun. "It will be dark in three hours, by then they will be
here."

"And camp here?"

"I am sure of it."

The rattle of drums betrayed their approach before a single
man showed. From overhead Sky Toucher counted twenty sledges
being drawn by teams of overworked horses, sending up great
clouds of vapor. The sledges held mortars of varying calibars and
a few cannon on their carriages. Sight of so many mortars did not
surprise him. They could be set up two miles or more from the
fort and hit it easily. He descended the tree. Wide Shoulders sat
just outside the lean-to, scraping the buckskin.

"How many fat guns?" he asked.

"With the cannons, as many as you have fingers and toes."

Wide Shoulders sheathed his knife. "I had better leave."

"Wait, I am getting an idea." Sky Toucher sniffed the air.
"Smell it, taste it, tonight it will freeze again."

"Who says?"

"It will, the wind is shifting, starting to blow from the north
again. They will be leaving their big guns on the lake for the night,
with their mouths covered up to keep them dry."

"What is your idea?"

"Remember back at the fort the day we left? The barrel filled with water that froze overnight and split, fanning out like a turkey spreads its tailfeathers? We must find an elm tree, we need bark. We need to make buckets, at least two big ones."

"Buckets? What for?"

"Line them with buckskin so they will not leak." Sky Toucher surveyed the sky. "*Nyoh,* tonight it will get freezing cold again and be overcast. No stars, no moon, as dark as a snake's hole. Good, very good."

"What are you talking about?"

Etienne Ramesay, governor of Montreal become commandant of the raiding party planning to eliminate Fort Anne and Fort Nicholson to open the way for a spring invasion of the valleys beyond, looked foward eagerly to his first clash with the enemy. Already, despite the discomforts, inconveniences and vicious cold, the assignment was proving refreshingly different. Ramesay found himself waited on hand and foot and giving orders all day. He quickly learned to delegate most of the preparation, the planning, the logistics and day-to-day duties to his experienced subordinates, thus saving himself for the battle. When they arrived and the fighting began, he would issue the commands, watch the action closely, be victorious and return home covered with glory. In the meantime, however, he resolved not to forego life's most enjoyable pleasure. He would not ride to battle without companionship.

He was married with nine children and a tenth on the way, but he had assured his wife that life on the march would be too arduous and dangerous for her. In her place he brought along his mistress, Paulette Lamaire.

That morning, after the expedition had arrived, Colonel Ramesay was snuggling under the blankets with his paramour when his orderly came bursting into his tent.

"*Mon commandant, catastrophe! Désastre!*"

"*Imbécile!* How dare you shove your ugly face in here? *Dehors!*"

"But sir—"

"Out!"

The orderly fled.

"Come to me, Etienne," cooed Paulette, "let me feel your manly arms, let me feel you hard inside me."

"You are *insatiable, ma fleur de pêche.*"

"I am cold. Make me hot! Where is it? Ohhh, ooo, I have it!"

"Easy, *mon amour.*"

Two more intruders showed at the entrance. One cleared his throat in embarrassment.

"Colonel, forgive the intrusion but we have dreadful news—"

"You must come at once, sir," said the other, covering his eyes with one gloved hand.

"What is this idiocy? Has everyone gone mad?"

"The artillery has been destroyed," said the first man.

"What the devil? Are you two drunk?"

"Every piece cracked, ruined . . ."

Ramesay sat up so sharply his nightcap fell off, but Paulette pulled him back down. "Etienne, Etienne, I am hot—"

He flung her arm off and fumbled about at the foot of the bed. "Where are my trousers? What happened? Speak!"

The first officer gulped, then stammered, "Last night while the whole camp was sleeping, even the sentries, someone dumped slush into the mortars and cannons."

"It froze solid," added the other, "cracking every piece like a walnut."

*"Impossible!"*

"Come and see."

"I am coming, damn you! Wait, wait, are you certain? *Every piece ruined?"*

*"Oui,* Colonel."

*"Mon Dieu!* I don't believe it! Hold on, I must think; my brother will scalp me for this. You don't know the *bâtard!* We must protect ourselves, concoct an alibi, find a scapegoat. Something! Every piece ruined, you say?"

"Beyond repair, Colonel."

"Who would do such a monstrous thing? Is someone looking for the culprits? Find them! Offer a reward, they must be apprehended, brought back in chains to face the music. Send out search parties, find them, hang them!"

"Etienne, Etienne," shrilled Paulette, "calm down, you will burst a blood vessel!"

"Shut up, you slut! Don't just stand there, you two, go, find who is responsible. Where in hell is my shirt? Where is my jacket? Find my jacket, *ma fleur de pêche!*"

"Find it yourself, you old goat!"

"Bitch!"

"*Cochon!* Fumbler! *Monsieur Souple!*"

"Whore! Slut!"

"Dog vomit! Wrinkled old *canaille!*"

The officers withdrew, unnoticed. Outside everyone within earshot stood motionless, listening, leering, stifling laughter.

# 39

FROM HIGH ABOVE the camp, with a clear view of the activity, Sky Toucher watched the French and their allies assemble and prepare to move out. By this time Wide Shoulders would be well ahead of them, having headed toward the lake on the fastest route back to Fort Anne. The wrecked mortars and cannon lay scattered about their sledges. Sky Toucher watched a fat officer strutting about like a *schwariwane,* a turkey cock, in dress uniform, wearing a poorly fitting wig, and beating his tricorn hat against his thigh every time he raised his voice. He stopped to survey the wrecked artillery pieces, then resumed haranguing his officers. He looked livid.

Gā̃oh gusted, bending Sky Toucher's perch beneath him, flapping the coats of those below and nearly whipping off the turkey cock's wig. The Mohawk smiled: it had been so easy. They had waited in the bushes clumped near the lake, watching until the campfires burned low, then sneaked like shadows out onto the ice and speedily plugged the touchholes of each artillery piece with chunks of venison. When they were done they scooped the buckets full of slush and filled each piece. Within the hour after they were done, the temperature began dropping and by the time the white sun produced its first feeble rays and sent them over the irregular crest of the Green Mountains, loud, metallic cracking sounds began echoing through the woodlands. The muzzles of the cannons split, fanning like day-lily petals, flaring outward, curving back inward. Awakened by the sounds, the sentries and men came running out to stand and watch helplessly.

Thinking ahead, Sky Toucher saw only one possible snag. What if the fat turkey cock in command changed his mind, and instead of continuing on up Lake Champlain to South Bay and heading forward, he turned east, or even turned west toward Fort Nicholson and came through the woodlands on the far side?

Assaulting the fort from either side rather than in a frontal attack, the turkey cock's men could take it even without artillery, then massacre the defenders, burn it to the ground and march on Fort Nicholson.

He descended the tree. Inside the lean-to he waited until he heard the expedition begin to move out before he headed for the lake. The bitter cold had refrozen the surface of the snow, making it slippery for snowshoes, though firm enough to support his weight. He stopped to remove his snowshoes and was tying them together to carry on his back when he was struck from behind. His head exploded in a crimson burst, into pitch blackness he plunged.

# 40

WHEN HE MANAGED to open his eyes, the first image was blurred; slowly it defined itself as the basket he and Wide Shoulders had made of elm bark and lined with buckskin. It was sitting on the ground. Pain struck sharply behind his left ear; he stifled a groan. Grins circled him above. Turning his head he saw dried blood on his shoulder. The pain persisted, it felt like a burning stick laid against his head. He shook off dizziness. The circle of faces parted and the turkey cock came forward, bending, capping his knees with his gloved hands and leering, his breath reeking of stale liquor. It was not until Sky Toucher recognized him that he realized his hands were bound behind his back.

"Look behind you," said the turkey cock.

Somebody shoved his shoulder, pushing him forward so hard
he nearly struck his forehead against his knee. Pivoting on his
buttocks, he saw, on top of a pole sticking upright in the snow, a
human head. The upper part of the pole was smeared with frozen
blood. The scalp had been removed; the eyes were rolled up to
the whites, the face was streaked with frozen blood. Sky Toucher's
heart sank.

"We have another pole," said the turkey cock, speaking in
English. "We can very easily arrange for you to share your ac-
complice's fate."

Sky Toucher glowered.

"Shouldn't we question this one first?" asked a tall, cow-eyed
officer, his mustache frosted, his cheeks ripe red. He was clad in
fur from boots to cap, as were the others, with the exception of
the turkey cock, who was all brass buttons and lace with a woolen
muffler reaching halfway up his round face.

"He won't tell us a thing, Colonel," said another man. "He
doesn't know anything."

The turkey cock's eyes bored into Sky Toucher's; the man
looked like he'd been drinking all night, and smelled like it as he
bent too close to Sky Toucher.

"How many men at Fort Anne, *Sauvage?*"

"We already know, sir," said a third officer. "About four
hundred."

The turkey cock grunted, clasped his hands behind his back
and began strutting back and forth. '*Sauvage,* I must commend
you two on your ingenuity. So simple yet so effective, every gun
disabled. The least we can do is render you useless in retaliation,
*n'est-ce pas?*" Sky Toucher said nothing. "The cat's got his tongue,
gentlemen."

A Caughnawaga stepped forward, drawing his knife. "Give me
his throat and his scalp."

The turkey cock fended him off with one arm. "*Mais non,* this
one we will keep alive. When we reach our objective, he will be
placed in the forefront of the action. His *compatriotes* will kill him
for us. *Sauvage,* are you listening? Do you understand? Make your
peace with your spirits. You will live only until the glorious battle
wherein we will demolish the fort, massacre your redcoat masters

and your friends and watch you die at their hands. Do you understand me? Does he understand?" he asked the man beside him.

"Look at his eyes, *mon commandant,* he understands every word."

Sky Toucher's glance strayed back to Wide Shoulders' head on the pole. For him it was over; for himself it would be at the fort. There would be no ambush, no warning for the defenders. He and Wide Shoulders had failed as scouts, except for destroying the artillery.

It was curious, he thought, that he felt only frustration at their failure. He had no fear of dying. Many Wounds had told them that death usually came too fast to think about or react to. Death was a cowardly snake hiding in the reeds that sneaked up on the unsuspecting and bit almost before you realized it was there. Still, it was not the snake he feared but dying without seeing Singing Brook one last time. He would not get to hold her, feel her heart beating against his own, and explain. She would not even know.

Or would she? Would her star tell her? She did have an intuition for some things. But he hoped she wouldn't know, at least not until they brought home his body, if anyone ever did.

The turkey cock and his long knives were all talking at once, ignoring him, except for the Caughnawaga who wanted his scalp and still stood glaring down at him, his hand resting on his knife hilt. Sky Toucher tested his bindings. They were cutting off the circulation. Without blood in this weather, his fingers would freeze and die. Now, two men pulled him to his feet, and to his surprise one cut his bonds.

His head throbbed so it all but numbed the pain of his wound. Singing Brook's smile floated before his mind's eye. They had vowed to marry forever; in all of their lives they would be inseparable. But that was not to be. He would never see her again. He would die and be reunited with his friends in the Village of the Dead while she lived on and the love they so cherished, so strong and so beautiful, would wither and die like a flower in the fall.

He reflected on Many Wounds, Wide Shoulders, so many other sacrificing their lives for the tribe, the Mohawks, Keepers of the Eastern Door of the Confederacy—siding with the English as the only hope for escaping extinction. Tiyanoga believed that, as he did, only here and now it suddenly seemed so unimportant. And self-centered. Who was he to think that his knife could make a difference? Thousands of warriors had given their lives before him, more would die after him. Boys not yet born would come into the world, grow into manhood and fight their way to the grave for the same cause. The rivers would run with Iroquois blood and the widows would become an army of their own before it was decided which Asseroni, which ax makers would rule North America.

Not the Mohawks, not any Iroquois, no tribe.

"Tenäte Oÿoghi," he murmured, speaking for the first time. "I love you."

"What did he say?" the turkey cock sputtered.

"It was Mohawk," said the Caughnawaga who so badly wanted his scalp. "Singing Brook."

"What the deuce does that mean?" asked the officer with the frosted mustache.

The Caughnawaga shrugged and spat at Sky Toucher.

No, he had no fear of death. It was too late for fear, he was already dead. Again he lifted his eyes and looked at Wide Shoulders' head. He felt the tiny arrow harmlessly striking his back. Saw the bear claw target suspended from a branch. First the bear claw, then a chickadee, then a turkey or a grouse.

# 41

THE PRISONER'S WRISTS were rebound in front of him, though not as tightly, he noted. A Caughnawaga led him by a rope fastened to a noose slipped around his neck. The detachment moved off, abandoning the ruined artillery and leaving Wide Shoulders' head atop the pole. Sky Toucher looked back only once, musing that as soon as the troops were out of sight, birds would come in and begin feasting. The Caughnawaga eyed him.

"Why do you fight on the side of the English dogs?" he asked.

"Why do you fight with the lace-cuffs?"

"The French are our friends. They are the army of God, the English the army of Satan. If they defeat the French they will overrun Canada, kill our women and children, make slaves of our warriors. They are the Antichrist. The black robes have told us so, and the black robes treat us well. See?" He showed a silver crucifix around his neck. "They give us many presents."

"They *buy* you."

"The English give *you* presents."

"*Nyoh,* but that is not why we fight on their side."

"Why then?"

"If you did not let the black robes pour their honey into your ears, if you never left the Mohawk Valley, deserted your blood, you would be fighting with us."

"You did not answer my question, why *do* you fight with the English? What have they ever done for any of the tribes that shed blood for them? They are all promises that are never kept, *neh?* What have *you* to show for your loyalty? Are you protected, safe? Your brain must be upside down in your head! You risk your life for a people who only use you and will end up stealing your land."

Sky Toucher could not think of a counterargument. *Was* there any real difference between the French and English? Did not both conduct themselves in the same way with respect to their Indian allies? The only difference was the words they used: the French called the tribes slaves and dogs, the English looked upon them as their children. Both lusted after all the territories and their bounty, not just the areas they had already taken. Both drained the tribes' manpower, exhausted their resources, imperiled their future. Was Kettle Throat right after all? Was this war, like the others before, designed to exterminate the tribes?

They walked all that day, all the next day. The nights continued bitter cold, but the sun emerged during the day and no more snow fell. The clouds all but disappeared entirely, leaving a sky the gray of a warbler's back. Gä̃oh gusted often.

Sky Toucher was thrown scraps, mostly rib bones, the poorest of deer meat; it was normal to starve prisoners of war, so he did not complain. His captors gave him a thin blanket against the cold nights but tethered him too far from the fire for any warmth. He reckoned they were within five days' march from the entrance to South Bay, holding to their present route. It was late afternoon, windy and freezing, he could feel his energy level dropping. They saw figures in the distance coming from the south. It was a small party of tribeless Indians led by a white man whom he recognized, having seen him previously near Fort Anne. Sky Toucher could not recall his name, but the turkey cock called out greeting.

"Mynheer Van Brocklin, my soul. What are you doing out here in the middle of nowhere?"

"Looking for you, Your Excellency. Forgive me, Colonel. I bring critical news of your enemies."

"Speak."

Van Brocklin hesitated. Reaching into his pocket, he brought out a hard-boiled egg and proceeded to peel it. Ramesay laughed. "Still eating your eggs, are you?"

"They are all I eat; they account for my prodigious strength." Van Brocklin offered him his biceps to feel; Ramesay declined.

"What news?"

"Ahhh, my dear friend, when I think of all the trouble my friends and I have gone to: exposing ourselves to danger in such weather, evading Mohawk scouts who would as soon lift our scalps as look at us, absent from our fires and our beds. But it is all for you and good King Louis."

"Vergennes." A stout little officer stepped forward handing a small drawstring bag to Ramesay, who held it out for the Dutchman. He moved to snatch it but the commandant deftly flicked it out of his reach.

"There are ten crowns in here. I'm curious, how much is Dorr paying you?"

Van Brocklin looked pained. "You think I am double-dealing? You disappoint me, *mon colonel*. Have I not proven my loyalty to your side time and again? Only ten crowns?"

"Money is tight, my friend, our wars have impoverished us. Take it and tell me what you've found out."

Van Brocklin counted it before he responded. "Albany is dispatching reinforcements."

"A number, a number."

"Six hundred colonials, a handful of regulars. Two hundred will join the garrison at Fort Anne, the remainder will go to Fort Nicholson."

"And artillery?"

"They've added a few six-pounders, no more than four or five."
Van Brocklin glanced about. "Where is your artillery?"

"We—did not bring any."

Up went one of the Dutchman's eyebrows. He grunted, made
a face and swallowed the last of his egg. "You expect to take Fort
Anne with muskets, bows and arrows?"

"Fire arrows," corrected Ramesay, "in the dead of night. Four,
six, eight hundred men, what difference? The more we face, the
more we roast, *n'est-ce pas?*"

"Providing you get close enough."

"I've devised a most masterful plan of attack."

"Oh! Tell me."

Ramesay hesitated, waggling a finger under his nose. It was
clear to Sky Toucher, listening with the others, that the turkey
cock shared Graham Hasty's opinion of the man.

"Well, whatever you intend," Van Brocklin went on, "knowing
your brilliance I'm sure it's masterful."

"Where are you heading?"

"North to Shawinigan."

"Join us, why don't you?"

"Ahhh, I fear we cannot. We Dutch are neutral in this—affair,
*n'est-ce pas?* But rest assured, we will be with you in spirit when
you attack and annihilate them. God is on Louis' side. *Goedandag,
goedandag,* gentlemen."

Off he went with his men toward the lake. Ramesay peered
after him. The cow-eyed officer with the red cheeks stared until
Van Brocklin and his companions vanished into the trees.

"I don't trust that fellow, sir."

Ramesay turned on him in mild surprise. "*Mon Dieu,* you think
I do? Snap to, La Forge, give the order to proceed."

Sky Toucher had taken in their every word. His thoughts
churned. The dark of night and battle would both be helpful in
any attempt at escape—only he would have to get away long before
they reached Fort Anne. Dorr needed time to mount his defense.
Possibly an ambush near South Bay, as he and Wide Shoulders
had originally conceived? Whatever Dorr planned, he must make
his move tonight. It wouldn't be easy. The closer they were getting
the closer they watched him. Out of the corner of his eye he

surveyed his Caughnawaga guard, whose name was Onea Canonou—Stone Pipe. He stood a head taller than Sky Toucher, out-
weighed him by a good four stone and looked as if he could tie
him in a knot. He eyed the Caughnawaga's tomahawk in his belt,
hoping to seize it while he slept, knock him out. Both of which
assumed he could somehow get free from his bonds, for as usual
he would be tied hand and foot when they bedded down for the
night. What could he find to use to sever his bindings?

Another problem loomed: his waning strength from lack of
decent food since his capture. He was beginning to drag one stone
leg after the other. *If* he got away he would have to travel at top
speed to avoid recapture. And once they discovered he was gone,
knowing he had overheard their plan of attack, whoever pursued
him would exert every effort to catch up and kill him on the spot.

Maybe he shouldn't try to outrun them, maybe there was a
safer way to avoid recapture. Whatever he worked out, time was
vital. Dorr and his men needed all the time he could give them to
prepare.

## 42

THE WIND SHOOK the longhouse, but the cold stayed outside.
Margaret and Swift Doe were in Margaret's chamber busy
making burden frames, using two plain sticks of hickory, bent in
half-circular shape, brought together at right angles and fastened
to each other by means of an eye and a wooden head. Two Eagles
lay on the bunk on his side, watching them.

"Did your cousin and his wife ever get back together?" Swift
Doe asked him.

Thinking back on the *baggataway* match, how Singing Brook
had tended to the injured Sky Toucher, Margaret smiled to herself.
"They did," she said.

"When we left there, they had not," said Two Eagles.

"They did, all right," said Margaret. "He went off to scout for
the English. She may not have given him her blessing but I'm sure
they parted amicably. *De-so-ka-anna.*"

"Maybe," said Two Eagles.

"Definitely."

"I hear that the lace-cuffs are sending a raiding party up Lake O-ne-ä-dä-lote," said Two Eagles, "to attack Fort Anne and Fort Nicholson. O-ron-ia-ke-te is probably out scouting for Dorr."

Swift Doe wove strips of the inner bark of the basswood between the hickory bows of her burden frame both lengthwise and crosswise, fastening them to the rim.

"Such a fool," murmured Margaret.

Two Eagles sat up. "Because he disagrees with you?"

"Because he can't see beyond his nose. Think about it: the English will do everything in their power to keep the French in Canada, with or without Iroquois help. Whoever's prime minister now will keep up the fighting. They want this part of North America so badly their bloody teeth ache. And they'll drain the Royal treasury to get it."

She readied the carrying strap for her burden frame, preparing to attach it where the strip of basswood passed across the upright bow from side to side and from there diagonally across to the horizontal part of the frame. When it was done, every strap would be carefully adjusted to the wearer.

"If the English win—and they likely will—and send the French back up to Canada to stay, their next job will be to take over our lands."

"You seem very sure," said Swift Doe.

"She thinks, she does not know," murmured Two Eagles.

"I know. And you two will see." She tapped her temple. "I know how they think and it's past time the Iroquois found out."

Swift Doe's eyes said she believed her. Margaret glanced at Two Eagles; did he? He wouldn't say if he did, and his eyes told her nothing. She stretched out the long frame ropes, used to attach the burdens.

# 43

THE WIND SHRILLED and tore flames from the campfire embers, a chorus of snoring surrounded Sky Toucher, the cold shrank his muscles in their sheaths, Stone Pipe lay mumbling in his sleep.

When it came time to bed down for the night, along with tying Sky Toucher's ankles, they retied his wrists behind his back. All day into what remained of the afternoon, into Van Brocklin's arrival and departure, he had shuffled along with his head down, looking for something he might use to cut his bindings while his captors slept. Periodically his eyes wandered to the Caughnawaga— the man's knife was under his jacket. During the day on the march he wore his tomahawk on the outside, but took pains to slip it inside his jacket before falling asleep.

About fifteen feet from Sky Toucher lay the remains of a buck which had been cut up, the choicer parts roasted for the officers' supper. Among the scraps and bones sat the head. Sky Toucher eyed the rack; the antlers were not sharp along their surface, only slightly rough, actually rugose, owing to their grooves. But they were as tough as bone. He inched toward the head and was about five feet from it when the sound of crunching snow reached his ears. A sentry walked by him, waking up the soldier lying nearest the head. The man sat up yawning and got up. The other picked up the buck's head, holding it before him by the antlers.

"What a handsome fellow . . ."

He flung it twenty feet from him, just missing a sleeping Abnaki. The off-duty sentry lay down in the other's spot and his replacement shouldered his musket and trudged off. Once more Sky Toucher began inching toward the head.

By the time he got there he was panting from exertion and covered with sweat. While the camp slept on and the wind continued teasing the dying fires, he fumbled behind his back and was on the verge of giving up when he finally managed to get an antler positioned next to the rawhide that bound his wrists. As he sawed away he realized to his dismay that although he was slowly abrading the rawhide, at the same time the movement was smoothing the rough surface of the antler. He managed to get a second antler into position and sawed until a single strand parted; others quickly followed and his hands were free. When he brought them around, they were covered with blood. He rubbed the circulation back into his wrists and untied his ankles. He sat a moment, the crisp air sending clarity to his brain. The snoring around him kept up. He looked off to the east. In the faint light of the bow moon, he made out a white pine a good eighty feet tall standing sentinel-like among other trees.

He began crawling toward it. Directly ahead of him, in line with the tree, a man stirred, rolling over onto his musket and awakening. Sky Toucher stiffened and held his breath. The soldier resumed snoring. Inching by him, he eyed the bayonet attached to his musket. He removed it, shoved it into his belt and went on.

Singing Brook awoke sweating furiously, instantaneously elated, discovering that she felt better than she had since being stricken. There was no soreness in her throat, her head did not throb and the aching in her joints had all but vanished. She felt so good, her first impulse was to get out of bed.

She couldn't understand it. After nearly two full weeks, had virtually all her symptoms disappeared in the space of a few hours? Had Endathatst's cure finally taken effect? Whatever the cause, Endathatst was welcome to the credit.

Anther good sign showed itself: her appetite. She felt she could down the whole kettle full of corn soup cooling in the corner. Filled with energy, she wondered how many hours it would be till daylight. Should she wake Green Water and tell her the good news? Suddenly pessimism flitted through her mind. Maybe it was only a temporary respite. How long *would* it last? She decided to let Green Water sleep.

Singing Brook lay back down and closed her eyes, but excitement kept her awake. She thought about Sky Toucher. How was *his* health? Was he outside in this cold—the coldest, snowiest winter all the elders remembered? How could they fight in such conditions? He didn't have to get shot, he could freeze to death.

Where was he?
What was happening?

Dawn arrived bitter cold, dissolving the darkness, graying the land, slowly awakening the camp underneath him. Looking down, hidden by thick, snow-laden branches, Sky Toucher could see the buck's head with which he had freed himself. Stone Pipe had awakened, saw at once that his captive had escaped and began shouting. The turkey cock came flying out of his tent, fumbling on his sword, his wig askew, as the other officers assembled bleary-eyed and yawning. The turkey cock began shouting orders. Two search parties quickly set out east and west. He knew they would only go so far in each direction before turning south; everyone in the camp knew where he'd be heading.

The turkey cock raged on, summoning Stone Pipe and berating him so, Sky Toucher imagined the officer might pull out his pistol and shoot him. It wasn't just the captive's escape that upset the colonel—it was knowing that he had overheard the lace-cuffs' plan of attack.

He would wait, giving the troops a mile or so head start before he descended. They moved very slowly, but he would be patient. Then he would head for the isthmus that separated Lake O-ne-äh-dä´-lote and Lake Andia-ta-roc-te before he turned south. It shouldn't be difficult. He could foresee only one problem: it would take him at least four days to make it back to the fort. What would he find to eat? He fingered the bayonet in his belt. Would he be able to get close enough to any small game? Would he even see any in such cold?

He wouldn't starve to death, he could survive on basswood bark, if he found nothing else, but for such a long and arduous trek in this weather he really needed meat of some kind. For four days he had eaten only scraps. Climbing the tree his arms felt so weak he had to rest half a dozen times before he made it to the top.

Evading pursuit shouldn't be a problem. Both search parties were Indians led by a single soldier. The ones heading west would probably go no further than the woods fringing the lake before turning south. Hopefully, it wouldn't occur to them that anyone would be foolish enough to climb up into the mountains in winter.

Once more he looked down. They were done eating, had broken camp and were assembling to start out. He waited and watched until they shrank into an irregular line of black dots disappearing into the trees.

# 44

H E DID NOT climb as high into the mountains as he had hoped to. Exhaustion overtook him about a third of the way up, but even there he could see anyone who might be following through the thinly wooded, boulder-strewn lower slopes. So thickly crusted was the snow, he left no tracks; he satisfied himself that the two search parties must be heading southward. The one on this side of the lake was his only worry. He rested briefly, then looked for small game, even a squirrel out of its drey. But that seemed a far-fetched hope in such bitter cold. By the time twilight settled over the mountain, he was so famished he began to hallucinate, seeing himself catch a squirrel, bite into it and chew until it ceased squirming in his grasp. Seeing no living thing, not even a bird, he looked for basswood. It was generally found only in the moist soils of valleys or in the uplands, almost never at higher elevations. Warriors, he knew, survived on the bark for weeks. A poor substitute for basswood was elm bark, hard to chew and very bitter; the one time he had tried it his stomach had rebelled and up it came.

He saw neither tree. He ate snow. Anyone could get by without food for as long as five or six days, even longer, but only if one was inactive. Traveling in these harsh conditions drained what little energy he had left. But he decided to continue on until nightfall, letting the search party below get well ahead of him. They would likely give up before dark and return to the turkey cock, to be bawled out for their failure. When Sky Toucher felt the last of his energy begin to run out, he would descend into the woods fringing the lake and find a place out of the wind to sleep.

He was making his way down the slope in the dark when to his left ahead two white luminous dots appeared. Crouching, moving slowly closer, he saw them vanish as the deer turned its head. In the faint light of the bow moon, Sky Toucher saw its white tail flick as it started away. Then it stopped. It was a doe; she had not seen him. He crouched lower, easing out the bayonet. Slowly he began circling to his left. The wind blew toward him; the doe could not detect his odor and, concentrating on chewing leaves, she still had not seen him. The snow was his ally, so slippery it did not crunch as he carefully slid one foot after the other. He was less than eight feet from her, his bayonet upraised to plunge into her rump, when she bolted, crashing away through the underbrush. He sat down hard, looking at the bayonet in his grasp. His hand was shaking.

He moved south the next day, the day after. It did not get any colder but he was too rapidly losing what little strength he had left. In the middle of the afternoon of the third day, with the cold sun as white as the snow around him, he sat down to rest on a deadfall. He felt disoriented, a sensation wholly unfamiliar. A minute before, he'd been barely able to move one leg after the other. They were stone, his whole body was; he imagined his blood as sludge in his veins, his heart pumping wildly to move it, his lungs laboring desperately.

Singing Brook and String-of-beads sat in the latter's chamber, the passageway fire framing the door flap with copper. The wind hurled itself against the side of the longhouse. They sat crosslegged, facing each other, weaving corn-husk lounging mats. Singing Brook started, glanced at her star and held it against her breast.

"What is it?"

"Nothing," she murmured.

It was pulsing, and when she held it against her it felt like a round-ended stick pushing hard against her breast.

"What?"

"O-ron-ia-ke-te, he is in trouble."

"*Neh,* he is not even *out* in this weather. It is too cold for birds to fly. Are you all right? How do you feel?"

"I am all better."

"You look like ashes."

"This husk is very dry, it does not bend, it breaks."

"Mine, too, let us get some water and soak them all."

Singing Brook's star continued to pulse, setting her heart beating faster. He was in trouble; very bad? Was he wounded? Dying? What?

It occurred to Sky Toucher that either the cold or starvation was hastening his death.

He rested his head on his crossed arms braced on his knees. Visions came. Voices.

*"You tell my sister and I will cut your heart out!"*

O´hute Onega's face replaced Tékha Ochquoha's. *"Knowing him, it did. He was his name, inside he was fire."*

Tenäte Oÿoghi frowned. *"All I ask is for you to tell me you are staying home. If Wotstaha Onirares goes, you will let him."*

*"She is* aghihi, *it is bad."*

*"If she is, what can you do for her? You are no Medicine Man."*

He raised his head. In front of him standing all by itself was a wretchedly deformed, blasted beech tree. Every branch was bare of the familiar dun-colored leaves except one. It stuck out crookedly as if testing the air, its leaves hanging on as they would until spring.

Except for the one branch the tree was as dead as the deadfall he was sitting on. But that branch, though blasted, relentlessly punished by the elements, clung tenaciously to life. It had no brain or even instinct: all it had was the will to survive.

"Will?"

Something. Some ingrained faculty that stubbornly refused to accept death. It was fighting to survive until spring thawed the earth, its roots unlocked and nurturing water came into it. The dried leaves would fall, the single branch bud; new leaves would appear and the battle would go on. Would it live? As long as it was determined to, so it appeared.

He took a deep breath, got up, went on. Moments before the sun began to lodge itself in the mountains across Lake Andia-ta-roc-te, through the mist rising from the ground he blinked and spied Kä-ne-go´-dick, Wood Creek. Beyond it rose the walls of Fort Anne. Descending the slope, stumbling across the frozen creek, he staggered toward the entrance. It swam before his eyes, he fell.

He got up on all fours, pulling himself forward. The gate melted and writhed like a dust devil. A voice called out.

"Who goes there?"

"Dorr's scout . . ."

"Speak up, I can't hear!"

"Scout . . ."

He fainted.

# 45

HE HELD HER so tightly she squealed in protest. They kissed hungrily.

"You are home, my husband."

"Does that surprise you?"

"I am relieved."

"Me, too."

"Twice you have gone, this is the last time, *neh?*"

"*Sky Toucher.*"

He grinned. "Until the next time."

She scowled. "It is not funny; you have no idea what I have gone through."

"What I *put* you through. It is over now. Tenäte Oÿoghi."

"*Nyoh,* and you are home to stay." She held him at arms' length and looked him over. "Any . . . wounds?"

"*Sky Toucher!*"

"One. To my heart that will never heal. Wotstaha Onirares is dead."

She caught her breath. "Do not tell me how, I have heard what they do to scouts when they capture them."

"*Sky Toucher!*"

He awoke to find himself lying on Dorr's bed in his office. He was covered with layers of blankets; nevertheless, every muscle, every organ felt frozen. Warm needles assaulted his feet and part-way up his left leg.

Seeing he'd awakened, Dorr pulled up a stool. Sympathy welling in his eyes, he patted Sky Toucher's shoulder. Hasty stood behind him grinning, looking relieved.

"How do you feel?" Dorr asked.

"One branch. Only one. You could see the leaves clinging to life."

"Shhh, take it easy, get your bearings. Hot soup is on the way. And solid food after that, all you can eat. And the doctor is coming."

Sky Toucher grunted. His mind cleared. He felt light-headed, as if about to pass out again. He hurried his words. "They are coming. Down Wood Creek. Less than a day from here. Moving very slowly. It was easy getting here ahead of them."

*"Easy?"* Hasty grinned.

Sky Toucher told them about Ramesay's plan of attack, and about Van Brocklin.

The colonel's eyes narrowed. He listened without interrupting, his expression somber, gently biting his lower lip, listening and thinking.

"Ramesay won't attack by night, O-ron-ia-ke-te," said Hasty. "He'll have to assume you reached here and warned us."

"What about an ambush?" Sky Toucher asked. "Perhaps up by South Bay?"

Dorr shook his head. "It's too late to start moving men up there. As slow as they're coming they've probably already passed there."

The door squeaked, Major Carver came in, beating the cold out of himself. His eyes widened at sight of Sky Toucher.

"My word, he looks frozen to death."

"Alden," said Dorr, "they're less than a day from our front yard. What do you say we abandon the fort, get off a ways to, say, the northwest where the woods are good and thick, and when they show up come at their rear?"

"If we abandon the fort they'll burn it to the ground," Carver protested.

"They will if we stay, they'll try to. Assemble the officers in the mess, we'll discuss it. Whatever we do we've got to decide fast."

"They are coming," said Sky Toucher.

"That's not your worry now," said Hasty.

"Rest," said Dorr. "Your job is done. And nobly."

The door opened and a man came in carrying steaming soup. The doctor followed. Dorr greeted him.

"Alden, Graham, let's go. Sky Toucher, I can't begin to express my gratitude. You've saved us all."

"We hope," added Carver.

"If you need anything," Dorr went on, "don't hesitate to ask. I'll be back soon."

The door latched behind them, the doctor took Dorr's stool, smiled benignly and removed the blankets. At sight of his feet, Sky Toucher saw a frown.

# 46

A SQUAD WAS dispatched in the direction of South Bay, under command of Captain Hasty, three hours after sunrise. Orders were to keep clear of Wood Creek; Dorr assumed that if the raiders planned to complete their march by night down to a position where they could be deployed for attack, they would follow the creek up to the fort's "front door." Hasty's assignment: reconnoiter the area particularly to the east, ascertain where Ramesay would leave his reserves and pinpoint the site for the artillery on the map he carried.

The officers agreed unanimously that Ramesay would not risk his entire detachment in a single frontal assault; chances were therefore good that he would leave some of his force in the woods, probably to the east where the terrain was reasonably flat and the trees thickest.

"We'll blow their reserves back to Quebec," declared Dorr. "That should strike blue fear into the attackers' hearts."

Sky Toucher was not as persuaded as the three officers that the turkey cock would alter his plan of attack. He could see no need for Ramesay to do so. Fire arrows by night would be devastating, forcing the garrison to evacuate. The men would run for their lives and be picked off easily by the Caughnawagas and other French moccasins waiting in the surrounding woods. And the English artillery would be virtually useless in darkness.

Revived by food and a few hours' sleep, Sky Toucher got up at reveille, found the colonel and asked to take part in the defense. Dorr agreed, mindful that his only scout to return thus far had a personal score to settle with the raiders. Sky Toucher's feet ached from his ordeal, but miraculously they had not frozen and he suffered no lasting ill effects. His state of mind speeded his recovery. He wanted Ramesay's scalp. He owed it to Wide Shoulders. As the first scalp he had ever taken in combat, Sky Toucher would treasure it and present it to Wide Shoulders' parents. His vengeance would hang on their wall. He had yet to see the turkey cock without his ridiculous wig; was he bald? That would be determined before sunset.

Midway through the morning, as Hasty and his men hurried northeastward, Dorr was struck with an inspired idea. So he described it, but it was actually, a reprise of his original idea: sacrifice the fort. When the enemy arrived, Ramesay would find it empty.

Some of the officers objected, until he ordered the garrison and the reinforcements assembled outside and explained his idea in detail. He pointed toward the distant creek, the very spot where Sky Toucher had crossed on his return.

"They will most likely come at us from there. Before then we will have withdrawn every man Jack to a distance of two hundred yards, forming a horseshoe around the fort with the open end toward the creek. We'll move forward firing; in effect, net the whole school of fish, except the reserves of course. With no avenue of escape, except the way they came in, if the attackers are so foolish or so panicked as to move back down it we'll follow and annihilate them."

"Can't we use the artillery on the hill?" asked an officer, pointing to a rise a short distance from the fort to the west, on top of which howitzers and mortars had been mounted in Sky Toucher's absence.

"We'll keep the guns fully manned and hope that none of the

enemy makes it up the hill. Sturges, you see to it that men are positioned so that they can pick them off if they try."

"Yes, sir."

Sky Toucher approached Dorr.

"Ready?" the colonel asked.

"*Nyoh,* I will follow Hasty's trail. Keep out of sight and when he sends the man back with their position I will get it from him and bring it back to you."

"You'll stand a better chance of getting back than he will, I'm sure. Mind you, it will be risky."

"Everything today will be for all of us."

"Take a musket."

"*Neh,* a shot would give away my hiding. They are bringing many Algonquins, Abnakis, Hurons, Ottawas, Mississaugas besides their Caughnawagas. None will fight beside the lace-cuffs or the farmers. They will be on their own and all through these woods."

"Just keep out of their way."

"I will," Sky Toucher promised.

"Find that messenger and get back here fast as you can. If Ramesay attacks before you do and brings in his reserves, we'll never get a crack at them with the artillery."

Sky Toucher started for the creek. *Find the messenger.* Find a fish hook at the bottom of a lake? A better idea came to him: find Hasty. By the time he did, the captain would surely have found where the reserves were—waiting. He hurried his step, surprised at how much energy he had.

# 47

SKY TOUCHER MIGHT have passed for a Caughnawaga or an Algonquin were it not for his roach, the distinctive band of hair strapping the center of his head front to back. From a hundred yards away, he could only be a Mohawk, warrior of no other tribe in North America. In tribal ceremonies many warriors wore the *gos-to-weh,* a cloth headdress with feathers, but it was never worn in battle, and it or any other cap would draw attention to his identity as quickly as his distinctive haircut. The best he could do, sneaking among his enemies, would be to keep his head down.

Following the path of Hasty's squad, crossing the southeastern edge of the frozen Champlain marshes, choked with alders and swamp maples, he made it to the woods. Almost at once he instinctively felt the presence of French moccasins. But as he pressed on, he saw no one. Where had Hasty and his men gotten to? Had they blundered into the reserves' temporary camp and been massacred? By now, at midday, the turkey cock would have separated his reserves from the main body of his troops. The tracks in the old snow continued as a path, with no clear-cut footprints. Why was the squad sticking together, when by now they should have dispersed to search in all directions? He followed their path across a small glade into deeper woods. In his haste to catch up he nearly tripped over an obstacle. He caught his breath, his hand going to his knife as he saw the body of a colonial, stripped of his scalp and weapons, his jacket and boots, and bleeding in a dozen places. He knelt to examine him; he was definitely an English, Sky Toucher could tell by his clothing. Unlike the French and the Canadians, the English militia did not usually wear fur outer clothing.

Knife in hand, still crouching, he looked about and saw a second corpse, a third. His nerves tautened, he moved up the path, heard bushes swishing and looked up. Staggering toward him came Hasty. He had been scalped; clotted blood streaked his face and had dripped down his uniform. His eyes were wild and in them Sky Toucher could see the glazed look of death. Babbling, he looked through Sky Toucher and reeled. Sky Toucher caught his arm. Hasty stopped, looked straight at him and down he fell. Sky Toucher cradled him in his arms.

"Where are the reserves?"

The captain went on babbling. Sky Toucher repeated the question. Hasty tried to speak but could not get out one coherent word. Slowly his eyelids came together, he went limp, he died.

Sky Toucher eased him down and looked around. He had yet

to see a single enemy, nor had he heard any sound to betray their presence. But they were here all around him.

Maybe not. Maybe they had congregated in one spot: Indians, French, Canadians, waiting for word from the turkey cock to join the battle. Sky Toucher cocked an ear listening intently; he could hear no gunfire coming from the fort. Had the enemy approached as Dorr was so sure they would?

The position of the three bodies forming a jagged line toward the northeast, and Hasty staggering from that direction suggested that the reserves were just beyond, possibly dangerously close. He searched the captain and found his map. It was an exact copy of the area on Dorr's map, only enlarged. Distances were measured in yards, which to Sky Toucher were paces. He had counted six hundred paces from the fort. He could not have strayed off the path the squad had followed up to this point, but the snow was mussed around the three bodies and beyond the third one, heading toward the northeast he could see moccasin prints. The snow was no more than a few inches deep here, snowshoes were unnecessary; in any case they were never worn in battle.

He moved furtively from tree to tree, pausing frequently to listen. He counted his paces and was up to seventy when he heard a low rumbling: many voices all talking at once. Another twenty strides brought him close enough so that he could make out words. But he did not understand any of them. He studied the map; they were encamped about a hundred and ten paces from where he had left Hasty's body. Good enough. All Dorr would need to know to aim his big guns. Sky Toucher must get back to the fort as fast as he could and hope that in the meantime the reserves would stay put.

He turned. And came face to face with a warrior. A second one moved out from behind him. They wore beaver-fur robes, thigh-high leggins, moose-hock moccasins. Their hair hung long and loose, without feathers or headbands. Their empty knife sheaths were at their chests, suspended from their necks. Their upraised knives gleamed in their hands.

Abnakis. They grinned evilly. One licked his lips, tasting the pleasure of forthcoming murder. They separated as they came toward him. The one coming at his left lunged. Sky Toucher side-stepped him and a vision of Burning Wolf flashed across his mind.

The footing here looked to be as unsure as that on the mountaintop. Sky Toucher set his feet into a crouch and whirled, striking out at his attacker, stabbing him lightly. He could feel the tip find flesh. Blood surfaced, glistening. The man grunted and ignored the wound. Once more Sky Toucher spun, moving to the other man's side, away from his knife hand. The Abnaki turned while his wounded friend started for Sky Toucher's back. Caught between them, he ducked as the man behind him started his knife down two-handed in an arc.

Moving out from under its path, Sky Toucher slammed his lower right leg against his attacker's knees, pitching him forward, widening the arc of the descending knife. Into his friend's chest the blade plunged. He bellowed, staggered back, dropped his knife, sent both hands to his chest. His eyes swam, he choked, blood threaded down the side of his chin, he fell. Sky Toucher turned on the other but he wanted no more, turning, running toward the low babble of voices behind a thicket.

Sky Toucher turned and ran in the opposite direction.

He had covered less than half the distance back to the fort when ahead he spied colonials in a straggling line, with their backs to him. He remembered Dorr's strategy, the trap into which he hoped the French would wander approaching the fort. He slowed his step as he came up to the line, but still men heard, turned, aimed muskets at him.

"*Neh!* No, I am Mohawk, the colonel's scout. Look—" He held up the map. "I must get this back to him."

A man snatched it from him. Others crowded around to look at it. The one who had taken it threw it away, and, sneering, cocked his musket, bringing the muzzle up under Sky Toucher's chin.

"You stinking, lying savage, you're dead!"

Another man had retrieved the map. "Wait, Joe, this looks for real. He got to be with us like he says." He handed the map to Sky Toucher. "We best let him through."

Sky Toucher swallowed hard and ran on. He was fighting for breath by the time he was done circling the marsh to avoid being seen by French snipers in the forefront of the attacking force. Now within sight of the fort, he had seen no French, no Canadians, no Caughnawagas. Where were they, coming from another direction, as they had the previous fall?

He found Dorr with three officers just inside the entryway; they looked to be the only ones around. One pointed off toward the creek.

"There's a flag!"

"I don't see anything."

"I did, the white standard with the fleur-de-lis. They're coming, marching straight into the trap!"

Dorr, meanwhile, was studying the map, his hands trembling with excitement. Sky Toucher pointed out the path through the woods, the place where he had found the bodies and the hundred and ten paces he had counted off from that point forward toward the bay.

"They are here."

Dorr marked the exact spot with a Cumberland pencil. "Roughly how many, would you say?"

"I could not get close enough to see."

"All right, good enough, good job as usual. A damned shame about poor Graham and his men." He pondered soberly for a moment then caught himself. "Let's get out of here."

Sky Toucher accompanied them through the fort to the rear entrance and outside. Above them and to their right the artillery-men waited beside their guns. After Dorr handed Sky Toucher the map, up the slope he raced; he showed it to the battery commander, explaining the directions and distances. Every gun was loaded and ready; they were directed at the distant woods and their positions double-checked. Sky Toucher had almost reached the bottom of the hill when they fired as one, the sound so deafening pain hammered his eardrums. The echo was still dying away and smoke was collecting above the battery when musket fire began, coming from the woods where the officer had seen the French flag. Ramesay had marched into the trap! Though Dorr should have been de-lighted, he did not look even pleased.

"Damn Ruggles! I told him explicitly to let them pass in force before opening fire! Catch them like they caught our lads in that ambush last fall."

The action exploded into furious firing as the French fought back. Sky Toucher followed Dorr and the others into the woods, joining the ambushers positioned where the trap began circling around to the opposite flank. As they ran, the colonel continued, livid.

"They'll run for open ground, make it to the fort! Great God, they'll defend *it* against *us!* Damn, damn, damn Ruggles!"

The artillery had let loose a second, a third fusillade, but Canadians in the forefront of the attack had found cover and were shooting at the artillery crew who stood in plain sight, with only the protection of their mortars and cannon.

Meanwhile, unbeknownst to Dorr, the first volley aimed at the reserves had overshot their encampment, killing no one but creating pandemonium. The reserves ran for the woods, straight at the line of ambushers Sky Toucher had made his way through earlier. War-whoops rang through the trees and in seconds a wall of smoke obscured the line of colonials in the charging Indians' path. Masses of shocked and infuriated militia now milled about in confusion, firing on enemies hiding behind bushes and trees, in gullies and ravines. The crack of firearms tore the air; balls drilled the surprised colonials with devastating effect. Within minutes the ground was littered with the dead and wounded as the continuous firing mixed with screams and war cries.

Through the decimated line the Indians swept, wielding their tomahawks, killing and scalping with wild abandon, sweeping on toward the fort where the artillery battery continued, beset by sniper fire from the well-hidden Canadians. At sight of the masses of screaming Indians crossing the frozen marsh, the lieutenant ordered the mortars and cannon reaimed. Within seconds they blew the oncharging savages to bits, creating more destruction than they had wrought moments before against the line of colonials.

Meanwhile the well-hidden colonials on the west side of the trap made short work of the main body of attackers, despite their undue haste in opening fire. The battle lasted less than thirty minutes. The attackers were repulsed with ruinous losses. The victorious defenders suffered heavy losses as well, but when the smoke cleared, Fort Anne stood defiantly intact. Not a single attacker had gotten within twenty-five yards of it. The English survivors began tending to their dead and wounded and the waiting prisoners.

# V

# THE VANE OF FATE

# 48

A RAGGED-LOOKING COLONIAL approached Sky Toucher as he was standing outside the magazine with Quane Onawy—Big Teeth—one of the other scouts. He and Sky Toucher were preparing to leave for home together.

"The colonel is asking for you, soldier," said the man, smiling through broken teeth.

"I am no soldier," Sky Toucher retorted.

"You sure 'nough preformed like one 'gainst them frogs and Injuns."

"You go on," said Sky Toucher to Big Teeth. "I will catch up with you."

Dorr was at his desk with Flood and Carver seated in front of it, their backs to the door. All three smiled broadly as Sky Toucher entered.

"Come in, come in, O-ron-ia-ke-te," burst Dorr. "See, your Mohawk name, Captain Hasty taught it to me." His smile fell. "Frightful loss, Graham, he was . . . like a son. Fine, fine soldier. They've brought his body in."

"He was a good man."

"Indeed." Dorr paused, then smiled at him. "I expect you're getting ready to leave us."

"I must get home."

"Of course. My friend, I don't have to tell you that if it weren't for you, up above and here in the woods, they would have massacred us. If you were a captain I'd make you a major. As it is I can only show my gratitude with a little something." He opened his drawer and brought out a number of silver coins. "Ten pounds sterling," he said.

"Money. What do I do with it?" The others laughed.

"It'll come in handy. To buy anything your heart desires from some trader passing through. They all prefer money to goods. Just see you don't get cheated. Two of those'll buy one of these." From the floor beside his chair, he brought up a brand new musket. Sky

Toucher's eyes widened. "I take it you know how to use this."

"*Nyoh.*"

"You might use some of your money to buy powder, ball, flints."

"Sparingly," cautioned Carver. "Don't go paying a fortune to some scoundrel like Two Tongues Van Brocklin for what's only worth shillings and pence."

"Him I know. I will stay away from him."

"There's more to come," said Dorr. He brought out a knife. "Sheffield steel, my friend, finest in the world. It'll hold its edge longer than any knife you've ever seen."

"It is wonderful."

They laughed.

"It is that," said Dorr. "And last but not least, this." He held up a gleaming silver medal.

"Medal?"

"Richly deserved. For your exploits, your heroism. It was struck to commemorate the Battle of Culloden ten years ago. Every hear of Culloden?"

"*Neh.*"

"It's in Scotland."

"What is that?"

"A magnificent piece of the world north of England, where I was privileged to be born and raised. I'd tell you about the House of Stuart but I'm sure it'd bore you. Suffice to say this will serve to proclaim you the hero you are to all who see it. Your people, our people. Wear it proudly, my friend." He stood up and placed it around Sky Toucher's neck. "These are your gifts in sincere appreciation. When will you be leaving?"

"Now."

"Good, good. Be careful, there may be a few French stragglers or their Indian friends lurking about the woods between here and home. Keep your eyes peeled. I'd suggest you keep your musket loaded."

"I'll fetch you powder and ball," said Carver.

"I have a question, Colonel," said Sky Toucher. "What news do you have of the other scouts?"

Dorr sobered. "Some were killed."

"*Some?*"

"We've yet to ascertain how many. You survived, as did Copper Man. And another one, Big something. I'm sure others are still up around the lakes."

"We can only hope for the best," said Carver.

Sky Toucher grunted. They shook his hand in turn. The knife in his belt, the medal around his neck by its silver chain, his money in his new belt pouch. Hefting his musket, he waved his free hand and went out.

"Good man," muttered Dorr.

"Why do they always go home after a battle?" Flood asked. "I've never been able to figure it out. All that way, when the shooting could resume next week."

Dorr smiled. "Wouldn't *you* go home if you could?"

"You certainly lavished gifts on him," commented Carver.

"An investment."

"I don't follow . . ."

"In the future. When we summon him again he'll come running. He'll feel obligated to."

"Graham told me his squaw fought tooth and nail to keep him from coming this time," Carver said.

"Oh, I'm sure the others' squaws felt the same way. Fortunately for us, their men have the final say. Yes, he'll be back when we need him. And we will, he's very good, very lucky. And best of all, committed."

# 49

SKY TOUCHER HURRIED his step to catch up with Quane Onawy. Both could have waited for Christittye Etsi, who had also come in from the field, but he did not seem in a hurry to get home. Sky Toucher thought about Wotstaha Onirares, seeing again his head atop the pole, the whites of his eyes, the look of surprise. His death alone would be enough to persuade Tenäte Oÿoghi that coming back a third time was out of the question. But he'd deal with that later.

Now, his wife's disembodied smile appeared, hovering before his eyes. Four days, maybe three if he hurried and slept only briefly, and once more, he would hold her. And life would resume.

"Will begin for us!"

It was milder out, almost as if the cold had concentrated all its force during the battle and then let up, resting for its next assault.

On a rock barren of snow he sat to remove ice he felt in his moccasin. Suddenly shadows fell across him. He looked up. Van Brocklin smiled down, vapor curling upward from his piglike nostrils. With him were four warriors—two looked like half-breeds to Sky Toucher. His heart sank. He reached for his musket lying on the rock beside him but one of the warriors snatched it up. Van Brocklin took it from him.

"What have we here? Do my eyes deceive me or is it Colonel Ramesay's favorite Mohawk? *Ik begrijp het niet.* Wait, I do understand. This musket is English. Look there, 'Made in London.' That medal is. You escaped from Ramesay and came down and warned your English masters. How very clever. *Zilver,* the Battle of Culloden." He studied the medal. "Reward for services rendered."

"Give me that," snapped Sky Toucher, reaching for the musket. Van Brocklin held it away and with his other hand jerked the medal from around Sky Toucher's neck causing him to wince.

"What else did Dorr give you? What's this?" He pulled off the belt pouch, handed off the musket and poured the money into his hand. "Ten pounds." One of the Indians snatched the knife from Sky Toucher's belt. "You've done very well, Mohawk."

"Give it all back. Now! I have to go . . ."

"What's your hurry?"

The man who had taken his knife held the point at his heart, grinning sadistically. Sky Toucher thrust out his hand.

"Give it to me."

"He will give it to you blade first." Van Brocklin studied him, canting his huge head to one side. "You've done yourself proud, Mohawk. Escaped from Ramesay, come down and warned Dorr, and who knows what else you did during the fighting? And now you're headed back to Tenotoge, right?"

"*Nyoh.*"

"Wrong, you are coming with us. There is somebody waiting who wants to see you."

"I am going nowhere except home."

"You'll come with us or die where you stand. Which?"

They marched him down the path and off into the woods in the direction of Fort Nicholson. No one spoke, not even Van Brocklin. Sky Toucher's eyes darted left and right. Should he try to get away? It would be foolish. They'd put a ball or knife in his back before he got two steps. His heart sank. He could hear voices ahead, many voices talking unintelligibly. They came to a clearing. French soldiers and Canadians milled about, and more than three times their combined number of Indians. Sky Toucher recognized Stone Antler talking to his woman. Then he saw the turkey cock, who came waddling over.

"Mynheer Van Brocklin!"

"Colonel, look what I found, an old friend of yours."

Ramesay squinted, his face darkened viciously; he seemed ready to pounce on Sky Toucher and strangle him.

"*You . . . !*"

Van Brocklin chuckled. "In the flesh, my friend. I'm in a hurry, let's make this short. How much do you offer?"

"I have no more money," replied Ramesay testily, his eyes continuing to rivet Sky Toucher.

"Oh dear, what a pity." The Dutchman grinned. "He's not expensive. A pittance actually. How about fifty crowns?" Van Brocklin got out a hard-boiled egg and began peeling it.

"Preposterous, I'll give you twenty."

"Sold."

He was paid, Van Brocklin touched the corner of his hat in salute, bowing slightly and was preparing to leave when instead he turned to Sky Toucher.

"Don't look so downcast, Mohawk, this is just not your lucky day. Chalk it up to the fortunes of war."

Ramesay watched him leave with his companions then called out. "Lieutenant Savard!"

A lieutenant came hobbling up, his leg heavily bandaged. "Sir?"

"Find the Caughnawaga who guarded this prisoner before, what's his name?"

"Stone Pipe, sir."

Hearing his name Stone Pipe came up. "There you are. Recognize this fellow?"

"*Nyoh.*"

"He's all yours. Again. We'll be taking him back with us." Wagging a finger at the Caughnawaga, he went on. "He's responsible for our defeat. Wholly and directly. If he hadn't warned them we'd have caught them by surprise and massacred them. I'm taking him back to Quebec to give to Governor Vaudreuil—living proof that we did nothing disgraceful, that we were undermined in our purpose by this *sauvage.* He'll be given over to the wives and children of the men who fell in the battle—to be drawn, quartered and his remains burned."

"*Nyoh.*"

"Watch him like a hawk. If he gets away from you a second time you'll be the one to be drawn, quartered and burned, *comprendre?*"

"*Nyoh.*"

"Excellent. Welcome back, Mohawk, and prepare for a long journey. Ever been to Quebec? He's not talking. Marvelous spot, you'll enjoy it. Take over, Caughnawaga."

Nearby, peering from behind a tree, was Christittye Etsi, Copper Man. Hearing the voices, his curiosity aroused, he had taken up his position and watched Van Brocklin bring Sky Toucher into camp, the money paid for him and the lace-cuff surrender him to the Caughnawaga.

"Poor O-ron-ia-ke-te, what bad luck."

# 50

T WO EAGLES SAT in counsul with Carries-a-quiver and He-swallows-his-own-body-from-the-foot in the latter's chamber. Two

Eagles had called the meeting. Since his return from Fort Anne he had been thinking long and hard about the tribe once again allying with the English. It was a policy rejected only once in the past; was it time to drop it altogether? He had returned home less than impressed by the colonel. Still, Dorr's evasiveness, the way he had fawned over them—which all three suspected was only a mask for the prejudice most English officers tried to hide—and the insincerity Quane Onente saw in his eyes were not, even taken together, sufficient reason to renounce an alliance nearly a half-century old.

The problem with the English transcended Dorr. It was bigger than any single officer or even group of officers. It was pivotal to the whole future of the Five Iroquois Nations. And critical to the most vulnerable, the Mohawks and Oneidas.

The two older chiefs smoked, Two Eagles did not. Smoking provoked unpleasant memories. Sa-ga-na-qua-de—Anger Maker—had smoked his foul pipe for the many years of their friendship up until the Montagnais captured them and tortured him to death. Two Eagles used tobacco only as a gift for when consulting his óyaron.

"My wife makes an interesting point," he murmured.

Carries-a-quiver and He-swallows stiffened. Only slightly, but Two Eagles noticed. Neither disliked Margaret, but they were ill-prepared to give much notice, let alone value to her opinions regarding tribal affairs.

"She is . . . English," said Carries-a-quiver in a tone that suggested he was revealing a dark secret.

"She is Oneida," retorted Two Eagles. Both smiled but caught themselves when he frowned. "Curiously, she has no liking for the English. Not that she hates them, she has no reason to. But she knows them, how their brains work and why. Much better than any of us."

"She cannot tell me anything about the English that I do not already know," rasped Carries-a-quiver.

Two Eagles shook his head. "She *can*," he insisted.

"What does she say?" He-swallows asked.

"That in the end, if the English defeat the French, our fate will turn out no better than if the French win."

"I disagree," said Carries-a-quiver. "Besides, who we side with is a decision we made a long time ago for all the reasons you know."

"All of which, if you examine them—and I have—are not good enough. Not to her. And I am beginning to think not to me, either."

He-swallows grunted. "Explain."

"I already did. It is simple. Both want our lands. What makes you think that if the English win they will leave us alone? I tell you, they are two sides of the same flat stone. And the Dutch no better. They want what we have."

He-swallows bunched his lips and corrugated his brow in thought. "So Mar-gar-et is saying . . .?"

"So *I* say we stay out of it. Completely. That way we at least keep the strength we have now."

"You want to go back to Dorr and tell him?"

"*Neh,* go to Tenotoge and tell their chiefs. And they will tell Schandisse and Onekahoncka."

"If they agree," said Carries-a-quiver.

"*Nyoh.* So what do you think?"

"I think I will think about it," said Carries-a-quiver. He-swallows nodded.

"Think long and hard as I have," said Two Eagles. "And as you do consider two things: her knowledge of their thinking and our history fighting by their side. What they promised us and what they have given us."

He-swallows smiled ruefully. "There is certainly a difference there."

"And for a minute forget the French and the English, we are surrounded by old enemies, *we must preserve the strength we have,* do you not agree?"

"I said I will think about it," said Carries-a-quiver.

"I would give you some advice, Tékni-ska-je-a-nah," said He-swallows and puffed on his pipe. "Do not tell people that this thinking comes from Mar-gar-et's head. As far as either of us is concerned it comes from your mouth, your head."

Two Eagles grunted. His knees cracked as he got up. "When you decide, if you agree, I will go with Tyagohuens to Tenotoge. *Na-hó,* I have done."

# 51

SNOWFLAKE WAS NOT feeling well. The cold she had contracted lingered stubbornly despite her efforts to rid herself of it. Red rimmed her single eye; she sniffled and coughed repeatedly, despite dosing herself with black-birch syrup and drinking great quantities of tea made from elderberry blossoms.

"I tell you I am all better," insisted Singing Brook.

"You do not look it," said Snowflake. "You were very very sick. Endathatst is boasting like a turkey cock over his success in treating you."

"I wonder," Singing Brook murmured, "did he cure me?"

"Is he not the Medicine Man?"

Singing Brook saw no point in discussing it. She had seen Endathatst on the way over. She *had* been his prize patient and now he was making sure that news of his success reached every ear. People stared, embarrassing her. She glanced at her star.

"Are you feeling something there?" Snowflake asked.

"It started abruptly a few days ago, as if something sudden and terrible was happening to O-ron-ia-ke-te."

"And since then?"

"It is on and off. Something is not right . . . Ó-klaʔ. As for you, you should stay in bed until you are well."

"It is a cold, nothing." Loud shouting erupted outside, filtering through sliver openings in the bark wall of the chamber. "What is that? Go and see."

Singing Brook made her way down the passageway. A crowd was gathering quickly inside the entrance gate. She caught a glimpse of Quane Onawy—tall, ungainly, his scalp badly scarred, he was easy to identify. Her heart leaped, she ran out pushing through the tight circle of welcomers, coming up to him.

"Where is my husband?"

"Right behind me, Tenäte Oÿoghi, he should be here soon."

"Is he all right? No wounds?"

"Nothing." The crowd pressed in on them. They had to shout

to be heard. "He is a hero. Dorr gave him a medal, a musket, money—"

She grabbed his arm. "Come with me to my mother's longhouse and tell me all about it."

"Later maybe, I must first see my wife and *cian.*"

"You say my husband is all right and on his way."

"*Nyoh.*"

"How far behind you?"

"Not far, he should be here before the sun dies."

"Ohhhh, that is good to hear. Thank you, thank you!" She sprinted back to the longhouse, spying String-of-beads coming out of the one behind it. "He is all right, he is safe! He is on his way home!" she shouted.

String-of-beads started, then grinned and nodded.

## 52

MARGARET HAD MIXED emotions. She was pleased that she had persuaded Two Eagles to accept her views on the alliance with the English. Indeed, he'd grasped the idea of his own volition. She was not pleased that he would have to sell his newly found conviction to the Mohawk chiefs at Tenotoge.

"It's freezing out. Can't you wait a week or two until it warms up?" she asked.

"I am not going to Quebec, only a few hours walk over and back."

"Half a day at least. What's the rush? You heard as well as I the fighting's over for now, the French raiding party was repulsed. There won't be anything further happening until spring."

Splitting Moon came in furred to the eyes, his snowshoes strapped to his back. "Ready?"

"Please wait outside, Tyagohuens, would you?" Margaret asked brusquely. "We're talking."

"I am leaving," said Two Eagles. He held her looking searchingly into her eyes. "This was your idea, *che-dagga-nä-we.*"

"Neutrality, I know, I just think it can be put off until decent weather. Have you seen the sky? It's going to snow again."

"We have to go now, this is not something their chiefs can decide overnight. They will have to talk long and hard about it, consult the elders, the clan mothers, just as we did. I want to tell them what I think of Dorr and then tell them your thinking."

"Don't you dare, they'll close their ears up like clams if they think a whiteskin English is behind it. It'll smell to high heaven."

"Smell—to—" Two Eagles looked blank.

"They'll be suspicious. They'll look for an ulterior motive. Tell them it's strictly your idea, yours and Carries-a-quiver's and He-swallows'. Just not mine. Don't even mention my name."

"It *is* clouding over," murmured Splitting Moon. "If we are going—"

"Go, go," snapped Margaret, ushering them out, flipping her hands. "And see you get back as soon as you can."

"I want to visit with O-ron-ia-ke-te for at least a day," said Two Eagles. "We both want to hear what happened at Fort Anne. He must have been in the thick of it."

"When are you coming home?"

"Two sleeps."

"Two. I'll hold you to that." She looked grim.

"Two, I promise, Margaret."

Swift Doe came in. "Are you two going out in this cold? Have you nothing better to do than freeze?"

"They are gong to Tenotoge," said Margaret.

"To talk more war?"

"To talk peace," said Two Eagles.

"*Che-dagga-nä-we,*" corrected Margaret. "Go."

They went out. Swift Doe snickered and frowned.

"That will be the day when those two talk against fighting. War is like milk from their mothers' breasts, they would die without it."

"Better that than with it," muttered Margaret.

# 53

COPPER MAN WALKED into Tenotoge about an hour after Big Teeth arrived. Singing Brook, waiting at the entrance gate for Sky Toucher, ran up to him. As earlier, a crowd quickly began gathering.

"Where is O-ron-ia-ke-te?"

His face fell, his eyes darted about guiltily. "He . . ."

"Where?"

"—was captured after the battle."

"What are you talking about?"

Big Teeth pushed through the crowd, listening as Copper Man explained.

"You *saw* the *kristoni asseroni* sell him to the lace-cuffs?" Big Teeth burst.

She turned on him. "*Ogechta,* let him speak!"

"They are taking him back to Quebec with them. I got close enough to hear."

"What did you do then?" she asked.

"I got out of there fast as I could."

"And went back and told Dorr."

Copper Man hesitated, licking his lips nervously, striving to avoid Singing Brook's stare.

"Speak up, *did* you?" asked Big Teeth.

"*Neh.*"

Singing Brook gasped. "Why not?"

"Why? He, Dorr, would not do anything. You think he would risk men for one Mohawk?"

"For him, the hero who saved you all," she snapped.

"Two times," said Big Teeth.

"I just got out of there before they saw me. Me they would not capture, me they would kill."

"What a brave warrior you are," muttered Singing Brook.

Copper Man held up his withered hand. "Brave enough. And with a brain."

Scowling, he pushed off through the crowd. Singing Brook and Big Teeth stared briefly at each other then she started back to the longhouse, her heart racing, sweat pouring. Bursting into her chamber, she found Green Water sitting on the edge of the bunk and she immediately began getting out dry food, her snowshoes, other travel necessities.

"Your face—what is the matter? What are you doing?"

"The French have taken my husband prisoner, they are on their way back to Quebec."

"Oh *neh* . . ."

"I am going after them."

"*You?* Is your brain broken? You have just gotten out of a sick bed!"

"I am fine."

"That bite has made you crazy, you cannot go after them."

"Who else will?"

"Alone?"

"I will get Quane Onawy and Christittye Etsi to come with me."

"You hardly know them, why should they help you?"

"They have to."

"You *are* crazy."

"Stop saying that! Keep out of it!"

"I will, gladly. Crazy, your brain upside down in your head!"

Singing Brook left her belongings on the bunk and went out, her mother's voice ringing in her ears, accusing, warning. She hurried to Big Teeth's longhouse. Finding him in his bed asleep, she shook his shoulder. He awoke groggily.

"I am going after them; will you come with me? Will you help me?"

"Tenäte Oÿoghi . . ."

"*Nyoh or neh?*"

"It is crazy, by the time you catch up with them they will have crossed over into Sokoki Territory."

"So? I am not saying there will not be danger. I need you, Quane Onawy, you know the way up the War Road."

"Anybody does, you just follow your *oneyatsa*. Even if you do catch up, how will you free him? You heard Christittye Etsi, there are hundreds of them. And he will be heavily guarded. It is impossible."

"When we catch up we will work out a plan to free him, one step at a time."

"You are not making sense, it is crazy."

"Stop saying that word! Will you come?"

"*Neh.*"

"You are afraid."

"I am being sensible, I refuse to chase after death and catch up with it. If the weather and the animals do not kill you, some lace-cuff will. Not me. Look, I am sorry for you and him, but there is nothing either of us can do. Getting him away from them would be like trying to get him out of a nest of snakes."

"You *are* afraid."

"Tenäte Oÿoghi . . ."

"Never mind." She stomped out seething, hurrying down the passageway, out and across to Copper Man's longhouse. He was standing outside talking to other warriors.

At sight of her his face darkened and he hung his head.

"I want to talk to you," she said, "privately."

He shrugged and came over to her. The other men stared. Singing Brook took Copper Man's arm and walked him down the side of the longhouse.

"I am going after them. Will you come with me?"

"Are you serious?"

"Do I *look* serious? They have my husband."

"I know, I sympathize with you. But it is useless to chase after them. Even if you caught up—"

"I know, I know," she interrupted. "Getting him away from them will not be easy."

"Easy? It cannot be done. You would need an army. Even if everything good happened on the way up and you got your chance, they would kill him before you got close. *Neh,* it is just too risky. Impossible, crazy."

She stared, swung about and strode away.

"*Tenäte Oÿoghi . . .* "

She stopped. "What?"

She stood glowering, he approached her. His conscience was in his eyes. Had he changed his mind or would he try to change hers? They stood staring at each other. Gâoh in March seemed determined to vent all his remaining fury in this single hour, setting the palisade groaning, attacking the trees, tearing limbs and whirling snow about. Copper Man studied the tips of his winter moccasins to avoid her eyes, and beat himself with his arms against the bitter cold.

"I am truly sorry I cannot go with you, Tenäte Oÿoghi," he mumbled.

"What about just part of the way? You know the War Road."

"Anybody can follow it, a blind *ochtaha* could."

Her eyes fell to his left hand. She could not question his courage, obviously, but he had had his fill of volunteering. Having done his duty, he had come home safely to stay. He was one of the lucky ones, and not about to press his luck. How many of the twelve volunteers would come home? And since he and Sky Toucher barely knew each other, why should he feel obliged to help her?

"What must I say to persuade you?" she asked, lifting her eyes and searching his. They held a strange glint, neither fear nor guilt.

"Please do not try. You should not be going yourself. I have just heard that you nearly died from sickness. You do not look well. You have no idea how hard such a journey can be. Impossible."

"If the French can make it I can."

"They are—*men*. At least hold off until *tegenhonid*."

"Spring is almost a whole moon from now. Every day, every hour puts him further away and in more danger."

"But think with your head. Even if you do catch up, how will you, a woman, rescue him?"

"You do not have much respect for women, do you? You think we are weak? We lack courage? We do not have your stamina, your endurance? Do not fool yourself, this has to be done and I will do it. I have the fire for it. And when I catch up I will rescue him. Not with weapons or strength but with my brain, with trickery if that is what is needed."

"What trickery?" he asked.

Frustration with him fired irritation. "You! Proud Mohawk warrior who walks into French guns, risks his skin—here is your chance to prove your courage and you back away."

"I am truly sorry, Tenäte Oÿoghi."

"So you have said. Keep your *sorrow,* and the milk in your stomach that quenches *your* fire!"

She walked off. With help or without it, she would leave within the hour.

A feeble sun, almost the color of the sky itself, was halfway up its morning path when she prepared to leave. She would need what was left of the day to get a good leg on her journey. She had dressed warmly: deerskin shirt, bearskin jacket, full leggins, moosehide winter moccasins, wolf fur hat and mittens, rabbit fur muffler, snowshoes with extra lacing. Salted venison and dry corn for rations, essentials for starting a fire, including a pump drill. A sharp knife, a tomahawk and a quantity of sweet-gum juice mixed with tallow, the ointment for preventing and treating frostbite. One factor was in her favor. It was March. *Augustuske's* heart had come and was going; cold snaps like this one yet to come would not last long. And if she was lucky there would not be much snow.

She scanned the sky. It was darkening. Maybe not so lucky.

She made her way to her mother's longhouse, down the passageway to Green Water's chamber, hoping that she was not still angry with her. Green Water was stirring a pot of *onīs´tagi,* parched corn coffee, over the fire just outside her door flap. Sight of Singing Brook's attire brought a frown to her face. She brought the coffee inside and got down two gourd cups.

"So you are going."

"You know I am, do not start."

"I start nothing. I do not have so much breath left that I should waste it. Talking to you is like talking to a stump to make it move out of one's way. Only tell the truth, you are well enough for such a hard journey?"

"I refuse to stay home and wonder if I am."

"Even in the best of health you are not used to such a distance. And all on foot, no canoe. And the worst time of the year. Have you bothered to look at the sky? It is the color of a mussel shell,

packed with snow, a blizzard. You could lose your way, freeze to
death before you even reach the first lake."

"*Distan . . .* "

"I know, I know, we have already talked this to shreds. But
there is nothing you can say that makes it sensible. You go, you
will never come back!"

"This is my husband, I have no choice."

"Is that what your star tells you?"

"What my heart does."

Green Water dismissed this with both hands. They sipped their
coffee in icy silence. It was bitter, suiting Singing Brook's mood.
What had either of them done to deserve this? And after all he
had already been through . . .

The flap lifted. Snowflake's face fell at sight of Singing
Brook.

"*Nyoh,*" muttered Green Water, "she is going after him."

Snowflake got her own cup and poured coffee, sitting down
between them. The wind struck the side of the longhouse, shaking
it full length.

"You really think you will catch up to them?" Snowflake asked.
"It will be like chasing a fish in the river, however hard you try
you will not even get close."

*A fine thing for his own mother to say,* Singing Brook almost
said, but held back. The bickering was already heated enough
without sending up flames.

Green Water was nodding. "Even if you do catch up, how will
you rescue him? You will not, they will capture you, rape you, slit
your throat; all before his eyes just to torture him. You are going
to your certain death."

Snowflake touched her arm. "Tenäte Oÿoghi, he is my son, I
do not have to tell you that I never let him out of my heart, but
this is wrong, completely wrong. Face the truth, he is already
dead!"

Singing Brook started, Green Water gasped softly. Snowflake
nodded. "As good as. Ask yourself, why must you die, too? What
good will that do him? Your eyes say that you think I am cold,
unfeeling. I am a Mohawk woman, I know how to bury my pain,
I have had much practice.

"Something else. You did not send him out in the first place, you were against it, he cannot be on your conscience. What goes on in your brain?"

"He is on my heart, that is enough, O-kla?. Besides, if they have killed him, why would I want to go on living?"

"That is stupid talk!" bawled Green Water, throwing down her cup and getting to her feet. "O-kla? is right, this whole thing has turned your brain upside down, foolish girl!"

"I am not a girl, I am his wife."

Singing Brook started for the flap. Snowflake stood in her way. When Singing Brook eyed her appealingly, the older woman made way.

"You are still not recovered from your illness. Do not be surprised if you do not even make it to the first lake!"

"I will make it to Canada."

"Not halfway!"

Singing Brook went out. The few people outside watched her head toward the entrance. Some shook their heads. The wind rested but overhead the sky still glowered. Green Water was right, it would snow before nightfall. She hurried her step. The crust was thick, her snowshoes slid easily without breaking through. Outside the gate she turned to look back at the longhouse, expecting to see the two of them at the entrance. Neither was there.

She sighed. Had she not expected both to disapprove of this? As they saw it, it was a fool's errand in every respect: like chasing the little blue-green ghosts that rise over the marshes on summer nights. She pulled one mitten off part way to look at her star. Was he looking at his? Could he sense that she was coming? She hoped not; he would agree with their mothers and both scouts, it *was* a fool's errand, and it would only add to his worries.

Someone called her name. Again she looked back. Four Otters came gliding up on snowshoes.

"I am coming."

"You do not have to."

"Your husband is my friend. Do not try to talk me out of it."

They slipped along in silence. He seemed to have plunged into thought.

"And a good friend you are, Cayere Tawyne," she murmured.

More silence, then he spoke, his tone sounding guilty.

"There is more to it. I did not go with them to scout."

"Because you thought they were wrong."

"*Nyoh,* but ever since my conscience has been pricking. And when word came back that Wotstaha Onirares was killed . . ." He shook his head. "A true friend does not let his friends down, even if he does not agree with them."

"You did what you thought right. *I* thought it was."

"We will catch up with them, Tenäte Oÿoghi, rescue him."

"*Nyoh.*"

"We will! You have a plan when we do catch up, *neh?*"

"*Neh,* we will first need to see what the situation is then figure the best way."

At this he seemed disappointed but then his cheerfulness returned. "It is not all black clouds, Tenäte Oÿoghi. We will have surprise on our side. They will not be expecting anyone. They will not guard him closely at night, right?"

"That we will find out when we catch up."

"We will, we will. Something else, they are in no hurry to get back."

"How can you be sure of that?"

"Because, because it is not like when they came down to attack the fort. Then every hour counted, *neh?* Now the fighting is over, they can relax, take their time. I hear, too, that there are many of them. Big groups move slowly, as slow as the slowest among them."

"You could be right. One thing *we* can do, when darkness falls keep going. Go until we are so weary we cannot move another step. Then sleep, but only for a short time. Eat for energy, go on."

"But will you be strong enough?"

"I will surprise you," she said.

"If your strength fails you we can cut a big piece of bark, make a sled, I can pull you."

"It will not come to that."

She glided on. Already, so soon, she could feel a slight tugging inside her thighs, muscles that had not been used so for too many moons.

# 54

BILLIONS OF SIX-ARMED stars floated down. Plodding along gazing upward into them, they looked to Two Eagles and Splitting Moon like falling feathers descending in eerie silence. Ahead through the gray of late afternoon rose the dark eminence of the castle of Tenotoge. It appeared abandoned. Splitting Moon returned his gaze skyward.

"This is no blizzard and it will not last."

"It has lasted too long already," muttered Two Eagles. "This is the worst *augustuske* since the time of the red days."

"*Nyoh*, long and harsh and still nearly a whole moon to go. Look at the snow heaped against the picket." Splitting Moon pointed. "It is almost to the top. And it is cold, my bones shrink in their cases. The first fire we find inside I will lie down in it."

Two Eagles merely grunted. "My *rackesi* O-ron-ia-ke-te is lucky he got home before this started, *neh?*"

"You are going to see him first?"

"*Neh,* Tiyanoga—Hendrick—and the others are expecting me. They would be insulted if I made them wait."

"You do not like Tiyanoga."

Two Eagles stared accusingly. "Who says?" He didn't, nor did he want to talk about it.

"Oh, it is not like it was between you and To-ah-no-ge-na— Two branches-of-water. Not hate with fire in it, just . . . dislike. You should see your face when the two of you talk. And you know he is all for the English, him crossing the Wide Water last year with those other chiefs to visit London. Her with the gold hat giving them gifts, bribing them."

"You sound jealous."

"I think you are. Of Tiyanoga."

"And I think you should think before you give your mouth to such jabbering." They moved on in silence through the descending snow up to the entrance, pounding and calling out loudly. It was opened and they were escorted to Winter Gull's longhouse. Their single Mohawk meal of the day they had consumed earlier at noon, but *sagamité,* succotash, bubbled temptingly in a kettle on the passageway fire and they could smell *onīà´tá‘dǎ',* made from minced meat and crushed green corn.

"*Sedĕkóni, sedĕkóni,*" piped Winter Gull. "You will eat, you will eat." He spoke to his wife, Owanisse·nekwaŕ—Yellow Tongue—who got into her furs and went to fetch Kettle Throat and Hendrick. They arrived shortly, Splitting Moon ate quickly and left the chiefs in privacy.

The three Mohawks got out their pipes and lit them, prompting Two Eagles to edge backwards to remove himself from the foul smoke that would presently gather thickly and assault his eyes and nostrils. Splitting Moon, with his chronically weak stomach, was lucky to get out of the chamber, he reflected.

"At Onneyuttahage," said Two Eagles, "we hear that Dorr has repulsed the lace-cuffs that came up the lakes to attack Fort Anne. They are now on their way back to Quebec, dragging their tails like beaten dogs."

He pointed out that at least for the moment all was peaceful down the full length of the War Road, giving Mohawks and Oneidas opportunity to reexamine their long-standing policy toward the English. He detailed the reasons he had given Carries-a-quiver and He-swallows, the elders and the clan mothers, in favor of neutrality.

"All things considered, it is in the best interests of all the Iroquois to keep sheathed our knives."

Repeatedly, his glance wandered to Hendrick squatting, sucking on his pipe, his shaggy head down, hiding any reaction that might find its way into his eyes.

"There are two points that are of special importance and should be weighed seriously," Two Eagles went on. "The Englishman's mind: he does not think of our interests, of anyone's, he centers on himself. He is no more to be trusted than the lace-cuffs, perhaps even less. Secondly, think about our experiences with them over the past sixty years. They do not keep their treaties, they do not keep their promises. They are no better than the French; in some ways, worse."

Hendrick raised his head for the first time. "Your woman is an English—"

"So?"

"What does she think of your thinking?"

"She agrees."

"So is it *your* thinking? Or hers?"

Two Eagles scowled.

"Easy," murmured Kettle Throat, "we are all friends here. We can speak frankly."

"Margaret knows her people better than you ever could, Ti-yanoga, you who only look at their faces and not into their hearts."

"Does she know the sickly chief with the gold hat? I do. Does she know little Lord Go-dol-phin,* her chief minister? I do."

"If you have something to say, say it," snapped Two Eagles.

"You speak of two things to keep in mind about the English. I will give you two more: one, they will win this war with the lace-cuffs. Not next week, not next year but in the end."

"And turn on us and take our lands, our trade—"

"Let me finish. Two things and still the first: they will win because they are in the best part of the land. Up by the Kanawage in New France is colder, the growing season shorter. Fewer people, fewer guns against the English. There is never enough food, many starve."

Kettle Throat laughed. "Because they bring over their wooden islands full of *oneharadeseoengtseragherie* instead of food."

"Liquor made of the juice of the grape, *nyoh*," added Winter Gull nodding vigorously.

Hendrick did not smile. He waved a crooked finger at Two Eagles, to whom he had moved so close that if he bent forward his forehead would have touched the Oneida's chest.

"Second, the lace-cuffs will lose because their king with the gold hat does not have the fire in his belly or the money, for more fighting."

Two Eagles sniffed. "You can see inside his pocket?"

"I know. *I* know something else you either do not or do not want to know. The English and French are not the threat to us, the French moccasins are. The Petuns, the Neutrals, the Sokoki

---

*Unbeknownst to Hendrick, Sidney, Lord Godolphin, died the previous August shortly after the Iroquois chiefs returned from their visit to London.

Abnakis, the Hurons, Ottawas, the Montagnais—so many tribes we have defeated, a solid circle of enemies around our Five Nations, all hating us. They, not the *asseroni* are the threat to us in the suns to come."

"*Nyoh!*" burst Two Eagles, "I was getting to that. We must keep our strength, what we have left, and not sacrifice our warriors in the *Asseronis'* squabbles. If we side with the English in the years to come, our warriors will be reduced to a handful. How then will we protect ourselves against our moccasin enemies?"

"If we do not side with the English, all the castles we have left will be destroyed and our people massacred!"

"You do not know that! You think like you always do, that the English have come to help us, protect us. That is dreaming!"

"Shhhh," said Kettle Throat. "We are not deaf."

"Margaret *knows!*" Two Eagles burst.

A mistake. Admission that the idea of neutrality had not originated with him.

"*Mar-gar-et* knows," repeated Hendrick, leering.

"Are you done?" Kettle Throat asked Two Eagles.

"Done talking to *him!*" he shouted.

Two Eagles made a second mistake. He started to shove Hendrick, who sat uncomfortably close, in the chest. He caught himself but not until he pushed him slightly. Hendrick retaliated with a push of his own. Kettle Throat separated them.

"Enough of that."

"You see?" Hendrick said, "he has to have his way." He smirked. "His *woman*'s way."

"We will consider what you have proposed, Tékni-ska-je-a-nah," said Kettle Throat, while his eyes warned him to leave.

Two Eagles heart cooled. It was useless, Hendrick controlled them; the mere suggestion that the tribes remain neutral would never get to the Mohawks outside for consideration, let along to Schandisse and Onekahoncka.

"The English are our friends," droned Hendrick. "But no one is saying they are reliable. Some lie. Many abuse our loyalty, and they are only the lesser of two nuisances. But when it is over, at least they will let us live, not turn loose on us a pack of wild dogs."

"You are dreaming," muttered Two Eagles.

"It is so. I have it from Lord Go-dol-phin and his chief with the gold hat herself. They think of us as their children."

"You like being thought of as a *cian?*"

"I like being protected like one," he responded.

"That is the difference between us, Tiyanoga," snapped Two Eagles. "I am a man, I can protect myself."

Hendrick bellowed and lunged at him. This time it took both Kettle Throat and Winter Gull to hold him back, quickly exhausting the older Winter Gull. Two Eagles stared contemptuously at Hendrick as he got into his furs and left.

Hendrick called after him. "Tell *Mar-gar-et* we are sorry—" He laughed.

It had stopped snowing, but the bitter cold persisted. Splitting Moon stood beating himself with his arms and stomping his feet, twin columns of vapor issuing from his nostrils.

"Why do you wait outside, Tyagohuens?" Two Eagles asked, still upset. "You like your arse frozen?"

His friend grinned. "So Tiyanoga got the best of you, eh?"

"*Ogechta!*"

"He did." Splitting Moon's smile fled. "I have more bad news. Your favorite *rackesi* never came back from Fort Anne. He was captured by lace-cuffs and is on his way to Quebec to be executed."

"Where did you hear that?"

"I overheard some warriors talking."

"We will see about this! Come!"

Splitting Moon loped after him as he hurried toward Snowflake's longhouse. Green Water was visiting her. Both wore the same dejected expression.

"Tékni-ska-je-a-nah," said Oʹklaʔ, "what are you doing here?"

"Doing nothing, it turns out. Aunt Oʹklaʔ, what is this I hear about O-ron-ia-ke-te?"

"It is true," she said. Even worse, his wife Tenäte Oÿoghi has gone after him."

"In this weather?"

"By herself," said Green Water, and threw up her hands at Singing Brook's rashness.

"This is her mother, O´hute Onega," said Snowflake.

Green Water nodded. "She could not get anybody to go with her so she went by herself. How is that for stupidity?"

"I will go after her, bring her back," said Two Eagles.

"I will come with you," said Splitting Moon.

Green Water snickered mirthlessly. "She will not come back with you or anybody. You will have to knock her over the head, tie her and drag her back."

"We can do that," said Splitting Moon, bringing mild shock to Green Water's face. "But we cannot leave right away. You cannot, Tékni-ska-je-a-nah. You promised—"

"I know, I know, that I would only be away two sleeps."

"We can go back to Onneyuttahage and leave from there," suggested Splitting Moon.

"I hate to lose the time . . ." Two Eagles pondered his options, torn.

"You go back, I will go on," said Splitting Moon.

"*Neh, neh, neh,* O-kla?, O´hute Onega, we will catch up with her, I promise."

"What about O-ron-ia-ke-te?" asked Snowflake.

"Him, too."

"You make it sound as easy as breathing," said Green Water.

Two Eagles bristled. "I do not make it sound anything. It has to be done and we are the only ones to do it." He turned to Splitting Moon, expecting a nod of agreement. All he got was a worried expression as his friend looked off into space.

Outside, Splitting Moon caught his arm. "I can leave from here and you catch up with me."

"What would we gain? We still have to catch up with her. And she does not know you, she would not come back with you, she would not even stop."

"I guess."

"And that is what we have to do, convince her that we can rescue him and talk her into letting us."

"Without her help."

"*Nyoh.*"

Splitting Moon sighed.

# 55

BOTH ONEIDAS WERE near exhaustion by the time they arrived at Onneyuttahage. It was within an hour of dawn, the castle was beginning to awaken. Two Eagles unintentionally woke up Margaret as he fumbled about the chamber, accidentally dropping a basket close to the bunk. She yawned as she came awake.

"You're home early."

He explained. Disappointment darkened her face as she listened but sympathy slowly began displacing it.

"Of course you have to go . . ."

"And right away."

"You could use a few hours' sleep."

"Tomorrow night we will sleep. By then we will have at least caught up with Tenäte Oÿoghi, maybe even O-ron-ia-ke-te. Catch up with the lace-cuffs before they cross the border into Sokoki Territory. Everyone at Tenotoge thinks they are in no hurry to get back. And bad weather will slow them even more."

"As it will you two," Margaret pointed out.

"Two can travel faster than three hundred."

"And how will you rescue O-ron-ia-ke-te?"

"I cannot answer that now. We will have to see what the situation is."

"The *situation* is hundreds against the two of you, and poor Tenäte Oÿoghi. They grab you, they won't take you to Quebec, they'll slit your throats then and there. And hers."

"Please, we are not stupid, we will not take unnecessary chances." He sighed silently. Words. Empty-sounding as old gourds. He couldn't argue with a single thing she'd said so far.

"Will you be taking your gun?"

"Of course."

"I wouldn't. Even if you surprise them you'll only get off one shot. Just enough to betray your position."

He smiled. "Are you going to instruct me on how to fight?"

"But you won't be fighting, you'll be sneaking into their camp, trying to bring him out—whatever shape he's in, assuming he's still alive when you get there. Meanwhile what'll you do with her?"

"Talk her into going back before we catch up with them."

"Small chance of that. That girl's got gumption. I can't imagine she'll give up just because you two come along. I'm sorry, I sound like I've all the answers when obviously no one has any."

"Cheer up, it will not be so hard. We will have surprise on our side, the darkness for cover. We will be careful, get in and get out with him and by the time the camp wakes up we'll be halfway back to Tenotoge."

"Assuming they don't post guards . . ."

"Why would they? They do not expect anybody to be following them."

"*I* certainly wouldn't: two men trying to rescue one from three or four hundred is too farfetched even to conceive of. There I go again, Miss Optimistic." She reached to massage his neck.

He managed a grin through his weariness. "There you go again."

The flap lifted. Splitting Moon came in yawning. "If we do not leave right away and get some wind in our faces, I will fall asleep and you will have to carry me."

"I am coming, I am coming."

"Wait . . ." Margaret sat up. "Don't go." Both reacted, startled. "I mean not right away. First get some sleep, even just five or six hours."

"We are all right," said Two Eagles.

"Please, at least start out refreshed. At this stage will five or six hours make any difference?"

Splitting Moon thought it over, nodded and left, Two Eagles undressed and climbed into bed beside her.

"What'll you do for food?" she asked.

"We will bring dry and shoot a deer."

"Promise me one thing. Don't try to go on when the weather gets beastly foul; why waste the energy? The French won't, she won't. Hole up somewhere, use the time to catch your breaths."

"Mmmmmm, go to sleep, I am sorry I woke you."

"You mean you'd leave without waking me?"

"*Neh, neh, neh.*"

# VI

# ENEMIES, TIME AND DISTANCE

# 56

TWO EAGLES AND Splitting Moon pushed on. Heading eastward, they moved toward Da-yä-hoo-wä-quat, the Carrying Place, and then cut northward away from the Te-ugé-ga river toward the south short of Lake Andia-ta-roc-te, Lake St. Sacrement, which paralleled the southern half of Lake O-ne-ä-dä-lote, Lake Champlain. The raiding party would most likely be heading up Lake Andia-ta-roc-te.

"I knew you were fond of O-ron-ia-ke-te," bawled Splitting Moon above the wind, "but not this close."

"*This* close? You mean to go chasing after him? He is blood and yes, I am fond of him. Since he was ten, Benjamin's age. His father died before my *rackesi* grew out of his cradleboard."

"And you saw yourself taking over."

"I saw no such thing. Is it wrong to be fond of one's relatives? He is a fine young man, would that Benjamin could have grown up to be just like him. Do you really want to know why I have become so fond of him? For one thing because he is loyal to his beliefs. I may not agree with him, but I respect him. He does not merely *talk* about fighting on the side of the English, he goes out and does it."

"To get away from his woman's voice stabbing the channels of his ears."

Two Eagles scoffed. "Her opposition only makes his loyalty stronger."

"His *loyalty* got him into a big mess this time."

"That was just bad luck, running into the lace-cuffs after he left Fort Anne. Those other two scouts did not."

"He is dead."

Two Eagles stopped, glaring. "Do not say that!"

"Be practical."

"Be *quiet!* Think before you spill out such hollow talk. They want him alive until they get to Stadacona. All we need do is catch up with them before they get that far."

"*All* we need do."

"If you do not think we can do it why did you come?"

"I wish I could answer that. Getting back to O-ron-ia-ke-te, I do not remember you two seeing much of each other."

"We did before Margaret came. Now I do not go visiting, do not travel nearly so much."

"Ha, because your wife has a rope around your neck."

"How would you like a rope around *yours?* Nice and tight to silence your rattling tongue?" He shot out his arm, stopping Splitting Moon. "Look."

They were passing through a stand of hemlocks. Many showed evidence of chewing. The telltale ragged cut betraying deer molars low on the tree.

"*Aque,*" said Splitting Moon.

"*Tantanege,* too. Look where their sharp teeth slice the stems at an angle."

"I do not see rabbit shit, only scut. Two-toed tracks as long as your hand is wide, *aque.*" Splitting Moon glanced about.

"It is too cold, they are sleeping, feeding only at night. How are your legs?"

"Strong as a bear's, why, are yours starting to hurt?"

"Did I say that?" asked Two Eagles.

"Why ask about my legs?"

"Just curious." Splitting Moon grunted and smirked. "Just curious!"

"How far do you think she has gotten?"

"With almost two sleeps' head start we will not catch up with her until the lake, I think. Then spot her easily. The lace-cuffs with him are a good quarter moon ahead."

Two Eagles looked grim. "A long way."

"So stop lagging, pick up your feet."

On they pressed all day without stopping to rest, without eating, but continuing their banter. They kept going after darkness fell when the stars came out and flung their spears at each other while the moon stared heedlessly. And Two Eagles' pessimism deepened.

The raiders made camp about two-thirds of the way up Lake St. Sacrement, which stretched for more than ten leagues from Fort Nicholson up to the Upper and Lower Falls west of the rise from

Fort Carillon. At that point the northern expanse of Lake Champlain began, carrying all the way to the headwaters of the Richelieu River, a distance of nearly thirty-six leagues.

Sky Toucher sat tied by a campfire, Onea Canonou, Stone Pipe, gazing down at him. He seemed overly conscientious in his duties this time, keeping a constant close eye on the prisoner. The turkey cock came by often to check. Sky Toucher could easily see that defeat in his first battle lodged less than comfortably in Ramesay's craw. To add to his discomfiture, his war companion Paulette had taken a ball in her pretty left eye, so Stone Pipe told Sky Toucher, rendering the colonel's portable bed no longer as inviting as earlier.

In simmering anger Ramesay glared at Sky Toucher as if he were solely responsible for the colonel's woes. Often he took advantage of the prisoner's bindings and slapped him. Sky Toucher could not be bothered to protect himself, even on those rare occasions when his wrists were untied.

The raiders left a trampled road twenty yards wide in their wake. Sky Toucher was still surprised at the number who'd survived the doomed attack. Though Ramesay's reserves had been slaughtered by Dorr's artillery, nearly four hundred Canadians and Indians had come away from Fort Anne with their lives. And already, even before departing Mohawk Territory, they began attracting wandering Abnakis, including women. Abnaki women were short, stumpy and most of them as plain-faced as an empty bowl, showing the years of trial and privation that had shrunken them and gnarled their limbs and bodies. They all looked alike to Sky Toucher. He could not find one that approached Singing Brook's beauty. They grunted like men, smeared their faces with bear grease against the cold and behaved like pack animals.

Onea Canonou did not appear to hold his earlier escape against Sky Toucher; he didn't abuse him, raise a hand, or taunt him. Did the Caughnawaga admire him for getting away the first time? Was that important? Getting away this time long before they reached Quebec was. Once behind bars he would surely end up with dirt in his mouth. And his death, as promised by the turkey cock, would be agonizing.

When they stopped earlier the women had cut down long poles of spruce saplings, raising them in structures with roofs covered

with birch bark which they carried piled on crude sleds, built narrow to enable them to be pulled through the dense woodlands
more easily. Then the women unrolled more sheets and assembled
them to make the walls. Green spruce boughs were collected to
spread about the floor. Though the work was arduous, the men
merely stood watching. A few ventured into the woods to hunt the
meager game that the bitter cold had not sent to ground.

The fires were lit, the nearly full moon reflected by the snow
lit up the encampment. The raiders turned in, quiet settling over
the area. The turkey cock's tent had been put up as had those of
his subordinate officers. His orderly prepared Ramesay's bed while
he sat on a keg smoking, now and then casting a menacing glare
at the prisoner. Sky Toucher ignored him: he *was* a *schawariwane,*
all puffed up with his own importance, all noise and fuss, and
under his feathers as cowardly as an Abnaki. Ramesay finally retired to the comfort of his covers and his bottle. Up to where Sky
Toucher sat came Stone Pipe with an Abnaki woman. She stared
blankly.

"She has never seen a Mohawk warrior before."

"Where has she been, down a hole?"

She spoke, pointing at him.

"She says you do not look like a warrior, you look like a beaten
*sateeni,* a bone chaser."

"Tell her she looks like . . . never mind."

Why give Stone Pipe reason to dislike him? She looked like a
chipmunk with its cheek pouches stuffed, huge black eyes and a
voice that whistled and chattered. Where was her tail?

"Can you get me another blanket?" Sky Toucher asked.

"Where? Steal one? For you? Ramesay would order me shot."

"Can I move nearer the fire?"

"For that, too, I would be shot. Can you not get it through
your head you are his prisoner of a lifetime, his excuse for the
defeat?"

"You want me to last until Stadacona, *neh?* If I freeze to death
before we get there, he will surely order you shot."

Stone Pipe looked thoughtful. He spoke to the woman, who
berated him. Then he shouted, drawing the attention of those
around them. She finally, grudgingly, went off.

He looked after her, muttering, "Jankanque Karackwero . . ."

"Very-beautiful-sun? That is her name?"

"*Nyoh,* why? She will try to find you something."

She came back moments later with a blanket even thinner and more holey than the one he had. As Stone Pipe took it from her, she reached for Sky Toucher's blanket.

"*Neh,*" he burst, straining at his bonds. "Tell her I need both."

She spoke.

"She says she cannot, she did not 'find' it, it is an exchange."

"That rag is not as good as the one I have."

Stone Pipe spoke to her. They began arguing, she threw up her fat arms and left fuming.

Stone Pipe scowled. "Good, fine. Now, thanks to you, I get no fuck tonight."

"I am sorry."

" 'Sorry' is fixing the trap after the rabbit gets away." He came down on his haunches and arranged the second blanket over the one Sky Toucher was wearing. Then he narrowed his eyes. "You are not going to try to get away, are you?"

"Of course not."

"I would have to kill you. It is me or you."

"*Nyoh.*"

Stone Pipe unsheathed his knife and drew the flat of it across Sky Toucher's throat. He did not flinch, nor did he take his eyes from Stone Pipe's eyes.

"Do not make me kill you, Cousin. I do not know why but I am getting to like you. Maybe because you have *karístatsi yon,* iron guts."

"I am a Mohawk."

"Maybe that, too. Go to sleep."

"Untie my wrists, leave my ankles."

"*Neh, neh.*"

"I am starving, I have not eaten since early yesterday."

"Maybe tomorrow. Not now, I am busy, I must go find her. This cold night, *she* is *my* blanket."

He laughed and walked away. Sky Toucher watched him disappear into a crowd. So now the turkey cock had two people keeping an eye on him, and she definitely disliked him. How could

any Abnaki not dislike an Iroquois? Over the years the Five Nations had decimated both the eastern and western tribes.

Lying on his side about thirty yards from the nearest fire's
warmth, he thought about the threat the turkey cock had made to
the Caughnawaga's life. Stone Pipe's leniency would stretch only
so far, not far enough to endanger his own hide.

Sky Toucher knew he had to get away soon. How? He could
not see his star but felt it pulsing lightly. Was hers doing the same?
How was she? Still furious with him for "deserting" her? *Neh,* she
might rail and rage; she could be as stubborn as a taproot but she
never held a grudge.

Did she sense that he'd been recaptured? How could she? No
one had seen Van Brocklin and his men stop him in the trail, then
take him straight to the turkey cock's temporary camp. The other
scouts, those who had survived, were long home by now, and when
he failed to show what could she assume but that he'd been killed?

Stone Pipe dragged him, bound hand and foot, into the nearest
bark hut. He lay on his side, burying his face in the sweet-smelling
boughs. Their fragrance failed to lessen the sickly stench of body
odor. As the onslaught of snoring slowly began, he heard giggling
and the movement of bodies as couples found each other.

He slept.

He dreamt.

Of her.

# 57

SNOW THREATENED BUT held off. Gã'oh showed unexpected le-
niency, playing about rather than blustering. Singing Brook and
Four Otters slipped steadily northward past ice-locked Round
Lake. They would eventually cross the twisting upper reach of the
Shaw-na-taw-ty, the river the Asseroni called the Hudson, that
sprang to life in the Tree-eater Mountains, and Lake Tear of the
Clouds, the source of the river's main headstream, the Opalescent
River. According to Four Otters, they should reach Fort Anne in
a little over two-and-a-half sleeps, taking them out of their way

for the trek up Lake St. Sacrement. But Singing Brook was determined to talk to Dorr, from whom she hoped to get help.

"The pitchfork soldiers made a road from Fort Nicholson to Fort Anne," he remarked.

"O-ron-ia-ke-te calls them mil-itia."

"I call them hay pilers with muskets. The road is three whiteskin leagues. Once we start up it we will move faster. It is where we were ambushed, where Gä-nä-esi-tas-i-go, Many Wounds, was killed and too many others. So many of our warriors sleep today with dirt in their mouths because of that place. The grass got red." The wind rose, snow powdered the woods around them. "It was all so . . ."

"*Ke-assa-te?*"

"*Nyoh,* futile. They fight and fight, we bleed and bleed. Because we are caught between them."

He stopped, nocked an arrow and let it fly uncomfortably close past her. Turning, she saw a cottontail rabbit lying pinioned to the snowcrust, a sumac stem still in its mouth. Four Otters retrieved the arrow, restored it to his quiver and held his kill up by the ears.

"Not much meat for the two of us, but something hot will taste good."

"It was getting dark. She recalled her earlier recommendation that they continue well into the night. It seemed sensible when she said it, but now her legs and thighs were aching furiously. She simply couldn't go on. She had never walked so far, even in summer, rarely venturing more than half a league from home.

Using their tomahawks they cut poles and pine boughs and built a lean-to, its entrance nearly blocked by a huge snow-capped boulder. They had just enough room to slip inside the structure, but the rock would keep out the wind and snow, and the entryway was sufficient to let smoke from their cookfire rise freely.

She skinned the rabbit, skewered it with an arrow and roasted it. Four Otters was right. It was not nearly enough meat for two ravenous people. Each also ate a handful of parched corn.

"I think we should put out the fire," said Four Otters as they prepared for sleep.

"It is only embers and it is very warm."

"There could be hunters wandering around."

"Mohawks," Singing Brook insisted, "This is Mohawk Territory and we do not hunt at night."

"Mohegans do," Four Otters reminded her. "Sometimes they cross the Shaw-na-taw-ty to hunt on our lands. With the river frozen, it is easy to get back and forth. I will put out the fire."

From her waist down, the separate achings joined in one great assault, gripping and squeezing every muscle. It would take her two or three days to work them into shape. As tired as she was, discomfort made it difficult to fall asleep, though Four Otters' was snoring so loud it shook the bough roof. Sleep finally came to her, but it seemed only minutes later that she felt his hand shaking her shoulder.

"The sun is already up; if we want to make Fort Anne in daylight we should get moving. I cannot wait to get there, get hot soup, sit near a roaring fire for an hour and chase *augustuske* out of my bones."

"I dressed as warmly as I could, and I am still cold."

"It turned very cold late last night, the trees cracking sounded like a battle."

"How could you know? you were asleep."

"I sleep, I wake, I sleep, that is how I have always been," he said.

They started forth into the frigid, bleak morning, Four Otters leading the way. They moved along without speaking, sharing the silence of the woodlands. Not a bird, not even a creaking limb, no wind stirred the naked branches, but the coldness continued to fist the land. She had all she could do to keep her teeth from chattering. Curiously, he did not appear nearly as cold as she did. Perhaps her fear was exacerbating the chill. She had a growing dread that they might catch up to find Sky Toucher's corpse. She knew his captors would not trouble themselves to keep him alive. Her sweat felt like ice pressing against the small of her back. In spite of her bearskin jacket and leggings, she felt frozen, her bones so brittle she imagined they would snap like dry sticks.

"When we get to Fort Anne we may get some news of the raiders and O-ron-ia-ke-te," said Four Otters, striving for optimism.

"Only Christittye Etsi knows he was captured."

"But the colonel must know that the lace-cuffs that survived are heading back north."

"How far up the War Road does Mohawk Territory go? Where does Abnaki Territory begin?"

"Between the two are the lands of the Sokokis, but they are Abnakis, too. The sunset tribe."

"Western."

"*Nyoh,* as much our enemies as the sunrise tribe. Their lands begin up by Fort Carillon."

"Between the two halves of Lake Champlain," she added.

"*Nyoh.* From there on it will not be easy. Maybe we should hide out of the wind during the day and travel by night."

"I would rather we travel both. As far as we can, as many hours. Have you been to Fort Anne before?"

"I saw it from the outside when we passed through there last year. The pitchfork soldiers had just started building it, after they cut the road."

"The road to Fort Nicholson near lake St. Sacrement?" she asked.

"That is what everybody calls the lake now; the lace-cuffs and the redbacks even take away our names." He grinned. "As you do— 'Champlain,' 'St. Sacrement.' "

"How old are you, Cayere Tawyne?"

Unprepared for the question, he stopped in surprise. "Twenty-four summers, why?"

"The same as O-ron-ia-ke-te. Do you ever think about marrying?"

He shrugged.

"Do you like women?"

"Some. I have not thought about *a* woman, about marriage." He chuckled. "I am still young. Besides, I do not know if it would sit well in my stomach."

"Does marriage for O-ron-ia-ke-te sit well, do you think?"

Again he shrugged.

"Has he discussed it with you, I mean since we were married?"

"*Neh.* I do not know what he thinks. When you see him, ask him. It is getting warmer."

She shivered. "I do not feel it."

The soreness in her legs was less severe today. How far had they come? How far had he and his captors gotten? Up past Fort Carillon by now, into Sokoki Territory—so that even if he somehow managed to get away he would have French moccasins to contend with. She had heard that the Abnakis were not as warlike as the Iroquois, but in earlier battles with them the Abnakis had lost many warriors. Would they take their bitterness toward his tribe out on him? What about her and Cayere Tawyne? Their clothing gave them away as Mohawk, the country ahead could prove as dangerous for them as for O-ron-ia-ke-te.

"You look even more worried than before," said Four Otters. "Relax, we will get to the fort, and maybe there you will hear some good news."

How was that possible? she was tempted to ask, but kept silent. Since he was voluntarily risking his life for them, he was entitled to his optimism.

# 58

SPLITTING MOON CAUGHT a cold, which helped neither his disposition nor his outlook, not that cheeriness was ever something that he harbored in quantity.

Two Eagles studied him. "You must feel weaker with all your blowing and wheezing."

"I am not blowing, I am not wheezing."

"You sound like a moose dying after a long chase."

Overhead the raptors streamed north in defiance of winter's continued dominance, a changing ribbon of hawks, eagles and falcons, guided by the valley. Two Eagles knew that most birds avoided the larger lakes, following the lakeshores hundreds of miles out of their way, funneling into a narrow corridor.

"They fly so easily," he murmured.

"So fast. They will pass her in no time and pass the lace-cuffs before dark, *neh?*"

"You sound like you envy their wings." Two Eagles smiled grimly.

"*We* could use wings."

"It is so cold up there you, without oil on your feathers, would freeze to death and drop."

"It is *warm* up there. They are following the winds that bring them up from below the Ganagawehas."

"It is colder than down here."

"You are wrong."

"I am right," Two Eagles insisted, then paused. "Let us stop before we start," he added wearily. "Arguing takes too much out of me."

"*Nyoh* let us stop. All this water in me, this fire in my head and throat, weakens me. I need rest. Besides, it looks like snow again. Maybe we should build a lean-to, eat and really rest. Sleep long."

"And let them get to the second lake, *nyoh?*"

Splitting Moon plumped down on a rock. He was sweating heavily, breathing hard. He *looked* sick. Two Eagles decided: they would stop.

Yellow evening grosbeaks, strawberry-colored redpolls, purple finches, sedate, dark-eyed juncos, lent tiny swipes of vivid color to the stark landscape. Singing Brook admired them. They knew how to cope with the harshest winter, fluffing their feathers for better insulation and pulling their feet up to their breasts to warm them.

As she and Four Otters pressed on, the sky gradually solidified into the gray of a mourning cloak's wings. Soon, snow fell thickly, quickly becoming a blinding wall of white driven by Gä̃oh. Overhead the bully from the north howled and swirled and trees around them exploded like cannon. So heavy was the snowfall, Singing Brook could barely make out Four Otter's back only a few paces ahead. She could not recall ever wanting to reach any destination as badly as this whiteskin fort. When they got there she would ask for blankets, undress and wash and dry every stitch of clothing, put hot stones in her moccasins to dry them and stick close to the fire as she ate. She guessed it would make her sleepy, and warm indoor beds would be inviting, but they had to go on.

Only not before she talked to Dorr. Could she get help from

him? If he had any conscience, he'd give her men. Dorr had rewarded Sky Toucher for his help and his heroism, could he turn his back on him now?

"They are sure to have deer heart or rabbit soup at the fort," said Four Otters. "And whiteskin coffee. It is good and strong. Everything hot to chase the cold out of our bones."

"Where *is* the fort?"

He pointed off to the right and ahead. "I have been thinking . . ."

"What?"

"This weather is so bad maybe we should stop first at Fort Nicholson, get hot food and dry out our clothes there. Fort Anne is only three leagues east of there."

It made sense, she agreed.

"Are you sure this is the right trail?"

"*Nyoh,* it is all familiar."

"What?"

"The trees, the rocks, everything. This is it."

How could he recognize a trail he had never seen in snow? She hesitated to ask. On they slid. It was not even noon yet, but already she was feeling tired. Such exertion after lying abed so many days was proving a shock to her body. The new snow slowed them, tending to pull their snowshoes, like mud. It finally stopped snowing, and she could see clearly ahead. The wind whirled a final cloud of powder, it dissolved, her heart thudded.

Rising out of the trees like a phantom monster was Fort Nicholson. Sight of it sent a tremor up her spine. Four Otters shouted happily. Moving closer, she could see that the fort was constructed of vertical logs and earth, with enclosed lookout platforms at the corners.

"I told you, I told you!" he shouted.

But something was wrong. There was no flag, no sentries in evidence, no sign of life.

"It is abandoned," she murmured.

His expression agreed, but he resisted acknowledging it. "Maybe not, maybe not."

"What then, are they all asleep? In the middle of the afternoon?"

"Let us look inside."

"Why bother?"

"If no one is there we can still build a fire. Maybe find food, maybe there is rum."

She made a face. "Let us just go on to Fort Anne."

"It is more than three leagues that way. Are you sure you are up to it? It is getting late; by the time we get there it will be dark. And much colder."

"It cannot get any colder."

"Are you shivering?"

"We will keep on."

"*Neh,* better we stop here, make a big fire, warm ourselves. I am cold, too, my hands are so red they are purple."

"You should see your nose."

He grinned. "*Ska-noh,* Tenäte Oÿoghi."

She managed a weary smile. "More power to you, Cayere Tawyne."

Her feet were swollen, her cheeks tingled above the edge of her muffler. She applied more of the ointment to prevent frostbite, offering him some. She finally managed to get control of her shivering, relieving herself of one worry. For if she failed to, difficulty with her speech would follow, her thinking would become sluggish, her skin puffy and bluish. It could be fatal.

Would they find Fort Anne deserted as well? Had Dorr and his men left when Fort Nicholson was abandoned and returned to Albany? The possibility struck panic in her. Four Otters noticed, his face darkening.

"Nothing," she murmured. "A cramp in my leg; it is gone now."

They started up the road to Fort Anne. The snow concealed low stumps, which slowed them as they stumbled. The road stretched as straight as a hawk dives. Out on the lake the flat whiteness persisted, losing itself in a mist that looked as if it concealed the end of the world. The sky glowered, but even as Singing Brook studied its sullenness, it slowly began brightening, taking away the threat of more snow.

"They will take good care of us at Fort Anne," said Four Otters.

"Dorr and the other whiteskin long knives will remember me. We talked many times."

"Mmmmmm. It is so frustrating when you think about it."

"About what?"

"That Christittye Etsi came straight home to Tenotoge after he saw them capture O-ron-ia-ke-te." Singing Brook shook her head disconsolately.

"What could he do, one man against hundreds?"

"He could have gone back to the fort and told Dorr. They would have pursued and rescued him that very day."

"*Nyoh,* even before the lace-cuffs left the place where Christittye Etsi saw them. It would have been so easy . . ."

*Nyoh,* she reflected, rendering all this chasing wholly unnecessary. "Christittye Etsi's brain is too tiny to be believed." She scowled.

"I know but since it did not turn out right for you it is not worth black thoughts now. Eh, feel, it is getting warmer."

He had said that many times the past three days in between storms, as if trying to drop a hint to the elements. This time she agreed. The sun came out, setting the crystalline landscape dazzling. He got out a dead coal taken from last night's fire and blackened the flesh under her eyes to lesson the glare. Overhead, crows that had gathered in the treetops during the bitterest cold were flying off their separate ways, a sure sign that it would be milder for some time. As well, the wind was fast losing its edge.

The white road lengthened behind them. Into view came Fort Anne, its four bastions built of timber cribbing filled with earth and gravel, and faced with stout logs. At sight of smoke rising from all four chimneys she cried out joyfully. To the right of the fort a wood-chopping detail was pushing and pulling a huge sledge piled with logs. Beyond the fort, the whitened path of Wood Creek undulated into the mist.

The sun was setting, sending pale swaths through the trees to bind earth to heaven as they started across the parade ground. A voice called from a corner lookout tower, Four Otters waved.

"Cayere Tawyne, Mohawk warrior who has fought on the side of your woman chief-with-the-gold-hat's soldiers against the lace-cuff dogs! Come from Tenotoge to speak with his friend, your Colonel Dorr!"

They were ordered to wait. The wind whipped her skirt and leggin fringes, her shirt was damp with sweat front and back. She felt as if her bones were slowly separating from fatigue. The gate swung wide, two soldiers in homespun britches and blue coats, their lapels faced red, came marching briskly out, then halted to salute their muskets. For all her weariness, she had to make an effort to suppress a grin, so serious did they look.

Inside Dorr, bundled in crimson and white with wincingly bright brass buttons, greeted them.

"Two Otters, what a pleasant surprise! What in God's name are you doing up here in this wretched weather? And would this fair lady be your missus?"

"This is Tenäte Oÿoghi, missus of O-ron-ia-ke-te: Sky Toucher, your very best scout."

"Who? Oh yes, yes, Sky Toucher. He's not here, he's gone home with the other scouts. But come in, you look frozen to the marrow. And famished, I'll wager. Sergeant Horrocks, go wake up the cook, tell him we have guests. Tell him bring hot soup. Come into my office, madam, come, come."

A fire blazed cozily in the grate. Dorr gave her two blankets, but she held off retiring to the adjacent small room he indicated, content for the time-being to remove only her mittens, hat, jacket and moccasins.

Sight of Dorr again stirred her resentment. She decided she disliked him even more close up than the last time she saw him, at the castle when he had singled out Sky Toucher: the first step along this dangerous trail. There was cunning in his smile for all its warmth; unscrupulousness in his eyes despite their twinkle. But as he looked at her, his focus wavered. Was his conscience troubling him?

Why wouldn't it! Didn't his responsibility for his pitchfork soldiers extend to his scouts? Weren't they just as much *soldiers?* The French considered their Moccasin allies *soldiers;* their Mohawk prisoner, as an enemy soldier, she was certain.

Dorr sat drumming his fingers and smiling tirelessly. "So tell me, Two Otters, what brings you here in such beastly weather?"

"We are after Sky Toucher. He was on his way home from here when lace-cuffs captured him. They had gathered in the woods not far from here. He walked right into them. Christittye Etsi saw it all from hiding."

"Who?"

"Copper Man."

"Oh yes, yes, the hand in the fire," Dorr recalled.

Suspicion stirred Singing Brook's mind. He already knew all this! Only how could he? Christittye Etsi had told her he'd come straight back to Tenotoge after seeing the capture. He hadn't mentioned seeing anyone who might be heading up here. Still, that didn't mean anything. Dorr could have learned of it in any one of a dozen ways. Traders came through here, friendly hunters. Anyone could have seen Sky Toucher with his captors farther up the line; how could they miss seeing such a large party? Four Otters droned on, almost apologetically, it sounded, as if preparing to ask a favor.

"You knew he was captured!" she burst, interrupting.

Dorr cleared his throat and studied his fingernails. "I . . . well, there *was* a rumor . . ."

"You have done nothing."

"We learned of it just yesterday, in fact; well, by now they have to be halfway down Lake Champlain."

"That is your excuse?" She pounded his desk and leaned over it, bringing her face uncomfortably close to his. "Why have you not sent a party to rescue him? The best scout you had. That is what you called him, I heard you!"

"And he was."

"Only now that you do not need him anymore, he is not worth bothering about, is that it? He volunteered!"

"That, dear madam, is the nub of it. I didn't force him to join us. There were no demands, he volunteered. He knew the risks, all of them did."

"Which should make you even more eager to rescue him—his bravery, his willingness to help you. Why do you not send someone!"

"I cannot."

"Why not!"

"If you'll please try to control yourself, I will explain."

"Tenäte Oÿoghi," said Four Otters.

"Explain!"

The soup arrived. Though it was venison and smelled delicious, she ignored it. Four Otters tasted his eagerly. Dorr went on, his tone taking on weariness.

"I haven't sent anyone after them because, as I have said, I cannot."

"You are the commander."

"Only of this garrison. I take my orders from headquarters in Albany. Tell her, Two Otters."

"His name is *Four* Otters."

"Sorry. I'm sure you're not aware of this and it may surprise you, but Nicholson is abandoned. The entire levy was relocated here only two days ago. Didn't you notice how crowded we are? Orders are to sit tight until spring, every man jack, sparing not a soul. I have that in writing. When winter is over an expedition will be setting . . ."

"Are you saying you cannot even ask men to volunteer, the way he did?"

"I'm saying I cannot spare . . ."

She shot to her feet. "Then forget I asked. We do not need your pitchfork soldiers." She swept her hand, sending the bowl clattering to the floor. "Or your soup. Cayere Tawyne, we are leaving!"

"But this soup is . . ."

"Leaving!"

"I am dreadfully sorry, madam." Dorr spread his hands appealingly.

"Keep your *sorrow*. The truth is Sky Toucher is not one of you. He is only a savage, and what is one savage's life, more or less? What is a *dog*'s!"

"That simply is not the case!"

Fumbling on her outer clothing, she glared at Four Otters. "Put on your shoes!"

"*Nyoh, nyoh.*" He glanced longingly at the steaming soup then began lacing on his snowshoes.

"You think you were wrong not to go with them?" she asked Four Otters. "They were the wrong ones!" She scowled at Dorr. "And all the while you smile and sit by your fire drinking your rum. You are as bad as the French! Worse. At least they do not abandon those who help them!"

"I tell you my hands are tied."

"Your neck should be! She growled, whipped out her knife and started for him. Four Otters sprang between them, but Dorr was already on his feet. Unruffled, he focused on the overturned bowl, the soup sinking into the dirt floor. He did not take his eyes from it as he went on.

"I'm beginning to feel foolish saying 'I'm sorry' over and over and trying to explain my position. Obviously, you're incapable of grasping it, so instead let me give you some advice—out of fondness and respect for your husband, greater, madam, than you can imagine.

"Don't do this. Don't continue to chase the wild goose. Even if you catch up you'll be helpless to rescue him. They'll capture and kill you."

"*Isa-ka-we!*"

"What?"

"Ingrate! Thankless whiteskin dog!"

She got on her snowshoes and clomped out, pulling Four Otters after her. Outside she hurried ahead of him as he struggled to catch up.

"That soup was so good," he muttered.

"*Ogechta!*"

"All right, all right."

"I will show him, I will show them all. Move!"

# 59

THEY HAD BEEN moving along steadily for hours under the stars, Singing Brook's indignation, her disgust with Dorr firing her stamina. She fumed and muttered. Four Otters finally called a halt.

"I am finished for today, I cannot go another step. Look, over there is a cave."

"With an *ochquoa* in it."

"There are more caves than bears," he said. "We can tell by the stink without going inside. I will look."

"Be careful."

The cave was unoccupied but reeked of dead vermin. They built a fire at the mouth.

"At least we get out of the wind tonight," murmured Four Otters.

"*Onewachten!* That is Dorr!"

When they had gathered fuel, he started the fire. He held his bare hands over the first flames. "Liar, *nyoh,* when we first got there he pretended he do not know O-ron-ia-ke-te had been captured. And he lied about his orders from Skä´neh-täh´de not to send anyone out until spring. His eyes gave him away."

"Filthy liar!"

"But not wrong," murmured Four Otters. "Look at it with his eyes. He has to count lives. O-ron-ia-ke-te is one life; to send out four or ten or twelve to try to rescue him would risk all their lives. They might not even get close to him. Men who send men into battle understand that."

"It is stupid! Heartless! This is his fault!"

"If you like. But that is how he has to think."

"You, too?"

She was going wild, glaring, working her fingers as if preparing to tear his eyes out. His heart went out to her.

"O-ron-ia-ke-te is my friend. When friends are in trouble you do not think of the risk. Let us get out some food. I wish an *aque* would cross our trail."

"Chasing it, cutting it up would take too much time. I have a feeling we are catching up to them. As you said, such a big party moves slowly."

"We need meat in us, Tenäte Oÿoghi."

"Eat your venison."

"It is salt, it is not enough and I am sick of it. You must be, too."

"I put it in me. I do not think about it. My stomach is grateful. Eat some, maybe tomorrow we will see another rabbit."

"That soup was so good, I can still taste it—"

"Don't you dare say that once more!" she hissed.

"All right, all right." A pause, they began eating. "They made it through the marshes and up to here. They may stop at Fort Carillon or further up at Fort St. Frédéric."

"Traveling at any pace they please knowing that Dorr cannot be bothered chasing them, he is too lazy, he does not care. And on top of all his other faults he carries a coward's heart. How could O-ron-ia-ke-te and Wotstaha Onirares join such a *kä-sa-de?* They knew what he was. *Nyoh,* worm, slimy, crawling . . ."

"At any rate we are going, three sleeps from now we will cross over into Sokoki Abnaki Territory. There they will be easy to follow."

She scanned the sky, still clear but the extreme cold persisted. "They will be if it does not snow again. We are wasting sleep time. Eat, sleep, get up, go on."

"How long can you go on?"

"How long can *you?* My strength comes from a deep well, Cayere Tawyne."

"Mine, too."

"*Nyoh.*"

Silence, save for the wind punishing the trees, tearing at the fire. They were almost done eating.

"You must be at a point where sleep does not restore you," murmured Four Otters, eying her worriedly.

"I am fine." She threw a handful of dry corn into her mouth and lay down.

Again he held his hands over the fire. "Should we let it burn?"

"You are the one who worries about fires being seen. Do as you like with it, I do not care."

"There is less risk down here than up above the border."

She sat up. "Oh? Are you suddenly afraid?"

"Not suddenly. Christittye Etsi said there are hundreds of raiders."

"And you wait till now to speak? So go back, I will go on alone. I planned to starting out."

"I would not desert you."

"No one is forcing you," she reminded him.

"I am sorry I brought it up. *Nyoh,* I am afraid. So are you. So what, I have come this far, I will go on."

She lay back down. He extinguished the fire and lay down beside her.

"I am sorry I snapped at you," she murmured. "It is not you but Dorr who upsets me. I could kill him! But why should we expect anything different? They hate us as much as the French do. To both we are no better than dogs. Only put here to bleed and die in their stupid wars. Liars! I hate them!"

But she was talking to the wind. He was snoring. She studied his face. He had every right to be afraid. It would be unnatural otherwise. What were they doing up here? Chasing Dorr's wild goose. Only what was the alternative, stay home, wait, wonder, worry herself back into a sickbed? Sky Toucher would never get away from his captors on his own. Somebody had to help.

She closed her eyes, the wind lulled her to sleep. Vines strangled the trees, twisting their dripping limbs grotesquely. The ground on which they stood was black, marshy and the trees themselves smooth-barked and gleaming with moisture. In the feeble light given off by the ground the trees stood about like crippled and wounded old warrors, too frightening-looking to evoke sympathy. Far ahead a bluish-green light appeared, rising slowly, a will-o-the wisp. Reaching its full height it curled at the top waving lightly, like a finger beckoning: a soft, slender rod of spectral light suspended just above the ground, the top bending slightly downward and to the side, gesturing her to approach.

Suddenly it vanished, displaced by the figure of a man. A Mohawk. Sky Toucher! There was no mistaking his posture. She could even make out his face—pinched and ghastly, the face of suffering; from the waist up he was naked, his flesh bruised and lacerated,

oozing blood from the larger wounds. Sweat glistened on his forehead, his eyes were hollow, staring. He had been caressed with
firebrands and beaten with branches by enemy squaws. Not to kill
him then and there, nothing so humane; he was meant to die slowly
and in agony. He looked half-dead already, so weakened he could
barely lift his arm.

She started toward him but her foot sank in the soft earth almost
up to her ankle, forcing her to pull it free. She stepped ahead but
the result was the same, as if she were walking on the bunched
heads of a crowd covered by mu, hands reaching up through it
to grasp her by the ankles and pull her down.

He raised both arms, waving them weakly, and she seemed to
be drawing closer. But then he began retreating, floating backwards, arms still upraised, fingers grasping, struggling to grab hold
of branches that passed him just out of reach. On she plodded.
His suffering hollowed his cheeks and etched lines either side of
his mouth. In the first few steps before he began to pull back she
had gotten close enough to see the agony in his eyes, so intense
they threatened to burst into flame. For a moment, a tree hid him,
then he reappeared. She cried out but no sound came from her
mouth. The will-o'-the-wisp reappeared behind him. Unaware, he
backed toward it. A faint radiance formed around him, outlining
him, edging gradually over him, closing until only the center of his
face and body could be seen and one arm breaking through it
beckoning. Then the light consumed him and began shrinking.

On she trudged, fighting the muck, reaching for him, silently
crying out. The light vanished slowly from the top down. She
panicked but then it reappeared to her left, almost the same distance from her. Rising, pulsing, parting, it revealed him gesturing.
Still losing blood, he looked even weaker. She started toward him.
She had only managed a few steps when he again began to retreat,
only this time she got closer before he disappeared in the light.

Twice more he reappeared, each time in a different place. The
fourth time she got within ten feet of him and imagined she could
hear his voice. But it was instead the plaintive sobbing of an infant,
the universal, constant, unrequited voice of pleading.

She could still see him when it began to rain. Icy droplets struck
her cheeks and bare arms, plashing him, too, washing away his

blood, revealing his raw wounds. His skin looked waxen, bluish. He was dying. She alone could save him; in his eyes she could see he was thinking that. But exhaustion was overtaking her, every step was like pulling her feet now turned to stone out of clay. Her legs became stone up to her thighs. The rain increased in intensity, but had no effect on the light when it showed again. It did not hiss or smoke, only outlined him then slowly enveloped him.

She waited and waited for him to reappear. And waited, wild with fear, exhausted, helpless, feeling him slip slowly out of the orbit of her possession.

# 60

TWO EAGLES WAS deep in a dream of Margaret, reprising the early part of the long journey back from Quebec. In his mind he saw what had turned out to be the only hazardous sequence, portaging the long stretch past the Richelieu River falls through enemy territory.

A loud shouting awoke him. He jerked upright. Splitting Moon was yelling and stabbing some creature, bringing his blade down again and again, snarling, his face twisted with pain. Shaking off the tattered edge of his dream, Two Eagles went to him. There lay a dead raccoon, its little bright yellow eyes reflecting the moon, its needle teeth crimson. It had bitten Splitting Moon in the calf through his leggins. Two Eagles helped him pull the garment off and together they examined the wound. The punctures looked deep, as if they had reached bone.

The raccoon was fully grown and undoubtedly starving to come out of its den, although raccoons did breed in the dead of winter. Apparently the smell of food had attracted it to their campsite.

"The pain is like quills hammered deep," muttered Splitting Moon, attempting gingerly to massage his leg, only to quit abruptly.

"It should be washed out," said Two Eagles. "There is more sickness in a raccoon than in any teeth in the woods. We should have some bitter root."

He washed the injury with snow and bandaged it with a clean

strip of deerskin, while Splitting Moon looked on wincing and scowling. His eyes strayed to the furry ball.

"It got deep," he murmured.

"The holes will close up. I just hope that no sickness gets into your blood."

Splitting Moon grunted. Two Eagles could see that the pain was getting worse. Splitting Moon got to his feet and balancing on his injured leg, kicked viciously at the dead animal, hurting his foot. His yell echoed through the trees. He retrieved his knife, staring at the bloodied blade.

"I warn you, there is sickness in him," said Two Eagles.

"You do not know that for certain. Can you see it in his blood?"

"It is there, all are sick. It is from eating *teki-do-sah-wä,* vermin too long dead."

"He was not sick. Look at his eyes, are they sick eyes?"

"We shall see. Can you fall asleep?"

"*Nyoh,* of course."

"Then do, and do not wake me again. You ruined a perfectly good dream."

# 61

THE NEXT NIGHT the raiders camped on the west shore of the lake, as they had the night before. Stone Pipe relented and undid Sky Toucher's wrist bonds. Occasionally the Caughnawaga released him after the camp fell asleep, knowing that it was all but impossible for his captive to sleep tied up.

Stone Pipe spoke: "The usual warning, Cousin, do not try to get away. Do not repay my kindness by getting me shot."

Sky Toucher grunted.

"Is that *nyoh* or *neh?*"

"I will not try."

"There is still food in that pot over there. Untie your own ankles, but not until I am out of sight."

They were surrounded by snoring. Occasional laughter could be heard. The tremulous, descending wail of a screech owl heard earlier had not sounded since the onset of darkness. Stone Pipe trudged off. Sky Toucher watched him vanish in the trees, sat up and undid his ankles. The Caughnawaga would return before dawn to retie him, to avoid possible reprimand or worse, if the turkey cock himself found out.

If Stone Pipe believed Sky Toucher when he said he wouldn't try to escape, he deserved to be shot. Were they not at war? These days were as red as any bleeding days. He massaged his wrists. How far up the lake had they come? It was still barely a musket shot from shore to shore. At Fort St. Frédéric it was three times this width, only how far ahead was that? His captors knew, and they would likely head back toward the eastern shore to avoid it. The turkey cock would not want to explain his disastrous defeat to the post commander. Sky Toucher reflected how the French called it Fort St. Frédéric when they took the area and built a fort and stone tower, and how the English had tried to take the place any number of times since but so far without success.

He crept over to the pot and dug out a handful of stew. It tasted slightly bitter, not deer—maybe otter? It was cold and greasy, with small bones, but he was starving. He began to gorge. It hit his stomach and back up it came. He melted snow between his hands and sipped it to cleanse his mouth and throat, then attacked a second helping, this time more slowly. The stew sat like a stone in the pit of his stomach, but he kept it down.

By this time, other than the guards posted in a circle around them, even out on the lake itself, the entire camp slept. Sky Toucher heard only snoring, no laughter, no talking. Time to leave. Being left untied at night at least three times previously, he had hesitated to attempt escape, knowing they'd assume he'd try. But now was as good a time as any. He resolved to head toward Fort Frédéric. When they discovered he was gone that would be the last direction they'd think he'd take. He would get up to within sight of the stone tower then cut sharply west for the mountains.

From then on he'd duplicate his earlier journey, in the same conditions, perhaps even more severe and more than twice the distance to Fort Anne. Too bad it was a clear night, but he could not wait for the overcast, which might not come until the Richelieu River. If only he could get hold of a knife.

From one cookfire he crawled to the next, about fifteen paces from the edge of the camp. He had no idea how many guards were posted or where, how far apart. All the sleepers he had passed so far kept their knives under their jackets. On he crawled slowly, the wind coming up loud enough to wake light sleepers, but no one slept lightly after walking all day under these conditions. He passed uncomfortably close to a sleeping Abnaki who rolled over and stared at him. Sky Toucher's heart stopped, the man's eyes looked through him, slowly closed. He was asleep.

He sucked in an icy breath and crawled on. He came around a tree, pulled himself up to a sitting position and leaned against it gasping, as much out of nervousness as from exertion. He failed to hear the soft steps to his right and behind him until the last two. They stopped, he held his breath. A knife came around in front of him, moonlight striking the blade against his jugular vein. He stiffened.

Stone Pipe. Holding his knife in place, he came around front leering, kneeling before him.

"A question, Cousin, did you really think I was so stupid as to believe you?" Sky Toucher grunted and felt the edge draw across the pulsing vein roping his neck then the tip pricked it lightly. "That would be inexcusably stupid, so do not disappoint me and say *nyoh*." Again he pricked him. "You lied, Cousin, tell me why I should not open this big vein and dress you in red?" Again he pricked him.

"Do it."

"I am tempted."

"What are you waiting for?"

"*Ogechta!*"

"I know. You need time to think. Think what the turkey cock will do to you if you kill me."

"He will thank me, he will give me a bottle!"

"Will he? I am his prize prisoner, his excuse for defeat. He dearly wants me alive to show his long-knife chief. His proof that he did not fail in his duty, that he was lured into a trap and I was responsible. Think about it, *Cousin*."

Stone Pipe's eyes said he was thinking. "I could kill you and tell him I had to, to keep you from getting away. His orders, *neh?*"

"*Neh*. What he said was 'Do not let him get away, if he does *you* are dead.' He said nothing about killing me. Kill me and he will shoot you."

"*Neh*."

"If you are willing to take that chance, slice away. Or we go back to your fire, back to sleep, pretend none of this happened."

"You really think I *am* stupid."

"Not at all, just caught in the middle."

"Freeing you was not my idea, it was Jankanque Karackwero's. She said 'Untie him, watch him take the bait.' It took a while but you finally did. She said, 'Follow him, stop him just before he tries to sneak between the guards.' I said he knows better than to try. He is smart like a crow, he will know it is a trap. I was wrong. And you are right, I may be jumping into a snake pit if I kill you. Besides, I owe you to her."

"*Owe?*"

"I told her if she was right she could have you tomorrow for her and her friends to caress."

"Thank you." He raised a hand against Stone Pipe's wrist and gently pushed away the knife. "How sad it is for us."

"For *you*," Stone Pipe corrected him.

"You, too. We would be together in the Mohawk Valley, perhaps even in Tenotoge, and close friends if not for the whiteskins. They break us apart, Onea Canonou, *they* make us enemies."

"That is true, O-ron-ia-ke-te, but what can we do about it? The hole was long ago burnt in the blanket. What is really sad is that one of us is sure to end up killing the other."

"I have killed Abnakis but never a Caughnawaga."

Stone Pipe grunted. "I have killed Valley Mohawks, maybe some from your castle." He squinched his dark face. "I did not enjoy it at the time, it put a taste in my mouth like grapes too old, but the black robes explained that it was not a sin. To destroy one's enemies will not prevent one from entering God's heaven."

"You believe that?"

"*Nyoh*, why would they lie? Lying is a sin."

"They are whiteskins, have you ever known one to tell the truth? Maybe Tékni-ska-je-a-nah's English wife, but none other."

Again Stone Pipe grunted and looked off over the lake. The

sky appeared to be losing its darkness over the snow-armored Green Mountains, the stars were fading.

"Up."

Sky Toucher got wearily to his feet.

"Move fast and low back to the fire. From now on you sleep tied hand and foot."

## 62

NORTHWARD DOWN LAKE Champlain ventured Singing Brook and Four Otters. Since he'd confessed his fears inside the cave, guilt had crept into her conscience. Was he going through with this merely to preserve face? He insisted that Sky Toucher was all the reason he needed to help her, he could not let his friend down. He no doubt believed that, but it failed to ease her misgivings. Though friends helped friends, they didn't necessarily lay down their lives for them.

Perhaps she wouldn't feel so if she could convince herself that they had a fighting chance at rescuing Sky Toucher. Plain common sense declared they didn't. Still she had to try, and if she was destined to die in the attempt, so be it. That would solve everything, for she couldn't go on living without him.

Only this failed to consider Four Otters. It was almost as if he were intruding into their personal showdown with fate. She eyed him askance beside her. She could certainly use his skills—he was quick with a knife, accurate with bow and arrow—but to sacrifice his life . . .

"What are you thinking?" he asked.

"Nothing important."

He grinned. "You would rather not say."

"If you must know, I still feel guilty about dragging you along."

"Not as guilty as I felt about not going with them. So, are we even?"

"If anything were to happen to you . . ."

"If it happens to me it will probably happen to you. Forget

about me, Tenäte Oÿoghi, think of me as just a traveling companion who happens to be going in the same direction."

"You are a good man, Cayere Tawyne, a real man."

"Some would disagree with that."

"They do not know you like I do."

"*Do* you know me?"

"I think so."

"You know nothing about me. How could you?" He smiled. "I see the question in your eye."

"What question?"

"You are wondering if I am a berdache."

"I . . ."

He waggled a reproving finger. "*Nyoh*. It is all right, do not be embarrassed. You know what our people believe, that the moon appears to Iroquois boys during *o-sag-e-te* . . ."

"Puberty."

"That it offers the boy a choice: a bow or a hoe. If he hesitates in reaching for the bow, the moon gives him the hoe." He grinned. "I hate to disappoint you, Tenäte Oÿoghi, but I took the bow. And carried it ever since. I have never desired to lie with a man."

"I had no right to suspect . . ."

"You think you are the only one? It is funny—"

"What?"

A goshawk dove directly in front of them, heavy-bodied with a dark blue-gray back, black crown, pale underparts. The instant it came into Singing Brook's view, Four Otters whipped out an arrow and let fly. Missing, but just barely. She held his arm, keeping him from a second try. The goshawk had seized its prey, a snow-white rabbit neither Mohawk had seen; the bird flapped vigorously to gain altitude.

The speed of Four Otters' reaction amazed Singing Brook. They moved forward, he retrieved the arrow, restoring it to his quiver.

"I should have hit him; there goes a good meal."

"I think he is hungrier than we are. I did not even see that rabbit."

"White on white."

"You said it is funny, what is?"

"I should not say it."

"You have to now."

"You will think me an *odasqueta,* an old squaw spreading nonsense, only this is true."

"Speak."

"Christittye Etsi." He nodded.

"I—"

"You do not believe it? It is true."

"Copper Man? Well, his eyes . . ."

"If you look closely they give him away, *neh?* Not so. Anyone can be one, they do not have to show anything."

"O-ron-ia-ke-te never said . . ."

"He does not know. Christittye Etsi hides it well. I would never have known myself if I did not accidentally stumble upon him. I was swimming by myself in the Te-ugé-ga, I came out and was putting on my breechclout when I heard a rustling in the bushes. I looked. He was there with Tali—Crane—who died in the ambush on the road between the forts. Do not ask me what they were doing."

"Christittye Etsi, he stuck his hand in the fire," she said.

"Should a berdache be any less brave? Maybe that's enough talk about it."

They went on. Afternoon was surrendering its brightness to the shadows when suddenly, bounding out of the woods onto the lake came a doe. From her movements, she did not even see them. His arrow drove cleanly through her neck, she lay sad-eyed, crimson droplets beading the snow.

"Now we have to stop," he murmured. "I will skin it and cut up the good parts in no time. Leave the rest for the goshawks and other birds."

She set a skewer stick holding fat chunks of the meat across two forked sticks. The meat was delicious, they ate to near bursting, tempted to discard the salt venison they had packed, so much more savory was the fresh venison. They shared a haunch and the tender tongue of meat found under the bone of the saddle.

It was growing warmer, there was no wind. Under the bright

sky their aches and pains seemed diminished. As well they were making excellent time.

"How long is this half of the lake?" she asked.

"From South Bay a little more than ten leagues."

"We should be nearing the end."

"*Nyoh,* across from where Andia-ta-roc-te ends on the other side of the mountains between." He sobered. There, we will be entering Sokoki Territory."

"How long is the northern half of the lake?"

"Longer. To the headwaters of the O-chog-wä, at least four sleeps, even moving fast." He shook his head resignedly. "Look at us, Tenäte Oÿoghi."

"What?"

"We look *too* Mohawk."

"I thought about that, but what can we do?"

He shrugged. "Hope that it is dark when we meet any Sokokis. Have you eaten enough? Can we sleep now?"

"No need to ask, just lay back."

He surveyed the trees across the lake. "The wind may come up. Shall we make a lean-to?"

"*Neh,* I am too tired to work. Let us take a chance it will not. It does not look like snow. Should we not pack the rest of the *aque* to take along?

"Leave it uncovered, it will freeze faster and not get rancid."

"You know so much that is helpful, I would never have gotten this far without you."

"*Nyoh,* you would, you are like a mother lynx: tough, fearless, and you do not hesitate. You make up your mind quick, like a goshawk going for the rabbit. Too bad you are a woman, you would make a fine warrior, even a great one."

"I am content to be a woman. Not expected to run off and fight with the whiteskin dogs."

"Are we on that again?"

"*Neh,* I will spare you."

"I had a dream last night," he said. "I dreamt that you saved him."

"*We.*"

"*Neh,* only you."

"Where were you?"

"I did not see me in my dream, I do not know."

She nodded "You will be there when the time comes."

"I wonder."

"I had a dream the other night, too. I saw him bruised, bleeding. He had been caressed. It frightened me. If only he survives until we can catch up."

"He is very strong, very stubborn. He will not give them the satisfaction of dying." Four Otters nodded determinedly.

She yawned. "I wonder how far ahead they are . . ."

"Soon we will be passing their fires. They will be warmer and warmer. We will catch up before the O-chog-wä River. Go to sleep, tomorrow this meat will carry us twice as far as we made today, you will see."

Catch up. And what then? What clever trick could they pull to bring the outrageous odds against them better into balance?

# 63

SO FITFULLY DID Splitting Moon sleep the rest of the night, Two Eagles kept waking up. Dawn arrived milky and cold, with not a breath of wind. The crows in the treetops looked frozen to their perches. Two Eagles glanced over at his friend, and gasped. Splitting Moon's leg was badly swollen and the uncovered area an ominous shade of blue. Feeling Two Eagles' eyes he came fully awake wincing, clenching his teeth.

"Your leg . . ."

"It is all right."

"It looks like a melon. Let me see." Two Eagles pressed closer.

"Never mind. If I say it is all right it is! Let us get out of here."

They started out, Splitting Moon in the lead, his teeth set so hard Two Eagles feared he would crack them. His pain was excruciating and obvious, despite his best efforts to hide it. He walked about fifty yards before his leg gave way and down he fell. Two Eagles knelt and examined it.

"Are you thinking what I am thinking?" he asked.

"And how would I know what you are thinking?"

"It is filled with poison."

Splitting Moon scoffed, "The good blood will drink up the bad and weaken the poison to harmlessness."

"It will climb up your leg past your knee, up into your body and stop your heart, take your life from you like a quick knife in the gut. My friend, it has to come off."

"*Neh!*"

"Do you want to live?"

"Not with one leg, not like Do-wa-sku-ta with his hands and feet lopped off. He did not want to live. Me, either. Not a cripple, not me. Leave it alone!"

"Tyagohuens, look at me. I have to cut it off."

Two Eagles could see illness glazing his friend's dark eyes. He was pale, sweating, running a fever. His leg was even larger since he had awakened and the flesh as hard as stone. But it was the bluish-white color that worried Two Eagles. He had seen the condition before in men's arms and hands. If he removed the leg right away, cutting it off just below the knee, he could save his life. If he waited . . .

"We will make a fire."

Splitting Moon sat shaking his head from side to side, gnawing his lower lip against the pain.

"Look at me, listen," said Two Eagles. "I will have to break the bone before I cut."

"*Nyoh.*"

Splitting Moon's sudden willingness to cooperate surprised Two Eagles. "Break the bone, cut through and *je-na-gah* the wound with fire. There will be pain like you have never known before."

"*Nyoh.*"

Two Eagles started a fire, cutting the limb of a hemlock to use as a brand. He hated this, destroying his best friend's leg and with it his heart. His own hand rendering him a cripple, relying on a crutch to drag himself about. Ending his days as a proud warrior with one blow of the tomahawk.

But Splitting Moon would live. Once cauterized, the stump would close and heal. Two Eagles pondered, if only he had a Dutch cutter, the piece of steel with jagged teeth that the *kristoni Asseroni* traders used to cut wood. His eyes strayed to Splitting Moon's tooth-ball tomahawk. He would break the bone with it and with his own sharp-edged tomahawk chop through, then finish with his knife.

He tied a tourniquet tightly just above the knee and handed Splitting Moon a stick. "Bite down hard and do not look."

"I want to see . . ."

"Bite, bite!"

He bit hard. Two Eagles swung. The tooth-ball tomahawk smashed his leg just below the knee. Splitting Moon shrieked, the echo assaulting them from the woods, the stick dropping from his jaws. Quickly, Two Eagles struck with his own tomahawk, shattering the broken bone so that he could cut straight through.

He slashed expertly, blood spurted, crimsoning his hands, as Splitting Moon screamed in agony. Snatching up the brand, Two Eagles cauterized the wound. Splitting Moon felt nothing. He had passed out.

Splitting Moon did not regain consciousness until the sun was well up the sky. Two Eagles sat on his haunches patiently waiting, watching. When at last he woke, he looked down at his stump and grunted. While he was unconscious Two Eagles had fashioned a crutch for him. Now he turned his back to pick it up and show him. In that instant Splitting Moon jerked out his knife, set the point against his stomach and rolled onto it, jamming it up to the hilt.

"*Neh!*" shrilled Two Eagles.

He lunged. Too late, it was all over.

Two Eagles sat back gawking in disbelief. "*Neh, neh, neh . . .*"

He cradled Splitting Moon in his arms, staring down at him. In his face was a serenity, relief that the pain was no more, that he was to be spared the frustration and embarrassment of living on as a cripple. Two Eagles' mind whirled back over the years to the day he, Margaret, Splitting Moon and the others traveled by canoe down the Kanawage. Again he saw Thrown Bear sitting on the rock, his remaining hand and both feet cruelly severed, all four stumps blackened with pitch.

*"Di-wä-tah-le-ä-na!"*

Kill me! Spare me this pain and misery, spare me the cripple's helplessness! Without hesitation he had nocked an arrow and let it fly. Straight into Thrown Bear's heart it sped. It was all he could do for his friend, the best he could do.

Once more he looked down at Splitting Moon in his arms. Death was the only solution.

"Good-bye, old friend."

He set a hand against Splitting Moon's cheek then slowly withdrew the knife. He looked about. He could cut poles, erect a scaffold. Using his clothing he would cover his friend's body, especially his face, to protect his eyes from birds. When spring thawed the ground, he would return, and retrieve the body. Bring it back to Onneyuttahage and bury it properly.

Until that time he would mourn his friend.

# 64

THE SQUAWS HAD been gathering slender branches before daylight. Now they formed a circle around the still sleeping Sky Toucher. Stone Pipe awoke first, prodded his captive and untied him. Sky Toucher sat up, massaging his wrists and ankles. The gathering stared.

Stone Pipe snickered. "Now it is Jankanque Karackwero and her friends' turn. I must keep my word, *neh?*"

Sky Toucher grunted.

"Stand up, take off all your clothes except your moccasins."

"You want me to catch a cold before I die?"

"They will not kill you, only caress. You tried to get away, you do not expect to go unpunished. Let me help you with your jacket."

Sky Toucher grunted. "You are too kind, Cousin."

As he stripped, the stinging cold struck his sensitive areas. Warriors and French Canadians joined the circle of onlookers. The turkey cock came out of his tent yawning, stretching, bleary-eyed.

"What is going on?"

"The prisoner tried to escape last night, Colonel," said Stone Pipe. "I caught him."

"Lucky for you."

Ramesay approached Sky Toucher. "And what are you up to, *sauvage,* going for a roll in the snow?"

Stone Pipe explained. Many of the women had lit torches. Flames licked the frigid air. The colonel's fat face furrowed as Stone Pipe rambled on.

"*Mais non,* they will destroy him!"

"*Neh,* only give him enough pain so that he will hesitate to try again. His skin will taste the fire, he will see his blood, he may pass out—they usually do—but he will not die, Colonel. Caressing does not kill."

"I'll take your word for it, only let's just call a halt anyway. You, Mohawk, put your clothes back on. You are not a pleasant sight before breakfast."

"But, Colonel," persisted Stone Pipe, "caressing is a sacred ritual. It has been decided."

"*You* decide about *my* prisoner? Don't be *ridicule!*"

"His actions invited it, the women have every right, they will be very disappointed."

"Think how disappointed *I* will be if someone accidentally kills him. *Mais non,* out of the question, we've no time for such *sottise.* We must be moving on, I want to make it to the headwaters of the Richelieu by nightfall."

"Colonel . . ."

"Enough! You are beginning to annoy me. They can have their *partie,* but not now, not till we're well down the river. Then, if somebody should overdo it, they can carry him the rest of the way. This sort of foolishness can easily get out of hand. You, put your clothes back on. Tell them, Caughnawaga."

Stone Pipe relayed the order. A groan raced around the circle. Faces darkened and fell, the women glared contemptuously at Sky Toucher. One old squaw moved to heave her torch at the colonel. Her friends caught her and quenched the flame in the snow. Very-beautiful-sun came striding over to Stone Pipe, furious, scowling at the prisoner. She spat at him; Sky Toucher ignored her, adjusting his breechclout before restoring his leggins.

"Now, now, Jankanque Karackwero, do not blame him," said Stone Pipe. "Go spit at the commander." She turned, he caught her shoulder. "*Neh, neh,* please, you heard him. He is not forbidding it, only postponing it until we get closer to Stadacona. Then he will be all yours, you can caress him to your heart's content."

Reprieve. Sky Toucher sighed inwardly, he had never been caressed, though he had seen it. It was a spectacle reserved for prisoners of war and could be excruciatingly painful for the victim. If the victim was a despised enemy whom his antagonists knew had murdered their son or father, they could be merciless, flaying and searing him for as long as a day and a night before he passed out for the last time. Generally, though, caressing was considered public amusement, producing bleeding and burns but rarely any lasting damage. If the victim died, it was accidental.

Now fully dressed, Sky Toucher tried to control his shivering. The gathering dispersed and the raiders broke camp and were moving before the sun had stretched the width of a man's hand above the ridge of the Green Mountains.

So the turkey cock planned to reach the Richelieu today. If they did, and camped in the woods near either bank, that night he would try again. He'd failed to induce Stone Pipe to untie him at night, but his captor had relented in one respect: he now tied Sky Toucher's wrists in front of him, which made it more comfortable lying down. Unfortunately he was tied expertly, with so much rawhide, that he would be wasting his time trying to bite his way free.

His ankles, however, were another matter. Because they had to be untied each morning, Stone Pipe fastened them much less securely. And with his hands now in front of him, even with his wrists tied, Sky Toucher found he could easily reach down and free his ankles. It seemed unforgivably careless of his captor. But perhaps it was deliberate. Perhaps he wanted his "cousin" to make a second try.

Very-beautiful-sun did. She wanted him dead. He read it in her greasy face every time she looked at him. Was she thinking of attacking him while he slept? She couldn't care less about the turkey cock. Stone Pipe was the only one who could control her.

Taking her knife in his heart was not a death a self-respecting

Mohawk warrior would choose. To die at the hands of such a homely, disgustingly dirty, smelly, pebble-brained Abnaki *cannawarorie* was a fate, consideration of which, greatly disturbed him. Yet it did give him another reason to escape.

Stone Pipe pushed his shoulder, hurrying him along.

# 65

THE TURKEY COCK realized his hope. Just as twilight came softly fingering through the woodlands, they reached the north shore of Lake Champlain and the headwaters of the Richelieu River. From there it meandered about seven leagues to where the rapids began, tumbling wildly for about four leagues. Where the rapids ended, a fourteen-league stretch began, terminating in the St. Lawrence at Sorel. Stockaded villages called *cotés* were built along both banks of the river, becoming numerous just past the midway point between the headwaters and the St. Lawrence. Where Lake Champlain ended and the river began, there were a number of islands, chief among them Ile-aux-Noix. It was uninhabited. An attempt had been made to erect a fort there—to command the lake much as Fort Frontenac commanded Lake Ontario at the headwaters of the St. Lawrence—but the work was halted for lack of funds. In time nature regained possession until now wild growth all but totally concealed the partially erected walls.

Even before the island came into view, Sky Toucher decided that he would wait no longer. He would escape that night before the raiders started down the river and past French settlements. The more deserted the woods, the better his chances in spite of his unfamiliarity with the area.

As before, he would head west before turning south. It would be many days before he reached the point where he started south after his last escape. From that point, as he recalled, it had been only five days to Fort Anne. He dreaded to think how long it would take this time. To add to his difficulties, he was in poorer physical shape. He had lost weight, he had eaten little substantial food since his capture. It was just as cold as the last time, conditions perhaps even harsher. Worst of all he was deep in enemy territory. He had no idea how close to the river the north-south trail might be, nor did he know the location of Abnaki villages, Jesuit missions, French settlements and forts.

In such unfamiliar surroundings, traveling by night would be out of the question, at least until he found a trail. As well, the cold would be much more severe at night. He had only the two tattered blankets for protection. His moccasins were holding up well, but he had no snowshoe, though his leggins were in good condition and protected him all the way up to his crotch. His jacket was fine, but he had no protection for his head or his hands, no muffler to stave off frostbite. He had no fire, no food, no weapon.

He could not fish or trap. He could only catch an animal by hand, sneak up on it, brain it with a stick, eat it raw. That would take precious energy.

Happily, even in the dead of winter there was other food out here, if one knew what to look for. *Akoanti*, straight coral fungus, could be found on exposed decaying wood. Tough and bitter, it was even harder to get down than *tripes de roches,* the lichen resembling tripe, which could be found clinging to stream rocks. Boiled down *it* was slimy and tasted like glue, with an even fouler odor. Starving *coureurs de bois* ate it; its solitary virtue was that it went down fast. A starving Mohawk would prefer to fall back on basswood bark, as he had himself on more than one occasion. *Tripes de roches* and *akoanti* were last resorts.

He might find berries, dried out but still edible. And like *akoanti* there was ashy coral—white fungus turned gray in winter, but still edible. He would look out for *oněň sǎ wá ně*, stalked puffball, delicious when young, slightly bitter by now, but edible. Most puffballs were, but the stalked were one of the few funghi that survived the winter cold. Brown-capped *oněňsǎ* were tasty, with white gills and smooth, silvery-gray stems that thrived in dead leaves.

He reflected on other potential obstacles: it was late March, and despite the cold bears were beginning to emerge from hibernation. He might also encounter an occasional lynx or a wolf: even the worst weather did not discourage wolves in their search for food.

But within a few days, as the earth tilted and the northlands once again angled toward the sun, the temperatures would warm. By that time, he hoped, he would be close to where he started south the first time. From that point on traveling should be easier, something he'd desperately need when his stamina and endurance would have all but given out.

He did not doubt that he would get away this time. Now the sky was overcast, the oncoming night promised to be starless and without a moon. Still, once he got a mile or two from camp his problems would begin. In his weakened condition, weariness would overtake him early. Four, even three nights from tonight, he could collapse from exhaustion, plunge into sleep curled up like an opossum and freeze to death before morning.

He had to be supremely patient, he told himself, resisting the temptation to walk too far, and at the first sign of exhaustion quit— while he still had the strength to seek a place to sleep out of the wind and find food.

Dangerous animals didn't worry him, nor did finding food. But the cold did. What he wouldn't give for a bear robe to wrap in while he slept. What he wouldn't give for a knife!

He thought about her. By now she must have given up on him and gone into mourning. How could he blame her? Making her suffer so pinched his conscience. Why did he volunteer when nobody urged him to—other than Wotstaha Onirares—particularly when she was so set against it? If she'd been the least bit agreeable to the idea, would he have had second thoughts? What was he doing, blaming her? Clearly, it boiled down to one fact: nobody, least of all his wife, could tell him what to do.

What a fool he was, she deserved so much better. Stone Pipe came over.

"The river at last, Cousin. At this end, Abnaki lands; at the other end, New France. A word of advice, if you are planning to escape do not wait until the other end. You might get away from me, but you would never get through the French settlements. They are as thick up there as mosquitoes on the Te-uǵe-ga in July. But what am I saying? You will not try a second time." He squatted and smirked. "You would not do that to me, your cousin, your friend. Force me to cover my knife with your blood."

"That could be very costly for you, Cousin."

"Do not think I have not thought long and hard about that. I have decided that in your heart, you could not bring yourself to leave me to the colonel's anger."

"*Neh,* I would much rather stay and end up being hung like a deer for the amusement of your masters."

"What masters?"

"You Praying Mohawks have put yourselves under the black robes' thumbs and so under the lace-cuffs'. Do you deny that?"

"You are wrong, you have been with the English so long your eyes are turning blue. We are the Canadians' allies, their friends, not under their thumbs. The black robes you so like to sneer at have opened our eyes, have brought us to Christ. Their cross is our cross, their God and heaven, our God and heaven. It is you godless sinners we left in the Valley who are under the thumb— of the English. You would be home in bed with your woman if you were not under their control, doing their bidding, their slaves."

"Mohawks are not slaves," Sky Toucher snorted.

"What do you call it when your life is not your own, when you do as others order you, even walk into guns?"

"We are their allies as you are allies to the French. It is the same."

Stone Pipe chuckled. "How blind you are, how stupid. It is not the same. The French have brought us to Christ. Whatever we may do for them in appreciation—that, Cousin, is our great reward. His most precious blood is our most precious gift, not guns, not cloth or useless trinkets. Your English cannot bring you to Christ because they are unbelievers."

"They are Christians."

"Not true Christians, not Catholics."

"Whatever happened to your own religion, the Religion of the Spirits, so sacred to all our people? Is it all forgotten, tossed into the kettle and boiled away, the religion of your fathers and their fathers? Tell me, Cousin, what do your friends the black robes say about our religion?"

"Nothing."

"Ha!"

"All right, they say it is worthless, that Christian is the only religion, Jesus our redeemer, God Almighty, our Father who rules in heaven. And once we are baptized, if we keep free of sin, if we confess our sins and they are wiped away, when this life is over we will enter the kingdom of heaven. As surely as my nose is in the middle of my face. What do you say to that?"

"I say help me inside, I want to sleep."

"Sleep well, you have two more days."

"Until what?"

"Your caressing, have you forgotten so soon? We will be half-way to the St. Lawrence. Any time from then on the women will come asking for you and I will have to hand you over. Not that I am eager to, but . . ."

"You must keep your word to Jankanque Karackwero."

"*Nyoh.*"

He dragged Sky Toucher inside, letting the bear robe flap fall behind them.

"Good night, Cousin, sleep well."

Sky Toucher grunted.

# 66

TWO EAGLES PRESSED on alone, carrying the tragedy like a boulder on his shoulders, hurrying more often than common sense would advise, as if to escape the horror of Splitting Moon's death even as he fled the site of it. His friend had not hesitated; the instant Two Eagles turned his back to get the crutch, into Splitting Moon's gut drove his knife. And so began his long journey to the Village of the Dead to join Thrown Bear, Bone the Mohican adoptee, Anger Maker, Red Paint and Fox.

That left Two Eagles the lone survivor. All his friends were dead. He knew everyone at Onneyuttahage, but no others were his friends, warriors who had fought by his side, with whom he hunted and fished and traveled to Stadacona to restore Margaret to her husband-by-proxy. Their friends' shades would welcome Splitting Moon's shade. There by day they would sleep, by night hunt and fish, do whatever they pleased except make war.

The Village of the Dead: where skillful hunters, brave warriors, men of influence and consideration went after death, while the lazy, the cowardly and weak were doomed to eat snakes and ashes in dreary regions of mist and unending darkness.

When would his life be snatched from him? When would he set out on the long journey through the dark forests to the Village of the Dead? Arriving there he would sit all day in the crouching position of the sick, and, when night came, hunt the shades of animals, with the shades of bows and arrows, among the shades of trees and rocks: for all things, animate and inanimate, were alike immortal, and were to be found there? There was O-na-geh, the swift river that had to be crossed on a log that shook under your feet, while a ferocious dog blocked the way, driving many into the abyss. The river was filled with fish, which the shades speared for food. Beyond was a narrow path between moving rocks that each instant crashed together, grinding to bits the less agile travelers.

But when his time came *he* would make it, pushed forward by the knowledge that he would be reunited with Splitting Moon and his other friends.

He stopped, lifted his eyes straight upward and let forth a primal scream. It tore his throat; so loud was it, he fancied he tasted blood. When the echo had died away he turned and looked back. He had come much too far from the scaffold to be able to see it still.

"Tyagohuens, Tyagohuens, what have I done to you?"

Murdered him. Turned his back, giving him two blinks of an eye to kill himself. How could he be so careless? Why had he not foreseen it? Knowing him, how proud he was, how fierce in combat, how could a man like that go on unwhole, a cripple? The pain he could bear—the shame of it, never.

"Tyagohuens."

He thought of the others: Do-wa-sku-ta, Thrown Bear, who wore his severed hand hanging from a string of rawhide around his neck. Closer than brothers they had been from childhood. Closer, to be sure, than he ever was to So-hat-tis, Long Feather, his only surviving brother, surviving until a Mohawk warrior had taken his life, for which Two Eagles had made him surrender his own.

Sa-ga-na-qua-de, Anger Maker, He-who-makes-everyone-angry, with his booming voice, foul-smelling pipe, his argumentative ways, his talent for stirring up trouble between even his friends. O-kwen-cha, who had spilled more lace-cuff and French moccasin blood than any three other Oneidas. In a single battle during the seven years of red days he had killed fourteen Ottawas and then tortured to death two French dragoons.

Sku-nak-su, Fox, who wore proudly a French major's scalp dangling from his belt and around his neck a crucifix taken from a black robe whose throat he had opened when the man pressed him too hard, too loudly, to embrace the cross. Fox had married Teklqʔ-eyo, Two Eagles' Aunt Eight Minks, who had brought up him and Long Feather after the deaths of their parents. Eight Minks was three times Fox's age and longed to chase the loneliness from her life with a husband, only to lose him two moons later to the Montagnais up on the Kanawage.

And Bone the Mohican adoptee, his friend from across the Shaw-na-taw-ty who had married Swift Doe after Long Feather's death and who had himself died at the hands of the renegade Ossivenda Oÿoghi, Blue Creek.

All of them gone, even small Benjamin, his son. All, leaving him and Margaret and a dwindling number of Oneidas to confront an uncertain future.

# 67

THROUGH SLITS IN the birch-bark siding Sky Toucher could see that it was black out. He yawned, fully awake. The Abnakis around him slept the sleep of the predawn, huddled tightly together. In the darkness he could not see Stone Pipe nearby, but from his distinctive wheezing snore, Sky Toucher knew he was there. He figured that while he slept, the Caughnawaga had left the dwelling to seek out Very-beautiful-sun to lie with. Sky Toucher wished he could have left while his captor was away, but he was too tired to stay awake.

An old woman, the one who had threatened the turkey cock

with her torch, lay beside him, her face inches from his own, her fetid breath invading his nostrils. Slowly, he sat up, easily undid his ankles and let his eyes grow accustomed to the darkness. He was barely able to make out Stone Pipe's hulking, huddled figure.

He waited, hoping his eyesight would sharpen further. It did not. He tested his wrist bonds. When he was well on his way, he would find an exposed sharp stone and sever them.

The stench hanging in the air was nauseating. Settling back down on one shoulder, he flattened his cheek against the floor and filled his lungs with the fragrance of the spruce boughs. Then getting to his feet, taking care to avoid disturbing the old woman, he probed gently with his toe, picked his way through the sleepers to the entrance.

Outside, so fresh was the air he filled and emptied his lungs repeatedly. It was bitter cold out, much colder than when he'd gone to sleep. There was no light, no wind, no night sounds—the silence was a giant fist closing on him. He held his breath and looked about; he exhaled in relief as he established that he was the only one awake. Now that the raiders were deep into Abnaki Territory there was no longer any need for night guards. Clear of the camp, there would be no one to stop him, at least in front of him. Turning this over in mind, he started as the moon slid into view like a malevolent eye, its beams painting the snow-encrusted floor of the woods in a deathly sheen.

He started out at a lope, threading through the trees, moving directly west, sending up great clouds of breath, the cold clamping and stinging his face. He rubbed his bound fists against his jacket to generate warmth.

Stone Pipe would be the first one to come after him, having the most to lose by his escape. Stone Pipe—"Cousin." The little things he said confused him. Why had he mentioned that the French settlements became more numerous about halfway down the Richelieu? Was that a warning? Then there was his habit of tying his ankles so carelessly. A child could free them.

It was obvious Stone Pipe had come to like him but would he risk his life for Sky Toucher? Mohawks, "Praying" or Valley, knew that giving in to their feelings was not just a sign of weakness but begged trouble.

On Sky Toucher struggled through the snow crust. If only he had snowshoes. Ahead of him, still out of sight, the Tree-eater Mountains ended in a broad, sweeping plain. Should he keep straight on and cross it, or head southwest for the mountains? It would be slower going, but just as hard for those pursuing him, although their snowshoes would help them to move faster. Still, in the mountains, there would be places to hide where he could rest protected from the elements and animals.

*Nyoh.* Cut southwest now. Get up into the mountains, head south, cross the Saranac River, keep on until he reached the place where he started for the fort last time. On he plodded, the moon fading, the sky at his back beginning to lighten over the Green Mountains. Exhaustion came slowly, insidiously, his strength seeping from him like sweat. He was fighting for breath, the trees swimming in his sight, when he stopped to rest, nearly falling over a dead tree. It had fallen against a snow-clad outcropping on which there were bare spots.

He sat for a long time, having no choice but to risk it, before he could get his breath and feel strong enough to go on. Inspecting the outcropping, he spied a fissure about a foot wide and began scraping his bindings against the sharper edge. Up and down he sawed, one strand parting then another. He had almost freed himself, in his haste bloodying both wrists, his upper arms aching furiously, when behind him a heard a throat clear. He stiffened and turned slowly, his heart thundering.

# 68

WHAT ARE YOU doing way out here? murmured Stone Pipe, pretending incredulity. Strapped to his back was an extra pair of snowshoes. "I wake up, you are gone, I am overcome with worry. And look at the blood . . ."

"I do not understand you."

"What?"

"You made it so easy to get away."

"And so you think I am a *seronquatse*, a heartless dog who

teases you just to amuse himself. *Neh*, if you must know, you tear me in half. You make me fight with myself. I want you to get away but if you do . . ." He sent a finger across his throat. "We have a problem here, Cousin, any suggestions?"

"Just one. Let me go, and you leave, too."

"For where?"

"Back to Caughnawaga."

"You make it sound so simple. What would I do there, sit playing with myself until the big long knife sends a couple of muskets to fetch me? Wait for a rope or a bullet?"

Dawn was breaking fast, a frigid gray, the color of Van Brocklin's eyes. A rush of tiny slate juncos whirled directly over their heads, drawing Stone Pipe's attention. They watched them sweep away in a ball, dispersing among the treetops, twittering raucously.

"Then come home with me," said Sky Toucher.

"To Tenotoge? I am originally from Onekahoncka."

"Come anyway. I will show you the way back."

"I know the way," said Stone Pipe.

"Take it."

"*Neh.*"

"Why not?"

"There is no place for me there, no place for any Catholic. And I *am* a Catholic. I know you do not believe that, but it is true."

"If you really are . . ."

"I am!"

"Then you have to let me go. I have heard that you forgive your enemies, so forgive me."

"It is not that easy." Stone Pipe explained. "Father Dubois says that you who refuse baptism in the Holy Mother Church are in the army of Satan. You can only be in one or the other. Do you know Satan?"

"I may have heard of him, I do not remember." Sky Toucher held out his fists. "Cut these last few strands so I can pull my hands up into my cuffs."

Stone Pipe complied, explaining: "Satan is evil. He is Christ's and God's enemy. He denies them. As you do, Cousin, as all of you we left behind in the Valley."

"You believe everything your black robe tells you."

"Of course," Stone Pipe replied.

Sky Toucher narrowed his eyes. "You think he speaks for your God? *Neh,* Cousin, he speaks for the French chief with the gold hat, for the lace-cuff long knives. They have you, they want us, they want our lands, our furs, our women, everything we own. Mostly they want us dead, out of the way."

"It is a little cold to stand here discussing it," the other admonished him. "Put on these snowshoes. I borrowed them for you, you cannot keep them. We will go back. When we walk into camp keep your hands up your sleeves. Maybe no one will see the blood. They will think we just went out for a walk."

"Let me go, Onea Canonou."

Stone Pipe stared at him without saying anything, without moving. His expression was solemn. No trace of a smile played about his mouth, and the usual friendly twinkle in his eyes was noticeably absent.

"I wish I could, O-ron-ia-ke-te," he murmured at length. "I would like nothing better. But I cannot."

"He will not kill you."

"Maybe not, but should I take the chance? Would you? Answer me, Cousin, would you?"

Sky Toucher finished strapping on the snowshoes. He sighed. "Lead the way."

"*Neh,* Cousin, you. And do not look so discouraged. It saddens me."

# VII
## THE TEST OF DEVOTION

# 69

WITH RENEWED VIGOR, Singing Brook and Four Otters made their way up northern Lake Champlain, following the raiders' tracks along the west shore with the Tongue Mountains fronting the Adirondacks to the west. Sky Toucher's captors, who had now crossed over into Sokoki Territory, were able to travel in the open with no fear of aggression. Not so their pursuers.

When the black bird of night settled its great wings over the woodlands and the fat moon ruled, they camped, ate and slept, awakening to the feeble light of the new day. Four Otters ventured off to replenish their dwindling supply of fresh venison while Singing Brook readied their packs for the day's journey. Starting down northern Lake Champlain, certain that they were steadily closing the gap, lifted Singing Brook's spirits immeasurably. Still there remained the problem of how they would help Sky Toucher escape. But she was confident that when they caught up and were able to judge the situation, some workable strategy would come to mind.

Four Otters came running back. "Come see, come!"

"What is it?"

"Hurry!" he whispered hoarsely.

He pulled her deeper into the trees, following the path he had just trod to a stand of snow-burdened spruce.

"Look."

Around a campfire set in front of a large, well-made lean-to were three Sokoki Abnakis, a man and two women. The man had killed a moose and was preparing to butcher it. Singing Brook and Four Otters watched in silence as he stripped off the hide, laughing and joking with the women. He handed the dripping hide to one, who with snow began cleansing it of blood. Watching them, Singing Brook failed to notice Four Otters nock an arrow. He let fly, thumping the man in the chest, knocking him sprawling. The women screamed, dropped what they were doing and ran off into the woods.

"Why did you do that?" she asked.

"If he saw us first, what would he do? Look at the meat."

They hurried forward. The dead man lay with the shaft sticking straight up, his hands crimson with moose blood halfway up his forearms. Four Otters bent to pick up his knife, a shrill cry sounded behind them. A second Sokoki came flying at Four Otters, knifing him in the shoulder before he could turn around. Grunting, grimacing in pain, Four Otters got his own knife out as the other struck again, burying his blade in the Mohawk's stomach. Four Otters' eyes bulged and he made a low rattling sound.

But not before he slashed his attacker's throat. The Abnaki sank to his knees, gurgling obscenely, falling over. Singing Brook dropped down beside Four Otters, also down on his knees, his hands gripping the knife. He whispered through his agony, staring at her, his eyes as blank as polished stones.

"It . . . wavers . . ."

"Do not try to speak."

"Your face, like it is under water . . ." She pushed his hands gently aside and took hold of the knife. *"Neh,"* he murmured, "leave it. It . . . already has my life. Oh . . ."

"What?"

"It is getting warm. I have been cold so long I had almost forgotten what being warm is like. But I am warmer now, all through me. Come closer, Tenäte Oÿoghi." She bent over him, her eyes beginning to mist. "Take this tooth and the other with you, theirs have bone handles. You must go on."

"Of course."

She eased him down on his back. He clucked disapprovingly. "Why do I challenge you? You are as stubborn as O-ron-ia-ke-te. Is that where you got it?" He tried to laugh, choked; blood trickled down his jaw. She took off her mittens and placed them beneath his head. "Warm, getting hot . . . rushing through me like fire . . . Listen, they have reached the Richelieu River by now and will be moving even slower. You will catch up."

"Do not talk . . ."

"I must, to say goodbye. It is getting dark, a storm is coming. It is so warm, tingly, even outside me on my face. I . . ." Again he choked, turning his head, letting the blood spill free of his cheek. His eyes had glazed like skin ice. "I . . . am sorry, Tenäte Oÿoghi, I mean to leave you alone out here. I . . ."

He shuddered, twitched, a groan escaped his lips and he was dead. She closed his eyes, retrieved her mittens. She looked about. The skinned moose lay staring dully into space, the fire crackled, the two dead Abnakis sprawled only a few feet apart. There was no sign of either of the women. She listened but could hear only the whispering wind.

She looked down at Four Otters. It had all happened so suddenly, only now was the shock of it beginning to sink in. The swift thrust of the knife, he was dead, she was alone. Should she go on? With him it was dangerous, perhaps futile, fatal. Without him, utter folly? Suicide?

*"Neh!"*

If his dying was meant to discourage her, it failed to. All it did was leave their mission in her hands. Having come this far, after enduring so much, it would be cowardly to quit. Sky Toucher did not deserve a coward for a wife.

Again she looked around the little camp. An idea came. She eased the Sokoki's knife from Four Otters' stomach, retrieved the other Sokaki's knife and tossed her own and Four Otters' into the bushes.

She went back to the hiding place in the spruce trees from which they had first watched the Sokokis. There she examined both knives. They were shorter than Mohawk knives. And because the Sokokis used moosehide sheaths, she exchanged them for her deerskin sheath. Curiosity would eventually bring the squaws back, possibly not the one who'd seen her husband killed by Four Otters' arrow but certainly the other, who had no way of knowing her husband had returned. At that, perhaps both would show up. She would be ready for them.

She waited and waited until she was almost ready to give it up, when she heard the soft, steady crunching of snow and spied the younger of the two coming warily back, looking about her like a frightened doe. Moving as quietly as she could, Singing Brook got around behind her, sneaking up on her holding her knife in front of her. She got so close she could almost reach out and touch her back when the Sokoki heard her and spun around screaming.

*"Ogechta!"*

The woman didn't know the word but its meaning was clear.

She stood trembling, staring at the upraised knife, her eyes saucering. She wore a cap made from the shoulder skin of a moose, the long white hair of the creature's hump forming a natural crest. Over the cap she wore a blanket draped like a shawl. Her full-length robe was beaver fur with buckskin leggings and moosehide winter moccasins. Continuing to menace her with the knife, Singing Brook jerked off her blanket and cap. Her hair hung in two braids; a flat coil on the crown of her head was tied by a thong, the ends hanging loose. Singing Brook gestured sharply, indicating her hair. She took it down.

"Now take off your clothes." The woman stared, confused. She was homely with a deep scar running vertically down her left cheek. Her nose looked as if it had been mashed by a stone. Most of her front teeth were missing. Singing Brook pulled at her robe then began removing her own jacket. "Take off your clothes!" she repeated.

She exchanged clothes with her, keeping on only her leggins, since they were all but identical to the Sokoki's. Lastly, she forced her to change moccasins with her. The woman appeared mystified but readily complied. When they were both once more fully dressed, Singing Brook edged close to her, waving the knife, sending her screaming back into the woods. Returning to Four Otters' body she began covering it with snow but gave it up. Instead, she got out her knife and cut poles for a scaffold. Lifting his dead weight up onto it was harder than she imagined it would be. But she finally made it, taking pains to cover every inch of his body against the depredations of the birds.

In the spring Sky Toucher and others would come back to bring it home for a proper burial. After removing his snowshoes and strapping them to her back, she set about cutting chunks of moose haunch. She debated whether to take Four Otters' bow and quiver, but decided against it. Since she had no skill with a bow, trying to bring down a deer would be a waste of time and energy. Preparing to leave she touched her friend's cheek with her bare hand in a sign of farewell.

"Cayere Tawyne. Dear, loyal, good Cayere Tawyne."

Back at their temporary camp she buried his pack and then the remains of their fire in the snow, messing the snow to conceal evidence of their presence. Packing as much of the fresh moose meat as she could comfortably carry, and adjusting the tumpline across her forehead, she was about to set out when she suddenly gasped and froze.

While she'd been busy with her various chores a pack of wolves had appeared, no fewer than eleven. They sat their haunches in a circle around her, staring malevolently out of their slanted yellow eyes. The leader rose and came slowly forward, the others following, tightening the circle. He stood with his ears erect, his mane bristling, his long tail hanging down to the level of his hocks, his tongue lolling.

Her heart skipped and thundered. Hungry, aggressive, in seconds they would attack. The worst thing she could do would be attempt to run for it. She wouldn't get twenty yards before they brought her down. If a moose does not run when wolves approach, they cannot kill. They usually go away and leave it alone.

Did they sense her fear? Likely. She stood straight, turning slowly, her eyes fastening on the place where she had buried Four Otters' pack in the snow, only three steps away. Yelling to distract them, she lunged for it, clawing it out of the snow, digging her hand deep, bringing out four small chunks of deer fat. In nearly the same motion she flung two pieces in front of the leader.

He had sat down again, now he got up staring at her. He lowered his head and quickly gobbled up one chunk then the other. Blood glistened on his mouth and dripped, spurting as he continued chewing. In an instant the scent was picked up by the other wolves, and the whole pack was driven into a frenzy of madness, setting the wolves tearing the bloody-mouthed one to pieces.

Meanwhile, she slunk slowly away. Speedily distancing herself from them, the sounds of their savage fighting growing faint in her ears, she stopped to examine one of the remaining chunks of fat. In it Four Otters had pressed a number of blades chipped from chert. As sharp as the sharpest knife they were. It was an old trick Mohawk hunters used as protection against wolf attack.

It had warmed up, the trees glistened and dripped as she moved out onto the lake heading northward following the shoreline. Was Four Otters right?

Would the raiders be slowing, now that they were safely into friendly territory and approaching the next to last leg of their journey?

She hurried her step. She did not stop until well into the night, then lit a small fire, ate and after a couple of failed attempts, managed to redo her hair in the style of the Abnaki squaw, putting on the cap and blanket over it. She was now Abnaki down to her two knives.

For the next two days she pushed steadily onward, coming at last to within sight of Ile-aux-Noix. It had not snowed since near the Champlain marshes, which, as she thought thinking about it, seemed months ago. Sky Toucher's captors' tracks were easy to follow. She continued, convinced that she would catch up with them before they reached the St. Lawrence.

There the band would turn northeast, following the river on the long journey up to Quebec. Long before that, she would sight them, wait for dark and make her move. Catching up was not the problem. Freeing him without getting caught was. In fact, that would be the start of a whole new set of problems. They had to get all the way back down to Fort Anne. Though the weather was getting milder every day, Sky Toucher was probably in poor shape for such a grueling trek.

But if she could find some place where they could hole up for a few days, he might regain his strength. Only where could they expect to find such a place in enemy territory?

One thing was certain, she could not let pessimism trespass her thinking at this critical stage. Maybe luck would come their way. Maybe some kindhearted soul would shelter them while Sky Toucher recuperated. Maybe they would even hide out until warm weather broke *augustuske's* back, opening up the trails and rendering travel easier.

Who could say what lay ahead?

Only it was all so infuriating, so grossly unfair. And so outrageously unnecessary. All of this could be blamed on the whiteskins and their stupid fighting. And Dorr's failure to send men to rescue Sky Toucher.

"Go home you snakes, child killers, liars, thieves, all that is evil!"

The wind rose in agreement.

# 70

COLONEL ETIENNE RAMESAY was in an uncommonly expansive mood, so pleased with the progress of the journey back to Quebec that he charitably gave his weary band a two-day respite. A thaw had set in, the ice in the river began to break up, the sun took on color and dispensed warmth for the first time in weeks. When the travelers found an ideal place to camp, the colonel ordered out the Abnaki hunters.

Seeing his commander's buoyant spirits, Stone Pipe decided to approach him, although not before conferring with the cow-eyed Captain Dussault, who magnanimously offered to speak to the colonel for him.

Now outside Ramesay's tent, the Caughnawaga stood behind the captain, peering over his shoulder. The colonel had his boots off and his orderly, a tireless little man who scampered about like a puppy, was paring his toenails.

"Careful, Alois, the cuticle, the cuticle. What is it, Marcel?"

"A matter of some urgency, Colonel, the squaws are upset."

"Because we have stopped to rest? *Mon Dieu*, there is no pleasing these redskins."

"It is this what they call 'caressing.' "

"Ca . . ."

"Beating the prisoner, sir," the captain explained.

Stone Pipe cut in. "You promised the women that they could punish him."

"I did?"

"You said they could have their *partie* when we go down the river."

"I don't recall saying any such thing." He turned irritably to his orderly. "The cuticle, Alois, the cuticle!"

"Sir," said Dussault, "we all heard you."

"Oh?" Ramesay frowned at his bare foot. "The little toe, and slowly, carefully, don't cut it off at the first joint."

"Well," persisted the captain, "can they or can't they?"

"Describe again how they do it."

Stone Pipe's expression darkened as Dussault described the ritual, emphasizing that it was considered sacred and a long-standing custom, that not even the tribe's warriors could deny the women.

"He tried to escape," Dussault reminded the colonel. "He should be punished."

Sky Toucher sat a few feet away, his wrists bound in his lap, listening, marveling that none of the three seemed to realize he was eavesdropping. At that, did they care? Did "Cousin"? He looked uncomfortable. Very-beautiful-sun had been searing his ears with her complaints ever since the turkey cock ordered the caressing postponed.

Their heads turned as she came striding up babbling, throwing her fat little hands about.

The colonel stared, first dumfounded then annoyed. "*Mon Dieu,* what a mouth. Shut her up, Caughnawaga. You, *ferme la grande bouche!*"

She disregarded him, continuing to harangue and point at Sky Toucher. Stone Pipe finally calmed her. The turkey cock flared angrily. He jerked his foot away from his orderly and dismissed him, flinging both hands. Alois backed off.

"Boots, boots, *imbecile!*"

As Alois meekly compied, the turkey cock glared at Stone Pipe. "Tell her when I said 'down the river' I meant the St. Lawrence. Any *idiot* could understand that." He glanced at Sky Toucher. "Look at him, he looks half dead. I'm not about to set his corpse down in front of the general. Are we feeding him?"

"He gets the same rations as the Abnakis," said Dussault. "I think."

"He looks like he hasn't eaten in a week. You, Caughnawaga, tell her *later,* explain and get her out of here."

Stone Pipe translated somewhat timidly. Jankanque Kerack-wero exploded, she began clawing the air, trying to get at the colonel. Both Stone Pipe and the captain had to hold her back. Dussault sent the Caughnawaga away with her. When the orderly finished restoring the colonel's boots, he was waved away.

"Have any of the hunters come back yet?" asked Ramesay.

"Not yet, sir, it's still early."

"Whoever brings in the first deer, see to it that the filet is saved for me."

"Consider it done, Colonel."

"Dismissed."

Dussault clicked his heels, saluted, spun about and marched off. The turkey cock came over to Sky Toucher.

"Are they feeding you?" Sky Toucher looked away. Ramesay kicked his leg, the Mohawk started and narrowed his eyes. "Answer me, *Sauvage*. You have lost weight since we rescued you from the Dutchman. Your ribs stick out like a starving hound's. We must keep you healthy. Stand up."

Alois emerged from the colonel's tent, brushing Ramesay's dress jacket, as Sky Toucher got to his feet.

"Take this one to the cook," said the turkey cock to Alois. "Tell him I said to fill him up. And no dog scraps. We *will* fatten you up, Mohawk." He laughed. "For the kill."

Stone Pipe, now returned, and the orderly marched Sky Toucher to where six cauldrons were lined up. A fire glowed under only one, which contained a watery stew with chucks of venison, dried peas rendered only slightly less stonelike by boiling, and bits of bread. After Sky Toucher ate his fill, back at Stone Pipe's fire he was ordered to sit.

The Caughnawaga retied his wrists behind his back; the right one felt very sore. Stone Pipe went to get wood to feed the fire. Sky Toucher looked about. Abnakis walked back and forth all around him. He could see hatred in every face. The birch-bark huts had already been put up, including one close to Stone Pipe's fire, where he would be sleeping that night. Should he try again to escape? The food he'd eaten was filling, and the hunters would be bringing back meat in quantity. Perhaps he should wait two or three sleeps until he got back more energy. On the last try he was exhausted when Stone Pipe caught up with him.

The Caughnawaga knew Sky Toucher would keep trying, and had stinted him on rations to discourage him. All Iroquois starved prisoners, that was the rule: keep them weak, they will be submissive, easy to control. Not that Sky Toucher required much; like all Iroquois warriors, his body was used to only one daily meal, but being denied it for even one sleep took its toll. The meal he'd just eaten would hold him through tomorrow and, thanks to the hunters, everyone would feast that night.

He had cut one wrist badly trying to scrape through his bindings on the rock; it was infected, covered with hardened pus. It had been flaming red but now was plum-colored, painful to the touch. It was midafternoon, some of the hunters were already straggling back with deer and smaller game. Stone Pipe returned with wood for the fire, Jankanque Karackwero tagging along behind him. She spat at Sky Toucher, he pretended not to notice, Stone Pipe pulled her away from him.

"She says that it is your fault the colonel is postponing your caressing."

"Do I care what the stupid bitch says?"

"Shhhh, she understands a little Iroquois. Oooo, I see your wrist, it looks angry." He undid the bindings. Sky Toucher held up his arm and Stone Pipe clucked. "It should be cut out and cleaned before it spreads up your arm."

"It needs to be drained and snake-lily root juice rubbed into it."

"And where do we find snake-lily root?"

"It would cure it."

"I know, I am Mohawk, remember?" Stone Pipe examined it closely, probing it with his forefinger. Sky Toucher pulled his hand away sharply. "Hurts, eh? I will have to slice it off and clean it with snow. Very bad." He got out his knife. Others saw them and began gathering around to watch. "This will hurt very much. Will you scream for them?"

An older Abnaki spoke, the others laughed.

"He says he is willing to bet his moccasins you will scream your head open."

"Tell him to find a hole in the ice and fish with his mouth."

"I am going to slice off the scab."

"I will," said Sky Toucher. "Give me the knife."

"*Neh.* Not that I do not trust you, but I am very good at this."

"Do not cut any cords."

"If my hand slips yours will be useless. It will hang down like a dead trout." He wiped his knife on his haunch. "Are you ready?"

"Just do it."

"First I must cut a piece off your leggin to wrap around it."
He did so. "Get ready to see a lot of blood. Ready?"

"Do it!"

Holding his knife by the blade, he set the flat of it against the
infection and began slowly paring it off. Against the agonizing pain
Sky Toucher set his teeth so hard they threatened to shatter. Sweat
burst from his forehead, his vision blurred. Very slowly, Stone
Pipe scraped the wound, drawing his knife along under the scab,
separating it from the cut in a single piece. Sky Toucher battled
to stay rigid. The onlookers leaned forward, chattering excitedly.

"Hold still, Cousin."

"I am!"

"Shhhh, almost done. You should see your face. It is white like
snow. All your blood rushes to here, *neh?* You are bleeding like
a scalped redback. It is good, it is cleaning it."

"Look at it, not me," Sky Toucher muttered through clenched
teeth.

By the time he was done, Sky Toucher was fighting to keep
from passing out. His whole arm and hand felt on fire.

"Done, Cousin."

Stone Pipe set a handful of snow on the wound to staunch the
bleeding. It failed to and he had to hurriedly tie the deerskin strip
around it.

"Too tight," complained Sky Toucher.

"Just until the bleeding stops."

"Cut another piece, make a pad."

His captor did so, and Sky Toucher held the pad in place while
Stone Pipe secured it with the binding. Muttering threaded through
the crowd. As it broke up, Stone Pipe laughed.

"You disappointed them, they were aching for you to scream."

Sky Toucher grunted, his face proclaiming his thoughts.

"You do not like Abnakis very much, do you? They sure have
no stomach for you."

"For *us.*"

"*Neh,* you. We are on their side, remember? Here, let me tie
that again. The bleeding looks to be letting up. How do you feel,
*aghihi?*"

"I am all right. Thanks to you, Onea Canonou."

"It was *ta-do-ä-we,* a pleasure."

Again Sky Toucher grunted. He looked down at his other wrist. His star felt unaccountably warm. What of her star? What was she doing at that moment? Thinking of him? How long would she continue to now that he was presumed dead?

"It will *coenhaseren* nicely," murmured Stone Pipe, studying the binding.

*"Nyoh."*

"Any time, O-ron-ia-ke-te. That is what I am here for, to take care of you."

"For your master."

"For yours. It is your life your friend the turkey cock holds in his hand. And when you open your eyes and see Quebec, you can say goodbye to it. I, for one, will miss you. Look, more hunters are coming back. Meat, Cousin, can you taste it? Go and shit, make room for more. And do not look so discouraged. From now on we will be eating like bears after their long sleep."

# 71

SKY TOUCHER'S WRIST seemed to be healing. It was noticeably less painful to the touch. To protect the wound, Stone Pipe obligingly tied him further up the forearms.

The thaw persisted, suggesting that suddenly spring had arrived. On the second night of the stopover, many of the Abnakis slept outside their birch-bark dwellings, as Stone Pipe and Sky Toucher did. But for the diminishing snow, it was mild as a summer night. The ice in the river was unlocking and melting, the *o-jis-ta-noo-kwa,* the "spotted in the sky" swarmed, moonlight blanketed the sleeping company.

Sky Toucher stayed awake plotting a third attempt at escape while Stone Pipe snored nearby. After they had eaten that evening, the Caughnawaga neglected to retie his ankles. Was it an invitation? Or had Stone Pipe decided that he'd given up trying to get away?

So how far would he let him flee this time? It had become a

game with Stone Pipe a reluctant player. One curious thing, neither time previously when Stone Pipe caught up with him did he appear angry.

This time maybe he should steal snowshoes, although so rapidly was the snow melting it would likely be all gone in a few days. Should he head west again or in the opposite direction? Cross the river, head into the sunrise . . .

Lying on his side, debating which direction to take, he started slightly as he felt movement under him. So slight was it, he thought he'd imagined it. The air was unaccountably still, not a whisper of sound in the entire camp, other than the muted burbling of the river. Then ice cracked sharply.

*Had* the ground moved? If it did, he appeared to be the only one who'd noticed.

*Nyoh,* this time he would head east. Find a cave, maybe a deserted trapper's cabin, and hole up for a while. And what would he do for food? That could be his biggest problem, but at least at the moment his stomach was full.

Another tremor. He propped on one elbow and spread his hand over the ground. It did not move.

Many miles to the east, deep in the rigid lithosphere of the earth, tightly fitting sections of a fault in the mosaic of plates that formed the mantle under the outer crust had been steadily building up strain—until the tightly locked formation shattered. From the focus, the force detonating upwards to the epicenter ruptured, the path of movement violently flexuous, dislocating the rock masses.

The sound began like a multitude of muffled drums. Quickly it built into an earsplitting climactic burst, like a thousand cannon fired at once, convulsing the ground, rousing the camp. People began yelling and screaming, the shrill sounds lost in the roar of the explosion. Sky Toucher got up on his knees only to be thrown on his side and shaken like a husk doll. Others tried to flee but were flung to the quaking ground, rolling like an ocean under their feet. Trees swayed and fell, huge shards of ice in the river heaved upward. Then, as the explosion died away, there came an ominous cracking sound, the ground split, a great fissure opened. It came from the north, shooting through the camp parallel to the river, turning and heading southwest. The side of it furthest from Sky

Toucher rose ten feet and from the fissure's depths, water spouted high in the air.

Into the gaping trench fell trees, birch-bark dwellings and tents, and people, screaming as they plunged to their deaths. Sky Toucher watched in awe as the turkey cock's tent dropped from sight.

The sound diminished, the gushing water subsided, disappeared, the ground steadied and was still. Sky Toucher held his breath, his heart hammering his breastbone. He got to his feet. Stone Pipe crawled over to him, his face ashen, eyes protruding.

"Is it—over?" Sky Toucher shrugged. Stone Pipe's expression hardened as his fear gave way to self-possession. "Do not even think about trying to escape."

"What do you need with me now? The turkey cock is dead." He pointed at the fissure less than thirty feet from them. "He went down tent and all."

"I know, no matter."

"Nobody else wants me for the big long knife in Quebec," he reminded Stone Pipe.

"The others wanted to kill you before we even started."

"What can he do to you now? Let me go, Cousin, do what is right."

"*Neh*, the long knives would have my scalp. Gagne will. He is *oeuda*, shit, and now he is in command." He glanced about. "If he is still alive."

They spied Major Gagne up a way at the edge of the chasm standing with two other officers. He was pointing to where the turkey cock went down and looking across at the raised opposite side of the fissure. Younger than the turkey cock, he was broad shouldered, slim waisted, with a face that looked more like a woman's than a man's, his expression perpetually dismal. He always looked prepared to challenge anyone venturing near him, except the turkey cock, whom he seemed desperate to please. Dorr, too, had attracted such toadies who fawned over their superiors, while treating underlings like dirt.

Would Gagne follow through on the turkey cock's plan and bring him to Quebec? Or would he order his throat cut and his body thrown into the fissure?

Would Gagne let him go? *Neh*, that would be a sign of weakness. He was taking over command, he had to show authority firmly and decisively.

The ground trembled, nearly tumbling Gagne and the other two officers into the fissure. The Abnakis and Canadians again reacted fearfully, women screamed, men quickly distanced themselves from the opening, dragging their squaws with them. Would the ground open under him and Stone Pipe, plunging them into the belly of the earth? Sky Toucher stiffened, not daring to move; in seconds that seemed hours the tremor ceased, just in time for a third tremor.

"The earth is rearranging its bones," murmured Stone Pipe.

"The worst is over, I am going back to sleep."

"Who can sleep after this? I must find Jankanque Kareckwero." He undid Sky Toucher's bindings. "You come with me. Stay close. Try to get away and I will bury my tooth in you before you take two steps." He grinned. "You have survived this, you would not want to die that easy, would you, Cousin? Hey, there she is . . ."

Only seven bodies were recovered. Many Abnakis and Canadians, even officers, had fallen into the fissure. The ground was frozen, so scaffolds for the dead were erected, the corpses wrapped in birch bark and placed on them until spring, when the relatives of the deceased would return and bury them. A funeral song was chanted. The Abnakis mourned for one year, the widow wearing a hood as a sign of grief, the widower painting his face black.

About a third of the way down the Richelieu River, Singing Brook made camp for the night. She ate, fell asleep, then dreamed the same dream as before. She saw him naked and beaten in the same primeval setting. Again, when she tried to move closer to him he vanished, only to reappear in another spot. It was so frustrating and upsetting, she awoke.

What did it mean? According to the Iroquois, all dreams had meanings; the purpose of a dream was to give information which had to be properly interpreted. Was this dream telling her rescuing him was impossible? Not even worth trying?

She fell back to sleep and into another dream. The ground was shaking violently under her. She kept falling and getting up. Trees shook, swayed, fell, one after another narrowly missing her. She woke. The tremor was subsiding. Only two dead trees had fallen, neither near her. In the river enormous chunks of ice had broken free and were standing straight up like gigantic teeth.

# 72

BEARS WERE COMING out of their caves, lynx and wolves were out roaming, and raccoons, all of them showing their ribs in the wake of the longest and harshest winter in many years. Alone, on the verge of collapse from exhaustion at the end of each day's travel, Two Eagles retired for the night into sleep so deep that a gun fired close to his ear would not have awakened him.

He decided to climb a tree and sleep, to avoid roving creatures. In addition to his own, he had Splitting Moon's tooth-ball tomahawk and musket. The muskets he hid in the boughs of a nearby hemlock along with his pack before climbing a sugar maple, locating a fairly comfortable spot where two limbs stuck out close together before turning in opposite directions. He straddled them with his back to the trunk. Through the leafless branches overhead he could see the moon eying him sullenly, its dark edge slowly eroding the luminous portion. It resembled a ball of ice and the few stars in evidence appeared flat and lifeless. Clouds that during the day were as soft and white as the inside of a doe's ear looked bruised by the light of the moon and did not seem to move. Everything above appeared to be waiting.

"For what?"

He had promised himself that he would not dwell further on Splitting Moon's death, or allow it again to recall the deaths of all the others. He was, after all, on a lifesaving mission, and that was what he should concentrate on. The O-ron-ia-ke-tes of the tribes, Mohawk or Oneida, were their only hope for the future. He had to be rescued, brought home for her sake as well as his peoples' and his own.

Two Eagles thought about himself, a chief now, a leader among his people. If the Oneida were to become involved in the fighting again would he take part? He had long since passed his thirtieth summer. He was not old; Sho-non-ses, His Longhouse, chief of the bear clan whom he had replaced, had fought well into his sixties, as had others. Still, reflecting on his days before Margaret came into his life, he had probably seen more action before the age of twenty-five than any other Oneida, thanks to the seven years of red days. He, Splitting Moon, all of them except Bone, the Mohican, who had come to Onneyuttahage after the fighting.

Once more he eyed the moon and was studying it, striving to make out a face between his yawns, when a sound below drew his attention. He estimated that he was a little more than thirty feet up, able to look straight down and see the white ground. Below a dark shape was circling the tree, a bear, a she-bear from the size. He thought of the two muskets hidden in the hemlock only a few feet away and mimed aiming straight down and pulling the trigger. He shot her squarely between the shoulders.

She was marking her territory, rushing the reluctant spring. She caught his scent, raising her muzzle and eying him. Seeing the futility of trying to get at him, circling the tree two more times and then wandering away, the sound of her moving through the woods grew fainter until it disappeared altogether, restoring the silence.

He shifted his body, seeking a more comfortable position but could not find one. He fell asleep sitting up. It could have been minutes later, or hours, when he was awakened. The tree was shaking violently, as were all the trees around him. He saw one of the muskets fall to the ground. He thrust out both hands to grab hold of the two limbs but too late; thrown from the crotch he fell.

# 73

TREMORS PERSISTED THROUGHOUT the remainder of the night and well into morning. On pressed Singing Brook, following the raiders' trail and coming at last to their deserted camp. Seeing the fissure and the scaffolds supporting the Abnaki corpses, the upheaval all about, she realized that the raiders had experienced the full impact of the earthquake.

She estimated that she was now less than a day behind the

party. Before starting out that morning, fairly certain that it would
not snow again or at least not heavily, she had discarded her own
and Four Otters' snowshoes. She considered the next phase: what
she must do once she caught up with the raiders. Whatever the
odds on rescuing Sky Toucher, and they had to be daunting, she
must try.

It was still light out when the raiders stopped for the day. She
heard them before sighting their camp: shouting, a gun going off,
raucous laughter. Her heart quickened. Venturing closer, she could
hear fires crackling and unintelligible conversation. She stopped
behind a spruce and moving a branch she got her first glimpse of
the camp. She was surprised to see so many more Abnakis and
Caughnawagas than French Canadians.

She recalled the corpses on the scaffolds and gasped as a har-
rowing thought occurred. Had Sky Toucher been injured? Killed!
She could not see him anywhere. Was he inside one of the birch-
bark dwellings? She made her way from tree to tree around the
camp at a safe distance and finally spied him sitting on the ground,
his arms bound in front of him, a piece of deerskin around one
wrist. Joy lifted her heart. Then, as she looked closer, it sank. He
looked haggard, even ill. They had starved him. That was to be
expected, but had they beaten him as well? She could see no
wounds, no marks, not like in her dream.

But was he strong enough to escape . . . ? And how far would
he get before he collapsed?

Just beyond where he sat a number of women were talking to
a whiteskin long knife who towered over them, his brass buttons
glinting in the low afternoon sun. She could not make out what
they were saying, but his response appeared to please them. A few
yelled out happily as they dispersed. She let go of the branch she
was peering over and looked about. Removing the tumpline from
her forehead, she shoved her pack under a deadfall, heaping pine
needles over it, marking the spot by a spruce that was almost twice
the height of those around it.

Filling her lungs, she set out, marching into the camp, imagining
all eyes suddenly fasten on her—but in reality no one paid the
slightest attention. Straight for where Sky Toucher was sitting she

headed, then stopped short. She could hardly walk up and speak to him.

But she had to let him know she'd arrived. She walked around him, picking her way through groups standing talking and around dwellings and tents, until she got behind him. Then she boldly walked straight for him, passing only a few feet away, stopping, looking back. He raised his eyes. His jaw dropped, he started to speak and caught himself, his eyes darting left and right. She turned and went on.

By now the women she'd seen talking to the long knife who had scattered into the woods were drifting back carrying slender bundles of switches. A few were lighting torches. Singing Brook watched as two Abnakis jerked Sky Toucher to his feet and ordered him to remove his clothes. When he did not comply fast enough one pulled off his jacket while the other cut away his leggins.

Two squaws carrying switches came up to Singing Brook. One thrust a bundle at her, smiling toothlessly, nodding. Sky Toucher now stood naked except for his moccasins. A warrior with a tom-tom approached, sat cross-legged and began thumping it. The excited women formed a circle around their victim. Singing Brook had no choice but to join them. Accompanied by the tom-tom they began walking slowly around him. Then the circle broke into a serpentine line. Approaching him, the first one beat him across the chest, the others shouting encouragement. He stood motionless, his expression impassive.

His third caresser carried a torch. She was about to apply it to his shoulder when Major Gagne called out.

"*Attendez!*"

The woman hesitated. He strode forward and snatched the torch from her. "*Mais non,* he must live. Switches only. Switches only!" he repeated to the others. "Dussault, don't just stand there, tell them, explain."

The major's instruction was not well received. Very-beautiful-sun, who appeared to have taken charge of the caressing, exploded. She waggled her torch at the major who stiffened and scowled. Stone Pipe stepped between them, snatching away her torch.

"Tell her switches only!" rasped Gagne to him.

The caressing went on without torches. It was Singing Brook's turn. Standing staring at him, she hesitated. He nodded, granting her permission to strike him. She whipped him across the chest and gave way to the next woman. By now his upper body was crimson. Ugly red mouths streaked his shoulders and chest, but when he was struck he did not flinch, did not alter his expression. The tom-tom beat louder, more frantically, goading the women into a frenzy. Each screamed in delight as her turn came to beat him.

Now they attacked his back and buttocks. Within minues his entire body down to his moccasins was red and raw, all except his cheeks, from which the blood was draining. He looked as if at any moment his knees would buckle under him. Singing Brook closed her eyes, unable to look.

*"Cạ suffit!"* snapped Gagne, stepping forward, blocking the next caresser.

The women yelled protest. An ugly scene threatened, then the two Abnakis who had stripped Sky Toucher rushed forward and led him away to the nearest dwelling. Stone Pipe retrieved his clothing and followed them. He carried a pot of bear grease to allay the bleeding.

Singing Brook sighed. He had survived, barely, but now he was in no shape to travel. How long would it take him to recover? When would he be fit to leave? Dusk came creeping in, settling over the camp. In the darkness that followed, while the camp slept, she would go to him, they would talk, decide. Knowing him, he would insist on leaving that night. It would be foolhardy, she would have to talk him out of it. Her hand sneaked under her robe to her belt and the extra Abnaki knife.

For him.

# VIII
## FLIGHT

# 74

A RAGGED CLOUD SLID over the moon as Singing Brook moved stealthily, in a crouch, through the sleeping Abnakis and Caughnawagas toward where Sky Toucher lay. She was within ten yards of him when from behind a hand came down on her shoulder. She turned. A stubbled face leered.

*"Qu´ est-ce que c´est?"*

His breath was foul from stale liquor. He was drunk. Sputum glistened at the corner of his mouth, his little pig eyes undressed her. He let go of her shoulder, got her neck in the crook of his arm and kissed her, smacking her obscenely, slobbering all over her mouth.

She pulled free, swiping her mouth with the back of her hand. "Filthy pig!"

"Shhhh." He clamped a hand over her mouth. "You will wake the whole crew. Come, I know just the spot where we can be alone." For the first time she saw the bottle in his free hand. When he pushed it at her mouth, she dashed it to the ground. He chuckled, again covered her mouth, and with his free hand began fondling her breasts. "You come quietly and you won't get hurt, *comprenez?*" His mouth was almost in her ear, his tone rasping, menacing. "Such a pretty face, *jolie,* not like those others. Where have you been hiding?"

Abruptly, she ceased struggling. "Ah, that is better. Listen, I will take away my hand but do not scream. If you do I will snap your neck like a stick. Ah, your eyes say you understand."

He dragged her into the woods and flung her down. Her shoulder struck a protruding root sending pain sharply down to her elbow. She gave a little cry.

"I promise I will not hurt you."

He was breathing harder, his button eyes bright with lust. Down on his knees between her legs, he pulled open her robe and threw up her skirt, exposing her place. His eyes became wild at sight of it, his tongue hanging obscenely from his mouth, he panted and growled. But with her skirt thrown up, he failed to see her hand beneath it edging around her hip. He had pinned her legs with his shins, his hand gripping her throat. Fumbling at his crotch, he got out his member, erect, enormous. His head down, concentrating on entering her, he did not see her hand slowly emerge, in it, the knife.

He pushed the head in and was about to thrust into her full length when around came the knife in a blur, passing between them, slicing his member. Blood spurted, he gasped, his eyes pushed to the front of their sockets. His tongue hung from his mouth, pain exploded through him. He tried to scream, she was too fast. She slit his throat. Blood cascaded down onto her, down he fell, his head narrowly missing her as she turned aside.

She struggled to squirm out from under him. She stood up adjusting her clothing, closing and fastening her robe. He lay drenched with blood, his eyes gaping, his tongue half out of his mouth. She collected pine needles, working tirelessly, concealing him and heaping additional needles around him so that presently instead of a telltale mound it looked like a slight elevation in the ground.

She had not seen his member anywhere, nor did she trouble herself to look for it. She rested a moment then returned to the camp, approaching the sleeping Sky Toucher. She stood over him, sick at heart, filling with sympathy at sight of his condition. She touched his shoulder. He came awake, his face showing his discomfort.

She set a finger to his lips. "How do you feel?"

He grunted then, fully awake, saw the blood. "What happened?"

"It is all right, it is not mine."

"Whose then?"

"It is animal blood, nothing, a problem solved. I will wash it off later."

"You are amazing. How did you ever make it all the way up here?"

She told him about following his captors with Four Otters, about his death in the Abnaki hunters' camp. "No one else would come. I asked Quane Onawy, Christittye Etsi. Be patient, we must wait a few days for you to heal before we try to get away."

"*Neh,* we leave now, tonight, I have had all I can take. Cut my bindings."

"I have two knives, yours is in my pack."

"Good, good . . ."

"But look at you, you cannot leave in this condition!"

"I can make it."

"You cannot!"

"Shhh, do you want to wake the whole camp?"

"Listen to me, O-ron-ia-ke-te, we must do this sensibly. You would not get half a league, the shape you are in."

"Cut my bindings."

"*Neh,* I will not."

He was suddenly furious, so angry she thought he would begin shouting at her.

"Cut!"

She freed his arms, he untied his ankles. His face and neck gleamed with the bear grease applied to his cuts as the moon reappeared, casting down its blue-white light. She seized him, holding him close, feeling his heart beating against her own.

"You are alive, that is all that matters. You will heal, you must be patient."

"We are leaving. Give me the knife and get yours out, keep it handy."

"You think we will have to fight our way out of here?"

"Who knows what will happen? I have not had the best luck so far. Come." He started up.

"Please! You are in no . . ."

"I said *come!*"

There would be no dissuading him. At that, could she blame him? He had been captive too long, and, with her help, this was his first real chance to get away. Would will and determination make up for the punishment he'd suffered, his weakened condition?

He started upriver, she caught up with him.

"Wait, the other way. I hid my pack under a deadfall."

"We do not need it."

"We *do,* I have a fire bow, food, things we will need on the trail. It is a long way."

He hesitated then followed her in the opposite direction. Beyond the edge of camp they found her pack. She fitted the tumpline to her forehead, they started out. She could see that he was already breathing hard.

"How do you feel?" she asked.

He did not answer. The question was pointless, if he did answer he would lie. He had no spring in his step, he moved bent slightly forward, as if preparing to topple over. This was a mistake. They would not get five hundred paces before his strength completely deserted him. He had been through too much, and lost too much blood.

In their favor, however, the snow was almost gone. There would be no way for anyone pursuing to track them on pine needles—except that the raiders knew they would be heading south and probably west before turning in that direction.

He continued to lead the way. He had no leggins; the Abnakis had ruined them, cutting them off for the caressing. What if it turned cold again? Became as bitter as earlier? She would give him hers, if necessary force them on him. She had some say in this!

How far downriver had they come? Probably only two or three leagues to the rapids that churned the river for more than three leagues. This was the heart of enemy territory. They could run into Abnakis, Caughnawagas or French Canadians at any time. *She* could pass for an Abnaki squaw, but not him, not with that hair and those clothes. She should have brought along the clothes from one of the hunters Four Otters killed, including the cap to cover Sky Toucher's Mohawk roach. Yet knowing him, he'd refuse to disguise himself as one of his blood enemies.

They made their way slowly, steadily westward. It continued warm, with no wind and only patches of snow left mottling the ground. They traveled the rest of the night, into the gray dawn, encountering no one, no deserted campsites, no villages, no dwellings of any sort—only the wilderness, vast and threatening. It clouded over, it began to rain.

They were passing a series of caves; she insisted they take refuge in one. He balked, she demanded, he yielded. He had little choice. He was—she could see—perilously close to collapse.

The cave they chose smelled of bear but there was no sign of life inside. She cleared away vermin bones, leaves and dried feces, making a place for them a few feet back from the mouth, deep enough so that they could look out without being seen by anyone passing outside. She removed her beaver robe and his jacket, one sleeve torn all but completely off the shoulder. He took off his shirt, wincing with the effort, and she made him lie down.

"I have dried corn and moose meat in my pack."

He shook his head. "Not now, I just want to rest."

"We could stay here all day or at least until the rain lets up."

"Rain cannot hurt us."

"It will not help you, it is cold. In your condition it could make you *aghihi*. Your cuts are starting to heal. Do they hurt?"

*"Neh."*

"They do. Why do I bother to ask? And you have lost blood, that is why you are weak."

"Just tired, we came a long way."

"West. When do we turn south?"

"Not until tomorrow."

She bent over him and caressed his cheek. "We got away, my husband."

"So far. But we will not be safe until we are a long way from here. Down to Lake St. Sacrement."

"Andia-ta-roc-te. Why must you call it by the lace-cuff name?"

"What does it matter?"

"Do you think anyone is following?"

"Only one, Onea Canonou."

"Stone . . . Pipe?"

"A Caughnawaga. He was my guard. Twice when I tried to escape he caught up with me." He explained that Stone Pipe would forfeit his own life if his prisoner got away. "They planned to show me off to their general in Quebec as the reason why they were defeated at the fort. Because I warned Dorr."

"But how could this Stone Pipe track us? There is no trail. We left no footprints—there is hardly any snow left."

"He could track a snake over rock. Do not be surprised when he shows up."

*"If."*

"When. Which is why we should not stop here for long."

"If he shows up we will see him walk right by."

"*Nyoh,* he will want us to think that. He is very clever."

"How can he see us in here? We are far enough back from the mouth."

"He does not have to see us, he will know."

"*Neh,* we have come too far. If he was going to catch up he would have before now."

"We will see." He sat up and started to put on his shirt. "We should play safe, keep going."

"It is still raining hard."

"It does not matter."

"Please rest a while longer. I need it myself."

"Are *you* all right?"

"Just tired. It was a long way up and worrying about you made it even harder."

He set his palm against her cheek affectionately. "You have a warrior's heart, Tenäte Oÿoghi, I owe you my life." He averted his eyes. "I should have listened to you in the first place." He shook his head. "Poor Cayere Tawyne. As good, as loyal a friend as Wotstaha Onirares. I hate this knowing that he gave his life for me."

"He did not plan to."

"The worst of it is I know now, too late, he was right when he refused to go with us to join the English."

"Please, do not get me started on that."

He got his jacket back on. She put on her robe. They stared out at the rain pelting the ground and setting the naked trees glistening.

"Dorr *did* treat me well."

"He used you, all of you. So he won the battle, who will win the next one and the one after that?"

"It is time we left."

"Not until it stops raining."

He shrugged; they waited. The rain let up but did not stop altogether. Growing restless, he insisted they go on.

"It is already afternoon. We have wasted the whole day. We will eat and—" He stopped and listened intently.

"What is it?"

"Somebody is coming . . ."

They drew further back, bellying down, peering anxiously out. A man came by.

Sky Toucher groaned. "I knew it . . ."

# 75

TWO EAGLES LAY where he had fallen, afraid to move, almost afraid to breathe. Then he took a deep breath, gritted his teeth and one at a time tested his limbs. It was hard to tell if anything was broken, the pain filled his body like water in a moose bladder, starting at his neck throbbing down almost to his feet. Moving any more than he had already could aggravate a possible fracture. Satisfied that his arms and legs had escaped injury he lay perfectly still; he had landed on the side of his right buttocks, sending pain shooting up his spine to the nape. There could be damage to his hip, to his spinal column.

Was his spine fractured? He lay motionless, waiting for the overall pain to subside so that he could focus on specific areas. The blackness gradually gave way to gray, the stars faded and the moon and presently the ridge of the Green Mountains began releasing a sun the yellow of a mallard's egg. Slowly, he turned his head to look at the hemlock where he had hidden the two muskets and his pack. Pain struck but not until he spied both weapons and the pack, all lying less than ten feet from him. He needed at least one musket and the pack with the ammunition to protect himself against the return of the bear or any other marauding creatures which would instinctively sense his helplessness and not hesitate to attack.

He waited until the sun was well clear of the mountains before deciding he had no choice but to attempt to crawl to the pack and muskets. He started out, pain shot up his spine and his right hip felt as if a knife was being repeatedly plunged into it. He stopped short, lying on his side.

So there were breaks. How bad and where specifically? Maybe not, maybe he had just badly jarred his spine, and it needed rest.

But he wondered if his hip was fractured. Could it be just a deep bruise that needed time to surface? How bad was it? He speculated: he had moved his right leg, it might be just a break as wide as a hair, if that. Patiently, painfully, he undid his belt and eased his pants down. The cold air struck like a slap; there was no discoloration, a good sign. Unless it was too deep to show this soon.

His back was something else. Restoring his pants, he reached behind him and ran his fingertips up his spine, feeling nothing, but activating no new pain. His overall pain was diminishing until it reached a point where if he stayed still he felt none, except in his hip and at the base of his spine.

Once again he started out for the pack and muskets and this time, gritting his teeth, ignoring the shafts striking his spine, picked up by his nerves and sent streaking up it, reached the pack. The effort left him gasping and sweating.

"Now what?"

He felt safe holding the musket, looking about him, seeing nothing, no one. He opened the pack so that he could get at the powder and balls quickly. He ate a handful of corn, some salt venison and washed them down with snow, letting it melt in his mouth. He felt invigorated. His teeth ached again from the fall. He resolved to stay where he was, not to stir from this spot except to reach up, cut the lower branches of the hemlock and make a bed under him. It was warmer out, thawing, if he didn't get off the snow he'd be soaked through before noon.

*Nyoh,* he would stay where he was while the raiders and Tenäte Oÿoghi got further and further away. Trying to go on was out of the question, at least for the rest of today. He would give it until tomorrow morning before trying, he owed his body that much.

He sighed. It carried too many healed fractures, too many wounds: knives, arrows, musket balls, even a tomahawk chop down his left buttock. Sight of him naked, he recalled, caused Margaret to avert her eyes, and in damp weather, in the fall especially, his body released pain in as many places as he had fingers.

"*Nyoh,* wait."

And when he was able to go on—tomorrow, the next day, the day after—how fast would he be able to move?

Not fast. Like a slug.

What had shaken the tree, all the trees? Not one that he could see had fallen, but all around him had shaken like peach stones in the bowl game. And it struck so suddenly he hadn't a chance of catching hold. Out on the lake massive shards of ice had heaved up, fat swords brandishing, challenging the sky. Ataentsic's great island on the turtle's back had all but upended itself.

"Why?"

What caused it? What force from deep in the bowels of the earth? What trigger? And would it recur? Once more the ground shook slightly, was it building up for another great shuddering? Had the first one attacked the raiders up ahead? Tenäte Oÿoghi and her companion?

"Will I ever catch up now and find out?"

# 76

"ONEA CANONOU," MUTTERED Sky Toucher, staring out at the man passing and looking not in the least surprised.

"He is alone," murmured Singing Brook.

"He is always. It is between the two of us, no one else cares."

"How could he pick up our trail?"

"I told you he was clever."

"He passed by, he did not turn toward us, he saw nothing."

"He does not have to see, he *knows*. He will not keep going."

"What will he do?"

By now Sky Toucher had risen. He shrugged and thought a moment. "Maybe wait for us to come to him, *neh? Nyoh,* that is it, he will hide up the way and try to ambush us."

"I do not understand, you say he *knows* he has passed us? How could he?"

"Our trail leads up to this cave."

"But we left no tracks, there is so little snow. He is not a wolf, he is a man, he cannot know where our track ends when he cannot see it."

"He followed us here, did he not?"

Desperation seized her. "So what do we do?"

"Not worry about it. I cannot worry about things I expect. I say we eat, give him time to get well out of sight, then leave here, backtrack a ways, then turn south. Travel what is left of this daylight and all night, keep going until our steps are too heavy to move."

"You cannot do that to yourself in your condition."

"I will do what I have to do. You do not know this *rackesie!* He caught up with me twice before as easily as a dog tracks a hare. He cannot go back without me this time. The turkey cock vowed to kill him if I got away. So will the long knife who took his place."

"Your Stone Pipe is Mohawk."

"Praying. He could be my blood brother, it is his life against mine."

They ate the dried corn, wary of lighting a fire that might betray their whereabouts. A short time after eating, they left, heading back the way they came, traveling about three hundred paces before coming to a narrow path running north and south. They started down it.

"The further south we get, the closer we can move toward the lake," he said. "And when we reach Lake Andia-ta-roc-te we will be out of Abnaki Territory and can relax."

"Will others be out looking for us?"

"I do not think so, just him. Maybe it is not that he worries about the long knife, what he will do to him if I get away. Maybe just my doing it."

"What do you mean?"

"Beating him at this game of ours. That is what it is, a game: one against the other. I think that is why he made it easy for me to try, tying my ankles so carelessly, so that I could undo them with my teeth. He is a strange one."

"Strange? How?"

"Not once all the way up here did he strike me, and yet there were times he forgot to let me eat. We had long, friendly talks, he gave me bear grease for my face against the cold, got me a second blanket. We became close. But when the turkey cock was killed and he could have let me go he refused.

"He does not hate me like some Praying Mohawks hate us. He never did, still he is determined to get me to Stadacona where he knows they will kill me after they show me off to their general. I am their excuse for defeat. I warned Dorr, I caused it. And I helped him destroy the men they were holding out of the fight."

In the dank woods, as they went on, they could smell spring before they saw any evidence of its coming. Billions of living creatures invisible to the eye, unknown to the mind, stirred, became active in the thawed soil. Gradually the earth was coming to life. Then, as if to satisfy demand for proof, she spied the blunt, fat finger of a skunk-cabbage leaf breaking the ground, bringing forth its fetid odor to attract the overwintering flies. Everywhere as the snow continued to melt to a patchwork, freeing the upper frozen layer, nutrients came to life. The air hung warm and thick in a blanket above the ground, inviting the earth to awaken after the long winter's sleep.

On they pressed. He had rested and eaten but he still looked weary, his step labored. He would need more than a few hours to regain his strength. His skin had a grayish-white look, betraying his loss of blood. Would his heart and will be enough to sustain him? He seemed to think so, so why must she be pessimistic? The hardest part was over. Now all they had to do was widen the distance from his captors. From the Caughnawaga.

*Nyoh*, they would make it! In less than a week they would be near the fort called Carillon and the north shore of Lake Andia-ta-roc-te. A few days after, and they would reach the English fort where he could rest as long as he pleased for the last leg home. Looking back, their escape had turned out far easier than she expected. Of course her clothes had helped. Dressed in Mohawk garb she wouldn't have gotten near the camp without being seized.

Where had Stone Pipe gotten to? He looked to be the last pitfall in their path to freedom. She caught her breath. Was he behind them? Had he waited somewhere just beyond the caves, watching from cover as they left and followed them? She glanced warily back and touched his arm.

"What?"

"You think he might be following us?" Sky Toucher glanced past her back along the narrow path. She continued. "Let us hide behind those bushes over there and see."

"Let us keep going."

"Please."

He yielded. Getting down on her stomach she peered around the side of their concealment. She had a clear view of the path back up the way they had come. If he was behind them, did he have them in view and see them leave the path? Was he simply waiting for them to go on? It was all so annoying! They waited, Sky Toucher fidgeting, growing increasingly restless.

"He is not behind us, we go on."

"Shhhhh, listen."

Other than the raucous call of a crow far ahead, there was no sound. She made him wait a little longer before going on, he in the lead as before, beginning to drag his steps slightly, she noticed. They were passing under a large beech tree. A voice broke the silence.

*"Sha·wák!"*

Down he jumped, knocking Sky Toucher down, snatching his knife from his belt, holding his own knife with the point close to his throat. She forced herself between them, pushing Stone Pipe away. As Sky Toucher got to his feet, she angled her arms protectingly in front of him. Stone Pipe laughed and lowered his knife; Sky Toucher's knife he had shoved into his belt.

"So . . . you found yourself a woman, Cousin? Or did she find you? An Abnaki and a Mohawk, the wolf and the doe, *neh?*"

"She is Mohawk, she is my wife."

"Go away," she rasped, "leave us alone!"

"You, I will. Him, I must bring back. You can go on." He shoved her aside and again raised his knife to Sky Toucher's throat. His attention fully focused on him, he did not see her hand ease inside her robe.

"You did well this time, Cousin, you came a long way for a man who is only half himself. It will take us at least a sleep to get back. By the time we catch up with them they will have passed the rapids and be on their way down the Kanawage, *neh?*" He pulled two long strands of rawhide from his belt, holding them up, "Turn around."

Drawing and thrusting in one motion, she drove her knife between his ribs up to the haft. His face opened in astonishment, his knife slipped from his grasp, he stood teetering slightly, lowering his eyes, looking down at his afflicted side then at her in stunned disbelief. Death rattled his throat, he sank to the ground.

Sky Toucher sighed heavily. "Very good, Tenäte Oÿoghi." He caught her as she swayed, her cheeks suddenly ashen. "Are you all right?"

"I am not used to killing, but I am getting practice."

"What do we do with him?"

"Leave him and go on."

He stared down. "I feel like I am leaving a friend to the crows."

"A friend who did his best to make sure you die in Stadacona."

She retrieved Sky Toucher's knife from the dead man's belt, handing it to him. He was studying her, in his eyes a glint of near-wonderment, a look she had never see before.

# 77

THE EXERTION OF pulling the Caughnawaga's body into the bush tired them both. By the time they were finished Sky Toucher was panting heavily. Even so, he wanted to go on.

She wanted to rest. "There will be time enough to rest when we cross over into our territory."

They walked on into a woolly pink twilight. He was stumbling more often, moving as if his feet were stones. She forced him to stop. They sat on a boulder. He began coughing. By the time he got it under control he was flushed and sweating. She eyed him worriedly.

"I am all right," he insisted. "Give me your pack, I will carry it for awhile."

"You can barely carry yourself."

"I said—"

He stopped short and cocked an ear.

"What is it?"

Up on his feet, he pulled his knife, crouching slightly, looking around. The leafless undergrowth was unusually thick. Out of it Indians appeared, quickly encircling them. They were naked to the waist and wore breechclouts and warm-weather moccasins.

Though armed with bows and arrows, tomahawks, knives, their faces were not painted for war; they were a hunting party. There were at least twenty, standing stock still and staring. Sky Toucher wisely dropped his knife and gestured submission. This was Sokoki Territory; the Sokokis were a tribal branch of the Western Abnakis, blood enemies like all Abnakis of the Mohawks, who raided their villages, massacred their women and children.

For fully a minute no one uttered a sound, but in every eye Singing Brook could see hatred. A red-breasted nuthatch landed on a limb above Sky Toucher, emitting its tinny *yank-yank* call. Singing Brook's thudding heart felt as if it would tear loose from its bindings as she glanced from face to stony face. Then she heard a rustling and two of the Sokokis made way. A black robe appeared, a large crucifix dangling from his waist rope. He wore sandals, his hood was down revealing a round, creased and furrowed face. His skin was ghastly white and the pale gray eyes peering out of the shadows of the protruding ridges above them showed illness, as did his pallor. In contrast, his lips were almost crimson. The smile he managed threatened to tear his parchmentlike skin. He did not seem to notice Sky Toucher's Mohawk hair strip, for he did not react fearfully to it, as many whiteskins did. He spoke in French, but when neither understood, he repeated himself in English.

He had moved closer to Singing Brook, his arms crossed, his hands hidden in the voluminous folds of his robe. "You are Abnaki?" he asked puzzled.

"*Neh.*"

"Mohawk," said Sky Toucher. "My wife."

"Caughnawagas?"

"From the Mohawk Valley."

"I see. Then you are not Christians."

"*Neh.*"

"You are a long way from home. Permit me to introduce myself, I am Father Superior Antoine Valterie Sebastien Xavier Fresnais. And you?" They told him. "Forgive me for saying so, O-ron-ia-ke-te, but you do not look at all well." He eyed his bare legs. "Tsk, tsk, blessed St. Sebastian was beaten to death; you look as if you came close to the same."

Sky Toucher told him sketchily about his capture as a prisoner of war, and Singing Brook's rescue.

"How brave of you, Tenäte Oÿoghi, to risk your life against such overwhelming odds. But God in his charity was with you, I see. And now you are on your way home."

"We—" began Sky Toucher and passed out, slumping to the ground at the priest's feet. She cried out, stooped and eased him up on his side, feeling his forehead.

"He is *aghihi*, sick. He has suffered much, lost much blood."

"Obviously. He needs hot food and rest. And treatment for his wounds. Our mission is not far from here, the Mission of St. Joseph. Do you know of St. Joseph, Tenäte Oÿoghi? He was a secret disciple of our Lord Jesus. We will carry him to the mission, put him to bed."

He ordered poles cut and a crude litter fashioned. Sky Toucher was lifted onto it.

"He is young, strong, he will be all right," said the priest. "When he wakes up we will treat his wounds, feed him. And offer prayers for his recovery to Christ's Holy Mother and to St. Joseph. It may ease your mind to know that I once cured a warrior of St. Vitus's dance by commending him to St. John of God, Camillus de Lellis, patron saint of the sick, and placing a medal stamped with the saint's image in his mouth. In two days he was cured. Don't worry, we'll have O-ron-ia-ke-te up and about in no time!"

Singing Brook barely understood his words but thanked him anyway. He was the first black robe she had ever spoken to. She had only seen them at a distance, when she was little and they came to Tenotoge seeking converts. All she had heard about them painted them as wicked, agents of destruction, the monsters who had come on their wooden islands to steal the minds of the Mo- hawks, get them to desert and move up to Caughnawaga on the Kanawage. They preceded the lace-cuff invaders. The black robes were cunning, avaricious *seronquatses,* commissioned by the gold hat who ruled their country across the O-jik⸱ha-dä-ge⸱ga to steal the tribes' beaver as well as their souls, to render them helpless before the great wave of soldiers who followed them.

Only this black robe was no *seronquatse,* no scoundrel. He was kindly, considerate, his heart went out to O-ron-ia-ke-te. When all he need do would be to raise his hand, and a volley of arrows would strike them down. Out of the wilderness this kindly whiteskin had come to save his life. And protect them both against the So-kokis, their mortal enemies?

And convert them?

About twenty birch-bark wigwams comprised the settlement at the mission. Permanent homes, they were better made than the Ab-nakis' portable dwellings. Beyond the settlement a quadrangular fort was under construction. The mission chapel was built of logs with a bark roof. Inside at the far end was an altar, on it a brass crucifix, vessels and ornaments. Pictures hung above the altar, among them a primitive painting of Christ, and a well-executed likeness of the Virgin, both nearly life-size. There was also a paint-ing of the Last Judgment showing dragons and serpents feasting on the entrails of the wicked, while hideous demons scourged them in the flames of Hell. As Singing Brook gaped at the sight, Father Fresnais smiled benignly.

"The lot of the wicked, my child, the sinner, the unbeliever."

With her meager English she didn't understand "sinner" or "unbeliever." He didn't elaborate. It was dark by the time he ushered her out of the chapel. He insisted on walking her about the little settlement while Sky Toucher, still unconscious, was put to bed in the rectory, a small, low-roofed building across from the chapel. Singing Brook would have preferred to sit by his bed until he regained consciousness, and then tend to him, rather then min-gle with their enemies. But she didn't feel she should tell the kindly priest that. Children flocked around, some pulling at his robe until he good-naturedly shooed them away.

He brought her inside one of the wigwams. The people eyed her suspiciously, despite her clothing. Word had apparently already gotten around. Men, women and children crowded together with their dogs, squatting coiled like porcupines, or lying on their sides or backs, knees drawn up. A woman sat picking nits from a child's hair and eating them. Singing Brook suddenly could no longer feign interest. She was seized by concern that the hunters who had carried Sky Toucher back might be harming him.

"I must see my husband."

"Of course. I just thought that while he's unconscious I could show you . . . But come, come."

Sky Toucher was awake. His pallor gave his face the look of a death mask. He coughed lightly but no sputum came up. His face and neck glistened with perspiration.

"Congestion of the lungs," declared Fresnais, "brought about by a combination of exhaustion, pain and the dampness in the woods that always comes when the snow melts. You are a very sick man, O-ron-ia-ke-te."

She wiped away his sweat with her cuff. The room was sparely furnished, two beds, a washstand with a fragment of mirror standing on a shelf over it, a single stool. The only decoration was a large wooden crucifix, the lower end of its vertical bar badly cracked, as if it had been used to hammer something. Father Fresnais pulled down the bedcovers. Sky Toucher's clothing had been removed down to his trousers. Lacerations covered his body from neck to ankles.

The priest clucked sympathetically. "We must get that foul bear grease off you before we can tend to your cuts. I'll fetch a basin of water and clothes and you'll scrub him clean, Tenäte Oÿoghi. You must be very gentle."

Sky Toucher's immobile expression betrayed his discomfort but she washed him and was given ointment for his wounds. It was dark brown and smelled strongly of mint. She would have preferred the mashed root and juices of yellow dock for open sores, but perhaps, she reflected, this would work. Unfortunately, she used it up before she got halfway down his body.

Father Fresnais, meanwhile, had excused himself to go and read his breviary in the woods by the light of the moon. When he returned and she told him she'd run out of the ointment, his reaction was not what she expected.

"No reason to worry, my child, I've a much better treatment. I will pray to St. John of God, Camillus de Lellus. You will see a miracle take place before your eyes. Then a prayer to the Holy Mother, one to St. Joseph—"

"Mir-a-cle?"

"I cannot define it nearly as well as what you'll see happen.

First the prayers, then we'll feed you both." He chuckled. "The soul before the stomach, eh?"

# 78

IT WAS NEARLY six grindingly long and frustrating days before Two Eagles was able to resume the pursuit. He gloomily concluded that by now O-ron-ia-ke-te's captors had to have passed the mouth of the Richelieu River and were well down the Kanawage toward Stadacona, Quebec. It seemed pointless to even bother resuming the chase. Was O-ron-ia-ke-te even still alive? And what of Tenäte Oÿoghi? Had she and the warrior with her survived the shaking? Had they been killed even before it struck?

What if nothing slowed the raiders and he failed to catch up before Stadacona? In these clothes he looked obviously Oneida; earlier, he'd resolved to keep a sharp eye out for Sokoki hunters, follow them and when they slept, kill one and take his clothes.

Before starting forth he took time to hang as dead weight from a limb a few inches off the ground, to stretch his afflicted spine as well as his arms. His back continued sore, but with a dull ache rather than sharp pain. Which, when he lay down, gathered in a knot at the base of it. Again and again he set his hand back there, to grip it as tightly as he could, trying to relieve it.

He walked all morning without stopping and by noon was exhausted, especially his legs. Too long immobilized, the muscles softened and weakened. They could not bear his weight.

He rested repeatedly throughout the afternoon. It had clouded over and the night coming on threatened as black as a toad's eye when far ahead he spied two men ice-fishing about ten paces from the shore. Quickly, he got into the woods. The two fishermen sat opposite each other on their packs, their deer-sinew lines descending into the same hole. Two Eagles could see they had caught a number of fish; with the onset of darkness, they would probably quit.

He drew closer, his hand wandering to Splitting Moon's toothball tomahawk sharing his belt with his own spontoon tomahawk.

He was not eager for a fight, particularly two against one. He was tired, his body ached. His legs worried him—in hand-to-hand combat good legs are even more important than strength and agility in the upper body. He could see only one strategy: ambush the Abnakis when they came to shore.

He drew closer, moving from tree to tree. He was about a hundred paces distant when he heard shouting coming from the deeper woods to his left. Out of the woods came two more Sokokis, ostensibly friends come to help bring home the fishermen's catch. One man carried a small doe slung over one shoulder. Two Eagles sighed: could he overcome four? Would they head for their village or camp for the night? Together, the two fishermen had caught at least twenty good-sized fish—with the deer carcass as many as all four could comfortably carry. Two Eagles moved ahead, found what he expected, a recognizable, well-used path leading off to the northwest toward the foothills.

How far to their village? It was difficult following the path with his eye, the way it twisted through the trees, quickly vanishing altogether. He hurried up it. It was narrow, requiring any group traveling along it to keep in single file.

He could hear them behind him talking, laughing. The darkness settled in quickly, no moon, not a single star. He was well up the trail when he paused and looked about. Just ahead to his right rose a stout black walnut towering at least eighty feet in the air. But it wasn't its height that attracted his eye, it was the single limb that stood out at a nearly perfect right angle about seven feet above the path. He hid his pack and the muskets behind a stump and got out a length of rawhide salvaged from one of Splitting Moon's snowshoes.

He climbed the tree, crept out onto the limb and straddled it, reflecting as he did that it would suit his purpose perfectly were it six weeks hence and the tree dressed thick with foliage. But even now the darkness would provide sufficient cover. He waited, setting his knife between his teeth. Why didn't they come? He was too far away to hear them. His heart jerked, had they headed in another direction? He turned slowly, carefully, peering back down the path—but he could see nothing.

He was acutely aware of how his whole body ached with the

simple effort of climbing the tree. He recalled ruefully how easily he'd climbed the tree nearly seven sleeps earlier, before the great shaking had tumbled him out. He suddenly felt as old and decrepit as Carries-a-quiver.

Voices! A laugh! They were coming. Again turning he squinted but could see no more than two paces in any direction. His heart quickened, thudding like a shaping stone on chert; he would have just one chance.

They were coming close. He could hear the soft padding of their moccasins between snatches of conversation. He held his breath as the first man in line passed underneath, then the second—he could dimly make out the deer on his shoulders—a big man, as powerful as Splitting Moon and a foot taller. The third man followed, jabbering animatedly, his share of the fish slung over one shoulder. The last man approached.

Luck was with Two Eagles. The fourth man stopped short, two steps from directly under him, to kneel and fuss with his moccasin. By the time he got up and resumed walking, the man ahead had widened the separation between them to several paces. When the last man straightened, Two Eagles stiffened, looped the rawhide, dropped it, tightened it with all his strength. As he strangled him he slowly lifted him clear of the ground. The Abnaki gurgled softly, wrenched, kicked and went limp.

On walked his companions, jabbering away. Two Eagles waited, dropped lightly to the ground, divested his wrists of the rawhide and pulled the body into the bushes.

He crouched and listened. Any moment now they would miss him; one would speak, get no response, turn, and come running back to look for him.

Up onto one shoulder he hefted the corpse, heading for the deep woods as fast as he could. His pack and the muskets he would return for later. He glanced at the man's hair—dark as his and the same length. Two Eagles sighed.

He hated this, changing into the clothes of a blood enemy.

# 79

MORE FOR SINGING Brook than for himself, Sky Toucher worried over being in the midst of long-standing foes of the Mohawks. When Father Fresnais was out of the room, talking to one of his flock, Sky Toucher grudgingly agreed to stay the night.

"I will give in to you this once," he told her. "But tomorrow we leave."

"Do not talk nonsense. Look at you, you are even sicker than you were before you fainted."

"I will have to take my chances. Out there, at least, we have a chance, not in this place."

"The black robe will protect us."

"The black robe is only interested in converting us to his cross and his Jesus. If he can do that and they kill us it does not matter to him, he has our souls. The problem is they are not about to wait for him."

Singing Brook shook her head. "He did not save your life to throw it away so easily."

"You do not know, that is how black robes think. Only of the soul. They like converting sick children the best, there is no talk, no arguing, they sprinkle water on them, they mumble their secret words then let the child die. I tell you you cannot trust him any more than a lace-cuff. He *is* one, only with a cross instead of a long knife."

"I trust him." She did, she had told herself so from the first.

"How can you say that? Can you see inside his head? He answers to his god and to the gold hat who rules his country, not to his heart."

She rose from the stool and began pacing. "He could have let them kill you back on the path and taken your soul then and there."

"*Neh,* he has to take it *before* you die. After is no good."

"How do you know so much about black robes?"

"From Tiyanoga, O-ne-ha-tah, all who know them say the same things."

"But none of them knows this one. I trust him, I tell you."

"Your brain is turning, swinging upside down in your head."

"I know him, how he thinks, he feels."

He waved this away. "I do not. And I would rather not be around long enough to prove that what I am telling you is the way it is. We leave tomorrow."

"Why not tonight?"

"I . . . am too weak."

"You will still be tomorrow and the day after." She was suddenly angry. "We go when *I* say!"

His brow over his right eye arched. She meant it. He saw the futility of persisting and let it go. She pulled the stool closer and sat.

"Listen to me, his mir-a-cle will heal you. When you are fit to travel we will go on. Not before. We have too far to go, it will be hard on both of us."

"*Mir-a-cle?* Did he say what that is?"

"You heard him, when you are healed *we will know what it is.*"

He grunted.

"He says it will happen," she added.

"He says . . ."

"Shhhh, someone is coming."

Father Fresnais came in with two warriors. The Sokokis riveted their eyes on Sky Toucher. She imagined that in the next instant they would pull their knives and attack him; she sighed silently. It would be so easy, anyone could be a hero simply by sneaking in while they slept and slicing their throats. And the black robe seemed naively unaware of it.

"How do you feel, O-ron-ia-ke-te?" he asked.

"Better."

"Good, good. It is late, you should be asleep. You, too, Tenäte Oÿoghi. As for me, no rest for the weary. I must go to Shogahu, the next village. There is illness there. From what we are told it sounds like smallpox. I must do what I can." He glanced her way and saw the worry in her eyes. "You will be safe, no harm can come to you under this roof." He grinned. "It is not the chapel, not the House of God, but the house of his servant, the next best thing. Sleep well with pleasant dreams. I should be back before noon tomorrow."

They went out.

"If it makes you feel better, I will cram a moccasin under the door," she said to Sky Toucher.

"You want to stop them with a moccasin . . . ?"

"Please! They will not kill us while he is away."

"It is their chance to."

"They know they would have to answer to him for it!"

He stared and shook his head. "I love you, Tenäte Oÿoghi, my heart is so full of you sometimes it feels sore, but you think and trust like a *cian*. This is a hornets' nest we are in here, the death sting is the tip of a knife and they are as thick here as corn in August. Where is *my* tooth? I want it here in my hand." He gestured.

"In my pack with my own."

"Get it."

He held the knife outside the covers in plain sight. "Tonight I sleep one eye. You had better do the same."

"I refuse." She shook her head. "A shame you are not a woman."

"Me?"

"Just for now, so you could understand him as I do. He knows we are their enemies."

"He is a whiteskin," said Sky Toucher. "He does not know how deep the wound is that binds us in war, so deep it can never heal."

"The point is I am sure he did not leave here without telling them not to harm us!" He rolled his eyes. "I am going to bed."

"Do not forget the moccasin."

"Never mind."

"You may lose it in the scuffling when they break down the door to get in here. Better we say good-bye than good night; the next time we see each other will be in the Village of the Dead."

"You talk nonsense."

"*One* of us does."

She stood before the wash basin, bathing her face and upper

body. He watched her standing nude before the fragment of mirror. Moonlight swathed her back in a wide sash down to her hip.

"You are more beautiful than ever, Tenäte Oÿoghi."

She turned, managing a wan smile through her weariness.

"I want you under me."

"Better you sleep, not risk killing yourself. When you are healed and well, from then on we will get back all these nights we have lost."

He grunted. "We will if we get out of here alive."

# 80

THERE BEGAN THE long night in the camp of the enemy, a night which Singing Brook knew in advance would bring no sleep for her. He slept, dropping off even before she got into her bed. She lay staring at the rude board ceiling and thought of her knife in her pack stuffed under the bed. Looking over at him she could see the blade of his knife still in his hand, moonlight silvering it. What good would it do him if they did break in? They would be on him like wasps on ripe fruit before he got fully awake. She was not as naïve as he accused her of being, although she did believe that Father Frenais would protect them, even to warning the people against harming them while he was away.

But that didn't mean that what he told them went into every ear, and would be obeyed. There are always a few who go their own way, whose hatred toward the Mohawk set their blood simmering. What good would it do them if the black robe returned to find them both murdered and punished those responsible?

She was so exhausted she couldn't stop yawning, but sleep refused to come. She thought of getting up and setting the bed firmly against the door, though anyone bent on getting at them could get in through the single small window. Then, too, if O-ron-ia-ke-te woke up and saw the bed had been moved what would he think all her assurances that the black robe would protect them?

Again she looked over at him. How long before he'd be well enough to travel? He had to rid his lungs of what the priest called "congestion"; it stole his stamina and pushed sweat out of his flesh. In him, too, was fire, it leaped to her hand when she felt his forehead. His wounds would heal, but his loss of blood worried her. Time was needed to restore it, and his vigor. But having escaped one fire, here they were in another, and still a long way from friendly territory, where he'd no longer feel the need to sleep knife in hand.

Something drew her eyes to the window above the head of his bed. She started; two men were peering in, one laying the flat of his hand against the pane. She herself was in shadow, they could not see her, but they must have felt her eyes for they ducked and vanished. She pictured a wizened sachem talking to a group of angry-looking warriors, stirring hatred.

She lay awake until the pale lemon sun sent its first rays slipping through the trees. It was not the winter-white sun she had seen rising for so many weeks while the earth suffered in *augustuske's* grip. The chill had fled the air, the sunsets were golden warm, the snow and ice vanished from the woodlands. The ice on the lakes must have broken up by now and would melt quickly before *te-genhonid's* steady advance. That afternoon she had seen an early-blooming trailing arbutus flaunting two white bell-like blossoms.

Retracing in her mind their route from the river to the caves and south from there, this village had to be well above the north-west shoulder of Lake O-ne-ä-dä-lote. Below it lay Lake Andia-ta-roc-te. One could travel by canoe from the Kanawage all the way down to South Bay with only brief portaging between the two lakes. Could they find a canoe when they left this place? Like the other northern tribes, the Sokokis made their canoes of birch bark, lighter then the elm bark the Iroquois used. Could O-ron-ia-ke-te make such a canoe? Birch trees grew in abundance in these woods, unlike those surrounding Tenotoge. When was the best time of year to strip the bark?

*"Neh."* They would not build one, but find one or steal one if necessary. Getting home would be easier, even delightful! They would travel at their own pace, rest whenever they got the least bit tired, and on the lake there would be no paddling against the current.

She had not seen any canoes here. Perhaps the people had no

need for them. Perhaps there were no lakes conveniently close. Still, before it came time to leave, maybe she should talk the black robe into asking someone to build a canoe for them. As if they would! she thought cynically.

She fell asleep, awakening what seemed only moments later with a throbbing headache, aching in every bone and joint.

He was awake, sitting up. Her heart lifted. In his cheeks she could see faint color and his eyes did not have that foggy, sickly look so evident the night before.

"How do you feel?"

He coughed. "That is the first cough since last night. I am fine. Let us dress and get out of here."

"*Neh*, there is no rush. Notice anything?"

"What?"

"We are still alive. I told you not to worry, that no one would come. There is no danger."

"Like a *cian* . . ."

"Stop saying that! I will make a bargain with you. You look improved. If you really are with no more coughing, and you stay that way until tonight, and wake up tomorrow even better—"

"We leave. I will make a bargain with *you*. We leave now and I will do my getting better on the trail."

"*Neh.*"

He shook his head. "You are like a boulder that only shows a little above ground but underneath is as big as a longhouse. No one, nothing can budge it. I have never known anyone so stubborn."

"You see the glass over the place to wash?"

"What about it?"

"I will hand it to you, look into it."

Father Fresnais did not return from Shogahu until late afternoon. He came in looking desperately worried, all but wringing his hands. He set his broad-brimmed hat on the washstand and settled himself at the foot of Sky Toucher's bed.

"You look vastly improved. How do you feel?"

"He is much better," Singing Brook said.

"Good, excellent. Have you eaten?"

"A squaw brought us *sagamité,*" he replied.

"That would be Frances White Stone. I asked her to bring you something."

"Is anything wrong?" Singing Brook asked.

"Everything at Shogahu. As bad as it could be. Are you familiar with the pox, smallpox?"

"*Ge-sa-de-ek-ä-nä,*" muttered Sky Toucher, "in our language. The whiteskins' gift in trade."

"It has struck the people at Shogahu."

"How?" asked Singing Brook.

"It is hard to say, perhaps a Dutch trader brought it or a *coureur de bois.* Four people have already died." He studied his hands in front of him. "It is, as you may know, fiercely contagious, the most vicious of all, the Devil's disease. First comes fever, then the eruptions leaving holes when they dry up. It disfigures some poor souls so they're scarcely recognizable. With the fever come restlessness, delirium, even coma. Death." He crossed himself and set his hands together. "Even the unborn are susceptible. While I was there a baby was born with eruptions, having caught it in utero. I will have to go back. My people here are deathly afraid. The two men I brought with me left as soon as we were informed. I doubt if I can get anyone to go back with me."

"Is there a medicine for it?" Singing Brook asked.

"There are medications to stem fever and relieve the itching, but nothing I know of for the disease itself. It affects the oldest and the youngest, those not yet strong enough to fight it, the others at a stage when their strength is depleted. Forgive me, I'm rambling, but it really is so disheartening. And frustrating. I must go to the chapel and pray to St. John of God to allay the suffering of the stricken. I baptized the four who died earlier, thank heaven, and this time seven little ones who are in *articulo mortis. Dabit deus his quoque finem.*"

Again he crossed himself, got wearily to his feet, retrieved his hat and went out.

"There—is a good man," she murmured. "To risk his life to save others . . ."

Sky Toucher frowned. "He cannot save anyone's life, you heard him. All he can do is baptize."

"What is that?"

"I already told you. They sprinkle water, mumble secret words, make signs and that way get their hands on the soul to give to their god. To them life is nothing, the soul is all. And he wants yours and mine. A blind mole could see that."

"He does not take, he gives. He saved your life."

"*Because he wants my soul!* Watch him, he will begin working on both of us, to convert us."

"You are wrong. You do not recognize goodness when you see it in front of you."

"Watch."

She felt suddenly weary in her heart, fatigue building like sadness in tragedy. She yearned to be away from there, on the lake or threading through the woods, approaching the border and friendly territory.

# 81

FATHER JULIAN ALAIN Clouet was a sparely built man with narrow shoulders, a thin, slightly long neck and nondescript features. His congenital near-inability to grow hair produced but a downy fuzz on his upper lip and his chin. He stood only five-foot-six but what he lacked in physique he more than made up for in heart and spirit. An ardent patriot, he had enlisted in the army at age fifteen, rising quickly to the rank of sergeant in the Alsace Regiment, eventually to conduct himself with honor and distinction in the War of the Polish Succession. Unfortunately, in his final action he took a ball in the left hip, which injury crippled him for the remainder of his life. Awarded not one but two medals of valor, he was honorably discharged and returned home to his native Strasbourg, to discover that his beloved mother, his only living relative, had taken to her death bed.

Day and night Clouet prayed at the altar of the Cathedral of Notre Dame for her deliverance, pleading with God, vowing that he would take holy orders and commit his life to Christ, if his mother was spared. Six days after his return his supplications were answered, and his mother miraculously recovered.

Clouet lost no time in making good on his promise to God. He had always been a good Catholic; now, spurred by the miracle of *maman's* deliverance, he underwent an upheaval of the spirit, bringing together all the forces of his dogged nature into one single focus. Once more he would go to war. Overnight there came a change, not of spiritual commitment, for that had always flourished in his nature. Now, he saw a change of life and purpose. With the aid of the Abbé Delacroix, prelate of the cathedral, he was introduced to the Society of Jesus. His military background served him well from the outset, for the Society based its regimen on the principles of military discipline exalted to the highest degree. The Society was everything, the individual nothing, except insofar as he might prove himself a useful instrument for carrying out the Society's aims.

Having exchanged the red for the black, Clouet underwent a six years' course, was ordained a priest and, in the midst of his work in Strasbourg, was called away to a tertianship, as preparation for his solemn profession of the society's three vows: to perpetual poverty, chastity and obedience.

Seven years passed; having compiled an exemplary record of service, upon the death by natural causes of his beloved mother, Clouet was dispatched with nine other priests to New France to "work among the heathen."

Father Emile Hiroux, who was older than Clouet and younger than Father Fresnais, accompanied Father Clouet back from a visit to a Sokoki village located well to the north of Shogahu. Now Father Hiroux was not in one of his more sanguine moods. He was weary, his left heel had acquired a blister inside his sandal strap, requiring him to walk with the strap hanging loose and his sandal flopping at his foot. He had not enjoyed an adequate night's sleep since leaving the mission. And he was famished. Originally from Marseilles, he was unaccustomed to the severe cold weather of the region and was forever sniffling. He stood nearly a foot taller than Father Clouet; side by side they made an amusing picture. Hiroux considered himself as zealous a Catholic as Clouet and as staunchly dedicated to propagating the faith, but lacked the smaller man's extraordinary and unabating fire. Enormous black eyebrows shadowed Hiroux's heavy face and eyes, which held a warm twinkle, in marked contrast to the persistently solemn eyes of Clouet. At the moment, Clouet hitched along on his bad hip, Hiroux's sandal flopped and slapped his foot, the bigger man carrying a switch with which he beat at trees as they passed them.

"Can you hear it?" he asked.

"Hear what?"

"My stomach. Oh, what I wouldn't give for a fat gray mullet sizzling in the pan!"

Clouet turned and eyed him sternly. "You took a vow of poverty, deprivation."

"*Dep*rivation, not *starv*ation."

"It's all in your mind, Father."

"It's all in my stomach, Julian, where it should be. The mullet, that is. Is it a sin to be hungry?"

"It is to lust after mere food."

"There's nothing *mere* about food, my friend. Oops, there it goes again, didn't you hear? Would that I never see another pot of corn mush again as long as I live. What I wouldn't give for a nice fat gray mullet . . ." he repeated wistfully.

"So you said."

"How far from here, do you think?"

"Another two hours." Clouet sighed resignedly.

"Anything wrong?"

"Our lack of success, of course, what else?"

Hiroux smiled. "We converted seven of them."

"I was hoping for three times that. And of the seven, how many will remain faithful? And practice their faith? That one they called Long Lake only accepted Christ because his squaw did. You could look at his face and see there was no commitment. That's our biggest problem," Clouet said.

"What?"

"What? *What!* Converting them only to stand by helplessly and watch them backslide. What I really can't stand is having to give trinkets to win them over, even to get them to listen."

"What's wrong with a few gifts?"

"It's bribery. A man accepts Christ for what he has to offer, not for needles and thread or ribbon or a knife. It's disgusting!"

"It works."

Clouet shook his head. "It's wrong and it doesn't work. You don't really think Long Lake will pray every day and keep the sacraments? And when he doesn't, will his squaw lose interest?"

"No one said it would be easy, Julian," Hiroux reminded him.

"No one said it would be *impossible,*" the other snorted.

"It's not. More than half our converts back at the mission have remained faithful . . ."

"Only because we're there looking over their shoulders. Do you think if we weren't around they'd remain true to their faith, practice it, keep it strong in their hearts? I don't."

"We *are* in an optimistic mood today, aren't we?"

"I'm sorry. You're right, seven *are* better than none. And even if only three or four stick with it . . . It's the little things that are the problems. *They* don't have facial hair, so we have to try to explain Christ's beard, try to find a picture of him without his beard. Where? And their hideous superstitions. The way they deny the existence of one all-powerful God, a great spirit. I could go on and on."

"Do you know what your problem is, Julian?"

Clouet stopped a second time and turned. "I wasn't aware I had one."

"My friend, you are the most Catholic Catholic I've ever known, another Ignatius Loyola in your zeal, in the astonishing depth of your faith. It's impossible for you to understand why others don't run to embrace the faith, throw off all their primitive beliefs like wet clothing and—and engorge Christ."

"Engorge?" Clouet looked astonished.

"You know what I mean."

"You hit it, that's our biggest problem, their superstitions. It's easy to write on a clean slate, it takes time and effort to first wipe it clean before you can even begin."

"True, true."

"Their primitive minds are so cluttered with nonsense!"

"Cheer up, my friend, learn to take what comes your way and be grateful for that. I do. Seven converts, Julian, seven."

"In nearly four weeks. At this rate we'll be dead and buried. The priests who follow us will be, too, before we can make any claim to bringing the faith to this wilderness. So it sticks, I mean."

Hiroux grinned. "You love being a pessimist, don't you?" He shook a reproving finger. "You *expect* everything to turn out badly so when something good happens it verges on the miraculous. You're another Job, my friend."

"Job? Job? Do you hear me cursing the day I was born?"

"Hardly, but you're just as impatient as he was."

Singing Brook stood in the rear of the little chapel staring at the "Last Judgment" as if mesmerized. A few worshipers were seated on mats on the ground. There were no benches, no chairs. Two were saying their rosaries, others knelt in prayer. Votive candles flickered on the altar. She stood in shadow, her eyes fixed on the painting. What was hell? Did evil and wicked people really burn there after death? It was frightening. She knew nothing about the black robe's religion, about any religion brought across the Wide Water. Old Porcupine did, but Singing Brook had never been sufficiently curious to ask him anything about his change of religious heart.

This picture was so unlike anything she had learned about monsters and spirits it disturbed her. Yet these people, the Sokokis, accepted it, believed; at least some did. Hearing someone come in she turned. It was a black robe, smaller, younger than Father Fresnais, unlike him not at peace with himself, troubled looking. He stared at her, not with the look that she saw so often in men's eyes that undressed her, this look was pure curiosity.

"Do I know you?" he began in Abnaki. She didn't understand. He tried French. She stared blankly. He changed to heavily accented English. She was unfamiliar with the word "stranger" but she could see that she had aroused his curiosity.

"I am not Abnaki."

"Oh?"

"Mohawk."

"Caughnawaga, of course."

"*Neh,* from the Mohawk Valley."

His face darkened, only slightly, just enough to warn her that she'd made a mistake. Now she realized he saw her as these people's enemy. He no doubt shared with them their hatred for her people.

"What are you doing here?" he asked, his tone a trifle annoyed.

She explained as best she could what had happened, leading to her second blunder.

"Your *husband* is here, too?" He stifled a gasp but tried to change the subject. "Have you seen the father superior?" he asked.

"He has gone to Shogahu, where the *ge-sa-de-ek-ä-nä* is."

"The . . ."

She couldn't remember the English word for it. "Ah . . ." She poked her cheeks with her finger.

"Pox! Smallpox!" He gaped and gasped and flung his fingers in the sign of the cross. "Blessed Saint Anne, not again!"

"He came back from Shogahu and returned there a while ago."

"How many men did he take with him?"

"I did not see him leave but I think he went by himself. The men he took the first time did not want to stay there."

"Because it's so highly contagious." His eyes rounded, he clapped his hands together, shaking his head melodramatically. "It's a devastating disease, it can go through a village like fire through a forest, devastating." He glanced at the parishioners. "He won't be back tonight; I'll have to take evening Mass. This is ghastly, terrible, I . . . what are you doing in here, did you come in to pray? Are you a Christian?"

"*Neh.*"

"Your husband?"

"*Neh.*"

"You say he's ill, exhausted, his lungs, whatever. How bad is he?"

"Getting better. We will be leaving in a few days."

"Ahhhhh." Again his eyes narrowed, he assumed a threatening expression. This one, she knew, she could not trust like she trusted the older black robe.

"I must see to my husband."

"I'll drop in later, after Mass, I want to meet him. I've never met a Mohawk warrior, I hear all the stories . . . I mean . . ."

She went out. He stood in the doorway watching her cross to the rectory. He shook his head. I don't understand you, Father, how does your mind work? How can you give shelter to our peoples' sworn enemy? A red devil who'd just as soon scalp us all as look at us? Amazing, he must be losing it, he has to be.

## 82

SKY TOUCHER IMPROVED rapidly, doing so remarkably well that he insisted they leave the next day. Singing Brook talked him into staying an additional day. Father Fresnais came stumbling back that morning, a portrait of exhaustion and frustration.

Into the rectory he summoned Father Clouet and Father Hiroux. They sat on three-legged stools around a rude table in a room as barren as a cell. On one wall was the requisite crucifix, against another was a cupboard and a long table on which stood a number of candles in various stages of consumption.

Father Clouet was speaking. "We might as well be harboring English pirates!"

"I must go and see to my children," said Hiroux, flashing a look between his two colleagues. He was anxious to escape their contention before the sparks began to fly.

Fresnais waved him away, the door rattled shut behind him. The father superior returned Clouet's cold gaze. In it, unmistakably, was silent reprimand.

Clouet cleared his throat and began tapping nervously. "They're Valley Mohawks, Father."

"They made no secret of that."

"The people hate having them around; it's downright painful for them."

"It'll only be a day or two more, Julian. They keep to themselves, they don't bother anyone. Something's on your mind. Say it."

"I think both should be taken prisoner," Clouet blurted. "Take them to the nearest fort, turn them over to the soldiers."

"I've offered them my protection."

"They're *Valley* Mohawks! Murderers, cannibals, rapists, it's our duty!"

"You're getting red in the face."

Clouet glowered. "Don't make fun of me, Father."

"I'm not, I just don't want you getting all upset."

"I *am* upset. This is wicked, a sin and a crime. Gray Moose's two brothers and his cousin were captured by Mohawk raiders, tortured to death along with their wives and children!"

"And you would hold these two responsible for that?"

"I would, as would the governor general and the authorities, everybody."

"I see. But that's as far as it goes."

"What do you mean?"

"I mean, Julian, that you won't do anything about it. I've given you my position on the matter, I'm afraid that ends it."

"With all due respect it does not. What about my vow? 'In all things *except* sin I ought to do the will of my superior and not my own.' "

Fresnais bristled. His words came spaced, tinged with resentment: "You presume to quote Ignatius Loyola to me?"

"Further," rasped Clouet. "When I am commanded by my superior to do a thing against which my conscience revolts as sinful and my superior judges otherwise, it is my duty to yield my doubts to him. If submissions do not appease my conscience I must—"

" 'Impart your doubts to two or three other persons of discretion and abide by their decision.' 'Two or three.' I've no idea as to Father Hiroux's opinion but even if he sides with you you're still one vote short."

"The law says that any Iroquois not converted to Catholicism should be seized on sight and brought to the military authorities."

"Military law, Julian, not the Society's."

Clouet knew that his position was shaky if not untenable. In Loyola's *Letter of Obedience* the founder of the society made clear the superior's powers. The superior was to be obeyed simply as such and standing in the place of God, without any reference to his personal wisdom, piety or discretion; and any obedience that falls short of making the superior's will one's own, is lax and imperfect.

But Clouet could ill resist the challenge. He was right, and he burned with his rightness. Fresnais was wrong and was deliberately committing a sin. Clearly, Clouet had no choice: he must save the father superior from his own recklessness.

Despite being unable to make out what was being said, it was clear to Singing Brook and Sky Toucher from the black robes' tones that Clouet was angry. Over what was just as easy to deduce.

"He hates us," murmured Singing Brook.

"He wants to turn us over to the nearest lace-cuffs."

"You think he would disobey the old black robe?" she asked.

"Either that or talk him into seeing it his way. He will keep at him. You talked to him, what do you think?"

"Perhaps you are right, perhaps we should leave."

In the other room Clouet was furious, red-faced, the flames of his indignation leaping. But wisely he did not press the issue further. Father Fresnais got wearily to his feet.

"I must return to Shogahu, Julian. I'd ask you to come with me but that would be as good as saying I don't trust you. Nevertheless, let me caution you: while I'm gone don't do anything you'll be sorry for."

"Are you implying . . ."

"I'm not implying anything."

"With respect, Father, you offend me. Deeply."

"I'm sorry. We'll talk no more about it. Just please leave those two alone, and don't go stirring up the Sokokis against them. I mean it, Julian. I've talked to their leaders, explained the difference between Mohawk warriors on the warpath and harmless individuals."

"*That* one strikes you as harmless?" Clouet asked.

"Under the circumstances, definitely. Both are in temporary difficulty and ask only to be left alone. They'll be leaving here shortly."

"I've no intention of stirring up the Sokokis."

"Good. I don't know what we can do about the situation at Shogahu. It's a sad and sorry day for the Mother Church when we have to depend upon smallpox to get us converts."

Clouet grunted. He wasn't in the least interested, his mind was on other things.

# 83

N O SOONER HAD the father superior left for Shogahu than Father Clouet got the ears of two Sokoki warriors. They were eager to assist him. He decided to head for the fort on the Ile la Motte, located roughly midway between where the Saranac River emptied into the lake and the headwaters of the Richelieu River, a distance of no more than five or six leagues. There he planned to obtain soldiers, rush back and capture the two Mohawks, get them out of there and into irons before Father Fresnais returned. If the old man asked whether Clouet had any part in the disappearance, he'd simply deny it. A lie told in the furtherance of a righteous cause is no lie. Besides, Fresnais would assume they'd left of their own accord.

So simple was his strategy, he foresaw no reason why it couldn't be carried out before sundown, if he hurried. He sneaked a look through the rectory window to make sure the Mohawks were still in their quarters and was preparing to leave the mission with his two companions when Father Hiroux came hurrying up.

"Julian, where are you going?"

"To Telldaga," lied Father Clouet, referring to a Sokoki village just west of the mission.

"What for?"

"Mission of mercy," he said.

"*What* mission of mercy?" Hiroux asked.

"Never mind, I'll be back tonight."

"You're leaving me all by myself? Father Fresnais may not be back for days, I can't handle everything."

"For the short time I'll be gone you can, you're not crippled. I'll see you tonight, I promise."

Hiroux groaned histrionically and set out for the chapel, his broken sandal slapping his heel. Only when he went inside did Clouet turn south, the two warriors hurrying behind him: Ka-ta-kwa-je, It-was-bruised, and Na-wah-tah-toke, Two-moccasins-standing-together. Neither was particularly bright but both were strong, willing, accommodating and hated Mohawks. Sokokis, like all Abnakis, wore their knives in sheaths around their necks. Theirs bounced against their painted chests as they loped along. They knew the south trail and Clouet knew he could depend upon them for protection on his "mission of mercy."

Which was what it was, actually. Wasn't he saving his superior from himself? As well as from certain harsh discipline from the archbishop in Quebec, if it ever got out that he'd been protecting Mohawks? Poor Antoine, he was getting old, his judgment deserting him as rapidly as his memory. Just recently he'd left his missal on a stump in the woods and in the same week completely forgot a catechism class. Older men need the protection of young friends.

The beauty of this situation was that Fresnais would never know what happened to his two Mohawk guests. Clouet's narrow chest warmed. The *commandant* at Ile la Motte would commend him effusively for his patriotism and doubtless hang the pair within the hour. In time a written report would find its way to the intendant, to be lost in the files with myriad others of its kind. That would end that.

And Clouet would have done his duty. What earthly right did Antoine have to prevent him? Now that he thought about it in earnest, he'd be letting the old man off easily. He deserved to be punished. Of course, they *were* friends, and for all the father superior's faults Clouet was fond of him. But covering up this indiscretion—the most charitable way of putting it—wasn't right, it wasn't. He'd decide about the punishment when he got back.

Spring was bringing the usual rush of wildflowers. The vanguard of lilac and bluish-white hepatica was speedily being joined by delicate spiral-flowered rue anenome, thick little greenish-white floret clusters of saxifrage and white-petaled bloodroot with its golden-yellow centers. Clouet failed to see the flowers, was unaware of the intoxicating smell of spring rising from the damp earth around him. His mission commanded his full concentration. Father Hiroux came to mind. Poor Emile, such a narrow-witted plodder, so determinedly oblivious to the political realities of these turbulent times, the complex problems here in New France. Hiroux should have enlisted in the army before studying for the priesthood. The army taught one about the world, who and what moved it. Strange, Hiroux came from Marseilles, a good-size port. One would think he would have gained a smidgen of worldly wisdom.

Hiroux wasn't about to voice a syllable of objection to the old man's treason. *Was* it treason? Strong word, but what else could one call it? The enemies of the Sokokis were the enemies of the French. No red-blooded patriot protected his country's enemies or their defenders. Sedition in the guise of charity is not charity. And what of the old man's vows? Did harboring the enemy break any vow? Clouet wasn't sure.

"Still, he's broken faith with Emile and me," he murmured. Two Moccasins glanced toward him questioningly. "Nothing, let's go faster."

"I am coming, I am coming," growled Sky Toucher. "What is the matter? You look troubled."

"I worry about the one with the peach fuzz all over his face." She studied him, frowning. "Will you be up to this?"

"I am all right."

"You will find that out after you have been on the trail for a while. You must not overdo it."

"I am fine, do not talk to me like I was a *cian*."

They had packed the extra clothing given to them by Fresnais, and now they set out, all eyes on them, eyes filled with curiosity, with disapproval, hatred.

Leaving the rectory, she glanced back at the door.

"What?" he asked.

"It does not seem right to leave without thanking him for all he did for us."

"You heard him. He had to go back to that village with the *ge-sa-de-ek-ä-nä*."

"Mmmmm. He is the first black robe I have ever met and his heart is good. If all of them are like that . . ."

"They are not. Most are like peach fuzz who wants us dead. Hurry."

"I am coming . . ."

They headed for the same trail Clouet had taken two hours before. Again and again Singing Brook glanced behind them to see if he was following with armed warriors.

# 84

Fort Dion on the Ile la Motte was a crude vertical-log stockade thrown up in a few weeks. Now it bristled with cannon on three sides and offered a clear view of the lake up, down and to the east. As small as the installation was, it protected the French on the south-central border of their colonial empire. To besiege a fort required attackers to bring up heavy artillery and break a hole through a wall, forming a breech that could be stormed. Since Fort Dion could only be stormed by water—an all but impossible task—fewer than fifty soldiers were assigned to command half that number of cannon on the "vigil in the south."

The island itself sat less than a league from the west shore. It had a small dock, so boat traffic plied to and from the mainland. Clouet and the two Sokokis clambered into a leaky *chaloupe* and as they were ferried across, he considered that he should have simply sent the two Sokokis to alert the *commandant*. But very likely he wouldn't have listened or even believed them. With no priest to accompany them, they'd lack credibility.

The sun was about two thirds of its way down to the Adirondacks. If the *commandant* heard him out and gave him the soldiers immediately, he would indeed be back before sunset. As two shabbily dressed French Canadians helped him up onto the wharf, it was easy to see that discipline was something less than rigid here.

"The commander, at once," Clouet demanded.

*"Oui, Père, dedans en haut."*

They were led up two flights of stairs to an office at the end of a narrow hallway. As the soldier knocked, Clouet could hear the clinking of glass. They were admitted and introduced to Commandant Claude Piquet, heavy-set, in need of bathing, unshaven, slightly disheveled and more than slightly drunk. A half-filled bottle of cognac stood by his elbow. He lowered his tumbler.

Clouet made no effort to hide a sigh.

"Father . . ." the major asked thickly.

"Clouet. From the St. Joseph Mission."

"A chair for the father, Bousset. What can I do for you?"

Clouet returned his glassy stare and resisted the impulse to judge him, despite the heavy alcoholic fumes. As Clouet explained his mission, Piquet emptied his glass, setting it down so hard that it jumped from his grasp and tumbled to the floor. He bent over to search for it.

"Go on, I'm listening. Mohawks? So far north? They must be Caughnawagas."

"*Mais non, Commandant,* they're Valley. He's a warrior, killed dozens of our Indians I'm sure. Not to mention our people."

Piquet reappeared, breathing hard from the effort, setting his tumbler in the center of the cluttered desk. "And you want us to take him prisoner?"

"Both of them."

"Two men should be enough."

"I'd rather at least four."

"You expect trouble?"

"He's a Mohawk, Satan in moccasins!"

The commander sighed. "All right, all right, as long as they're back here with them right away. Bousset. Bousset!" Clouet winced at the loud voice. The corporal reappeared. "Go find *Sergent* Loubet, wake him up. Tell him to collar two men and yourself to go out on a prisoner pickup. The father here'll take you to them. Bring both back here. They're not to be harmed. I want to talk to them before we hang them."

Back at the Mission of St. Joseph Father Fresnais had returned unexpectedly early to be welcomed enthusiastically by Father Hiroux and informed that Father Clouet—

"Left with two men."

"Left for where?"

"Talldega."

"What for?"

"He said a 'mission of mercy.' "

"*What* mission of mercy? I know of no problems in Talldega."

"He didn't say."

"And the Mohawks?"

"They left sometime after he did. I think they were . . . un-comfortable here."

"I know they were. Did you see them leave? Was the man in any condition to travel?"

"He looked all right."

"Talldega you said."

"That's what Julian said."

"Mmmmm. Why, I wonder? What does he know that's going on there we don't? Which direction did he take?"

"I didn't see but, Talldega's to the west."

"Mmmmm. Let's go in the rectory."

Fresnais closed the door behind them. "Talldega. Let me ask you, did Julian say anything to you about the Mohawks?"

"No, why?"

"He couldn't stand their being here, couldn't stand the idea of us giving shelter to the enemy. He's absolutely fanatical in his hatred of them. I wonder . . ."

"What?"

"Is it possible he lied to you? That he went to get soldiers to arrest them? I wouldn't be surprised."

"Disobey you, his superior?"

"He wouldn't see it as disobedience. To him it's duty, to be ignored, avoided at his peril. Sometimes I'm so naïve. I specifically warned him not to stir the people up against them. It never dawned on me he'd sneak off behind my back and get soldiers to arrest them."

"I can't believe he'd do such a thing."

"I can. It was in his face. I paid no attention to it. How long after he left did the Mohawks leave?"

"More than an hour, close to two."

"That long? Of course they didn't realize he'd left, didn't sus-pect anything. Oh dear, I hope I'm wrong. Bless my soul." He crossed himself. "I pray I am."

"Father?" the other asked tentatively. "Perhaps Julian's right. It's for the best. They should be captured."

"No. I brought them here in their hour of need. They trusted me. They had my word they'd be safe. If they're caught the authorities will surely hang them both."

"Not the woman . . ."

"Yes, the woman. The governor general doesn't mince words about that. Their women have babies, boys who grow up to become warriors. Oh dear, oh dear. If only we knew in which direction he's heading . . ."

"He said west to Talldega."

"He 'said.' What's the nearest fort?"

"North of here, Fort Jean on the Richelieu River. South, the fort on the Ile la Motte."

"South, it has to be. That's the direction the Mohawks would be taking. He has to play it safe."

"Safe?" Hiroux looked baffled.

"Of course, in case they leave here before he gets back with the soldiers. Heading south they can't get past him. What do we do? What do we do?"

# 85

TWO EAGLES WORE his pessimism like war paint. Anyone looking his way would recognize it instantaneously. Catching up to Tenäte Oÿoghi, let alone O-ron-ia-ke-te, would be impossible; he'd squandered too much valuable time.

This bad luck—the fall and the consequences of it—he hated even more than the clothes he'd appropriated. They were rags and smelled putrid. He whipped off the headband, threw it away and dropped the blanket from his shoulders. It was getting warmer, even in the nights. He didn't need its protection. It smelled like *oeuda*.

"Shit!"

Too late he was getting his stamina back, finally able to cover three and four leagues without stopping for anything, other than to urinate. One other worry dogged his steps: It was *tegenhonid*, Sokoki hunters would be coming out by the hundreds. This was their main trail he was following, the War Road. Was she ahead of him, or on the other side of the lake? More likely, by this time, she had already passed the mouth of the O-chog-wä, the Richelieu River, and was heading down the Kanawage. Still, starting down from the headwaters of the Richelieu, how had she gotten through the settlements crowding the banks on both sides?

"Dressed like a Mohawk?"

If she'd made it to the river, which in itself was doubtful, they'd be captured, her companion shot and she'd be raped before she got within a hundred paces of the first settlement.

"Her brain must be upside down in her head to do this thing." The one with her had to be even stupider. As stupid as he himself was? He should not think that about any of them. This was O-ron-ia-ke-te, they at least had to try to rescue him.

The further he traveled, the more trees had fallen. Was *she* following any trail? She'd probably stopped at Fort Anne, and if nothing else, was advised to follow the War Road. And the warrior with her would know.

Longingly, he imagined Splitting Moon walking beside him on two healthy legs: Splitting Moon, his conscience, his voice of pessimism. In his head Splitting Moon spoke:

*Her brain must be upside down to even try . . .*

"He is her husband."

*He is dead, he must be by now. Too much time has gone by.*

"Maybe not. I cannot believe they would take him back and kill him on the way. That scout who overheard them told her they wanted to get him to Stadacona, that is what her mother said."

*What for?*

Two Eagles shrugged. "Must you ask? To execute him before all eyes. And think about this: if they did not intend to take him all the way, would they not have killed him when they bought him from that trader?"

*Ahhh, how do you know they did not kill him there.*

"Dorr's men, a scout, somebody would have found his body where he was handed over. *Neh,* they took him all right, he is with them."

*They could have killed him and stuck him in a tree. Or buried him.*

*"Neh."*

Ahead, an island rose, on it a ramshackle fort. Which one? What difference? Were they not all the same, all studded with cannon and manned with lace-cuffs? Off to his left the land rose in a ridge. He ascended it and presently was able to look down on the path he had been following. Passing the fort he shaded his eyes. The white standard powdered with fleur de lis hung listlessly at its mast, cannon barrels gleamed in the sunlight. Two boats were tied to the pier. No one was outside, the place looked deserted.

The mission of St. Joseph was now well behind Sky Toucher and Singing Brook. But still, glancing back repeatedly and hurrying her step, she could not relax.

"If only we were not so far from the border—"

"Not that far now," he said. "If we keep going all night, we will cross into Mohawk Territory before dark tomorrow."

Not once had they stopped to rest, for even a few seconds. Both were tiring. She had picked a handful of yellow lady's slippers with a few bluets. Ahead the trail narrowed before swinging around a huge boulder. They heard metal striking, they stiffened. She grabbed his arm.

"Back—" she snapped.

They whirled. Two soldiers, muskets upraised, stood leering. The other two, Father Clouet and the Sokokis, jumped up from behind the boulder and came running, encircling them.

"You are under arrest in the name of our sovereign, Louis the Great, Louis the Grand Monarch, Louis the Sun King!" bawled Clouet. "Do not move, do not even speak."

"You cannot do this," murmured Singing Brook. "We have the old black robe's protection, your chief."

"You *did* have, no longer. Out here you're fair game. Where's that rope, *Sergent?*"

A rope was produced with a noose already fashioned and draped around Sky Toucher's neck. He was to be led like a cow on a halter.

"Tie their hands behind their backs and stand clear."

"Hers, too?" Sergeant Loubet asked.

"*Oui!* If she gets away, she might come back with warriors. There could be bloodshed. All set, march them back to the fort. *Vite. Avancez.* One two, one two—"

"Why do you do this?" Singing Brook asked. "You do not even know us."

"You are the enemy. Wherever we find you, under whatever circumstances, you must be taken."

"And hanged," said Sky Toucher.

"That's not up to me, I'm only doing my duty as a patriot. March in step there, one two, one two." Two Moccasins shoved Sky Toucher, he stumbled, nearly falling. "Stop that!" snapped Clouet. "The prisoners are not to be abused. Keep moving everyone, left right, left right."

Above them, peering down through the trees, Two Eagles watched the ambush, the capture, the party start toward the fort. He had readied one of the two muskets for firing, bringing the cock back to full, aiming at the black robe.

He reconsidered, lowering his weapon. "Kill him, and my cousin and his woman will die."

Better he get ahead of them, ambush *them*. But he could only take out one at a time. Not the black robe, he wouldn't harm the Mohawks. Instead first one of the two Sokoki dogs.

"You understand," said Clouet, "I do not do this out of any personal enmity, it's strictly duty. To shirk one's duty in time of war is treasonous."

"Your conscience is *your* problem," muttered Sky Toucher. "We are not interested."

"What I'm trying to say is neither of us created this—unhappy situation. It's been thrust upon us, and we're forced to live with it. A loyal Frenchman never questions the rightness or wrongness of war."

"*What* war?" asked Singing Brook. "No one is fighting now."

"All the same, the war goes on. We all serve. Each of us must do his part: you, me, these Sokokis. Consider me: I have no personal enmity toward you. Bless my soul, I scarcely know you."

"You make my ears ring like a tree cricket stuck in the pocket. Can you shut his mouth?" Sky Toucher asked the sergeant.

Loubet scowled, shoved him with the stock of his musket. "Don't be disrespectful to the father, *Sauvage.*"

A soft whirring sound. The knife lodged, vibrating, in Two Moccasins' chest. Down he fell screaming. A shot rang, Bruised grunted, his tongue rolled out, his moose eyes bulged, he fell dead. Clouet screamed, Loubet began yelling hysterically, frightening the other French soldiers. They dropped their weapons and fled. He dropped his and ran off leaving Clouet, the two dead Sokokis, the prisoners.

Two Eagles emerged from behind a tree, smoke curling from the muzzle of his musket. Livid, Clouet snarled, snatched up a musket and was trying to aim it when Splitting Moon's tooth-ball tomahawk whirled crushing his chest. As his shot flew harmlessly into the air, Clouet toppled over dead.

"*Rackesi,*" murmured Sky Toucher, his expression amazed. "What are you doing here?"

Two Eagles showed a rare grin. "What are you? I was after Tenäte Oÿoghi."

"She caught up, rescued me. It is a long story."

"*You* rescued him?"

"Do not look so surprised, Tékni-ska-je-a-nah. It was not so hard, and he helped."

Two Eagles stared. "You rescued him?" he repeated. "Margaret will be amazed."

"Maybe not," murmured Singing Brook. "It takes a woman to know a woman."

Sky Toucher footed Clouet's corpse, bent over, jerked off his crucifix and hefted it. It was silver, its weight surprised him. It showed Christ on the cross. He studied it.

"A strange torture. Very slow, very good. Who did this to him, I wonder? What did he do to deserve it?"

Two Eagles shrugged. Sky Toucher offered it to Singing Brook. She examined it. "What do I do with it?"

"Keep it," suggested Two Eagles, "to remind you never to trust another black robe."

"We trusted one," she murmured and glanced at Sky Toucher. "And I would trust him again."

# IX
## DARK DAYS COMING

T HE THREE SET out leaving Clouet's body and those of the two Sokokis.

"Such a rash and foolish man," said Singing Brook to Two Eagles. "It was almost as if he begged you to shoot him."

"He did," murmured Sky Toucher. "He wanted to go to his God."

The cousins began firing questions at each other about their separate exploits. Both were impressed by Singing Brook's valiant efforts. So effusively did Sky Toucher praise her, she began blushing.

"She saved her own life in the camp, saved mine, saved mine a second time on the trail when she knifed Onea Canonou." Sky Toucher's eyes gleamed admiringly. "She thinks like a warrior, Tékni-ska-je-a-nah, and jumps into trouble like one. Amazing . . ."

"Stop it, my husband, you make my cheeks tingle."

"You are like Margaret," said Two Eagles. "In your blood there is fire, and all it takes is trouble or danger to light it."

They passed the Ile la Motte at a safe distance; from the time they left the site of the ambush, they saw no sign of the soldiers who had fled in confusion. They moved on at a brisk pace. Tender new leaves and fragile flowers dressed the woodland floor, greening and blossoming before the trees put on their foliage to block out the sun's rays.

Late the next day they passed the spot where Two Eagles had strangled the Sokoki to get his clothes. Passing the tree, he took a few minutes to search the bushes for the corpse, but it had been taken away, as had the clothing he left. He was disappointed.

"Sokokis stink worse than skunk cabbage," he muttered.

Singing Brook nodded. "I still can't get used to it. Tomorrow we will pass by the hunters' camp where I got these clothes, where I left Cayere Tawyne's body on the scaffold."

Sky Toucher nodded. "I must bring it back to Tenotoge. The ground is soft enough for burial."

"Further up the line I have Tyagohuens' body, which I must bring back to Onneyuttahage," said Two Eagles glumly.

Singing Brook frowned. "How can the two of you carry both?"

"In one litter," said Two Eagles, "easily."

"I will tell you who I would like to see buried," muttered Singing Brook, "alive: that lying dog Dorr. We must stop there, O-ron-ia-ke-te. I want a word with him."

"Forget him, Tenäte Oÿoghi, forget them all," said Sky Toucher.

"*Neh.* He caused all of this—Cayere Tawyne's death, Tyagohuens', yours, nearly."

"What good will it do to claw his ears with harsh words?"

"Has she not earned the right to?" asked Two Eagles. "Besides, I want a word with him myself."

It began raining early in the afternoon. The ice on the lake was now gray, with rapidly widening holes. The rain intensified the stench of Two Eagles' and Singing Brook's Sokoki clothing. Two Eagles squinched up his nose as he scowled contemptuously.

"The Sokokis are like the Ouendats, the Hurons: two-legged dogs who shun water like the poison shrub."

"Every tribe has its own stink," observed Sky Toucher. "Mohawks and Oneidas do not smell like clover."

"We do not stink to burn your nose like these animals," rasped Singing Brook. "I have a thought, Two Eagles. We stop here, all of us take off our clothes, wash ourselves with the rain, wash our deerskins, wring them out and set them to dry on that boulder over there when the sun comes out."

"You will *not* take off your clothes in front of my cousin!" snapped Sky Toucher.

"I will go behind the boulder." She held out her arms and lifted her face to the downpour. "It is cold but it feels good. Let us do it." Off she ran to the concealment of the boulder.

"She is so like Margaret," said Two Eagles looking after her. They watched her head bob up from behind the boulder as she removed her clothing. "No fear of anything, least of all what a man may think."

"She is funny," Sky Toucher remarked.

"*Funny?*" Two Eagles frowned.

"She is opposite things: tough as a hawk and soft as a dove. Calm as water when the breeze rests, wild as a river in spring. There is not a day goes by that she does not surprise in some way."

"Just like Margaret." They stood naked rubbing themselves down with sand, the rain washing it off. "Do you know something, O-ron-ia-ke-te? I believe you and I are better men because of our women."

"Because of their love."

"Because of their strength, their *orochquines*, spines that are steel. I think if our tribes had no men, only women, those two would be chiefs over women warriors. They would be the bravest and the best. We are luckier, you and I, than any warriors we know, I think."

"*Nyoh*, lucky, too, to be going home alive."

"To what, I wonder?"

"What do you mean?"

Two Eagles shook his head. "What does tomorrow hold for us, for the Five Nations? We are in our twilight, O-ron-ia-ke-te, the darkness coming slowly. And nothing can stop it. The storm cloud of our destiny."

"I do not want to think about that, I feel too good."

"You may not want to think about it, but it is something we all must deal with."

"*Neh, Rackesi*, I do not see the future as black as you do. I say we just take each day as it is given to us and see what happens. Maybe it will not be so bad for our people."

Two Eagles grunted. "Maybe it will be worse."

Their clothing dried quickly, the sun and fresh air taking away much of the stench. They dressed. Singing Brook reappeared. Two Eagles was scowling.

"What is the matter?" Sky Toucher asked.

"I hate dressing in my enemy's skins. I feel like they are rotting my flesh. I feel like a *ke-wa-sa-ne*."

"A traitor?" asked Singing Brook. "You must not feel that way. Besides, it is only for a few days more."

"It is risky," said Two Eagles. "It was crossing over into Sokoki Territory wearing Mohawk skins. And just as risky crossing back into Mohawk Territory wearing these."

"I did not think of that."

"I look what I am," said Sky Toucher, thumping his chest proudly.

"You look as if you are from the Rag Tribe," said Singing Brook laughing merrily.

RECOGNIZING THE AREA, Singing Brook led Sky Toucher and Two Eagles off the trail into the woods to the west.

"The camp is just ahead."

As they drew nearer they could hear the sound of many voices.

"Watch yourselves," cautioned Two Eagles, crouching and moving quietly forward, holding the branches ahead of him to keep them from snapping back.

At least a dozen hunters crowded the little camp. They had killed four moose and a number of deer. The mooses' tongues, a delicacy, had been cut out and laid on hemlock branches to dry in the sun. The fire sent up billowing smoke as pine boughs were laid on it. Singing Brook pointed to the far side of the camp. The scaffold she had hastily erected for Four Otters' remains had been burned. His badly charred corpse lay on the partially consumed rack which hung by one corner. His head was missing. Little was left of his body. Two Eagles turned to Sky Toucher; he looked furious, his hand went to his knife. Two Eagles laid a restraining hand on his arm.

"Easy, *Rackesi.*"

"Stinking dogs!"

"Shhhh," cautioned Singing Brook. "Blame me, I should have taken the time to find a well-hidden spot."

"They would have found it wherever you put it up," said Two Eagles.

"You do not do that to a dead man," muttered Sky Toucher, seething, "even your worst enemy. It is wrong, wrong!"

"Shhhh." Singing Brook placed her arms around him from the

back, leaning her head on his shoulder. "It is done, there is no way we can change it."

"I want his body! What is left of it."

"What will you do?" asked Two Eagles. "Ask them for it?"

"You think it is funny? It is not. It is depraved, their hearts are filled with *oeuda,* shit, to do such a thing!"

The two hunters closest to where Two Eagles and the Mohawks were hiding abruptly stopped talking and looked their way. Two Eagles duck-waddled backwards, pulling Sky Toucher with him. They withdrew, quickly returning to the trail.

"I cannot leave him like that," muttered Sky Toucher, "in this rotten place."

"What choice have you?" asked Two Eagles.

"We stay here, wait."

"For what?" asked Singing Brook.

"For them to leave."

Two Eagles deep-furrowed his brow. "What makes you think they plan to?"

"They will, either to return to the hunt or take what they have killed back to their village."

Two Eagles shook his head. "If they return to the hunt they will surely scatter. And wander all over this part of the woods. They could spot us easily, the last thing we need is a fight."

"He is my friend, I cannot leave him like that. A Mohawk warrior should not warm the bellies of crows and vultures."

"There is nothing left of him," said Singing Brook.

"There is enough. All there is should be properly buried. It is the least I can do. He died for me, Tenäte Oÿoghi, for you, too. It is wrong to leave him so, to take his head. They probably cut his heart out before they torched the scaffold. Dogs! Stinking animals!"

Sky Toucher's determination set his jaw, drawing the cords tight.

Singing Brook stared at Two Eagles, asking with her eyes, *What now?* "We can wait a while," she said. "Two Eagles?"

He grunted. "We could wait for days. Darkness is coming. They are not going back out to hunt, not at night."

"They will sleep," said Sky Toucher. "When all is quiet I will sneak in and out with what is left of him."

"If they catch you they will kill you on the spot." Singing Brook shook her head.

He scowled. "Are you saying I should leave him?"

Two Eagles shook his head. "She did not say that, only that you should be careful. Clear your mind of your fire and think about it, Cousin. You did not come all this way, down and up the lakes, going through all you have gone through to die here, with the knife of some Sokoki scum who sleeps lightly or maybe not at all."

"If you two are so dead against this, why do you not go on, leave me here to do what has to be done?"

"Do not take your frustration out on us," rasped Singing Brook. "We did not do this to Cayere Tawyne. Blame your friend Dorr, he started all this."

Sky Toucher sighed. "Let us not get into that again."

Darkness came quickly; stars enlivened the heavens around a drowsy-looking moon. As Two Eagles slept, Sky Toucher and Singing Brook crept back to the same bushes through which they had watched the hunters' camp. Some of the Sokokis were already asleep; others, four of them, sat talking in low tones. What was left of the scaffold was situated on the far side of the fire; Sky Toucher and Singing Brook could barely make it out against the undergrowth.

"You will have to circle," said Singing Brook.

"I know what I have to do," he muttered. "You stay here."

One of the Sokokis still awake was stretching and yawning.

"Why not wait for those four to fall asleep?"

"I could wait until the moon goes down."

"Be patient."

"I am going now."

"*Neh!*"

"*Nyoh,* they will hear nothing. Keep your eye on them. If I do catch their attention they will look my way. Pull back a branch and snap it to distract them. Then run back to Two Eagles, wake him and the two of you get out of here."

"And you?"

"I will be all right."

"I doubt that. You are too angry, too frustrated. You will hurry it, they will hear you."

"*Ogechta!*"

She bristled. "Do not tell me to shut up! No one tells me to. Go if you are going. Get out of here."

Knife in hand, off he went. She squinted, keeping her eyes fastened to the scaffold and waited, holding her breath for as long as she could. Her heart thumped wildly. Presently, she imagined she saw the scaffold move. It did. She could not make out Sky Toucher but the remaining corner was being cut down. She watched it lower slowly and cocked an ear to listen, but she heard nothing except the four Sokokis arguing, then laughing loudly. She saw one jab the man opposite with a finger.

Steps. Sky Toucher returned clutching a charred bundle and looking devastated.

"I could not find his head anywhere. His arms and legs are cinders, pieces fell off. All that is left is his trunk. I wish I could knife them all, every one while they sleep!"

"Please, let us just get out of here."

They had nothing to wrap Four Otters' remains in. Later that night, when they stopped to sleep, Two Eagles suggested they kill a buck first chance they got, skin it and wrap up the Mohawk's remains. Sky Toucher neither agreed nor disagreed. He was too far into himself, clutching the bones to his chest, shaking his head repeatedly, muttering to himself.

"It makes me want to go back to Dorr and scout again. Fight next time. Look for Sokoki dogs and kill every one I can!"

Singing Brook glanced at Two Eagles beside her. Neither spoke.

# 88

IN LIGHT OF what happened to Four Otters' body, Two Eagles grew more and more apprehensive as they drew nearer the spot where he had left Splitting Moon. They reached it at twilight. A quick inspection confirmed that it was undisturbed, save for the eyes. Birds had pecked through the deerskin covering them and emptied the sockets.

"You cannot prevent that," said Sky Toucher. "Crows especially will peck through wood to get at eyes."

Singing Brook averted her gaze as they lifted the corpse free of the scaffold and laid it on the ground.

"It is getting warmer out," said Sky Toucher, "and staying warmer longer. Soon now he will begin to stink." Two Eagles' glance said that this offended him. "We must pile pine boughs on him on the litter," added Sky Toucher hastily.

A litter was fashioned with two poles and Sky Toucher's two threadbare blankets; Splitting Moon was placed upon it. The Mohawks looked on in silence as Two Eagles stood staring down at his friend.

"All of his life people he knew were shocked whenever he found sunlight in anything. His eyes could only see the black side. In his great heart it started raining the day he was born and never let up." He let a low growling slowly out of his throat, a desperately melancholy sound. "But he was so good, so fearless, so loyal, always willing to help, to risk his life for a friend. In anything, even if he did not believe in it. He would carry on, make his ridiculous noise, hammer your ear pans so they ached, but in the end he would always go along. I will miss him like I would miss my arm if it was torn from me. Never to see him again, to hear his voice, his complaining. He leaves a hole in my heart that will never fill.

"Good journey, my friend, and when you reach there, when you are welcomed by all the others, shoot the shade of a fine buck with the shade of an arrow for me, in memory of our friendship. And your tomahawk is safe, I will keep it and from now on use it in place of my own, this old ball with a tooth. To remind me of Tyagohuens, Splitting Moon, Oneida warrior, the bravest heart, my comrade in battle, my friend." He turned to Sky Toucher. "Are we not strange, you and I?"

"How strange?"

"To do this, save the remains of our friends. As if we could preserve them, breathe life back into them, flesh that is charred, is already carrion, bones that will be bared, souls flown away, the

Village of the Dead waiting. Look at them, both are empty corn husks."

"Not so," murmured Singing Brook. "They are not empty. They are precious vessels in your keeping. If friends do not care for lost friends, who will? Both have earned their graves. What they do not deserve is fire, and birds feasting on them. And neither is dead." Both looked at her sharply. "Not in your hearts, nor will they ever die there."

"She is right," said Sky Toucher, setting a hand fondly on the bundled remains of Four Otters.

Two Eagles looked about. In the west, the teeth of the Tree-eater Mountains were cutting open and emptying the sun of its molten gold. The woodland shadows deepened, absorbing the amber twilight. A curious silence prevailed, singularly heavy, reverential, and then a wedge of early arriving Canada geese broke it with their rich, musical honking. All three glanced skyward.

"They can have their north," said Sky Toucher. "I never want to see the O-chog-wä again."

"Shall we keep going?" Two Eagles asked Singing Brook.

"You mean am I up to it? No need to ask my permission. We will go on until it is too dark to see our way. How far to the fort?"

"Three, maybe four sleeps," said Sky Toucher. "You do not still want to stop there, Tenäte Oÿoghi."

"I do," growled Two Eagles.

They went on for about two more hours, Two Eagles noting that Sky Toucher, for all his willingness to press on, was still not completely recovered from his ordeal. He, himself, was not at his best: his back ached dully, and now and then a needle of pain shot through his right hip. When he got home to Onneyuttahage, for at least a month he would stay close to the longhouse, to the chamber and bed. Sleeping in the bunk, he knew, would restore his back. Its comfort and Margaret's arms cured every ill. He thought back to the tree and the violent shaking that had awakened him. He was lucky he hadn't broken his neck. Yet for all their difficulties and tribulations the three of them had benefited from more than their share of luck down the lakes and back up to here, although Tenäte Oÿoghi had made the most of hers through daring and initiative. A warrior she truly was, if not in body in spirit.

Four days later, somewhat slowed by the cumbersome litter, they forded the chilly, ice-strewn waters of Wood Creek and approached the front gate of Fort Anne. Militia milled about outside, stopping their conversations to stare at them. The garrison looked to be bursting with troops. A voice called Sky Toucher's name—it was Dorr with Carver and Flood. They appeared to be returning from a walk. The colonel carried a baton, beating the dead grass along the creek bank with it.

"Sky Toucher!" He came bustling up all smiles and—to Singing Brook—acting as if greeting a long-lost brother. "You made it! You're safe. Praise be! A miracle, dear friend, my prayers have been answered. And here is your dear wife. We've had the pleasure, hello again—ahem, I trust you're not still upset with me . . ."

She grunted, a reaction so uncharacteristic it brought a smile to Two Eagles' face.

"And you . . ." burst Dorr, shifting his glance to Two Eagles and too obviously failing to recall his name.

"Two Eagles," muttered Singing Brook.

"Of course, right on the tip of my tongue. The Oneida chief. All of you must come in, relax, catch your breaths, put your feet up, share a libation. And what have we here?" He indicated the litter and made a face.

"Bodies of friends," said Two Eagles. "We do not leave our dead in enemy territory."

It was a deliberate dig; neither the French or the English bothered to retrieve their Indian dead from the battleground. Dorr smiled, oblivious of the affront. Flood and Carver saluted and withdrew, and the colonel edged upwind of the litter.

"I must tell you, Sky Toucher, it was plain bad luck we didn't hear of your capture until much too late to help." This prompted another grunt from Singing Brook, who looked away, unwilling to meet Dorr's eyes as he addressed her. "Madam, I swear on my mother's sainted head that is the unvarnished truth. If only we found out, I mean that afternoon within an hour or so. Unfortunately, Sky Toucher, O-ron-ia-ke-te, as it turned out, anybody we might have sent chasing after you would have been much too far behind."

Singing Brook stared. "Oh, but you could not send anybody, remember?"

"I beg your pardon?"

"Orders from Al-bany."

"That's right. The important thing to remember is that even if we did pursue, with all the time that elapsed, we'd never have caught up."

"*I* caught up," said Singing Brook.

Dorr gaped. "You?"

"And rescued him," added Two Eagles, "as you can see. With courage and cunning. A long story, one I am sure would not interest you. You and I must speak on another matter."

"Of course, whatever. Let's leave the bodies outside here." He touched the side of his nose with one gloved finger and made a face. "No one'll go near them. Come in, all of you."

# 89

To SKY TOUCHER's relief, Singing Brook's boiling resentment toward Dorr turned out to have nearly spent itself in her seething and bursts of vitriolic criticism before they'd arrived at Fort Anne. Still, she could not now bring herself to look at the man, much less converse with him.

Sky Toucher saw Dorr's failure to rescue him as all in the past, his conduct normal for an English long knife. He reminded himself that he had volunteered because it was in the Mohawks' best interests, not as any favor to Dorr.

But from the way Singing Brook fidgeted, studied the floor and twisted her fingers in her lap, he could see that she could not wait to get out of the stuffy little office. Dorr offered them rum; the Mohawks declined it. Two Eagles, who normally drank little alcohol, downed half a tumbler in one gulp. Sky Toucher watched him, his cousin looked like a hungry man who'd cornered a deer, so eager was he to get to the subject on his mind.

"A damnable pity they took your gifts," said Dorr, shaking his head sympathetically, "especially your medal. And I'm sorry I haven't any more money to replace the ten pounds. Since we last spoke, Sky Toucher, word has come up from Albany that we'll be launching a spring offensive. Huge operation, the biggest ever. It's tentatively scheduled for mid-May."

"My husband will not take part," said Singing Brook.

Dorr frowned, elevating an eyebrow.

*"Neh,"* said Sky Toucher, "I cannot."

"Don't be in a rush to decide, my boy, we've time to talk about it."

"We *are* talking about it," said Singing Brook. "And I am telling you not to count on him to scout. He is going home to stay."

"Tenäte Oÿoghi," began Sky Toucher. He could see her mind working. She was forcing him to defer to her wishes. *Ordering* him.

"We will talk about it, my husband, but not here."

Dorr smiled indulgently. "Which, I take it, means it's not absolutely decided."

Singing Brook's eyes, riveting Sky Toucher's, said that it was, prompting him to think better of saying anything further.

"Tékni-ska-je-a-nah," she murmured, getting up. "We will be waiting outside."

Sky Toucher rose from his stool. "One last thing, Dorr. Perhaps you know, where is the *kristoni Asseroni's* trading post from here?"

"The what?"

"The Dutchman," said Two Eagles.

"You mean Two Tongues Van Brocklin." Dorr swung around to his wall map behind him, but it was insufficiently detailed to show the location with any accuracy. "When you leave here heading down the trail that takes you around Round Lake, about half a league distant cut sharply right. Keep heading west."

Sky Toucher nodded. "That is where the Two Tongues captured me and took me to the turkey cock."

"Who?"

"The leader of the lace-cuffs. There is a clearing there . . ."

Dorr nodded. "Van Brocklin's trading post is just beyond that."

"I must stop there, he and I have to talk."

*"Neh!"* burst Singing Brook.

*"Nyoh!* I owe him a red bib."

"Be careful Sky Toucher," said Dorr. "He has at least a dozen redski—*Indians* working for him."

"You may get a red bib of your own, cousin," said Two Eagles, finishing his drink.

"Listen to them," Singing Brook said. "We are almost home, forget about him."

"I cannot do that."

Husband and wife left, bickering. Two Eagles cleared his throat.

"What can I do for you?" Dorr asked, refilling the Oneida's tumbler, which Two Eagles ignored.

"We talked last time about *je-na-kia-de-gä´,* alliance."

"Yes yes, about your joining us in this last great, decisive battle."

"Who says it will be the last? Who says it will be decisive?"

"It has to be, my friend, Queen Anne's War is nearing its end in Europe. The French are bankrupt, their armies exhausted. Here in North America all it's been for the past decade has been skirmishes, mainly in the east, in Maine, Acadia. Precious little action around here. But the high command in Albany sees this coming spring as an opportunity we should seize. To do what Samuel Vetch tried and failed to do: dispatch a large and powerful force down the War Road to Montreal, to Quebec and attack and destroy both. Obliterate them, break the frogs' hold in Canada, wipe New France off the map. From the distant South to Hudson's Bay, from the five lakes to the ocean forward to victory, for God, for England and St. George!" He pounded the desk.

"And the Iroquois?" asked Two Eagles quietly.

"With, with the Iroquois, of course, the fearless Oneidas and Mohawks. Absolutely. Our allies in war, our friends in peace."

"Of course."

"What?" Dorr cupped a hand to one ear, leaning forward.

"Nothing."

"Let's go back to the question, shall we?" He leaned even further forward. "How many warriors can your tribe provide us?

How many brave Oneidas willing to defend their lands, their hunting grounds in this last great battle for control, for peace everlasting?"

"None."

Dorr grinned. "You're being facetious."

"None. Since we talked last I have talked to He-swallows and Carries-a-quiver. They agree that we should stay out of any future fighting. And we are talking to the Mohawk chiefs, Kettle Throat, Winter Gull and Tiyanoga at Tenotoge. They, too, are not eager to resume fighting."

"Hendrick said that?"

"Never mind Hendrick."

"He said no such thing."

"Never mind the Mohawks. You ask about us, the Oneidas and I say again, do not count on our help."

"See here, old chap, aren't you being just a wee bit presumptuous? You ask me to believe that you speak for your whole tribe?"

"Believe it."

"We shall see. However you feel, however I may or anyone else may feel, it's the old story, my friend, when push comes to shove the Mohawks and the Oneidas have to come down on one side or the other. Which? What choice have you?"

"I must go. O-ron-ia-ke-te and Tenäte Oÿoghi are waiting." Two Eagles got wearily to his feet, cracking his knees. He hated this helpless feeling while Dorr smirked confidently, his threat dripping honey. Two Eagles knew he had to get out of here.

Dorr clucked. "You're angry."

"*Neh.*"

"You are. I dislike for us to part with bad feelings. We'll talk again, I'm sure. There are so many factors you should be aware of and consider before you and your fellow chiefs decide. Let's put these last few minutes behind us and go forward, shall we? After you left here the last time I discussed the situation with Major Carver. He suggested we come and visit you at Onna . . . Onna . . ."

"Onneyuttahage."

"Right."

"Good-bye, Dorr."

"Good-bye, Tékni-ska . . . ska . . ."
Two Eagles grunted and went out.

# 90

MARGARET WAS SO right. Why did I not see it a long time ago? Singing Brook was leading them. Two Eagles muttered, carrying his end of the litter. Sky Toucher held the front end. He turned to look back at his cousin.

"Nothing, nothing," muttered Two Eagles.

Sky Toucher glanced around looking for where Van Brocklin had left the trail for the clearing where the French had assembled. He recognized the rock where he had sat to remove the ice from his moccasin, where the Dutchman and his companion had come upon him.

"We turn off here."

Singing Brook stopped, they halted. They set down the litter. Two Eagles swiped sweat from his forehead. The afternoon had gotten unseasonably warm, the sun growing brighter by the hour.

"Before we go one step further," she said, "I want to know what you plan for the *kristoni Asseroni*."

"You already know," said Two Eagles.

"*Neh!*"

"*Nyoh!*" Sky Toucher's eyes blazed. "He started all this, his throat gets my tooth!"

She sighed, he could see that she had neither the strength or the desire to resume arguing.

"Look—" Two Eagles pointed ahead. About two hundred paces beyond, smoke rose above the trees, the breeze tearing it, flinging it about. "The trading post."

"They are burning brush," said Sky Toucher.

"That smoke is too black to be brush. Let us leave the litter behind those rocks there and go see."

"*Neh,* better in the clearing up ahead where Two Tongues took me."

Setting the litter down in the clearing, they hurried toward the source of the smoke. They could hear yelling, whooping. Peering through the undergrowth they gasped as one. The main building had been destroyed by fire. Flames still licked the far wall. Indians of no recognizable tribe were cavorting noisily about, dressing themselves in brightly colored cloth, swigging from jugs and bottles. The burning main building occupied the center of the clearing, which was somewhat larger than the one where they'd left the litter. The three of them could see a well, two small outbuildings—both leveled—three wrecked and burning wagons and goods scattered about: partially burnt bolts of coarse woollen shoddy, spools of ribbon in various colors, scarlet, green and blue worsted hose with and without clocks, which some of the savages had pulled on, hatchets with broken handles, axes and other tools, dented pots and kettles, broken baskets, a large spool of brass wire, a battered and smashed red-leather trunk, its contents strewn all about. They could see shattered rum casks and crates and in the charred remains of the house, pelts, bottles, boxes, barrels, fragments of sacking.

The plunderers continued their depredations, whooping loudly.

"Let us get out of here before somebody sees us," warned Singing Brook.

"Wait—" said Sky Toucher. "Look over there past the furthest wagon."

He pointed past the charred bones of a wagon at a sight so grisly Singing Brook took one look, gagged and turned her head. Two trees about four inches in diameter standing six feet apart had been stripped of their branches, pulled together about two-thirds of the way to the top and fastened.

A white man had been stripped naked and hung by his ankles. Then the knot was severed, the trees flying apart ripping him in half. Not evenly: most of his body lay on the ground close by a rectangular fire, its embers glowing brightly. The smaller portion, his right leg and thigh, still hung from its tree.

They moved off to their left, getting closer, finding better concealment in thicker brush. Realizing he'd been deprived of his vengeance, Sky Toucher's heart sank. And where, he wondered, had his medal and knife gotten to?

Parts of Van Brocklin's remains had been cut off, spitted and roasted whole, and now lay on the ground. As charred as they were, it was easy to see that his murderers had eaten most of his flesh. Large chunks were missing and a few ribs lay among the coals.

"He was fat," murmured Two Eagles, "they had a feast."

Sky Toucher shook his head resignedly, disappointed at being denied his revenge.

"Let us go back and get the litter," he said. "Get out of here."

# 91

IT RAINED A deluge all the way from near Round Lake to Teno-toge. They came sloshing through the entrance gate, the two men bearing the litter, looking like drowned squirrels. Green Water and Snowflake greeted them ecstatically; their joy hid their astonishment at seeing them returning safely, Singing Brook was certain. The two mothers were in the midst of making corn-husk dolls with cornsilk hair: the husks shaped tubelike for the bodies.

"Who is that on the litter in the passageway?" Snowflake asked. Two Eagles explained.

"And the bundle is what is left of Cayere Tawyne," said Sky Toucher, busy drying himself with a bear robe.

"There is not much left of you, either," said his mother. "So, we would both like to know, have you had your fill of playing on the War Road? Are you back to stay or just until the English crook their finger at you again?"

"He is not going back," said Singing Brook, eying him sharply. "Ever."

"No need to keep hammering that stone to everybody," he growled.

"What about the Oneida?" Green Water asked Two Eagles.

Having returned to her dollmaking, she was rolling first one then the other leg of her doll, winding them spirally with twine, and tying them tightly at the ankles.

"They are staying out of the fight, too," he replied, "as long as I have any say in it."

"How long will that be?" asked Snowflake. She shuttered her

single good eye and shook her head. "Maybe he will not go back to fight, maybe you will not, but the Mohawks and Oneidas will. They were spilling blood for the English long before I came into this world and will be long after I leave, until—"

"Until there is no one left to fight in either tribe," said Green Water.

"I cannot argue that," Two Eagles said, arising. "*Rackesie,* Tenäte Oÿoghi, I must get Tyagohuens home."

"I will help carry him," said Sky Toucher.

"*Neh,* you have done your part, I will carry him over my shoulder."

"That is foolish talk," said Singing Brook. "You cannot carry a corpse that size so far. You are as weary as we are."

"Wearier," said Snowflake, "because he is older." She cast a sly look at her nephew. By now, she had drawn the head-cover husks tightly over the form, tying them at the neck; later she would wind them tightly with a smooth husk. "Tenäte Oÿoghi, go and fetch Quane Onawy or Christittye Etsi. Neither would go with you last time, but there is no danger this time."

Sky Toucher smiled at Singing Brook. "Your rescuing me brings them shame. Helping Tékni-ska-je-a-nah will save one or the other a little face."

She shrugged. "They should not be ashamed for not going with me, they had no *ottis-ven-dä-gä,* no obligation to."

"They did to their manhood," observed Green Water curtly. "Come, I want to see the corpses."

Outside in the passageway both older women crinkled their noses and made faces.

"Give Cayere Tawyne to his parents to bury fast," said Green Water to Sky Toucher. "And you, Tékni-ska-je-a-nah, get your friend home and into the ground before the stink of him sickens your whole castle."

Two Eagles stiffened resentfully. "Fold your flapping tongue, old mother, you are talking about my friend."

"I am talking about a stinking corpse who used to be your friend. Get it out of my longhouse."

Singing Brook laughed lightly. Sky Toucher and Two Eagles

carried the litter back outside, after Sky Toucher removed Four Otters' bundled remains.

It had stopped raining. Singing Brook induced Copper Man to help Two Eagles carry Splitting Moon's body home. They left within the hour. As Two Eagles passed through the front gate at the rear of the litter, the breeze in his face, he thought that brave warriors and cowards, *Asseroni* gold hats and Sokoki vermin all had at least one thing in common when life fled their bodies.

He sniffed.

 **92**

TWO EAGLES AND Margaret stood over Splitting Moon's freshly mounded grave. She squeezed his hand consolingly. The sky was clear, harebell blue, the spring sun blazed radiantly; off to their right in a tall elm, male chickadees answered each other's *fee-bee* whistles, proclaiming their territorial boundaries to each other.

"O-ron-ia-ke-te has buried his friend by now, and here lies Tyagohuens," said Two Eagles sadly, "holding a part of my heart in his. Remember back when Benjamin died of the snake's poison, what you said?"

"I was angry then, bitter."

"But you were right. Life *is* too harsh here; everything, everyone dies too easily. Not even counting the wars. Though all warriors die because of the two-legged snakes."

"Indirectly."

"Who else would you say caused their deaths? There may be one hope. I think it has reached a point where most of our women feel as you do about the English, as O´-kla?, O´hute Onega and I am sure other women do at Tenotoge. It is like a chant of mourning that they have been performing for many moons, only the chiefs and the warriors have closed their ears to it."

"Perhaps this time they will begin to listen. You and Sky Toucher did."

"All he and Tenäte Oÿoghi want is to get back into their lives and have a *cian*." He sighed. "What am I talking about, it is past too late. For them, for us all. However we feel, the long dying will go on. The signs are dark and can be clearly seen. A chill wind blows."

She shook her head. "You don't believe that, it's your grief talking. The tribes can retake control of their destinies. It's in their power to if they want to badly enough. We go to bed tonight, wake up tomorrow and life goes forward. We can shake off their yoke, stay out of their fighting, survive, grow."

The chickadees fell silent, the wind sang briefly then was quiet. Margaret turned from Splitting Moon's grave, catching sight of Benjamin's a short distance away. She glanced at Two Eagles.

"We, you and I, could have another son."

His eyes rounded, he brightened. "Do you mean it?"

"How will we grow without children?"

"*Nyoh.*"

"They're the future, they're survival."

She took his hand, they started back to the longhouse.

# EPILOGUE

A WHOLE MOON AND half moon later, when the new leaf of the white oak reached the size of a red squirrel's foot, the hills were raised in the cornfields, the three kernels planted and around them, beans, squash and pumpkin, which would eventually sprout and send their vines spiraling up the rising cornstalks. On a perfectly splendid afternoon Colonel Douglas Dorr, Major Alden Carver and their escort appeared at the entrance gate to Onneyuttahage. With them were the three Mohawk chiefs from Tenotoge.

Despite Two Eagles' spirited opposition, he was to find himself outvoted by his fellow chiefs. The decision was made to supply warriors to augment the Mohawk forces preparing to fight on the side of the English.

Queen Anne's War ended in 1713–1714 with the Treaties of Utrecht and Rastatt. Neither Two Eagles nor Sky Toucher took part. The Oneidas as well as the Mohawks, however, continued to ally with the English and were to do so up to and throughout the French and Indian War (1754–1763), diminishing their manpower and steadily eroding Iroquois influence.

The total number of Mohawks in the late twentieth century is about five thousand.

The total number of Oneidas in the late twentieth century is about three thousand.

# AUTHOR'S NOTE

THE SPELLING OF virtually all Mohawk and Oneida words is open to dispute. Careful research has established that few scholarly sources agree on the spelling of place names in particular.

This is the case because tribal languages were exclusively oral and only written when transcribed by white men.

This story is a work of fiction based on the history of northeastern America shortly after the turn of the eighteenth century.

I am deeply indebted to my husband, Alan, without whose painstaking research this book would not have been possible.

—Barbara Riefe
Stamford, Connecticut